Matthew Francis

Created and Written By Matthew Francis
@matthewfrancisj
All text and art © 2021 by Matthew Francis and FrancisFilm, LLC
Illustrations by Megan McNamee
@_megelmac / megelmac.com

All rights reserved.

PRAX & all related characters and elements are ™ of and © Matthew Francis
PRAX publishing rights © Matthew Francis

praxseries.com
matthewfrancis.co

No part of this publication may be reproduced, distributed, or transmitted in any form or by any means, including photocopying, recording, or other electronic or mechanical methods, without the prior written permission of the publisher and author, except in the case of brief quotations embodied in critical reviews and certain other noncommercial uses permitted by copyright law. For permission requests, contact author Matthew Francis.

If you purchased, downloaded, or found this piece of art anywhere besides an official PRAX affiliated bookstore, website, or social media page, you should be aware that this content is illegally stolen property. It was reported as "unsold and destroyed" to the publisher or downloaded and resold without consent. Neither the author nor publisher has received any payment for this "stripped book." Please support the artists behind this story fairly and honestly.

First edition printing, February 2021
Published by Matthew Francis and FrancisFilm, LLC
Printed in the U.S.A. 2021
ISBN: 978-1-7366990-0-3

TABLE OF CONTENTS

Chapter 1   What A Stupid Name 1
Chapter 2   Chores of a Twisted Heart 12
Chapter 3   Two Hours 24
Chapter 4   Chocolate Pecan Pie 32
Chapter 5   Year 3451 43
Chapter 6   Breakfast at Quaker Cottage 52
Chapter 7   The Valedictorian & The Frozen Princess 65
Chapter 8   The Thirteenth Floor 80
Chapter 9   Day One 89
Chapter 10 Staffball Tryouts 104
Chapter 11 The Ambassador's Announcement 118
Chapter 12 The Squire 129
Chapter 13 The First Attraction 139
Chapter 14 Underwater Gratitude 147
Chapter 15 The Icy Match 162
Chapter 16 The Rally 179
Chapter 17 A Hazardous Threat Returns 189
Chapter 18 Cost of a Cure 200
Chapter 19 Countdown to Madness 212
Chapter 20 Morphing Memories 233
Chapter 21 Cheesecake 255

This book series is dedicated to:

The kids who society harms, violently or silently, because they dare to just be different.

May 31, 2005

Ava Harlow burst into the office and found her boss, neck snapped on the dirty floor, cold and dead. Terror was still plastered on Stephan Rock's lifeless face. Justin, the corpse's brother and business partner, whimpered with paranoid shock in the corner.

"Where is it?" Ava, their assistant, glanced around the room.

"It's not...," Justin wheezed, "it's not in the locked safe."

"Are there any other copies?" Ava fretted.

"No, none!"

"Did he move it?"

"No, no, no," the man stammered like a child. "Stephan always kept it here!"

Wailing screams of escaping employees barely covered up the brutal grunts of combatants fighting near the company's lobby. Ava desperately hoped Daniel would stay alive. The loud crash of a heavy body thrown against the break room wall made Ava jump and Justin clutch his thumping chest.

"In the closet!" Ava pulled her surviving boss into the storage chamber and locked the door from inside.

"Stay quiet," Ava whispered in the darkness. "We can't let you die, too."

The office windows shattered as more intruders swung into the room from the dark night outside. Broken glass crunched beneath heavy combat boots. The cruel intruders saw the corpse of the company's CEO and laughed.

"Find the formula. Now!" A deep voice snapped the snickering minions to attention.

The six thieves knocked over file cabinets, rifled through documents, and broke open locked drawers. They were so rambunctious Ava could no longer strain to listen for Daniel's voice. As the burglars tore apart the office, they found nothing but useless paperwork.

"They lied to us," the captain called out as the men paused their frenzied search. "It's not here."

One of the crooks fiddled with the doorknob of the locked closet where Ava and her boss were hiding. Justin struggled to muffle his fearful breaths. Ava knew they were losing options.

"This door is jammed!" the brute told the others. "It could be in here! Help me break off the knob!"

Ava huffed as Justin squeaked in fear behind her. Rules be damned. If she didn't act now, those killers would ruin everything. She had no choice.

"Mr. Rock?" Ava whispered as she turned around. "I'm so sorry…."

"Huh?" Justin Rock mumbled in scared confusion.

Ava placed her thumb on her boss's forehead. The frightened man immediately fell into a mystic trance and his eyes glowed a cloudy white. Ava wiped her thumb across his skin from left to right. Her boss crumbled to the floor, lying motionless next to dusty shoes and cardboard boxes. Ava cursed silently. *Where was Jerome? Where was Daryl?*

The terrifying men pounded on the closet's handle with a hefty metal object. Ava had seconds before they killed her too. If these assassins got the best of Daniel, she would never forgive herself. She couldn't fail, not now.

Ava kicked open the closet door so forcefully that it broke off its hinges and slammed against her attackers. They were blown back like debris and fell near the corpse they mocked.

Stepping into the light of the ransacked office, Ava looked over the minions and stared down the thieves' menacing leader.

"Who do you work for?" Ava demanded as she squared her shoulders and lifted her chin. The men on the ground all turned to look up at the short, brown, slender secretary in surprise. They scoffed as they rose to their feet.

"Out of the way, sweetheart. We just need the formula," the militant captain ordered without a second thought. "Leave now, before you get hurt."

"I'm not going anywhere," Ava objected, raising her voice. "Who are you and who do you work for? Don't make me ask again!"

"Your primitive mind couldn't grasp it," the captain snarled.

"I doubt that, old man," Ava retorted in contempt.

Ava reached under the back of her shirt with both hands and unsheathed two graphite-colored dowels. She slammed her two fists together, interlocking both ends to form a single staff over five feet long. Ava was so fueled with purpose, she and her moldable staff began to radiate a wistful aura of emerald-green. The glowing energy swelled so bright, the men were forced to cover their eyes.

"Leave!" Ava Harlow stood her ground. "Before *you* get hurt."

The joking smiles vanished off the faces of the assailants.

"She's an agent." The captain's eyes went wide. "Get her!"

All six brutes barreled toward Ava. She leaped toward a nearby cabinet, bounced off the wall, and backflipped over the cronies like an acrobat.

She came crashing down on the shoulders of one of the intruders, knocking him over into a second one.

Ava tucked and rolled under a third attacker, swiping his right leg to topple him. Now on the opposite side of the room, she charged right into the fray of battle.

The men swung at her with meaty fists and hefty kicks.

She expertly maneuvered around their thrashing arms and legs as she kicked a man in the groin, chopped another in the neck, and swung back to elbow his neighbor across his jaw.

Just when Ava was beginning to gain control, the captain snuck into the quarrel.

He slugged Ava straight in the face, breaking her nose.

Ava recoiled in pain, losing her balance. The captain stepped closer, breathed in, and kicked her in the stomach with a mountain of force. Ava screamed as she flew back and over the top of an office desk, crashing to the ground.

"AVA!" a worried voice bellowed from down the hall. "I'm coming!"

Daniel! Ava winced on the floor, disoriented. *He's alive!*

Still bloody and bruised from the lobby, Daniel Nockby barged into the room in mission mode. He twirled his own morphstaff masterfully as he plowed through Ava's attackers. Ava got to her feet with an aching grunt to join her partner in combat.

As she looked over the desk, Ava's heart froze. A mysterious new figure covered in a dark hood entered the chamber. The shadowy villain, barely visible except for its blood-red eyes, pulled a loaded gun from its side.

"DANIEL!" Ava shrieked, begging him to somehow avoid what she knew was coming.

A gunshot fired and Daniel collapsed to the ground, dead with one blow. Ava felt immediate devastation in her bones. Their soul connection was instantly severed, as if Daniel's life meant nothing.

Ava released a guttural battle cry and launched forward in vengeance. She refused to let their mission fail. The world's future was at risk, and the only person she loved more than Daniel could never survive if she was gone.

Time seemed to slow as Ava leaped off the desk into the air above her attackers. She mystically morphed a portion of her staff into eight floating daggers. She telekinetically hurled the blades like missiles deep into the chests of the captain and his six intruders. They all dropped dead. The eighth dagger darted toward the mysterious murderer with the glowing red eyes. But the stoic villain merely sidestepped to dodge the flying knife. As Ava landed back on the floor, the eight blades shot back to reattach to her morphstaff. The ominous figure was unfazed. It raised its hand and made a grasping motion. Ava went rigid. Her muscles were stone. She couldn't move. The murderer raised their weapon once more. A cracking gunshot fired toward Ava. Within milliseconds, the entire history of her short life danced across her mind.

Ava Harlow's final heartbreak was knowing she failed the boy she left behind.

Over 1,400 years later, in mid-August of 3451, the historic destinies of four young heroes crashed together, locking the past, present, and future of our world into a new timeline of inevitable destruction.

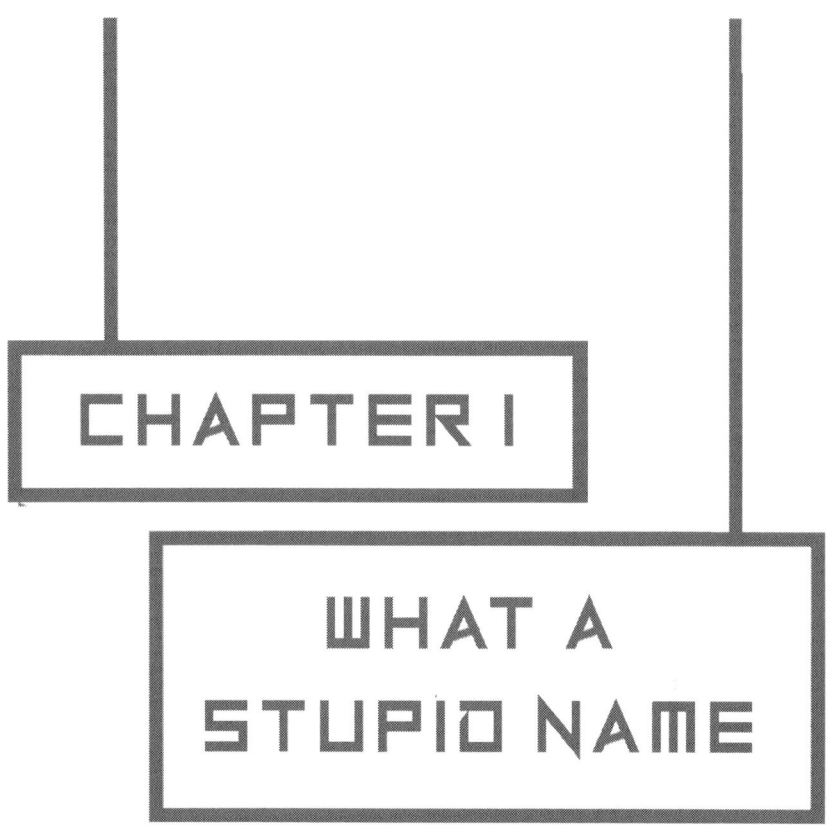

CHAPTER 1

WHAT A STUPID NAME

"**X**endo! Don't make me ask again!" the boy's mother threatened.

"Mom! Hop off! I've got one more round before the game's over!" he called back from his room.

"What?" she yelled up to him. "You told me you were packing for school!"

"Oh, shoot!" Xendo muttered with a laugh.

He took one last, glorious look at his dream man, Rory Michael, dominating the court in the instant replay. Xendo Quaker ran his fingers through his messy, silver-gray hair and grumpily switched off his holoscreen. The roaring cheers of the 3451 Grounded Staffball tournament vanished. Xendo turned to the mound of wrinkled street clothes on his bed. He stuffed the pile into his duffel bag and ran down the stairs.

"See, I'm done." Xendo plopped his bulky bag on the kitchen counter. "Mom?"

"Great, honey," Blinda Quaker called from halfway inside the oven she was scrubbing. "Can you go into town and pick us up some food?"

"You're a chef," Xendo replied. "Can't we just eat something here?"

CHAPTER 1

"We're saving the food I made for the superintendent's visit tomorrow. Do you want to help me clean or get us lunch?"

"Fine, I'll go." Xendo rolled his eyes and went to put on his shoes.

"Don't roll your eyes, it's rude," Blinda muttered without looking in his direction. She was going after an unruly grease stain.

"How could you possibly know I rolled my eyes?" Xendo asked incredulously.

"I'm Super Mom. I see all," she responded.

"Yeah, sure," he chuckled. "I can't believe I'm missing Rory's staffball match."

Blinda popped out from the oven and gave Xendo a cheeky grin.

"Ooohoo, the great Rory Michael!" she cooed in her sarcastic, mocking, mom voice. Blinda flexed her arm muscles as if she were the new model for Earth Digital's male fitness blog.

"I'm big muscle man, Rory! I wave sticks at glowing balls!" Blinda teased. "And my sport suit is too tight!"

Xendo glared at his frumpy mother with her blonde hair in a messy bun as she struck multiple muscle poses and tried not to laugh.

"Rory's the best staffball player this century and his suit fits just right, thank you very much," Xendo retorted with a playful grin. "Don't make fun of my future husband, Mom."

"Husband?" Blinda laughed. "Doesn't he have five different girlfriends each year?"

The two came to a stare down. Blinda cocked a smile, and Xendo went back to tying his shoes.

"Every cute guy is my potential husband until they tell me otherwise!" Xendo smirked. "He just hasn't met me yet!"

"Oh, is that so?" Blinda chuckled while staring at her son. His annoying confidence reminded her of his father. She softened.

"Well, any husband of yours is welcome here. Maybe he'll actually help me clean, unlike someone else I know!" she pestered while throwing her soiled towel at him.

"He won't. We'll just be making out upstairs!" Xendo joked as he dodged the dirty kitchen rag and exited their tiny cottage home.

Xendo plucked a Honeycrisp apple from the fruit trees that grew along the main road into Duluth. He enjoyed its crisp sweetness as he passed their community garden and tossed the core into the town's compost generator. He saw his neighbors chatting while gathering their

WHAT A STUPID NAME

weekly produce to cook at home with their families. Xendo smiled as their kids competed in elaborate virtual reality games in the park.

Xendo rounded the bend and was granted a gorgeous view of Lake Superior's rocky beach and its deep blue waves. Up above the green pine-forested hills were huge solar panels and colorful wind turbines, lazily spinning in the summer breeze. For centuries, both systems gave power to his whole village in Minnesota and left extra energy to spare. His city, like many others, was a harmonized mix of nature and technology.

Xendo arrived at the busy town square, entered his mother's favorite sandwich shop, and ordered some food. He waited on the store's patio and saw an elderly couple enjoying lunch with a younger friend. Xendo couldn't help but eavesdrop when he discovered they were discussing politics.

"I'll be sad to see Namid Kanosha go," the elderly woman lamented as she enjoyed some tomato gazpacho. "All the global presidents have been effective these past few decades, but she's been the best."

Her husband nodded while chewing a bite of his smoked lox sandwich.

"All community budgets were increased for infrastructure around the globe, employment is up, our monthly universal income increased, and her push to have education tech updated each year was great for the grandkids."

"Kanosha perfected the art of actually listening to requests made by the masses and bringing the world's origins together to solve our problems," agreed the younger friend, sticking her fork into her quinoa salad. "If the next president keeps doing that, they really can't go wrong."

"Do you think a trioka will ever run?" the cheery grandfather asked. His wife knocked his knee under the table.

"Marc! You can't ask her that," his wife chastised, "just 'cause she's trioka."

"It's fine!" The friend laughed with them. "People in this little dioka town ask me questions like that all the time!"

"I think a trioka should run!" the grandma expressed. "We've had multiple presidents of every sort except for trioka. They deserve a shot! They could run under the smaller Freedom Party."

The younger friend paused for a moment. Xendo leaned in.

3

CHAPTER 1

"Run? Yes. Win? No," the woman answered. "Listen, even that trioka widow here in town was outcast by her own origin just because her husband failed some government mission. If the world can't be kind to a trioka who makes mistakes, the world would never accept a trioka as its leader."

The elderly couple sank back in their seats. Xendo grabbed a menu to hide behind. They were gossiping about *his* trioka family. A server called his order. Xendo dashed to quickly grab the food before he was seen. He strained to hear the last of their conversation while leaving the deli.

"OMNI can't be around anymore," the older woman mused, "their ideologies died centuries ago."

"Nah, that's what they want you to think," the friend replied. "Look at history; hatred never goes away."

Xendo plodded the short journey back home to his mother. Instead of enjoying the scenery, Xendo was now lost in thought. *I'm trioka. Why are so many people afraid of us? Why would they hate me for something I can't change?*

Xendo held up his face to their front door's scanner. It beeped and let him in. Xendo forgot his troubles when he caught his mom shaking her bum to old lady music and sweeping the floors. Xendo chuckled and placed the food on the kitchen island.

"Oooh, what did you get me?" Blinda called out while turning the music down, not at all embarrassed of her weird mom dancing.

"A sandwich from Lakeside Deli," Xendo replied while his mother gasped in delight, "and a green tea kombucha to cool you down."

"Oh! Their salt beef with garlic mustard on einkorn sourdough!" His mother chirped with glee as she unwrapped the sandwich. "Is there—"

"Extra dill pickle spears are in the bag," Xendo cut her off with a smile. "I didn't forget. I chose their super-green salad."

"I love you," Blinda cooed while taking a huge first bite.

The pair ate their lunch before moving on to finish their last cleaning job: sorting through old belongings in Xendo's childhood storage pods. Blinda opened a pod that she hadn't seen in years and gasped with excitement as she looked inside. It had old photographs, Xendo's baby toys, and napkins with old recipes scribbled onto them.

"Why do you have so many printed photos, Mom?" Xendo won-

WHAT A STUPID NAME

dered aloud. "It's easier to just keep them in Earth's Database."

"It's like you and your old books! I like to hold them in my actual hands. A sweet way of saving memories," she purred while looking at each of Xendo's baby photos endearingly.

"After I started at the café," Blinda continued with a pout, "life became just a bit too hectic. I miss these easy days."

Xendo nodded. His mother was the hardest worker he knew.

"Aw, look!" Blinda whipped out a photo from a folder at the bottom of the pod. "Here's one of your father!"

"Really?" Xendo remarked while moving closer. "Oh, wow!"

Xendo rarely saw images of his father. He peered over at the photo to notice six friends posing in front of the large glass doors of SIYT. The school's name, "Superior Institute of Young Trioka," was scrawled above the entrance behind their beaming faces. A younger Blinda was on the very left, standing in the cleanest chef whites Xendo had ever seen her wear. She must have ironed them and everything. On the right side was a friendly-looking older woman in a sensible gray suit.

"Is that Superintendent Pearl?" Xendo asked, shocked.

"It sure is!" Blinda proudly replied.

"I didn't know you were friends *that* far back." Xendo looked to his mother.

"Of course! How do you think I got my job?" she laughed.

Next, Xendo's eyes moved to the four people in the center, dressed in all black, head to toe. They carried large backpacks and morphstaffs.

"This was taken before their mission back to 2005. We were all about thirty then. Well, except for Nova, of course," Blinda stated simply.

"No way!" Xendo said, grabbing the photo to peer even closer.

"Yep! It was still pretty hush-hush back then. They traveled back that afternoon, and then my life went up in smoke."

Sure enough, between Superintendent Nova Pearl and his mother, was the infamous 2005 team. Standing next to his wife was Xendo's father, Jerome Quaker. He was an incredibly handsome man with a sharp jawline and messy silver-gray locks, just like Xendo. It's funny how all the Quakers seemed to have messy hair. Xendo could barely remember his father at all. Jerome Quaker's team had failed their time travel mission when he was only two years old.

"And see," Blinda sighed solemnly, "there's Daryl Irwin. Poor boy. He was a bit younger than the other three. He didn't know how tragic

CHAPTER 1

the mission would become. He returned a completely different man."

The young Daryl Irwin was grinning from ear to ear. He had jet black hair, brown eyes, and a welcoming expression. He is now known as Ambassador Daryl Irwin and works as the Global Government's advocate for the trioka people of Earth. Xendo was always proud that the ambassador had been friends with his father before he died.

Blinda shuddered and placed her hand on her chest. Her voice wobbled as she recounted flashbacks of that fateful day.

"All four of them entered the time portal. We expected them to return in just a second so we could celebrate. But no, Daryl fell out the portal alone with his legs cut off, blood everywhere! It was horrifying, but not as terrible as the news about your father, Daniel, and Ava."

Daniel Nockby and Ava Harlow were the two other members of the 2005 team. They were in the very center of the photograph. Everyone had their arms around each other, except those two. His father and Daniel could have been brothers, they were so close. Daniel was attractive and strong. However, Ava was the most beautiful woman Xendo had ever seen. She had dark brown skin and chest-length passion twists strewn over to one side. Her lovely smile and intense hazel eyes made Xendo never want to look away. They were mysterious and kept drawing him in.

"You don't talk about any of them that much," Xendo muttered, not releasing the woman's frozen glance. "You must miss Ava."

"She was my best friend," Blinda sighed. "Even though we came from separate parts of the world and had no classes together, we were still inseparable at SIYT until our Primary Advancement. She stayed for SIYT's Human History when I left for my culinary graduate program. She also introduced me to Jerome."

Xendo had always wished his mother would share about his father more, but he never wanted to push. Xendo didn't even think to ask if she missed the other team members. He could tell his mother must have had many depressing nights after the day this photo was taken.

"Ava was the only person who told me if my food wasn't good enough. Jerome just ate everything." Blinda laughed as a tear fell. "With his mouth stuffed full of food, he'd spit out, 'Delicious, babe!' But Ava would tell me if she thought I could tweak something to make it better."

Xendo placed his hand on her shoulder. She reached up to hold it.

WHAT A STUPID NAME

"If the mission hadn't failed, what do you think they'd be doing now?" Xendo asked empathetically.

Blinda took a deep breath and looked up in thought. "Well, the public never knew they traveled to the past before Irwin's accident made it a huge scandal. Most historical agents keep working for the government after missions if they're not too worn out. Neither Daniel nor Ava were really the quitting type," Blinda muttered softly and smiled as she gazed into the photo. "Jerome would have retired, that lazy bum."

"It's really a shame." Xendo hugged her from her side. He put his head into her shoulder. "Maybe, if they had come back, Daniel and Ava could have worked their way up at Global, could have found cool spouses, and started families of their own. You could cook for dinner parties," Xendo nudged her playfully. "C'mon, you'd like that!"

"Yeah." Blinda snorted absentmindedly. "*Other* spouses."

Xendo felt her smirking and got confused.

"What's that supposed to mean?" Xendo chuckled as he took his head off her shoulder and looked for meaning in her smiling face. Blinda stopped suddenly and looked away from the photo.

"Mom?" Xendo asked curiously. Something was amiss.

Blinda ignored him and suddenly acted like her old crumbled up recipes at the bottom of the storage pod were like rare, ancient American dollar bills. Xendo stared at his mother and made a fed-up face.

"All right! She *has* been gone for over a decade." Blinda slowly flattened out a recipe for coq au vin, then raised her eyes to meet Xendo's gaze.

"Ava and Daniel were secretly dating," she whispered as Xendo gasped. "They used to hate each other. Daniel could be kind of cocky, and Ava never had time for that nonsense. But after their graduation, I guess they developed sparks."

"Mom!" Xendo couldn't believe what he was hearing.

"What? It wasn't my secret to tell. She'd only just told me the night before they left! They never got caught!" Blinda admitted while shrugging her shoulders. Xendo's mind was reeling.

"They could have been fired! Or their mission could have been given to different agents!" Xendo exclaimed in surprise.

"They were smart about it. Agents break that rule all the time!" Blinda waved her hand.

CHAPTER 1

"Not when they're on the same team! Did Superintendent Pearl know about it?" Xendo questioned.

"Nope, or else they wouldn't have been approved for 2005." Blinda looked up from the photo. "Damn, I wish Nova *had* figured it out." Xendo saw his mother's spirits falling again and tried to lighten the mood.

"Well, I'm impressed. They must be pretty darn crafty," Xendo concluded. Blinda gently set the photo on the countertop and tossed the clutter they didn't need into their incinerator bin.

"If all four of them had come back, Ava and Daniel could probably have gotten married publicly and had kids. Jerome and I could've given you siblings. Our families could have grown up together," Blinda pondered.

"Then I could actually have some friends," Xendo scoffed.

"Oh, don't say that!" Blinda responded, punching him lightly in the arm.

"Ow!" Xendo laughed while recoiling.

"If you took your head out of your books or away from Rory Michael for just a few seconds, maybe you'd make some!" she taunted.

"No one at school likes me, and I'm smarter than all of them, even the Skybornes. I feel like Daniel and Ava's children would have understood us more," Xendo complained.

"Once you start your graduate program this year, you'll have smaller classes with new kids that will be into the same subjects you are. All you have to do is talk with them. It's all about timing. People can surprise you," Blinda explained.

He looked at the photo of his father's team and their beaming faces on the counter.

"Wait!" Xendo's eyes lit up. "How long did the ambassador say their 2005 mission was? When did they actually arrive?"

"Hmmm. They landed well before 2005 and had to stay many months after. I think Irwin said it was about five years," Blinda stated blankly, stuffing the last of the "to keep" items in the pods for storage.

Xendo snatched the photo and scanned it rapidly like he was hunting for a clue. He gave his mother a look he always had when he was up to no good, or cracked a difficult math problem.

"No one knows what happened to them! Maybe Daniel and Ava ran off together? They could have had a whole other life in the past!

WHAT A STUPID NAME

Maybe they had kids?" Xendo's brain was exploding with ideas.

Blinda turned pink in the face. "Ava would never do such a thing. Don't be silly now."

"There are rumors the team split up for a large chunk of the mission, and the diokas in the 2000s would never have found their relationship problematic!" Xendo pressed on.

"Ava would never abandon their objective," Blinda assured defensively. "I've told you, don't listen to wacko conspiracy theories from strangers."

Xendo's excitement just kept growing. "What if they got, like, ancient digital-era jobs? What if their kids were *trioka*? In the early 2000s!"

"Xendo, stop, this is ridiculous!" Blinda countered, getting frustrated. Xendo didn't care. Anything to distract from cleaning was worth joking about.

"Hey! You never know! Let's search the ED." Xendo jumped up from the table and tapped his technoband. The small metal bracelet produced a blue holoscreen. Xendo selected the icons for Earth's Database and spread his personal display wider in the air. The search engine was ready for entry.

"Did she have any favorite kid names?" Xendo asked.

"I'm telling you, you won't find anything," Blinda stated adamantly.

"C'mon, let me have fun with this," Xendo grunted.

"Ugh, fine," Blinda relented. "She liked Regan, try Regan Harlow, I guess."

Xendo typed the name on the holoscreen. "No results, what else?"

They entered all of Ava's favorite names. They even tried them with Daniel's surname, Nockby. All the options had zero results.

"That's everything she's ever mentioned." Blinda was stumped. "I mean, I once told her that I liked the name Philo. Ava really loved my Greek food. It was—"

"*Philo?*" Xendo interrupted curtly. "What a stupid name."

"Shut up, I think it means 'loving.' It's sweet," Blinda argued.

"*Loving?*" Xendo blurted, shoving a finger near his mouth to fake barf.

"I also like Phyllo dough. It's a play on words," Blinda added.

"For the love of Earth, Mom!" Xendo rolled his eyes at how lame she was.

"Hey!" Blinda punched him again. "It made her laugh! I just men-

CHAPTER 1

tioned it casually when I made her dinner one night. But yeah, she'd never remember any of that."

"Yeah," Xendo scoffed, "I'm trying to forget it now!"

"Okay, Mister! We're done with all this kid nonsense, right?" Blinda lifted the first finished pod. "Help me carry these downstairs!"

"Is all this cleaning really necessary before I move out?" Xendo complained. "Primary Advancement isn't until tomorrow. School is just a ten-minute walk and one quick skytube from here."

"Now that you're fourteen, you'll be boarding full-time. I'm putting you to work while I still can. Let's go," his mother concluded as she carried the storage containers to the basement.

Xendo sighed. His distraction didn't stall long enough. While sitting alone at the kitchen counter, Xendo stared back at the empty database page. He typed "Philo Nockby" into the search engine looking for results in the early 2000s. The holoscreen remained blank, still nothing. That stupid name was as pointless as the others. Xendo stood up to leave. As he reached to turn off the display, the screen flashed briefly. A single information page lined up on the holoscreen. Xendo couldn't believe his eyes.

"Mom! Mom! I got something!" Xendo belted out to her. "Mom! Come here!"

"What?" Blinda yelled from the basement, not hearing him.

Xendo raised his voice to bellow even louder, "You were right! Ava had a kid named Philo!"

Xendo heard the clang of a metallic storage pod crashing to the floor beneath him, then the cantankerous sounds of his mother tripping up the stairs.

"No way! It's not possible," she huffed, out of breath when she re-entered the kitchen. Xendo pointed to the ED holoscreen. Blinda shook her head, "No freakin' way! I bet it's Daniel's fault!"

Xendo watched his mother rub her temples in stress.

"Well?" Blinda urged, "Click on it, already!"

"Oh, right!" Xendo chuckled. He touched the first link with his index finger and it opened up an ancient file from May 8, 2019.

"It's from an obsolete video sharing website from the digital era. Here, let's look," Xendo muttered softly while trying to convert the archaic data to be watchable on their modern holoscreen.

An antiquated red and white web page opened and a video

WHAT A STUPID NAME

popped up in front of them. The video title on the bottom read *Philo Nockby's Personal Essay Notes (First Draft).* It had zero views and showed a thumbnail of a small teenage boy with olive-brown skin, wavy, dark hair, and hazel eyes. Xendo touched the red play button. The boy started talking nervously in a strange, slow accent from the past. Xendo was immediately mesmerized the same way he had been with the woman back in the 2005 mission photo. With each passing second of the four-and-half-minute footage, Xendo and Blinda's jaws dropped millimeter by millimeter. The video finished playing. This mysterious teen just ruined their perception of reality, and yet, the mother and son couldn't stop smiling.

"Ava would be so proud," Blinda murmured, wiping tears off her cheeks.

Xendo felt an indescribable urge to understand this boy who shouldn't even exist.

CHAPTER 2

CHORES OF A TWISTED HEART

Philo Nockby breathed in the stale dustiness of his pillow and felt sloppy drool leaking from his lips. He opened his groggy eyes and peered around his bedroom to see three other foster boys fast asleep. Jonathan, the youngest at age four, slept on a spare mattress on the ground. He had dark, frizzy hair, and was clutching his little stuffed horse named Hercules.

Jonathan arrived only three months ago. He hopped around lots of foster homes just like Philo had. Jonathan did sometimes cry late at night. The whimpering made it difficult for all the foster kids to sleep. His whole life, Philo never had his own room.

Philo quietly sat up in his bed and his sweaty pajama shirt clung to him like cooked spaghetti to a wall. Philo changed into his ripped jeans and one of his six faded t-shirts. Most of his clothes became too snug a few group homes ago. What was left he kept in a black trash bag under his bed. Philo didn't own any other belongings because his parents died before he was even a toddler. As soon as he became comfortable in a new foster home, he would just get transferred again. Philo learned there was no point in saving what was worthless.

Philo snuck through the hallway and down the staircase. Their kitchen looked like it was straight out of a cheap 1980s sitcom. Philo

CHORES OF A TWISTED HEART

opened the refrigerator to find a carton of eggs, half a jar of salsa, apricot jam, and a nearly empty gallon of milk. On the counter was some overly ripe fruit and a bag of sliced Wonder Bread. Philo sighed. He had worked with worse.

As Philo grabbed the eggs and started cooking, he felt a finger poke his hip.

"Boo!" Jonathan shrieked behind him. Philo flinched and almost dropped the frying pan.

"Good morning, Philo," the boy laughed.

"You scared me!" Philo smiled, placing the eggs and a little bowl of salsa on the table. "Did you sleep well?"

"Kind of." Jonathan sat at the table, eagerly. "Hi, Gabby!"

A young girl of about eleven entered the kitchen. She was one of the other eight children at the group home.

"I didn't sleep well," Gabby complained while sitting down. "Monica came home super late and woke Jonathan up. Chelsea and Rachel were chatting about their friends until ten, but I guess I'm used to that."

Philo added the ripe fruit and milk into their shoddy green blender that luckily pureed their breakfast smoothies before calling it quits. As he poured their drinks into nine reusable plastic cups, the last three foster girls approached the dining room table. Rachel sat next to Gabby without taking her eyes off of her phone. Chelsea tousled Philo's hair and grabbed one of the smoothie cups.

"Hey! The guys aren't up yet!" Philo called out, hoping they could eat like a real family for once.

"It doesn't matter, Philo," Chelsea retorted with a shrug as she tasted the smoothie. "Oh, this is good."

Monica, the oldest, grabbed her backpack, and rushed to the fridge.

"Philo! Did you use all the milk?" she yelled at him.

"There was only a little bit. I used it in the eggs and smoothies for everyone," Philo replied, hoping it wasn't a big deal.

"I wanted cereal! I need to go with my friends early today," Monica scolded while glaring down at him.

"Um, sorry? I didn't know," Philo responded nervously.

"Ugh, whatever." Monica reached up to grab a box of sugary cereal. "How hard is it to make sure we have enough milk? You're supposed to keep track of the food. Do your chores right, or I'm complaining

CHAPTER 2

to Doug!"

With that, Monica turned on her heels with the box of Cocoa Puffs and slammed the door on her way out. No one was shaken by this dramatic outburst.

"Where *is* Mr. Kelly?" Jonathan asked.

"Who knows?" Chelsea said with a sigh. "He was probably at the bar last night."

"I know Jenna died like a year ago, but he needs to pull it together before I call social services," Rachel complained aloud even though her eyes were glued to her phone.

Doug Kelly was their assigned caretaker. He owned the house and was supposed to be at home when any foster kid was present. Robert, Monica, Topher, Chelsea, and Rachel all said he used to be funny and kind. So was Jenna Kelly, his wife. Jenna was a childhood cancer survivor and loved helping kids to have better younger years than her own. She had worked at the local orphanage in Philo's town for years before marrying Doug. Not being able to have children of their own, they decided to open their home to foster children. They took the kids on trips, helped them with homework, and had apparently been amazing foster parents. However, two years ago, new malignant cancer cells had regrown in Jenna's brain and killed her in a matter of months. She died just before Philo was transferred to Mr. Kelly's home.

Doug started neglecting and resenting the children he was paid to take care of. He demanded they start calling him Mr. Kelly and forbade them from mentioning his wife again. He turned to late nights of drinking for solace. Any troubling memories of Jenna must have stung worse than the alcohol burning his throat. At times, he would shout or even get violent, but usually, he just wasn't around. Philo didn't mind being in charge of making meals—he liked cooking—he just wished Mr. Kelly kept their food supply more consistent.

"Can I have some eggs and toast?" Gabby asked, eyeing up the plated food.

"Yeah, I'm starving," Rachel agreed.

Robert, the oldest foster boy, hustled through the kitchen, talking on his phone and wearing his letter jacket.

"Are you ready to eat?" Philo asked.

"I'm good. I have my protein shake!" the athlete waved a bottle with creamy liquid in Philo's direction. "Thanks anyway."

CHORES OF A TWISTED HEART

"Go ahead," Philo told the girls as Robert left the house. "Don't make a big mess, though. I have to clean the dishes before the bus comes."

The girls and Jonathan started eating as Philo grabbed himself a plate. Topher, the laziest of the house's teens, trudged into the room with a wide yawn, scratching his stomach. He brought his school bag to the table and sat down.

"Eggs with salsa?" he said with displeased eyebrows.

"It's all we had left," Philo stated. "I'll tell Mr. Kelly we need more food whenever he shows up."

Disregarding his own previous disgust, Topher took a huge pile of the scrambled eggs and doused it with the salsa. After everyone finished eating, They got ready to leave for school. Topher was the first to walk out.

"Topher!" Chelsea bellowed.

"What?" He poked his head back in, confused.

"The garbage!" Chelsea angrily grunted. "You're finally here, so I shouldn't have to do your job for you again."

"Ugh, fine," Topher moaned. He tied the garbage bag, threw the large mound over his shoulder, and followed Chelsea, Rachel, and Gabby out their dull, white door.

"Can I help clean?" Jonathan looked up at Philo.

"Oh, thanks, bud," Philo smiled as he finished clearing all the plastic plates to the sink. "Can you just put the jars back and wash the table for me, please?"

"Yep!" Jonathan chirped.

Philo handed a soapy towel to the boy and continued speed-washing the dishes. He knew the bus should be here any minute, but, luckily, it arrived just down the street. A sudden, loud sound shocked Philo. He whipped toward the noise.

Jonathan gasped, "Oops."

While making exuberant, soapy circles, Jonathan had knocked the condiments off the table, making them fly toward the refrigerator. Glass shards, apricot jam, and salsa were all over the wall and linoleum floor. As Philo's mouth fell open, Jonathan had tears welling up in his eyes.

"I'm sorry, I... I... was trying to help." The boy started whimpering.

"Oh, it's okay, don't worry about it. We all make mistakes," Philo

CHAPTER 2

comforted as he kneeled down at Jonathan's level.

"I'm so stupid," Jonathan mumbled feebly.

"No, you're not," Philo sighed, calming him down. "You just have to wipe tables a little less fast next time, okay?"

"Okay," Jonathan muttered. Philo glanced at the clock on the wall showing it was half past the hour.

"What should I do?" Jonathan looked at the mess again.

"Uh, nothing, I guess," Philo breathed. "You're going to miss your bus to St. James if you don't go right now. I can miss my first period. I hate gym class anyway."

Jonathan reached out and hugged Philo. Philo hugged back.

"Now, go catch up with Gabby!" Philo told him.

After the little boy left the house, the room was dead silent. Philo groaned. He now had to clean more *and* walk the five miles to his high school. As Philo started sweeping the messy floor, the back door opened. Philo turned and saw Mr. Kelly walk into the room. Startled, Philo stepped back and landed on a big chunk of glass. He felt a sharp pain hit the sole of his foot, but Philo dared not move an inch.

"I had a late night," Mr. Kelly called out to the kids that were no longer around. "You all better be off to school soon. I uh—"

He stopped in his tracks. All Mr. Kelly saw was the huge mess and Philo staring back at him.

"What the *hell* happened here?" Mr. Kelly yelled. "Where is everyone else?"

"It was an accident—," Philo started.

"You rotten kids!" Mr. Kelly bellowed. "I'm gone for just a couple hours, and chaos erupts in this damn house! Which one of them did this? Was it you?"

"Well, I mean—," Philo tried to explain.

"I'm going to the advisory board and telling them eight kids is too many. I can't handle this anymore. It's all too much. I should never have signed for more than four!"

Philo ignored whatever blood was surely leaking from the wound in his foot and continued to sweep while being yelled at. He wished he was invisible right now. A porcelain bowl whizzed by Philo's left ear and hit the wall with a loud crash.

"Hey! I'm speaking to you, dumbass!" Mr. Kelly yelled as the shattered bowl shards fell to the sticky floor.

CHORES OF A TWISTED HEART

Philo turned around, terrified, locking eyes with the furious Mr. Kelly.

"I swear, you're all more trouble than you're worth! Which one of them did this?" demanded Mr. Kelly, not giving up.

"I did it," Philo lied.

Mr. Kelly cursed and rubbed his forehead. "Didn't you learn from the last mess!? If you can't do your simple chore, you're transferred!"

"I'm sorry, I'll clean it up. You won't even notice there was a mess," Philo pleaded.

"Hurry up then." Mr. Kelly checked his watch and released an angry grunt. "If you don't get to school today, I'll get a call from that horrible principal."

Philo let out a sigh of relief and waited for any other commands.

"Well? Stop staring at me like an idiot and get scrubbing! I have to get to the office before they realize I'm late." Mr. Kelly stepped around the splatter and opened the fridge.

"Oh, and we're out of food again," Philo mentioned as quietly as he could, to minimize the blowback he knew was coming. Mr. Kelly swore and slammed the fridge shut, almost knocking the door off its hinges.

"More food? I don't have time for this! What has my life become?" He brushed past Philo and stomped to the front door. "Don't expect anything too fancy. Our budget is too low to feed eight ungrateful brats. Now, clean up that mess and get your ass to school!"

"Yes, sir," Philo responded.

With that, Philo was left alone again. He let his chin drop to his chest and released a slow, deep sigh. Philo winced as he remembered the painful glass shard stuck in his bare foot. He carefully lifted his leg to inspect how gross the bloody wound became during Mr. Kelly's tirade. As he scanned his sole, Philo was shocked to see no blood. *That's weird.* Philo tugged on the sizable shard until it released. He stared at it for a second, then shrugged his shoulders. That was a stroke of luck that Philo wasn't used to.

While scrubbing the walls and mopping the floor clean, Philo hoped Mr. Kelly wouldn't actually complain to the advisory board. Starting over now would be devastating. Philo threw the dirty wash rag in the sink with frustration, startling himself with the loud noise. Apricot jam splashed back to stain his school shirt. Philo scrunched his eyes and dropped his head in his hands. He didn't want to cry this

CHAPTER 2

early in the morning.

Whatever, Philo told himself. If he did get transferred, it would suck, but he'd been through worse. Philo put away the mop and grabbed his ratty, red backpack filled with outdated schoolbooks. He glanced at himself in the dirty mirror. The apricot stain on his shirt was never coming out. Philo groaned with annoyance at the mirror, hating his own reflection.

Central High isn't that terrible, Philo thought as he stared down at his grungy sneakers walking toward his last class of the day. The food wasn't as horrendous as the past three schools he attended and his classes were so simple he had extra time to read. Philo didn't feel upset. He was just bored and beaten down. He wanted more for his life, but also lost whatever curiosity he once had. Nothing ever worked out for Philo, no matter how hard he tried. He would finally feel like he belonged somewhere; then, like clockwork, he would be transferred. His foster family would tell him it was always supposed to be a "temporary situation," and he knew it was. They all said that.

Philo turned left into Mrs. Jofald's creative writing class and headed straight to the back corner. As the rest of the students corralled into the room like sheep, Philo glanced at his own face in the window on his left. He saw bags under his eyes. Copper skin. Pesky pimples. Even though it had already been a terrible day, he still mustered a smile just for himself.

"Four more years," Philo whispered. "Just four more."

When Philo turned eighteen, he could escape anywhere he wanted. Maybe he could get into a fancy college or look for a job in a big city. He could finally create his own life, whatever that may be. Philo stopped analyzing his own face and gazed through the glass toward the beautiful Hudson River underneath the distant hills of Hyde Park. He loved getting lost in the horizon beyond every window. The world out there must be so wonderful. However, to Philo, wonderful was always out of reach.

"Okay, everyone, listen up!" Mrs. Jofald announced, drawing eyes as she strolled to the center of the room. "As our creative writing class comes to its end this school year, I'm proud of all your thoughts and emotions we've explored through prose. I've enjoyed the time we've spent together, and I hope you have as well."

CHORES OF A TWISTED HEART

Some of the kids nodded along with the teacher, detecting her kind sentiments, but most gawked blankly at the chalkboard behind her like it was a news program they were forced to watch.

"I hope you all learned how powerful your words and voices can be. You may not understand it yet, but many of you have great talent," Mrs. Jofald continued, glancing at Philo. They made eye contact but Philo broke away to stare at his blank notebook. He sensed her compliment but didn't want anyone else to.

"One common trend I sense we could all improve on is honesty and vulnerability. When I read your papers, I sometimes feel like we are writing for a good grade or completion points and not trying to make the work the best it can be," Mrs. Jofald explained.

Even though it seemed like Philo was just playing with his pencil, rolling it around in his fingers, he was glued to every word she uttered.

"When we write, sometimes we exaggerate the positives and hide the negatives because we can finally edit our own thoughts. But I want us to be *better*, to find the truth in what we put on the page."

This is why Philo admired Mrs. Jofald. Other teachers didn't care if he had reread this semester's textbooks twice and that his classmates hadn't even cracked theirs open. They lost enthusiasm, just like their students, but not Mrs. Jofald.

"Tonight, for homework, I want you each to record yourself on a video camera. Explain who you are and what's important to you. Do it as if you were describing a mental picture of yourself to a complete stranger. No script, no pauses, just keep talking. Reveal a secret, tell a sad memory, remember the last time you laughed so hard your side cramped up. On Monday, you can watch them back and write me an essay telling me who you *really* are. What does your face look like when you're honest? How does your voice sound? What did you find out about yourself?"

Mrs. Jofald returned to her seat, and the students reluctantly pulled out their notebooks.

Philo didn't understand how recording himself would reveal anything he didn't already know. He also had a problem. All his classmates had a smartphone they could easily film themselves on, but Philo never owned anything that expensive. Some of the classmates were already recording selfie-style videos mentioning their annoying parents, a sick new car they wanted, or how much their many friends meant to

CHAPTER 2

them. The bell soon rang and the students herded out of the classroom to head home, Philo realized he needed to talk with his teacher. He couldn't do this assignment.

"Mrs. Jofald? I don't have my own phone to film myself," Philo whispered.

"Oh. Well, any form of video recording will work," she replied pleasantly. "Maybe someone in your family has one?"

Philo turned his head to the left. He couldn't look her in the eyes. "I don't have a family. I live in a foster home."

"Oh, Philo. I'm so sorry, I didn't know." Mrs. Jofald tilted her head in sympathy and reached out to him. Philo knew she was trying to be kind, but he was too embarrassed to take her hands offering comfort.

"See, this is what I'm talking about, Philo," Mrs. Jofald expressed warmly. "You're one of my brightest students this year. Heck, of all my years teaching! I've wanted you to open up this whole time, but I still don't know anything about you."

"I… I don't even really know… who I am, yet," Philo uttered softly.

"Ah," Mrs. Jofald smiled somberly, sitting back in her chair, "there it is."

"There *what* is?" Philo asked, confused.

"The truth, Philo," Mrs. Jofald stated. Philo had fallen into her clever trap. He smiled slightly as she leaned forward.

"None of us know who we truly are. It's a painful journey that takes our whole life to figure out. In your essay, show me this side of you, Philo. The honest side. You'll start uncoiling mental tapestries you didn't even know you've woven. You don't know who you are? Then ask yourself, *why? Why* don't you know? What are you missing? What do you need to *discover?*"

"I… I guess I need to—"

"Nope!" Mrs. Jofald cut him off, waving her finger in a funny way that made Philo forget his train of thought. "Save all the revelations for when you record yourself. You have to watch it happen on your own face in real-time!"

"I do think my caretaker has a laptop," Philo thought aloud.

"Wonderful! See! Things are looking up already!" Mrs. Jofald concluded cheerfully, hands up in the air. "I'm looking forward to your essay, Philo. And I hope you discover a wonderful new side of yourself that surprises you."

CHORES OF A TWISTED HEART

After his bumpy bus ride back to the group home, Philo noticed that Mr. Kelly had restocked the groceries. Philo half-expected the man to be there, ready to yell at him again, but the caretaker wasn't around. Philo knew he should ask Mr. Kelly to borrow the laptop. However, he didn't want anyone asking too many questions. What if Mr. Kelly wanted to sit with him while he recorded his video essay? Horrendously embarrassing. Philo decided to wait until everyone fell asleep.

After a few hours of distracting himself by reading a fascinating book on food history in his bedroom, Philo noticed the clock had just passed 11:34 p.m. The boys were snoring around him in their beds, and he was sure the girls must be sound asleep, too. His stomach growled. All the food from his book made him ravenous, but he couldn't risk making a snack. It was now the perfect time to record his video.

Philo tiptoed out of the bedroom and snuck down the stairs. He desperately hoped none of the other foster kids would hear him. Especially Jonathan, who had trouble sleeping. Philo sat at Mr. Kelly's cheap desk near the large family room window. He soaked in the quiet freedom of being the only kid awake in the foster house at night. Philo opened up Mr. Kelly's laptop, launched YouTube in a new tab, repositioned the camera angle, and pressed record. A little red dot appeared, signaling for him to begin.

"Okay, so, I'm Philo Nockby. I just turned fourteen in April, and my life is fine. I don't really know what I'm supposed to say exactly, but I guess that's the point. I've only gone to Central High for this school year, and so far, it's not that bad. Most of the kids around here have rich families. They wear fancy clothes and are dropped off in fancy cars. I won't ever drive because," Philo scoffed all alone in the moonlit room, "I'm broke, and where would I go?

"I might work in a small restaurant to earn some money one day if I knew I could stay in one city for more than a year. Maybe learn how to cook something interesting? That would be fun. Um... what else? I've never had a girlfriend. I think young romances are naive. There is no possible way you could imagine your whole future with someone when you aren't even fully grown yet. I barely know who I am now, let alone what I'll be in, like, ten years!" Philo checked his little notebook for bullet points and kept going.

"Oh yeah, I have a birthmark, right here on my chest," Philo pulled down the collar of his t-shirt to show the camera a strangely

CHAPTER 2

shaped brown spot.

"One of the foster kids here named Gabby said that it looked like someone drew a heart and then tried to twist it. I thought that sounded kind of weird, but then Topher joked that it resembled an upside-down ball sack!" Philo admitted with a laugh. "It doesn't really matter to me, but if anyone ever asked, obviously, I would prefer to say it looks like a twisted heart."

"Umm..., I'm intelligent, I like food a lot, maybe I said that already, and I find sports boring. I enjoy this creative writing class, even if I don't say I do. I don't like to engage in small talk with people. That's also why I probably don't have any friends; I just don't invest the time or energy. I can look people in the eyes and already know how they feel and that they don't want to speak to me. They think I'm poor and gross, a weird foster kid. If they want to avoid me, why should I bother with them?" Philo scratched his head, suddenly a little too self-conscious.

"Is something wrong with me? I mean, sure, I'd like to have friends or a girlfriend, but it just never works out. I can't control that I get shipped around to a new broken family every couple of months. Like, why did all this have to happen to me?"

Philo took a moment to collect himself. He gave Mrs. Jofald credit. She was right. He never would have written all of this in a paper.

"I've been in and out of different foster homes for as long as I can remember. I don't know if Mr. Kelly will keep me up until graduation. Which sucks, because that's all I need... Ugh. I just look at other kids, and they have it *so* easy. They've been in the same house with their parents all their lives. How is that fair?

"My parents died when I was really little. I don't remember anything about them. Nothing about who they were, what they looked like, nothing. Well, no, wait. I *do* know their names were Dan and Ava. I've tried searching online for something about them or any other Nockby, but there's nothing! It's like they barely even existed. I think about them every day. Who were they? Am I more like my dad? Or my mom? What did they do for a living? What did they do for fun? *Is it my fault they died?* And... and... I always wonder what my life would be like if they were still here.

"I don't know. I just... I feel like everyone around me has a headstart on life and that I'm miles behind. What if my parents were just like... awesome? And I missed out on getting to know them! I have the

CHORES OF A TWISTED HEART

worst luck. If they never gave birth to me, maybe they'd be alive right now. Why did I live, and they had to die? I feel like it's *my* fault. I do! I don't think I'll ever find out who I am because I don't know my own history. I...."

Philo sighed. That was going to have to be enough. He felt too worked up to keep rambling. Philo didn't usually talk about his past because it made him yearn for the impossible. He pressed "upload" on the open tab and waited for it to finish.

Philo felt miserable. Today had been too long. He closed the laptop, being meticulous enough to make it look like it had never been touched, and tiptoed back up to the boys' room.

Tomorrow was Saturday. He could avoid his thoughts by sleeping until noon and reading the rest of the day. He took off his clothes and relaxed into bed. Philo realized that most kids would already have exciting plans with friends or family after their school week was over. Philo wished he had loved ones, or literally anyone, to enjoy his weekends with.

While breathing in the scent of his stained pillow, Philo gazed out his bedroom window at the moon. The starry sky made it seem like the glowing sphere was in good company; the moon and its friends looked picturesque and peaceful. However, Philo knew those stars were all light-years away, and the moon was as lonely and melancholy as he was.

Philo wondered that *if* the moon, up there in the night sky, could have its own thoughts, what would it think about? Would it understand that it has fascinated astronomers and artists for centuries? That so many couples have fallen in love while gazing up at it from down below? That every person on earth witnessed its evening beauty each night? *Probably not,* Philo concluded. He closed his eyes and let a tiny yawn escape his mouth. *The moon would only know of its own isolation.* Philo finally fell asleep, dreaming about the stars.

The moon could never comprehend its own value.

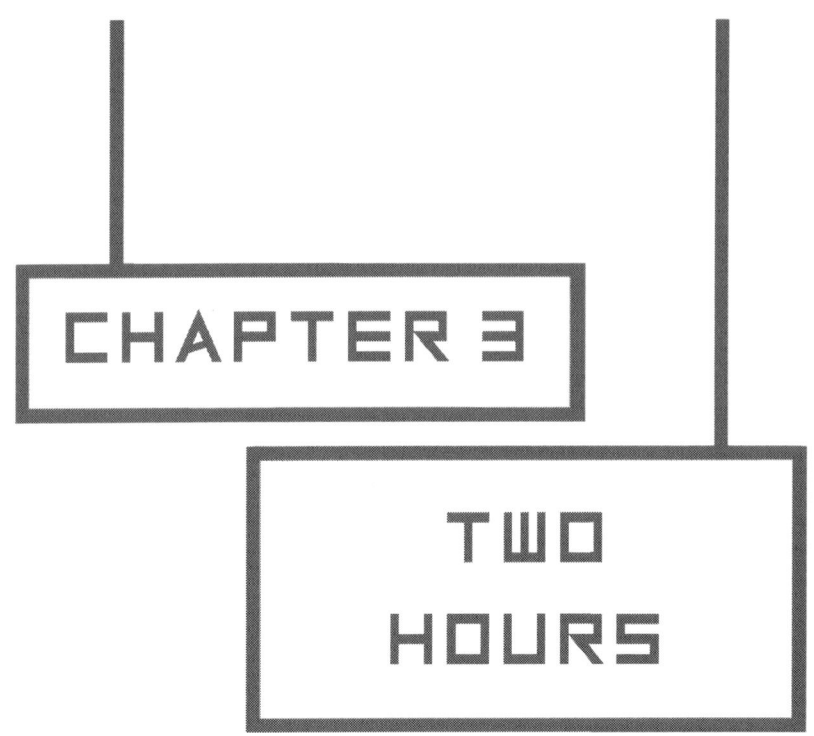

CHAPTER 3

TWO HOURS

"See! He's clearly more intelligent than most second-millennium dioka! He has that twisted heart-shaped genetic mark; he has to be trioka!" Xendo pleaded as he paused the video in Superintendent Nova Pearl's office.

"And he said his parents were named Dan and Ava," Blinda chimed in. "Nova, you have to see it. The resemblance is eerie."

Superintendent Pearl did not budge. The tall, solemn woman held power in every room she entered. Throughout the full duration of the video clip she never spoke a word or changed her unconvinced, quizzical expression. Ten minutes ago, she was awoken from slumber by loud knocks on her office door. She didn't have time to do anything but wrap herself in a magenta robe and fuzzy pink slippers. Mercifully, the door-knockers were just Xendo and Blinda. They had been trying to contact her all throughout her hectic day. Pearl's complaints about the inconvenience of this midnight meeting vanished when Xendo started playing the video clip. Superintendent Pearl would not be going back to sleep now, that was for certain.

"I don't know what possessed them to be so sloppy and conceive a child while on a mission, but here we are." Blinda sighed, trying to figure out what they should do.

TWO HOURS

If Superintendent Pearl was startled by any of this shocking information, she didn't show it. Xendo and Blinda stared at her with an unbreakable intensity, hungry for her help. Pearl gazed into the holo-screen and into Philo's eyes—his familiar eyes. She felt herself searching for answers to questions she abandoned long ago. Superintendent Pearl broke her concentration by standing up from behind her grand oak desk. She glided around to come closer to her two unexpected guests.

"*If* that young man is, in fact, the biological son of Daniel Nockby and Ava Harlow, and *if* he is, in fact, trioka, what are you proposing we do?" she stated in a firm whisper.

Xendo opened his mouth, but Blinda held up her hand to silence him.

"You should use SIYT's time portal to go back and retrieve him," Blinda urged with the most serious face Xendo had ever seen his mother make. Pearl chortled in shock as Blinda went on. "He obviously doesn't belong to an era over 1,000 years ago. He should attend classes *here*, finally use his brain to achieve more!"

"Everybody always torments us with rumors of what happened," Xendo butted in. "They say Jerome Quaker is the one at fault for making the mission fail."

"There's no proof of that, honey." Blinda looked at her son, worried.

"It's what everyone whispers around me," Xendo expressed. "So, what if Philo knows information we don't?"

Superintendent Pearl could not believe what she was hearing. Of course this had to happen tonight, the night before Primary Advancement, and just before the new school year. If this got out, the next week would be a disaster. Nova Pearl does not allow disasters. She had been Superintendent for the last thirty years. She ran the Superior Institute of Young Trioka with an iron fist and warm heart. She loved this school more than her own life.

The superintendent walked to the low-burning hearth in her office. She breathed in the nutty smell of the burning birchwood. Her office, positioned at the highest point of SIYT's Time Tower, overlooked the shops and neighborhoods of Superior Skisland. During the light of a standard day, she could observe much of the farms and villages surrounding Lake Superior. High up in the clouds, the view reminded her of the importance of her position. Rules were rules. Without them, society on Earth would collapse. However, this matter was one that

CHAPTER 3

has never been faced by previous SIYT superintendents. Instinct was all she had.

"I will reach out to the correct government time-travel managers in the HTPA and discuss our options," Superintendent Pearl concluded to her visitors.

"No! You can't," Xendo objected with a whisper. "That'll make it worse!"

Pearl was surprised with the boy's conviction. Blinda leaned forward.

"The global parliament would be in meetings about this for months, and it will certainly get leaked to the public just like last time," Blinda argued. "At best, they study him like a lab experiment. At worst, some crazy group like OMNI could send a contract killer back to terminate the boy. Either way, if anyone but us knows, he'll never be able to live in peace."

Superintendent Pearl exhaled in frustration. The dioka terrorist group Omnipotence was long gone, but secret extremists who claimed they had ancestors in the order still caused problems for society. These radicals kept popping up, secretly recruiting new cohorts to cause mayhem each year. Some of them attempt to illegally go back in time to swing history in their favor. Various horrible scenarios of the boy's fate bounced around in Superintendent Pearl's imagination. A decision would not come easily.

"The school's portal is not as precise. It must have an operator. I will have to find a trusted member of the Continuum Division to control it while I fetch the boy," Superintendent Pearl posed, mind racing.

"You *know* that any agent would be risking their career to do that, Nova, and we'd most likely be found out," Blinda confided.

Xendo glanced around Superintendent Pearl's expansive office. SIYT students were not usually allowed to enter her official chambers. Above the burning fireplace was the same physical photograph he and his mother found in storage this afternoon. Superintendent Pearl had a larger copy; it was framed and in a space of honor for all to see. Even after all that has happened since that fateful afternoon, Superintendent Pearl was still proud to show her support for the infamous 2005 agents. Everyone else may think him foolish, but at this moment, Xendo never felt prouder of his father.

Without thinking, Xendo spoke up, "You could just send *us*."

His mother and Superintendent Pearl whipped their heads his way.

TWO HOURS

"Xendo!" Blinda snapped, slapping him on the arm.

"My dear boy, this is not the time for jokes," Pearl interjected with a quick laugh to hush him.

"No, I'm serious," Xendo replied. "I think it's our best option."

Superintendent Pearl straightened her back and crossed her arms. She lowered her glasses and glared down at Xendo with exceptional sternness.

"Have you graduated from the Human History Program?" She asked bluntly.

"No," Xendo replied.

"Are you at least thirty years of age?"

"No, you know I'm not."

"Have you ever wielded your own Military Morphstaff?"

"I wish, can I?"

"Have either of you ever time-traveled before?"

"No, of course not."

"Then why, on Earth's honor, would I permit you or your mother to use the time portal?" Pearl finished.

Xendo looked down at his black shoes, second-guessing his outburst. To outsiders, Superintendent Pearl seemed as cold as frostbite. She was one of the most powerful figures on Earth. A kineoka master and former continuum agent who led multiple historical missions to success. Most people were too afraid to cross her. Her dominance gained the respect of both rowdy students and myopic government officials. However, Xendo knew he was right about this. He looked up from his feet.

"I mean no disrespect, Superintendent," Xendo responded politely.

She looked him up and down. Options, indeed, were slim at this point. She let her crossed arms fall, moved back behind her desk, and sat down. "Explain why your idea would be best."

"Like Philo," Xendo reasoned, "I'm also a fourteen-year-old boy. If a frightening man in a black suit and a scary glowing weapon banged on my door late at night, for *whatever* reason, I would run for the hilltops!"

Blinda sat forward in her chair, clutching the armrests. Her eyes kept scanning the expressions of the other two.

"*Or* if an intimidating woman I didn't know," Xendo proposed, subtly indicating Superintendent Pearl, "tried to explain to me how

CHAPTER 3

my parents died and that I belong in the future, well, honestly, I would think she's bonkers, no offense."

"None taken," replied Superintendent Pearl with a stern smirk.

"But if a boy my age came to see me and we simply talked about it, I don't know, I feel like the news would be easier to absorb," Xendo finished uneasily.

Superintendent Pearl released a slow, gentle shrug and reasserted, "The fact remains: neither of you have been trained in Continuum policy or procedures. It could be dangerous."

Blinda placed her hand on Xendo's right shoulder. He relaxed into her touch.

"Nova, we wouldn't need weapons," his mother carefully offered. "We don't need some government-orchestrated plan. We find the boy and bring him back. That's it."

Superintendent Pearl shook her head, "The school would be liable if something were to—"

"This isn't a typical mission that spans years. There's no espionage, no criminals, no timeline to correct. We can do this!" Blinda mustered confidently.

Superintendent Pearl closed her eyes and took a deep breath. Xendo could almost hear the whirlwind of thoughts crashing through her mind. She glanced at the clock on her wall and exhaled stubbornly, "For Ava!"

In the span of the next two hasty minutes, Superintendent Pearl dashed around her office gathering little books, gadgets, tools, and a black seamed cap. Pearl opened an old file folder and handed two photos to Blinda. She paused to give her longtime friend a somber, knowing nod, and stuffed the rest of the objects into a jet-black backpack. She picked up a steel bracelet off of a silver shelf and motioned for them to follow her to the room's exit. Superintendent Pearl turned off the lights, closed the electronic door behind her, and whispered, "Follow me to the Observatory."

The Portal Observatory was in SIYT's astronomy wing, housed under a huge glass dome in view of the stars. The mesmerizing classroom was wide enough to showcase SIYT's historic time portal. It was one of only two operational time portals that weren't destroyed by the government.

A few hundred years ago, when the trioka scientist Hardy Flep

TWO HOURS

successfully built the first "time machine," the idea of time traveling became immensely popular. Daredevils across the planet craved the ultimate adventure of sightseeing history. However, to prevent the pandemonium this could have created, the Global Government outlawed public time travel before it even began.

Xendo's father only traveled back in time as a trained government agent under the Continuum Division of the Historical Timeline Preservation Agency. The HTPA's time portal was rumored to be bright, colorful, and mesmerizing before it collapsed. Xendo was present in this very observatory when his father's team departed through the portal to 2005 and never returned. However, Xendo didn't remember any of it; he was too young. Xendo was secretly excited to witness the portal again.

While racing down the Time Tower corridors outside Superintendent Pearl's office, they dared not make a sound this late at night. The Human History students may still be on summer vacation, but SIYT's faculty were already on campus, sleeping in this building. If any of the professors awoke, Xendo, his mother, and the superintendent would be caught breaking global law. His mother would be fired from her position as head chef of SIYT's cafeteria, Superintendent Pearl would go to prison, and Xendo would be expelled before he even got to choose his graduate program. That would be embarrassingly tragic. The last thing the Quakers needed was more scandal surrounding their family.

Luckily, the valiant Superintendent Pearl understood the significance of this opportunity. This boy, Philo Nockby, changed everything. The 2005 mission now had missing holes in its story and new secrets to unearth. Philo might know absolutely nothing about Daniel or Ava. He might not help them at all. However, rescuing this boy was *worth* the risk. Philo could be the key to helping them discover what really happened in the past. Maybe Xendo's father was innocent! Maybe they could absolve Jerome Quaker from his disgraceful infamy.

Superintendent Pearl pushed open the doors to the Portal Observatory and, immediately, Xendo's eyes were drawn upward. The room was a grand, open glass dome that showcased the starry night sky above them. Superintendent Pearl attached the steel bracelet from her office to the control panel, inputted information, and flipped switches to power up the Time Portal Platform. Blinda rifled through the supplies in their backpack. Xendo took a moment to enjoy his first time in

CHAPTER 3

this historic wing of the school.

Xendo snuck toward the observatory's perimeter and got so close to the domed glass, his breath left a moist residue. He drew a heart in the condensation and chuckled to himself. Through his small drawing, he peered at the moon. Tonight, it was only at half its potential brightness. The moist dew evaporated and his heart faded away as the sparkling stars came back into focus. Xendo headed toward the departure platform to join his mother and Superintendent Pearl. In the dark of night, the large metallic platform was imposing and mysterious, but it was not as dazzling as he had hoped. Xendo preferred the moon and shining stars.

"Both of you go stand in the center of the platform," Superintendent Pearl urged them.

As Xendo and Blinda stepped onto the massive structure, they passed various multi-colored rings on the floor. They entered the smallest center ring as Superintendent Pearl's steel bracelet beeped, turning neon blue. She unplugged the bracelet and tossed it over to Xendo. He caught it and was shocked it was almost too hot to hold. He glanced down at the four-inch band in his hands. There was a timer at the base that read *2:00:00*.

"I only had enough time to charge the Return-Ring for two hours. Once you arrive in 2019, it'll start draining energy. I entered the coordinates from where the boy's video was recorded. You should land within a mile of his location. If you can't find Mr. Nockby and convince him to return within two hours, you'll need to abort, *no matter what*. I can't afford to have two untrained civilians stranded in the early digital era. You have my only Return-Ring," Superintendent Pearl informed the anxious pair. "Here we go!"

Pearl flipped a small switch and the heavy, metallic rings below them began to glow and rise up from the platform. The colored rings dragged a 360-degree holoscreen with them as they floated above Xendo and Blinda. Over their heads, four large numbers became visible, *3451*, indicating the current year. The holoscreen all around them flickered with bright rays of rainbow light. Xendo felt like a kid again. He was certainly impressed now.

"Hey," Blinda whispered to Xendo, "put this on."

Xendo snapped out of his glee as his mother gestured down to the black knit hat from Superintendent Pearl's office. Xendo hated

TWO HOURS

wearing hats.

"Why? I don't want to," Xendo asserted.

"Diokas in the 2000s didn't have silver hair, Xendo," Blinda reasoned.

"Oh… right." He took the hat and sadly pulled it over his shiny silver locks.

"I need you to focus," she said. "This is important."

"I know," Xendo replied, squaring his shoulders.

"Remember, the boy needs to trust you," Superintendent Pearl gave her final warning, "You can't tell him everything. Not yet."

Superintendent Pearl pressed a yellow button and a soft bell signaled the portal was activating. Both Superintendent Pearl and the observatory outside their holoscreen vanished. Xendo's body felt like it was floating in mid-air even though he knew the platform was beneath his feet. Blinda glanced up at the *3451* number as it started counting down. The holoscreen landscape outside began to morph like a time-lapse movie being rewound with increasing speed. The pair stood stunned as history's most dazzling moments of beauty and tragedy flashed past their eyes. As they reached 2019, Xendo felt a hot sensation on his leg. He reached into his front pocket and grasped the Return-Ring. He pulled the glowing steel bracelet out into the dark of midnight to show his mother.

The clock read *1:59:59*.

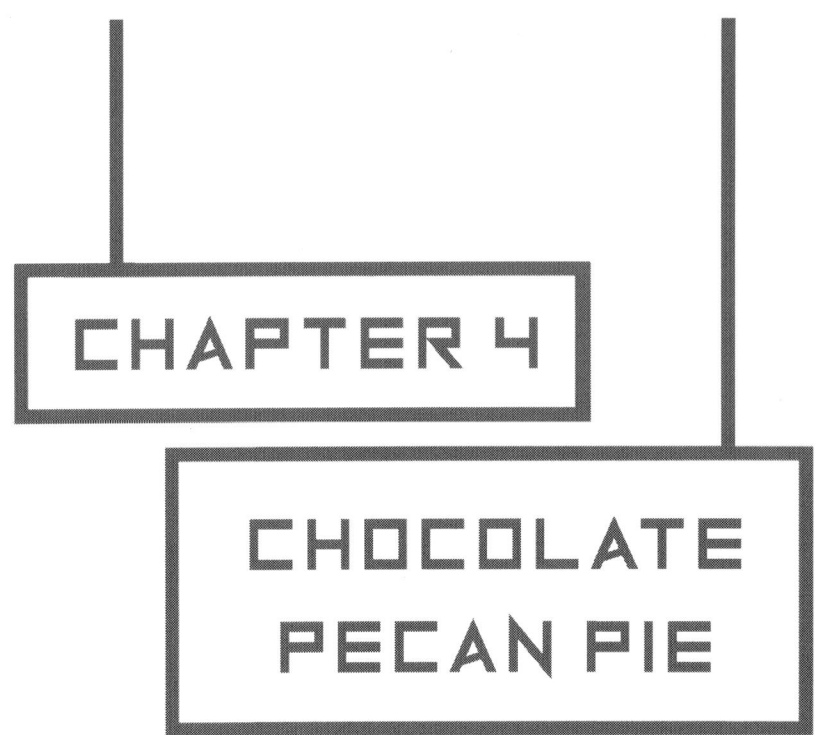

CHAPTER 4
CHOCOLATE PECAN PIE

Harsh shattering glass woke Philo from his short slumber. Philo's gaze focused on the clock on his wall. *Ugh, only two in the morning.* He already lost sleep tonight recording his school video. His eyelids had just started to feel heavy again when he heard strange whispers in the kitchen downstairs. *Damn it!* Philo thought.

He jostled around in his bed and looked past the other three foster boys… that were in their beds. *Hmmmm, that's odd.* Philo strained his neck to listen without leaving the warmth under his blankets. There were at least two people downstairs, and it definitely wasn't any of the girls… or even Mr. Kelly.

Philo grunted. He couldn't sleep now. He was too curious.

Leaving his bed, Philo put on his ratty dark gray jeans, white undershirt from the day before, and his favorite green hoodie. He slipped on his sneakers. If these people were actually dangerous, he might need to run out the back door.

Philo inched down the stairs as if each careful step could trigger an alarm. He didn't want the voices to know he was spying on them. *Shoot!* Philo didn't have anything to defend himself with in case these people attacked him. He scanned his dark surroundings to grab anything he could use to ward off the intruders. But there was nothing.

CHOCOLATE PECAN PIE

As he neared their small bathroom, Philo saw a bottle of sprayable air freshener. He rolled his eyes. That would have to do. Philo gripped the blue spray bottle and put his back against the wall behind the living room. He listened to the strangers whispering on the other side.

"Do you think you got it all?" a woman asked quietly.

"Yes," a boy's voice answered. "The wine glasses just broke in this corner of the floor. I know how to sweep, Mom."

"Be quieter!" the female voice hissed.

"Me? Why are you baking?" the boy shot back. "We only have *one hour* left!"

Philo guessed the whispering boy must have been around his age. He seemed annoyed with the female voice. *Are they related?* Philo hadn't the faintest idea why a mother-son criminal team would break into his group home. While gripping his "gentle rain" spray bottle like a dagger, Philo peered around the wall's corner to catch a glimpse of the intruders.

First, a plump, middle-aged, blonde woman wore Mrs. Kelly's old apron. Random ingredients were strewn all over the kitchen. They were using the food Mr. Kelly *just* picked up from the store! Philo was going to be in so much trouble. But why would strangers sneak into another person's home to cook food?

The boy gathering glass shards into their dust bin was the most abnormal boy Philo had ever seen. The young man was slim, but muscular with a discernible jawline. The boy grunted in annoyance and ripped off his black beanie to reveal short, silver hair with pushed-back bangs that bounced into a perfect quiff. His silver locks danced in the cool breeze blowing from the open window.

Philo blinked in disbelief. Who *were* these people? The way they moved and talked was so peculiar.

The boy dumped the glass shards into the kitchen garbage bin, stood up, and asked his mother, "Is this even the right house? There are no pictures of him anywhere!"

"Nova said the origin of the video's internet protocol came from this home," the woman answered. "The boy must have just finished making the video."

The young man shrugged his shoulders. "Well, we don't have much time left. Should I wake him up? I'll have to do it quietly. I think there are other people here."

CHAPTER 4

"Yes, but just wait until the pie's done," the woman protested. "It only has about five minutes more. These ancient ovens take so long!"

"Mom, that is *not* what's important here!" the boy whispered angrily.

"Put your hat back on!" she hissed back.

"Ugh!" the boy lamented. He pulled the black wool cage over his silver hair. "Pie or not, we need to find Philo, now."

Philo froze. They needed to find *him*. What the hell? That made absolutely no sense. Philo only understood a fourth of their conversation, yet they know who *he* is? *That's it,* Philo decided. He should wake up Mr. Kelly. An adult should handle this. Philo took one last glance at these weirdos and shifted his weight. The old floorboards beneath him creaked as he moved. Philo cursed in shock. The strangers whipped their heads Philo's way. He darted back behind the wall in fear.

"Is someone there?" the woman asked her son, shocked.

"Maybe, I'll go look," the boy responded.

As the boy's footsteps stalked toward him, Philo's mind was straining for exit strategies. He could run back upstairs and lock himself in his bedroom. He could escape out the back door. He could scream bloody murder to warn the others, but Philo failed to move any muscle whatsoever. All he could do was clench the blue air freshener bottle tighter in his fist. Just as the strange teen was about to discover him, something in Philo snapped. He stood up, whipped around the wall, and whacked the mysterious boy on his silver-haired head. Philo met eyes with his shocked victim as the boy fell backward. He instantly regretted the move as the mother gasped and covered her mouth in surprise. With a thud, the strange boy hit the ground hard.

"Xendo! Honey, are you all right?" The woman rushed over. Philo felt like a deranged serial killer.

The handsome boy, apparently named Xendo, rolled over to groggily face his bewildered mother fawning all over him. He turned to look up at his attacker. Philo saw a grin gradually appear on his victim's face.

"Well, that could have gone better." Xendo clutched the front of his head. "I'd hate to be on your bad side with a staff!"

Philo's fears faded as Xendo chuckled and got back on his feet.

"Hey, talk quieter. We don't want to wake the diokas," the mother whispered while checking the spot on her son's forehead where he was

CHOCOLATE PECAN PIE

hit. "It's turning red, but you should be fine."

What the hell is a dioka? Philo thought as he stepped back. He placed the air freshener down and scanned the pair in front of him. The two nutcases stared back with wide eyes and stupid grins as if *he* was the interesting one.

"Why did you break in here?" Philo asked. "We... we don't have money or anything you would want. Who are you?"

The odd pair exchanged glances and deep inhales. Philo knew this ritual. They were going to break news that he wouldn't be fond of.

"We don't want to frighten you." The boy stepped forward. "But, obviously, we're failing. This is my mother, Blinda, and my name—"

Ding! All three heads turned toward the oven timer.

"Ooh!" the woman squealed, "It's ready!"

The two strangers left Philo dumbfounded with confusion in the living room. The boy casually leaned on the kitchen counter as his mother opened the oven door. The most pleasing aroma graced Philo's nostrils. Thoughts of warm winter cocoa and caramel candies flooded his brain. Reluctantly, Philo peered into the kitchen as the giddy woman pulled out a dark-colored pie. She opened the refrigerator to grab a bowl of whipped cream that Philo was positive hadn't been there earlier. The baker woman seemed incredibly, if not overly, thrilled with both creations.

"Philo, it would be rude if I didn't offer you a sweet treat when we entered your home." The woman started cutting some slices of the pie. Philo looked at her with a confused face. Everything they were doing here was a bit rude.

"C'mon, aren't you hungry?" Xendo laughed. "The chocolate pecan pie isn't going to eat itself!"

Two and a half slices later, Philo made up his mind: he had never tasted a dessert more delicious. The mother named Blinda began to talk about Philo's parents as if she somehow *knew* them. Philo didn't believe a word this crazy woman was saying, but he was willing to tune her out while enjoying the rest of this succulent chocolate pecan pie. Philo *was* pretty darn hungry.

"And at age fourteen, Ava and I started going to separate universities, but we still spoke over holochat every day. She was one of the best friends I ever had. I wish you had been able to love her like I did."

Philo didn't know if he could trust this blonde baker or her son.

CHAPTER 4

They came out of nowhere, gave him food, and now they knew everything about his parents? Philo couldn't help but feel a pretense behind the woman's voice. She wasn't telling him exactly what she truly wanted to say. Could all this be because he just rehashed old thoughts before falling asleep? Philo hated dealing with what he couldn't change, and now his mind was creating stress dreams to make him suffer.

These old stories of his mother and father were what Philo always wished to hear, but they couldn't be real. He didn't trust anything these figments of his imagination were saying. Philo grunted as he finished his dessert and Blinda started a fourth story. Dream or not, questions were arising.

"If you knew my mom and dad so well, why didn't you find me sooner? I've been living in foster homes for as long as I can remember," Philo asked.

"Well, honestly, we didn't even know you existed. Tonight was the only date on record within Earth's Database, and the ambassador did not mention you in his briefing," the woman answered as if her meaning was obvious.

Were these people escapees from a mental hospital? Philo waited, hoping they'd clarify those odd statements, but the mother and son just kept staring at him.

"I...," Philo stammered, "I have no clue what that even means."

The pair looked at each other as if Philo wasn't as bright as they expected.

"Look, there's no way around it, Mom," Xendo exhaled with dissatisfaction. "Let's just get it over with."

The boy ripped off his black hat and plopped it on the table like a dramatic microphone being dropped. His shiny-silver hair flowed back to its messy natural position. The boy looked at Philo as if he had bestowed a mystical gift upon a curious tourist. Philo stared back without a changed expression.

"Xendo has *silver* hair," Blinda raised her eyebrows and nodded toward her son's scalp.

"Yeah, I have eyes," Philo admitted, shrugging his shoulders. "I saw it earlier."

"Well... it's pretty rare," Xendo clarified, a bit embarrassed.

"I suppose," Philo sighed. "Plenty of kids dye their hair like that. I don't know why you're acting like it's so special..., no offense."

CHOCOLATE PECAN PIE

There clearly was offense. Philo somehow broke their hopeful gimmick of impressing him. Xendo sat back in his chair with defeat and Philo felt the urge to amend the situation.

"It looks super cool, though. Is it new? I'm not saying it was a mistake or anything," Philo complemented pathetically. He decided it may be best to avoid angering the loony, and possibly violent, intruders.

"No, it's not new." Xendo smiled, glancing toward his mother.

"He was born that way," Blinda added, sharing the same growing grin. "He had less hair as a baby, but it was silver, nonetheless. Some Skyborne children are born with the recessive gene of metallic colored hair."

"What?" Philo let out slowly, almost with a chuckle.

Blinda reached out to Philo. Her gentle hands were warm; his were cold. He was unsure if he should pull back his arms or embrace the friendship within her touch. Xendo cleared his throat.

"In about a year, a viral pandemic is going to shock the world. Nothing like people in your era have ever experienced. Misinformation will run rampant, distorting what's reality and what's propaganda. Your elected leaders will incite violent division at home and attack outside nations who try to thwart their reign. In a few years, it will escalate to the biggest global war yet. The world, as you know it, will be over."

Philo stared blankly. This was madness. Who would say something like that?

"A year from now? How the hell would you know any of this?" Philo questioned, completely puzzled.

Xendo dropped his shoulders and tilted his head. He took a short breath.

"Philo, you are trapped in the wrong millennium. We've come to bring you back to our time, in the future, where you belong," Xendo insisted.

They couldn't possibly be serious. Philo was correct. They were psychos.

"Yeah, right," Philo scoffed. He wiggled his fingers to exaggerate, "the *fuuuuture.*"

The other two weren't laughing. They were completely serious. They also didn't seem to understand Philo's finger wiggling.

"We just time-traveled from 3451," Blinda told him. "We were only

CHAPTER 4

able to find you from the video you *just* made. Your parents had a mission that was supposed to end in 2005, and somehow they had an unplanned pregnancy…, or they possibly could have—"

"Gone rogue? Or quit, maybe?" Xendo interjected with an unsure facial expression.

"Maybe…? Again, not like Ava," Blinda responded, turning to Xendo and scratching her temple, "but there must have been some reason Irwin didn't know—"

Philo stopped listening. This dream wasn't a funny joke anymore. He wanted to snap awake and forget these crazy people ever entered his subconscious. But he couldn't make himself escape the nightmare.

"I'm out of here," Philo interrupted the characters his mind created. "I'm going back to my room."

Philo stood abruptly from his chair, tossed the pie in the garbage, and walked toward the kitchen's exit.

"Wait!" Xendo called out, reaching into his pocket. "We only have a few minutes left! We *need* to take you with us!"

Philo groaned and looked back for just a moment. The silver-haired boy pulled out an oversized, thick bracelet glowing with bright blue light. Out of curiosity, Philo stepped back to the table for a second glance. His subconscious never could have fabricated an object like this. The ring had holographic numbers counting down like a timer: 3:17, 3:16, 3:15. Philo looked back up at the two strangers waiting on his every breath for a response. He had no idea why, but Philo was furious.

"This is insane!" he spat in a higher pitch and pointed at the gizmo resting in Xendo's palm. "That *thing* can't be real. You two *wackos* can't be real. None of this makes any sense!"

"I know you're confused, Philo. But, please, just listen," Blinda asserted. "If this isn't proof, I don't know what is."

She reached into a black backpack and handed him, of all things, two heavy metallic photographs.

As he took hold of the oddly malleable and dense pictures, Philo's curiosity shifted to the strange people actually depicted in the two photos that he never should have known.

The first photo had six friends posing in front of huge glass doors. The building behind them read "Superior Institute of Young Trioka." On the right was a stern older woman in a boring gray suit. A young blonde woman wearing chef whites was on the left. She hugged the

CHOCOLATE PECAN PIE

man next to her and beamed toward the camera with so much positivity, Philo cracked a smile. There were three males and one female in the center wearing what reminded Philo of black ninja suits. The woman had darker brown skin, curly-styled hair, and hazel eyes, just like Philo.

In the second photograph, the same woman with hazel eyes was a few years younger and held a small plaque. She had her arms around the same blonde girl and older lady, now wearing a navy-blue suit. All three hugged each other so tight, they basically resembled a smiling mass of multiple limbs. Blinda first pointed to the blond girl hugging her best friend, saying, "This is me." Next, she pointed to the woman in the navy suit, "This is Superintendent Pearl." Lastly, she moved her finger to the girl holding the wooden plaque. "And this is your mother, Ava Harlow. She had just graduated valedictorian of Primary."

Philo's heart stopped beating. He didn't think his eyes could be seeing this correctly. He had wondered his whole life what his mother looked like. And now, here she was. So close, yet never further away. *It couldn't be true, could it?* Philo didn't want to believe these strangers, but after seeing how this girl's smile curled upwards, her dimples soft but distinct, and how her eyebrows raised at different levels..., it was like he saw himself in a handheld mirror. It *had* to be true.

Philo looked back at the first photograph to study the man standing next to his apparent mother. He had the same nose as Philo, the same jawline, and even Philo's reluctant and dorky half-grin for photos. He was stronger than Philo ever could be, but their bodies were shaped the same.

"Is this my father?" Philo wondered aloud, too afraid to ask directly.

"Yeah," replied Xendo. "It's the day of their mission. His name is—"

"Dan... Dan Nockby," Philo finished. His mind was putty at this point. Philo looked up, "I... I have so many questions...."

As Xendo and Blinda opened their mouths to speak, a bell-like, buzzing noise chimed throughout the room. The large bracelet in Xendo's hand vibrated vigorously. The numbers turned from light blue to dark red. The countdown read: *1:00, 0:59, 0:58.* Xendo handed the band to his mother.

"We have someone who can answer all your questions," Xendo declared while snatching the photos to stuff in the backpack. "But we have to go, like, now!"

CHAPTER 4

"Go where?" Philo fretted. His throat clenched from nerves. He was shocked that, for some reason, he now didn't want these strangers to leave.

"To SIYT. We came to retrieve you and take you back to 3451," Xendo answered, standing up.

"What's *SIYT*? This is nuts! I can't leave!" Philo cried. "My life is here! Everything is here!"

"Philo, my dear boy," Blinda reached her hands in to cradle his shaking face. "This place and this time can offer you nothing. You are meant for so much more! Come with us and live the life that was taken from you."

"You chose the wrong person. You can't want me!" Philo protested.

Blinda pulled him closer to make sure he heard her every word. "I can already tell you have the best qualities of both Daniel and my sweetest Ava. You can be the hero they spent their lives trying to become. We can prove everyone wrong! I lost my best friends, and I *will not* lose the last thing on this planet that can redeem their memory. We *need* you."

Philo stared into Blinda's eyes, seeing her as if for the first time. Even if this woman was crazy, at the very least, she would not abandon him. Philo experienced a small sense of security he had never fathomed before.

"We've got twenty-nine seconds!" Xendo whispered urgently, showing them the diminishing red letters. "If you don't come now, we will have to leave without you, and we won't be able to come back!"

Blinda let go of Philo's face and retreated back to stand with her son.

"We can't force you," Blinda stated, "but the future is where you belong, Philo."

She glanced at her son. He looked a little less serious.

"Plus, I know you'll *love* it," Xendo smirked. "Are you coming?"

Philo had his head down. His mind was racing. He still had millions of questions and millions of doubts burning through his skull. But if these intruders did leave without him, he'd *never* find any answers. Philo felt out of place everywhere he went. Maybe *this* was why! He looked up. Xendo and Blinda gave him big dorky grins full of warmth and possibility. Philo must have been just as insane as they were.

"Yes," Philo decided. "I'm coming."

Blinda dragged Philo in for a hug, Xendo pulled a fist toward his

CHOCOLATE PECAN PIE

chest with a celebratory grunt. As he was trapped in Blinda's tight embrace, Philo watched Xendo put his fingers inside the metal bracelet and tug outwards. The small band stretched to the full width of Xendo's wingspan as he raised it above their heads. Philo looked up and saw the flashing number pass *ten* and then *nine*. The stretched metal ring made a buzzing noise.

"This is the Return-Ring. It's going to send us to the future," Xendo explained with a cheeky smile like Philo had never seen. "Keep your footing and try not to vomit!"

Philo, completely lost, stood still as Xendo and Blinda both yanked the large hoop down over their shoulders toward the kitchen floor. With a whooshing noise, a ruby hologram wall rose from the ground, surrounding them in a glowing dome. The red timer above them had only three seconds left. *Three.* Blinda's eyes were shut as if she was bracing to get hit by a train. *Two.* Xendo wore a childlike grin, stoked for this rollercoaster ride. *One.* Philo peered outside the kitchen and saw his terrified foster brother, Jonathan, watching them from a distance.

Philo's stomach flipped. The little boy had silent tears streaming down his cheeks. He was crying out of fear and surprise, watching his only friend about to abandon him. Philo reached out to Jonathan in desperation. He wanted to bring the boy with them. However, as soon as Philo realized he would never see Jonathan ever again, the clock struck *zero*. Philo felt a wave of pressure hit him. The timer disappeared. Philo winced as they were propelled forward like a spaceship. As he opened up his disbelieving eyes, Philo saw that Mr. Kelly's kitchen was long gone. Young Jonathan was nowhere to be seen. He was viewing an entirely new sight.

Philo was peering down from the clouds as the world turned. It felt like he was watching a movie but someone was fast-forwarding the entire film. *They were traveling through time.* Night and day passed by so fast it gave Philo a headache. Cities below him grew wider, taller, and brighter. Out of nowhere, smoking balls of light torpedoed down all around him. Explosions drew his attention from one city's disaster to the next. Philo looked at his fellow passengers for their shock to match his own. However, they both watched the apocalypse with dead stares. Blinda squeezed his hand, leading Philo to accept the truth. They *were* right. The world he knew was collapsing right in front of him.

Small villages began to populate in the wreckage below them and

CHAPTER 4

grew outward like flowers in the rubble. Greens and blues eventually replaced all the gray. Each second in his sped-up vision must have represented decades. Philo saw specks of people, vehicles, and animals on the move. The time portal traveled over the country's landscape and approached a great body of water. Philo marveled as a beautiful city was built in seconds *over* the water. When a bright white light flashed, Philo covered his face with his arm. He felt dizzy as their portal slowed down. The pressure subsided and their hologram wall retracted into the floor.

They were now in a tall, grand dome made of thick glass. All around them were thousands of shining stars. Philo looked down to see they now stood on a metal platform. There were odd machines and artifacts everywhere. Xendo bumped his hips into Philo's side. The nervous boy looked over as Xendo laughed.

"Good, you didn't puke!" Xendo winked at him. "We made it!"

Philo inhaled a sharp breath, full of fear. Just like that, his old life in the past was completely gone. Philo couldn't go back.

"What a relief!" Blinda sighed, taking a step forward, then twisting back toward the boys. "Oh! Data be darned! I didn't clean up my mess from the pie! Philo, I hope none of your family gets ups—"

"Quiet, you two!" a hissing voice interrupted them.

Philo looked away from Blinda and saw a familiar figure behind a control panel staring directly at him. It was the same lady he had seen in the mission photos who wore sensible suits of gray and navy blue. Now, however, the woman wore a dark magenta robe and fuzzy pink slippers. She somehow still looked intimidating. Philo gulped.

The stern woman did not look pleased to see him.

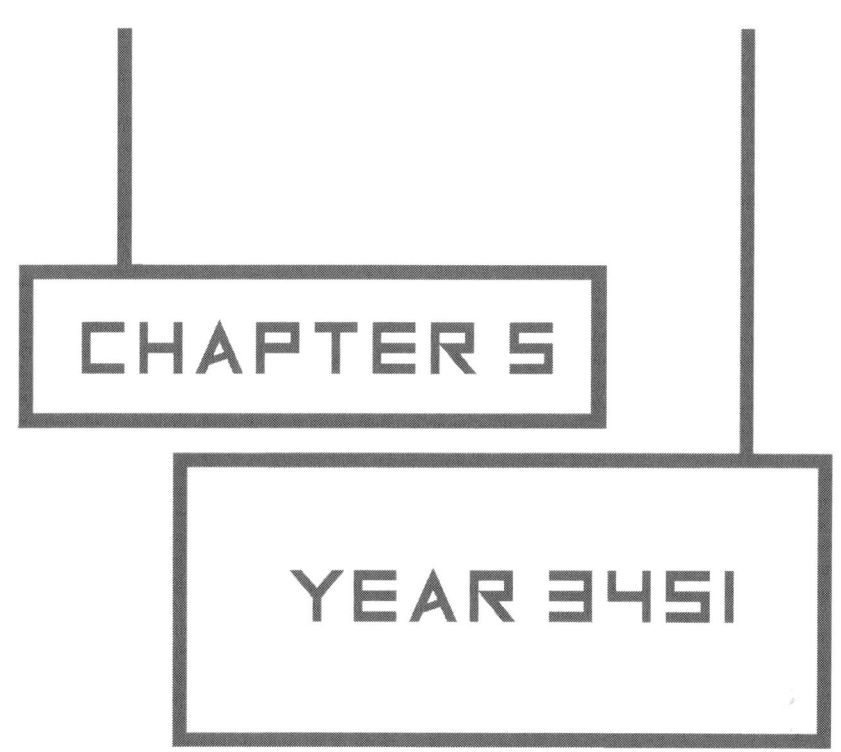

CHAPTER 5

YEAR 3451

"Sit down," commanded the woman in the pink slippers. She gestured to the seats across from the oak desk in her office. Philo, Xendo, and Blinda sat in the cushioned chairs.

The intimidating woman was perched on the edge of her leather desk chair staring at Philo. He felt like a nervous criminal waiting to hear his sentence. Philo had no idea what was even going on. Was he in trouble? Why was this lady so vexed by him?

"Welcome to the year 3451," the woman finally spoke. Philo was surprised to hear the kind words delivered without a smile.

"Thank you?" Philo replied, still unsure if any of this was real.

"How are you feeling?" the woman asked in a monotone voice.

Philo snorted. How was he *feeling*? He didn't know how to answer. His heart had only just stopped thumping inside his chest. Philo swore he had seen clouds *below* their vantage point as he was smuggled through this sky-building's dark hallways in secrecy. Everything changed so quickly; he never had a chance to process anything.

Philo took a moment to inspect this woman's penthouse office and gather his thoughts. A strange globe in the corner had extra land borders and ocean structures. There were antiques from every nation and

CHAPTER 5

tech objects Philo couldn't identify. Every mysterious thing his eyes fell upon seemed historical *and* postmodern, as if this room had centuries of stories he forgot to read about. Philo didn't know if he was excited or terrified, curious or dejected. He had no idea if he could trust any *feelings* he was experiencing, much less articulate them on the spot.

"I'm just… confused? I don't know why I'm here," Philo conceded.

"Do you know anything about your parents or how they died?" the woman asked.

"No, nothing," Philo answered.

"As I feared." The woman looked disappointed. "I apologize for not retrieving you myself, but a wise young man advised me I'm not the best bearer of surprising news."

Xendo let his face exhibit a subtle, satisfied smile.

"Do you know who I am, Philo Nockby?" the woman questioned.

"Uh…, I uh…," stammered Philo. For the life of him, he couldn't remember any of the names Blinda had mentioned earlier. It had been an extremely long day.

"You knew my mother? You were her friend," Philo offered, remembering Blinda's photographs. The woman cleared her throat but never broke her gaze with him.

"Yes, Ava was very dear to me," she noted apathetically. Philo was unsure if the woman was incapable of showing emotion or if she had mastered how to control it.

"My name is Nova Oliviana Pearl, and I am the superintendent of this institution."

"Institution?" Philo asked.

"The Superior Institute of Young Trioka. It is the most rigorous academy on Earth, specifically designed for gifted trioka like yourself," informed Superintendent Pearl with a proud half-grin.

"What is a 'trioka'?" Philo questioned. Superintendent Pearl turned a vicious glare toward Xendo and Blinda.

"For logic's sake!" she lamented, "Did you inform the boy of nothing?"

"We ran out of time to talk," Xendo exclaimed. "And—"

"It took too long to find the house!" Blinda joined in.

"One of us got distracted!" Xendo recalled. "She—"

"I *wanted* to make him pie!" declared Blinda, gesturing to Philo. "He had three slices!"

Philo wasn't sure who to look at during this quick exchange.

YEAR 3451

Superintendent Pearl, however, stared straight ahead at Philo. She had zero interest in how their conversation was derailing.

"The Return-Ring went off before we could go more in-depth," Blinda finished. "Besides, we knew you would be the best to explain everything."

Superintendent Pearl said nothing. She held silence in a room as deftly as a chef wielding a knife. Everyone else leaned forward, waiting for her input.

"Fine, I will untangle this predicament," Pearl concluded.

She took a thin, steel bracelet out of a desk drawer and walked over to the fireplace. Superintendent Pearl tightened the waistband of her robe and faced her guests.

"Philo, I have been Superintendent of the Superior Institute of Young Trioka since the year 3420. I have had the pleasure of witnessing the education of thousands of talented youth, including Xendo, Blinda, and, yes, even your parents. Some of our graduates live regular lives, but most go on to become important figures in various industries all over this great planet. Students begin their studies at age three and graduate from the Primary Program at the end of their thirteenth year. They then advance to a Graduate Program to specialize in a field of their choosing. All fundamental academies on Earth are organized this same way."

"But SIYT is by far the best!" Xendo interrupted with a tap on Philo's left shoulder.

"We are not better, just advanced academically," Pearl continued, silencing Xendo's outburst. "Some other dioka academies are just as exceptional, but our institution is the only one available for trioka-specific studies. You are *trioka*, Philo. It is unfortunate that you were not able to attend this school for these past ten years. However, to explain trioka history, and why you never learned any of it, we must go back about a thousand years."

Philo's face was awestruck as he tried to absorb all this new information. Pearl put on the steel bracelet and tapped her wrist. The band activated as she held it up to her mouth.

"ED, gather all files on Continuum Preservation, Human Antiquity, Trioka Anatomy, and the Historical Timeline itself, please," she instructed.

A beeping sound answered her. The white wall behind Superin-

CHAPTER 5

tendent Pearl lit up like a giant screen. Philo gasped as a hologram-like monitor populated with hundreds of photos and text on its surface.

"This is what we call a mounted holoscreen," Pearl continued as Philo remained flabbergasted. "The closest invention in your time, I believe, would be a television, or possibly a projector. I'm now accessing Earth's Database, which is like your internet, only less juvenile and more factual."

"Woah," breathed Philo in wonder.

Blinda leaned over, "That's the least surprising news you're about to learn."

"Brace yourself," Xendo agreed with a chuckle.

An image of tiny spheres connected in three spiraled lines popped up on the holoscreen.

"You are familiar with deoxyribonucleic acid, correct?" Superintendent Pearl questioned.

"Yes, DNA?" Philo answered.

"Correct. In the same way that DNA carries all genetic information for dioka, normal humans, TNA or trioxyribonucleic acid, carries all genetic information for trioka," she explained as the triple helix image slowly rotated behind her.

"You—," Superintendent Pearl opened both hands to Philo, "we—," she gestured to Xendo, Blinda, and herself, "are all trioka. We each have TNA, as well as *these* modified helix structures in every cell of our bodies."

"What?" gawked Philo. "That's not possible."

"It is," she pressed on. "After a viral pandemic contaminated the globe in 2020, it led to political turmoil and nuclear airstrikes sparking World War III. Millions of people were killed because of government negligence. The small population of survivors, affected by both the pandemic and radiation, had irreversible changes to their genetics. Generations later, some humans started to be born with strange, illuminating genetic marks. When tested, the children exhibited abnormal blood, skin, bone, and muscle tissue.

"Geneticists soon discovered their shared trait. These children had TNA and a triple helix structure as opposed to the oxygen-free DNA with just a double helix. These unprecedented humans, born all over the globe, caused mass hysteria. They— we— were considered freaks of nature, especially trioka who couldn't control their developing men-

YEAR 3451

tal abilities. Many were mocked, attacked, or hunted for centuries. Young children hid if they were trioka from everyone they knew.

"Eventually, our ancestors grew tired of living in the shadows and fought for equal protection under global law. A movement of outspoken trioka emerged in the 3200s and made progress in cementing our positive place in society. SIYT was built in the year 3213. We trioka are still only about five percent of the world's population. Some groups still fear us and misunderstand us, but by and large, we proved we are as human as anyone else."

On the holoscreen, Philo saw images of all the trioka history he time-traveled over. Activists on podiums spoke to large audiences. Little children lay in hospital beds surrounded by doctors. People of differing ages, races, and genders held signs at protests that read, *"Triple helix? More to offer!"* and *"Trioka Rights are Human Rights!"*

Philo broke his silence to ask, "How do you know I am one of you? A... 'trioka'?"

"Do you become ill easily?" Pearl questioned without pause.

"Uh, no, I don't think so," Philo wondered why that was relevant.

"Have you ever had broken bones or bruises?"

"No, I don't get hurt very often."

Philo watched the superintendent turn back to the holoscreen and move files around with her fingers.

"Are you smarter than most of your friends?" she persisted.

"I don't really have friends," Philo sighed.

"And you have that genetic mark on your chest, yes?"

"My what?" Philo was confused.

"Your twisted heart? As I believe you called it?" Superintendent Pearl clarified.

"Oh, okay, yeah, I have a birthmark," Philo confessed, remembering his stupid video.

"Well, unless you were never exposed to an ounce of danger your entire life, you have all the characteristics of being trioka," Pearl finished turning back to face her three guests. "We just have yet to find out if you develop telekinetic abilities."

Philo was speechless. *Telekinetic abilities?* He turned to look at Xendo and Blinda. They shared big, dorky grins, relishing in the revealed secrets. Blinda rubbed Philo's right shoulder tenderly. Xendo then punched that shoulder.

47

CHAPTER 5

"Welcome to the club, dude," Xendo laughed.

Superintendent Pearl sighed. "If you need the specifics, I can explain more."

She pinched images behind her to enlarge them on the wall. The pictures showcased multiple charts, a triple helix graphic, and the musculoskeletal figure Philo recognized from school. This time, the anatomically perfect man-without-skin was drawn broader, taller, and his muscles were darker in color.

"Since trioka have different cell structures that soak in more oxygen, every component of our bodies evolved faster than diokas. We have thinner yet more durable muscle fibers, which give us augmented strength and flexibility. We have increased stamina and pain tolerance because of our wider blood vessels, thicker skin tissue, and denser bones. We have twice the synapses within our nervous system and triple the connections in our brains, which allow us to process stimuli at a quicker rate."

With each statement of medical claims, the superintendent pointed to a corresponding graphic as proof.

"Fascinating," Philo whispered by accident.

"Basically, compared to dioka, we're smarter, stronger, faster, and live longer!" Xendo bragged while adjusting his silver quiff.

"Xendo! Rude!" Blinda knocked him upside the head.

"No," Superintendent Pearl stated, "that's only true when comparing a trioka and dioka in their peak mental and physical prime. Plenty of dioka are strong, ingenious, and active. Plenty of trioka can be unmotivated, sedentary, or vapid."

Philo got the sense the superintendent had to defend this argument many a time before. Xendo nodded his head sheepishly and slumped back down in his seat.

"We have more in common than what divides us. We're all human. That's what's important," Blinda chimed in.

"Exactly," Pearl agreed with a thin smile.

For years, Philo always had questions only his deepest subconscious dared to ponder. Why was he bored in his classes when his peers were overwhelmed? How was he able to heal from the punches of bullies and foster siblings so quickly? *The shard of glass in his foot this morning?* He finally had answers! Suddenly, Philo felt squeamish and lightheaded.

YEAR 3451

"Is there a bathroom nearby?" Philo asked, losing color in his face.

"Yes, down the hall," Superintendent Pearl replied. "The pressure imbalances are kicking in. Xendo?"

"On it!" Xendo leaped up as Philo tried not to fall over. Xendo put his arm around Philo and helped him to the bathroom.

"Of the three of us, I thought Mom would be the one who got time-sick." Xendo laughed back at the two ladies.

Blinda nodded to Superintendent Pearl. "I did too! It's a pleasant surprise I didn't, actually."

"Blinda, not now," the superintendent replied with a wave of her hand. "Get the boy some water, please."

"Right, no problem," Blinda responded.

Philo feared passing out as he staggered across the pristine hallway floors of this strange building.

"Hold on there, Phi, I've got you. Don't worry, we're almost there." Xendo hoped his mother would catch up soon.

"I'm going to hurl," Philo spat. He had never felt so dizzy in his life. The room wasn't spinning, the whole building was. Philo felt like his intestines were trying to escape his mouth.

"Here we are!" Xendo proclaimed as they reached ten tall black rectangles in the hallway. Xendo pressed a button and one black rectangle shot up into the ceiling, revealing a tiny bathroom in the wall.

Philo lunged at the toilet and projectile vomited wet chunks into the bowl. Xendo turned up his face in disgust and plugged his nose.

"Oh no! I'm really bad with throw-up!" Xendo whimpered nasally with his back turned. Philo hurled again.

"Oh, no, I can't!" Xendo screeched. He nudged Philo's foot hanging out of the bathroom, and the door shut him in.

"Xendo!" Blinda cried, appearing with a glass of water.

"It was gross, Mom," the boy replied with sounds of retching a foot away.

"Philo? Honey?" Blinda knocked on the door. "It's common to get nauseous after exiting through portals. I, myself, usually get sick."

Philo ignored them and puked again. He inhaled a deep, long breath and tried to relax with his exhale. Finally, he took in his surroundings. His face scrunched up in bewilderment. There was a tiny sink, soap dispenser, and a mirror on the wall *behind* the toilet. There were cabinets, drawers, and secret hiding spaces all around him. No

CHAPTER 5

inch in the teeny bathroom was wasted. Philo searched around and found copious amounts of first aid items, free hygiene items, and electronic buttons he was too terrified to push. A strange projection sat across from the toilet that contained electronic articles flashing by. Philo saw titles such as "The Hottest Fashion Trends From the 503rd Oceanite Showcase" and "How to Find Love in the 35th Century." People were posing under headlines wearing strange clothing and holding objects Philo had never seen before. *The future is so weird.*

"Hey, hun? Are you okay?" Blinda asked kindly. "Press the button to open the door."

Button? Philo thought. *Which one?* There were so many that seemed to do a thousand different things. He had no idea what to do. He was so tired, so confused. And now, he was getting increasingly claustrophobic. The bright walls, slim cabinets, and bowls of hygiene products were closing in to suffocate him. He was going to die in this mini futuristic toilet trap! Philo sat down on the white bowl's lid. He put his face in his hands, but the room still felt like the inside of a whirling blender. Everything was spinning and closing in on him. Philo never felt lonelier than in this moment. He finally understood that he wasn't sleeping; he really was in the future! Philo couldn't help himself as the tears started flowing, no matter how hard he tried to hold them back. Xendo and Blinda heard him whimper.

"Oh! Philo! Don't feel bad, it's okay!" Blinda tried her darndest to leak maternal love through the door. "We know you're nervous—"

"We are too!" Xendo chimed in.

Philo sniffled. *Were these wackos really all he had?* Both mother and son strained to hear Philo with their ears plastered to the door. Philo looked up from his hands. He rubbed the tears off his cheek, defeated.

"Just take me back!" Philo pleaded in a soft sputter. "I don't belong here!"

"Oh, sweetheart. I know you don't see it now, but you *do* belong here," Blinda tried to reason through the metal. "You will find new passions that challenge you and friends who love you."

"Also, there's no way Pearl will let us use the portal again," Xendo scoffed.

Philo heard Blinda slap Xendo's shoulder through the door.

"All I know is my past world; I don't understand this future!" Philo cried. "How do you know this will all work out?"

"Honestly, we don't," Blinda responded. "But now, we are in

YEAR 3451

this *together!*"

Xendo assured, "Whatever happens, Philo, we've got your back! And so will the superintendent, she'll help us find out what really happened to your parents and my dad!"

"You're Ava's son, Philo, which means we're family now," Blinda said, tears welling in the corners of her eyes. "And don't you forget it!"

"Oh gosh, Mom, don't cry again!" Xendo groaned.

"I am feeling emotions right now. I am trying my hardest!" Blinda snapped back as she wiped her eyes, sloshing Philo's cup of water on herself. "Oh great! Now I'm out of water."

Xendo started chuckling. Philo smiled.

"Okay. Okay. I can handle this." Philo tried to calm himself. He had to move forward.

"Which button do I push?" Philo asked. "I have no idea what I'm looking at."

"On the screen, swipe until you see a menu of options," Blinda instructed. Philo gestured through even more futuristic articles that made absolutely no sense. The screen labeled "Menu" eventually came into view.

"All right, I did that," Philo responded. "Now what?"

"There should be a button that says, 'Open Door.' Hover your finger over that and the door will open," replied Xendo curtly. "It's not that difficult, really."

The door opened up, revealing Philo's shocked expression and his finger still pointing toward the futuristic menu screen.

"There you go!" Xendo chuckled.

Blinda rushed to give Philo a big hug and Xendo joined in. The hug wasn't forced, premeditated, or some sort of cruel joke. They embraced Philo with warmth and friendship. The lingering hug gave Philo a flooding of contentment he hadn't felt in a long time. In fact, he couldn't remember ever being hugged like this. It was vulnerable and awkward but pleasant at the same time. He melted into their kind embrace. He wondered if this would become a habit of theirs. Philo decided he wouldn't really mind if it did.

Blinda kissed Philo on the forehead. "Let's take you home."

CHAPTER 6

BREAKFAST AT QUAKER COTTAGE

The smell of something sweet hit Philo's nose. His eyes opened to see a red book spine with glowing lights in a curvy pattern two inches from his face. Philo lifted his head to read the title: *Each Second Counts: The Greatest Staffball Tactics Since 3168*. A jolt of realization about being in the future shot through Philo's body, forcing him to gasp and sit up. As he looked around, the memories of yesterday came flooding back into his brain.

"Oh, right," Philo muttered to himself.

Books and techy toys were strewn about the cluttered attic bedroom he had slept in. He was sitting on a gray pad on the floor no thicker than cardboard, yet it felt softer than any of Philo's previous beds in life. A pair of black stretchy pants and an emerald green shirt were folded near his feet for him to borrow. Philo heard Xendo and Blinda arguing downstairs.

Philo changed into Xendo's outfit laid out for him, headed down a spiral staircase, and entered a dining room that opened to the house's first floor. Scents of buttery sweet pastries, zesty citrus fruits, and salty garlic-caramelized onions filled Philo's nostrils. Sizzling fresh eggs and browning sausage were melodies to his ears. The boy's stomach rumbled with hunger. Philo saw Xendo sitting on a slender barstool with

BREAKFAST AT QUAKER COTTAGE

his feet up on the kitchen counter and Blinda was busy over the stove. They didn't see Philo at first.

"More? I don't think they need all of this food!" Xendo groaned as if he's made this complaint thousands of times before.

"Why do you say that?" Blinda asked innocently as she cracked what must be her twelfth egg into a black skillet.

"He's going to balloon up to five hundred pounds if he keeps eating what you cook him," Xendo reasoned.

"Nova hasn't been here in ages. Breakfast *has* to be impressive," Blinda fought back, "and I can tell Philo loves food as much as I do from how he ate that pie."

"Or he was just hungry and didn't want to hear us talk anym—"

"Good morning," Philo quietly interrupted as he approached the babbling duo.

Blinda looked up in shock while in mid-flip of a fluffy raspberry pancake. Xendo retracted his feet from the counter and gave his bedhead a fresh shuffle. All three individuals smiled awkwardly.

"Morning!" Xendo greeted, standing from the barstool.

"Welcome to Quaker Cottage!" Blinda opened her arms.

Philo glanced around their bright beach home. The walls were made of lake stones and the floors of sand-colored wood. A leather sofa and two chairs sat in the living room near their quaint-but-impressive kitchen. The space was cozy and warm, even though a fresh, lake breeze blew through the windows. Diverse tchotchkes, agates, driftwood, and pictures of the mother/son pair decorated the home.

"I hope you're hungry." Blinda smiled, gesturing toward the dining room. "Sit down and eat."

Philo scanned the table and saw a feast foreign to a foster kid like him. There was savory bacon, sausages, eggs of all sorts, cheddar asparagus quiche, and fresh-baked oat bread. Glazed kringle, fresh fruit, homemade jams, and syrup-doused pancakes added sweetness to the table.

"Woah," Philo's stomach pulsed with yearning.

"Don't get Mom too excited, Philo," Xendo cautioned.

Philo grabbed a strip of crispy brown sugar bacon and snapped it in half. It tasted so delicious he moaned out loud. So meaty, smoky, and rich.

"This bacon is insanely good!" Philo gushed, forgetting that he

CHAPTER 6

was chewing with his mouth open.

"Yep! The lab-grown meat from the South Pole really is the best quality!" Blinda called out from the stove. Philo's eyes widened and he spit the bacon out on his plate. Xendo and Blinda first looked shocked, then chuckled.

"Lab-grown?" Philo was disgusted. "This isn't *real* meat?"

"It's real!" Blinda expressed, trying to calm him down. "It's just grown from stem cells of animals, so it's slaughter-free."

"What?" Philo was still wary. "What do you mean?"

"Well, the government banned barbaric slaughterhouses and unhygienic factory farms centuries ago when scientists finally mastered growing meat more sustainably."

"*Grow* it?" Philo squinted in thought, eyebrows furled, "How?"

"With the right conditions," Xendo reasoned, "stem cells from happy and healthy animals can be cultured to grow meat, fat, and bone tissue just like any animal would naturally."

"There's zero pathogens or disease, it has all the same nutritional benefits, it's cleaner for the environment," Blinda added, "and a few centuries ago, they started getting the flavor and texture perfect. So, it's a win-win!"

"Hmmm," Philo mulled it over, "I guess it *is* better than hurting animals."

"Exactly," Xendo agreed. "Some people still raise their own livestock or hunt or fish for special occasions, if they want primal cuts, but there's a government-regulated cap each year, so the animal populations stay healthy."

"Yeah, almost all of the meat we eat is grown by culture now, Philo." Blinda smiled as she put a new batch of brown sugar bacon in front of him. "You liked the flavor, right?"

"Yeah." Philo gave in and grabbed another piece. "It's really tasty."

Blinda gave him a pat on the head and returned to the stove to keep cooking.

"Mom! I think that's enough food," Xendo complained to her. "Superintendent Pearl isn't even here yet."

"Hmmm..., Nova *is* running a tad late." Blinda checked her technoband for the time. "I wonder what's keeping her."

"She's coming here?" Philo asked,

"Yes, she is! We have much to discuss. Today's a big day,"

BREAKFAST AT QUAKER COTTAGE

Blinda responded.

"What's so important?" Philo inquired as he reached for an oat muffin spotted with blackberries and lemon zest.

Xendo smiled. "It's Primary Advancement today."

"What's that?" Philo replied.

"It's a traditional ceremony at SIYT that honors recent graduates of the Primary Program and allows the students to announce their chosen university and field of study," Blinda informed as she brought over the last platter of food and sat down with the boys. "Xendo is receiving an award!"

"Oh cool! Good job!" Philo congratulated through bites of his goat cheese omelet.

"It's not a sure thing yet," Xendo breathed in anxiously.

"Oh, no? I thought you secured Principal Scholar?" Blinda looked confused.

"I, for sure, have the best grades out of the other Skyborne, but I was told they were still *deliberating* between the top scholars in other origins," Xendo explained. "They're going to announce who's actually the valedictorian at the ceremony right before we all declare our majors."

"I guess we have a surprise to look forward to then!" Blinda beamed.

"I hope not!" Xendo laughed. "I really want that title! I worked so hard for it."

"Oh, honey, I'm sure you'll get it," Blinda comforted.

"Other origins?" Philo questioned. "What does that mean?"

"Oh, uh…," Blinda's face scrunched up as she cut herself a slice of the asparagus quiche. "There's Grounded, Oceanite, Frozen, and Skyborne origins. They're like our ethnicities. It's kind of like a person's people. Where you were born and where you're raised helps define the person you become."

"What? Like countries?" Philo asked.

Xendo took over as only an avid reader of history could.

"Sort of! The world's nations are just much smaller than the larger origins. The countries you know of still exist as territories of the Grounded origin, and even the three new origins have their own nations and cities. We still honor traditions in our families' heritages and pass down national customs. However, those differences aren't divisive anymore. As populations grew, education increased globally with fact-

CHAPTER 6

checked data. Instead of fighting each other, humans began working together to solve shared goals. They expanded beyond only land and constructed civilizations at the arctic poles, in the skies, and under the oceans. Our whole planet is full now. The Global Government granted each origin their independent recognitions around, what?" He looked to his mother. "Maybe 2400?"

Blinda tilted her head to think while chewing her scrambled eggs, then nodded. "About then, I think."

"In our time, if you're born to any of the villages of Earth's land, oceans, arctic poles, or islands in the sky, you belong to that respective origin in addition to your home nation," Xendo explained.

"Wow, that's strange," Philo let out.

"Not really," Xendo posed. "Each origin has its own culture, food, beliefs, traditions, values, and personality traits they respect."

"I guess." Philo shrugged.

"If a person is born to one of the ancient cities on land, they belong to the Grounded origin," Blinda began. "They're hard workers and good with their hands, I think they're wonderf—"

"Unless you count the Frozen. They're also born on land territories, just down in Antarctica, or at the Northern Palace. They love everything scientific and athletic. They're also known for being icy, in every sense of the word," Xendo joked.

"If you're born in any of the huge metropolis domes under the planet's oceans, you are considered Oceanite," Blinda continued. "They're creative and free-spirited artists. And if you're born on a skisland, you're Skyborne."

"Like us!" chirped Xendo.

"Yes, but we're not typical Skybornes. Our people obsess over competing new technologies and global politics. But I've chosen to raise Xendo on the ground here in our cottage to escape the hustle and bustle of skylife."

"More like shunned from skylife," Xendo scoffed. "I still go to school up there. All they do is trash dad and look at us sideways."

"True, but I think living down here has preserved your unique identity. Those Skyborne kids can be ruthless," Blinda pressed. Xendo shrugged his shoulders and relaxed back into his chair. Philo's mind was racing!

"People live in the sky? Underwater? And at the North Pole?" he

BREAKFAST AT QUAKER COTTAGE

spat out, shaking his head but thoroughly amazed. "That's wild!"

"Well, mostly near the South Pole for the Frozen, but yeah! We'll have to show you them all sometime." Xendo nudged Philo from his left.

"What origin am I?" Philo wondered aloud.

"We were talking about that with Superintendent Pearl," Xendo sighed as he began to ponder. "We're not sure what you'd qualify as, because we don't know the circumstances of your birth, and you weren't raised with any of the origins' cultures as we now understand them."

"Your parents were both Grounded, though, Philo. Ava was of Mexican and Native American descent, and your father's family was Greek and Italian. Ava had a work ethic like no other and was very inventive. Daniel, while cocky, came from a warm and caring farm family. Being Grounded was the only thing they had in common while at school," Blinda reminisced.

"Mom, can you pass me the orange juice?" Xendo asked.

"Sure. Here you go, hun!" Blinda reached for the slender pitcher of fresh-squeezed orange juice. Philo noticed the silver band on her wrist was starting to flash.

"Um… your watch is blinking," Philo interjected, pointing as the juice passed him.

"Oh my!" Blinda exclaimed, stopping mid-pour.

"They're called technobands, Philo, not watches," Xendo corrected.

"Do you think it's Nova?" Blinda asked as she placed the pitcher back down and looked at the boys. Philo shrugged and Xendo groaned because he now had to finish pouring his own drink.

Blinda tapped her wrist and a small hologram screen grew from where the band was first touched. The holoscreen read, "Superintendent Nova Oliviana Pearl," and the powerful lady Philo had met last night appeared on the screen. This time she was wearing a dark crimson pantsuit instead of a robe and slippers.

"Blinda, good morning," the woman stated more like a simple fact than a warm greeting. She spoke to them while busy typing on a separate display.

"Hello, Nova, will you be arriving shortly?" Blinda asked. "I made your favorite pastries! Fresh from the oven."

"The walnut kringle?" Superintendent Pearl tore her eyes from her second screen in delighted surprise.

CHAPTER 6

"And the blackberry muffins," Blinda stated proudly.

"Oh, how the odds curse me! It has been too long since I have enjoyed those. Unfortunately, I cannot make it this morning."

"What?" Xendo called out.

"Too much is happening with today's festivities for me to step away from the event's committee," Pearl informed as she resumed typing. "I'm re-working my commencement address as we speak."

"This breakfast was supposed to take your mind off the ceremony because everything was set to go," Blinda stated quietly, bummed her culinary efforts had gone to waste.

"Some royal guests from the Northern Palace arrived out of the blue and His Majesty has requested a tour of the institute's grounds, guided by me."

"That's a little rude to not give notice," Xendo responded with an up-curled lip.

"It was a surprise, but pleasing the King of the Frozen is in the institute's best interest. However, this is not the reason I'm calling. Philo, may I ask you a question?"

Philo, startled, stopped chewing his breakfast sausage. He swallowed it all in one painful gulp. He called out, "Uh, yes, ma'am!"

Pearl peered into her display at Blinda. "I hear him, but I do not see the boy. Can you rotate your display please, Blinda?"

Blinda used her fingers to tilt the floating holoscreen in Philo's direction. Xendo raised his eyebrows and pointed toward his cheeks gesturing for Philo to smile from across the table. Philo sat up straight and flattened his emerald shirt as the display faced him. Superintendent Pearl squinted at the boy.

"Philo, I've decided the best-case option to give you a positive life within our time is to have you attend school at SIYT," she stated as Philo's mouth fell open.

"You would be vastly behind our other students but may be able to catch up if you choose Human History as your graduate program. In fact, it's probably the only one you qualify for because it has no prerequisites."

Philo didn't know what to do besides awkwardly nod his head. Xendo was beaming and bouncing in his seat on the other end of the massive feast.

"This is slightly against protocol," Superintendent Pearl contin-

BREAKFAST AT QUAKER COTTAGE

ued, "but I will enroll you as the first transferring student from the Grounded Primary Program. If anyone asks, you adore Human History and just *had* to study it with us at SIYT." She paused from typing. "Philo?"

"Um, yeah," Philo answered, mustering courage, "I can do all that."

"'Philo Nockby, 'Human History Major.' It has a nice ring to it!" chimed Xendo, enjoying this.

"Oh, Nova!" Blinda gasped. "He can't go by Nockby. It's too obvious."

"Oh, right...," Xendo nodded, feeling dumb.

"For logic's sake!" Superintendent Pearl muttered and rubbed her forehead. "I'll have to enroll him with a different surname. Ideas?"

"Wait! Why can't I use my last name?" Philo asked.

"Uhhh...," Xendo chuckled, "your parents were famous Continuum agents, top of their field, who traveled back in time, went missing, and apparently had a secret love child in the past.... Pretty sure if you told people you were Daniel Nockby's son, you'd be trampled by a mob and torpedoed with questions."

"It's illegal for active agents to date, wed, or procreate, Philo," sighed Blinda while rubbing his shoulder in support and spooning him some more corned beef hash.

Pearl shifted her glasses and looked away from her second screen to face the trio again. "Romantic entanglements of agents inevitably confuse emotions and motives, resulting in blundered assignments. Ava and Daniel's apparent relationship and failed 2005 mission is just additional proof of why the ordinance is in place," stated Superintendent Pearl.

"Oh, so I have to lie to everyone?" Philo asked with a sigh. He already knew the answer, but he hoped he could be rescued from yet another obstacle to overcome.

"For now, you will need to, yes," confirmed Superintendent Pearl. "In the meantime, you'll go by a different surname to protect your anonymity. Do you have any particular preference?"

Philo thought about what he could choose. When he thought of family, the only names he ever thought of were those of his parents. He first read their names on a police report he was shown when switching foster homes as a kid. For years, he became obsessed with trying to actually feel like a true Nockby. Now he had to give that up, too. There was only one other person Philo felt was sort of like family, one thing

CHAPTER 6

he did miss from his past.

"Jonathan. I guess I can go by Philo Jonathan," Philo finally announced.

Xendo nodded his head in satisfaction and Blinda tilted hers in thought.

"That will do just fine. When you start classes, you'll be with the rest of the first-year history majors. Just aim to blend in."

"I'll do my best," Philo responded as Xendo patted his back.

"Blinda, my dear friend," Superintendent Pearl apologized, "I owe you yet *another* sit-down dinner, with my full attention, at a later date."

"I'll hold you to that, Nova." Blinda smiled solemnly.

"I must go," Superintendent Pearl stated with an almost-emotional inflection. "I will see you all at the ceremony this afternoon. Until then, farewell."

And with that, the holoscreen went dark and dematerialized. Everyone at the breakfast table settled in their seats. Philo had already eaten three plates of food, but it seemed like they had hardly made a dent in finishing the entire breakfast feast.

"That woman works too hard," Blinda remarked with a shake of her head.

"What about all this food?" Xendo groaned. Philo chuckled and took another bite of his lab-grown bacon.

As they walked through the Quaker's Grounded village, there were no paved roads, no cars, no big buildings. Instead, blooming berry bushes and flowering fruit trees grew along their stone path. Each home they passed had a lush vegetable garden in the front yard. Philo watched a man in a formal suit give his kids a hug goodbye, step on a metal platform, and vanish into thin air. Philo couldn't believe his eyes. *Did he just vaporize himself? Or was he just leaving for work?*

Xendo and Blinda turned around a corner on the edge of town, and Philo's neck craned back as he looked upward. A mile overhead was a gigantic island city in the sky over Lake Superior. The massive structure stood on columned legs mounted beneath the waters. Most of the city's huge tech towers and colorful lights were wrapped by cumulus clouds, but Philo still marveled at the beautiful view. They approached a lighthouse standing on the edge of a rocky cliff overlooking the blue waters. The lighthouse must have been over a thousand years old. On the lake's horizon were green islands filled with pine and birch trees.

BREAKFAST AT QUAKER COTTAGE

An ultramodern bridge connected the ancient lighthouse to one of the giant columned legs of the sky city. The giant white pillar was thick and jutted straight up through the clouds with no end in sight.

Xendo saw Philo's confused gawking and pointed, "That is Split Rock Lighthouse. It's been here forever. We're going to take that skytube to go up to SIYT on Superior Skisland. Cool, right?"

Philo nodded, pretending those sentences made sense.

"The skytubes are buried into the ground underwater and hold up the skislands," Blinda said.

"And they take you all the way up in only thirty seconds!" Xendo added.

When they stepped into the skytube, a soft beeping sound went off, the doors closed, and a calm female voice spoke over the speaker, *"Now leaving the ground of Duluth Village."*

The platform shot up the skytube. Philo had a brief queasy millisecond in his stomach that subsided to a frictionless feeling of being lifted. The clear wall to their front allowed Philo to watch the village's vibrant farms shrink exponentially as they rose.

The doors opened and the steady robotic female voice stated, *"Welcome to Superior Skisland. The smallest of Earth's Skislands. Home of the beloved artisan market, Superior Bazaar, and the world's only graduate program of trioka-related studies, Superior Institute of Young Trioka."*

"We're here!" Blinda stated, "Now we just need to hurry over to the auditorium before the ceremony starts!"

"So, let's get moving!" Xendo urged, putting his arms around their shoulders, and wrangling them forward.

They exited the tube and Philo had to remind himself they were above the clouds because he saw shops, eateries, buildings, signs, and people walking in every direction. The "ground" was the same metal-like white substance the skytube was built-from. Philo could hardly believe he was on the same planet as the simple, peaceful village they just came from.

Each person he saw wore a different style of fantastic outfit or used some sort of outlandish technological gadget. Some were typing into holoscreens, listening to tiny earpieces, or placing their purchases into floating storage pods. Children were smacking glowing orbs of white light back and forth to each other through the air. Each sight was more captivating than the last. Philo felt overwhelmed, but he also wanted to just sit and watch this town square for hours.

CHAPTER 6

A busy stranger bumped into Philo's shoulder by accident.

"Oh! S-sorry!" a quiet voice cried as a yellow SIYT uniform jacket fell near Philo's feet.

Philo turned to see a short boy his age with thin black hair, a small nose, and a graduation outfit just like Xendo's. Philo bent down to pick up the dropped item.

"No worries," Philo offered as Xendo and Blinda walked ahead in the busy town square, not noticing him fall behind. "Here's your jacket. Do you go to SIYT?"

"It-it's not mine," the boy stuttered sheepishly, taking hold of the uniform. "But, y-yes... I do."

"We might have classes together soon," Philo mentioned with a smile. "I'm Philo by the way, Philo... Jonathan."

"I'm... Luther," the boy hesitated. "N-nice to meet you."

"What origin are you?" Philo asked.

"Oh...," Luther seemed distracted. "I'm Skyb—"

"LUTHER, WHERE ARE YOU?" a voice bellowed over the crowd of tourists.

Luther tensed up. Philo's shoulders jumped in surprise. An angry teen with sandy-brown coiffed hair, arched eyebrows, and a Skyborne suit stomped past Philo.

"What took you so long?" the boy yelled at Luther. "That fat dioka shopkeeper better not have ruined my dry cleaning."

Philo was shocked by the crudeness of the angry teen. The boy's fancy mother trailed behind wearing ornate jewelry and gold-rimmed sunglasses. She was stunning, but sort of dazed, like she didn't exactly realize where she was. She didn't say a word as her son continued to bellow at Luther. The mean boy didn't even bother to look at Philo as he snatched the dry-cleaned garment.

"Did you drop it on the filthy ground?" the teen griped, disgusted as he slipped into the SIYT jacket. He turned and marched away in a huff. "Luther, you always mess everything up! Let's go before SIYT is riddled with the land-dwellers."

The young Skyborne stomped off to mow through the bazaar square, and his mysteriously elegant mother followed behind. Luther released a sad sigh.

"Umm," Philo reached out, "You shouldn't let that guy ta—"

"S-Sorry," Luther interrupted him. "I have to go before they get

BREAKFAST AT QUAKER COTTAGE

too far ahead and leave me stranded here."

"Oh! Okay…, good luck!" Philo muttered as Luther jogged off. Philo was now alone, stuck in the busy center of Superior Bazaar. He had no idea where to go without Xendo and Blinda. His stomach flipped.

"Oh! Thank goodness! There you are," Blinda came back through the crowd, and put her arm around Philo. "We thought we lost you, we have to stick together on these busy market days."

"Did you talk with Jasper Finn?" Xendo inquired, eyes narrowing.

"Who?" Philo asked, confused.

"The guy that was stomping around here a few minutes ago? He brushed by us and we heard yelling?" Xendo explained.

"Oh right," Philo made the connection. "No, I didn't speak to him, he sort of just yelled in my direction." Philo shrugged. "I did speak with a kid named Luther."

"Luther Wyatt?" Xendo looked surprised. "He spoke to you? I don't think I've ever heard him speak."

"Those Skyborne boys bullied Xendo for years," Blinda interrupted and shook her head. "Kids can be so cruel."

"Mom!" Xendo complained, "I… handled it. They're just dumb." He rolled his eyes.

"Luther seemed pretty kind," Philo admitted.

"Maybe. He's sort of the squeaky extra wheel in Jasper's gang," Xendo groaned. "So glad I'm graduating primary so I never need to see them again."

"Sorry, the bazaar is so crowded right now," Blinda apologized, noticing Philo's panic. "Usually, it's a calmer place to buy food or barter with shop owners, but Primary Advancement draws so many trioka families from around the globe."

"Alright, now that no one is lost, let's head to school." Xendo led the way as they turned around.

Half a mile ahead, their white path sloped down to reveal a huge campus of five buildings that took Philo's breath away. This must have been the Superior Institute of Young Trioka. He didn't realize he would be so nervous witnessing the important place first hand.

The first building on the left had a round, wave-like architecture that ebbed and flowed throughout its blue walls. It was surrounded by a moat of water. The second brown edifice was flat, wide, and made of brick walls sprouting with ivy. Many green trees barricaded the build-

CHAPTER 6

ing from its whiter surroundings.

On the far right was a domed, dark steel building with high, icy white walls to guard it. Somehow, snow surrounded the building without melting. The fourth edifice was a perfectly square glass cube with golden yellow molding. It was both nondescript and frightening at the same time. The focal point in the middle of the four buildings was a crimson-and-purple-hued estate with a collection of towers that reached even higher into the sky. At its base, Philo noticed, were the same glass doors from the photograph taken of his parents before their death. The building was powerfully striking, ancient, domineering, and royal.

Blinda opened her arms with a smile, "This is it, the Superi—"

"We don't have time!" Xendo cut her off. "We can do a tour later, Mom."

Blinda laughed and followed Xendo hustling toward the front doors of SIYT. Philo stood outside the doors, taking a moment to finally be by himself. He breathed in with apprehension and looked down at his feet. His parents once stood in this exact same spot. They had been smiling, laughing, and *alive*. Crossing this barrier into this ominous place where he didn't belong seemed like a betrayal.

Philo couldn't help but feel a stab of guilt. If his parents never came to the past, if they never gave birth to him, maybe they wouldn't have died. It was *his* fault his parents weren't here with him today. It was *his* fault they weren't joyously celebrating the graduation of their kids like Blinda. A sense of overwhelming dread bubbled in Philo's stomach. Would he bring his bad luck here as well? Screw up the hopes Xendo and Blinda had for him? He seemed to always ruin the rare opportunities that life dangled in front of him.

Blinda and Xendo called to Philo from inside the building; he didn't want to fall too far behind. The SIYT glass doors were heavy as he pushed them open. Philo crossed the threshold of the crimson school, entering the Superior Institute of Young Trioka.

This place held the answers to who Philo was always supposed to become, and that terrified him.

CHAPTER 7

THE VALEDICTORIAN AND THE FROZEN PRINCESS

They entered the noisy oval-shaped SIYT auditorium filled with thousands of enthusiastic guests. Young children and happy parents chatted over each other while proud teachers, stoic security, and older students were scattered around the space working the event.

"Mom, I swear, this is the embarrassment line." Xendo drew an imaginary line on the floor of the auditorium's aisle. "Once we walk past here, you have to take your fawning from fourteen down to two."

"Don't tell me what to do, I'll fawn as much as I want over *my* son," Blinda responded with a greedy grin. Xendo rolled his eyes more dramatically than Philo ever thought possible.

"I'll see you guys after the ceremony," Xendo called back as he jogged ahead toward the row of other skyborne teenagers wearing stylish gray-yellow suits like his own.

"Oh, that boy," Blinda laughed to Philo with a shrug. "When is he going to realize embarrassment is a wasted fear? No one is actually watching him that closely to care."

Philo and Blinda strolled down a center aisle toward the raised crimson stage with a bright purple podium. Each auditorium section had different colored seat cushions: blue, white, green, and yellow.

CHAPTER 7

Philo peeked around the room in wonder. Blinda caught him glancing about.

"Oh right. This section is for us Skybornes. To our left, sit the Oceanite students and their families. To the right, the Grounded, and across the stage is the Frozen section," Blinda explained loudly over the crowd. "SIYT is the only place where everyday trioka from different origins around the world are all in the same room. I love Primary Advancement!"

All the sights Philo observed so far on the skisland were now making sense. In the blue Oceanite section, the fashionable families were wrapped in sea-colored tunics or soft swimwear of purple and cerulean. Music played from devices they carried as they chatted away with glee. The Grounded people in the green section were quieter, but still whispering with excitement. Their earth-toned attire of rough fabrics matched their warm and peaceful personas. The Frozen guests across the room wore materials of white or black stitched with geometric patterns and were draped with exotic animal furs. The fierce soldiers with clenched jaws made Philo glad there was a stage separating them.

At the front of the white section sat a domineering mountain of a man and a beautiful young girl. Dressed in royal attire adorned with jewels and vibrant furs, the pair had solemn faces framed with intricately-shaped black hair. Both wore crowns constructed of rainbow-colored jewels and icy crystals. The young girl sat still; she was the only person in the auditorium who looked downtrodden and out of place. Surrounding the mighty man and his daughter was a border of muscular women wearing militaristic white uniforms. They had stone-cold faces and scanned the room as if danger was all around them. However, most of the Frozen families had rosy cheeks and glowing smiles. It was clear they were just as wowed by this auditorium as Philo was.

Their Skyborne section was quiet and stoic compared to the others. As Blinda stretched on her toes to find seats, the Skybornes nearby glared as if she was an eager rabbit that crashed their business meeting. Their slicked-back hair topped electronic body suits or gray corporate attire. They sat bored and distracted as if their time was being wasted. Philo couldn't believe Xendo and Blinda were from the same origin as these people who looked like walking androids.

Blinda grabbed two spots in the very back of the auditorium. Up so high, Philo couldn't see Xendo anymore. Scanning the arena, Phi-

THE VALEDICTORIAN & THE FROZEN PRINCESS

lo noticed the clear divide between origins. Each section resembled a loyal family that cheered fiercely for their own members. If his parents were alive, Philo wondered if they would be happily chatting with their neighbors in the Grounded section. He pictured them telling stories of Philo's childhood and bragging of how proud they were to see their son graduate. Philo released a depressed exhale. His chin fell. There's no sense in lingering on fantasies.

"Look, there's Nova!" Blinda shrieked, pulling Philo from his thoughts. "Oh! Her crimson suit is stunning!"

Philo squinted to where Blinda was pointing as Superintendent Pearl strutted onto the stage. Her crimson pantsuit laced with gold details was tailored to show off her powerful form. As she passed professors sitting in matching crimson and maroon robes, the floating spotlights followed her to the podium. In an auditorium full of eye-catching people, the superintendent still commanded enough attention to silence the crowds. Without a wisp of worry, the superintendent began her speech.

"Good afternoon. I am Superintendent Nova Oliviana Pearl, and I am pleased to preside over this historic ceremony today. Primary Advancement is a proud and bittersweet day for us, here at the Superior Institute of Young Trioka. It is the day that we say farewell to our precious students and launch them into their bright futures yet to blossom. Every day, our graduates prove that starting their education here at SIYT has allowed them to forge a positive change in the world. It is our youth who enhance our legacy as trioka."

The entire auditorium roared with applause and cheers. Even the inexpressive Skyborne people nearby clapped in agreement. Philo leaned over to a cheering Blinda.

"Is *everyone* in this room a trioka?" he asked.

"Hmmm, I'd say maybe 95 percent," Blinda responded. "The students graduating are all trioka and most of the parents would be. Maybe some friends of guests here are dioka? You never know unless you ask, or see a trioka person's genetic mark."

"Oh okay, so we blend in still," nodded Philo.

"We're usually the minority in most places, but not here at SIYT," Blinda finished as Superintendent Pearl continued.

"First, I would like to welcome the other superintendents of our sister dioka universities that actively recruit trioka students. Let's start

CHAPTER 7

with the origin we all stem from, the Grounded."

With more applause, Superintendent Pearl left the stage and an elderly woman in dark green robes took her place. She had styled hair with streaks of black and gray, wide glasses, and big earrings.

"Hello, my brethren. I am Moira Goodwillow, Superintendent of the Shanghai College of Trades. SCOT was the first origin-specific Dioka University on Earth. We were founded in 2350, a mere eighteen years after world leaders finally coalesced after the pandemic, wars, and the expansion. Seeking peace and independence, the Global Government decided to classify our four separate growing civilizations as 'Origins.' At SCOT, official trioka students first enrolled in 2705, as soon as the evolving genetics were confirmed and accepted in society. We are proud to teach both dioka and trioka students the trade skills humans have passed down since the dawn of civilization. These trades include Agriculture, Culinary Arts, Healing, and Craftsmanship. Our aim is to teach our students to help build a sustainable future for humankind. After all, my dear students, as we Grounded believe, *You are what you create!* Thank you!"

Steady applause sounded around the auditorium. Blinda clapped more enthusiastically than everyone else around them. She leaned over to Philo.

"That's where I went. I studied culinary arts at SCOT for five years. Such wonderful memories!" She reminisced.

"But you're Skyborne, right?" Philo asked, a bit confused.

"Oh yes, but you can choose any graduate program you like. Most students do stay within their own origin, but there are always a few, like me, who want to branch out, and see more of the world. They want to follow their passions, even if they differ from their origin's usual skill set."

"Ah, that makes sense. So these students could choose anywhere?" Philo whispered back.

"Exactly," Blinda nodded, "there's always a few surprises!"

The pair faced forward again to see a bald, middle-aged man with gadgets in both ears and an electronic monocle walk toward the stage. This is the type of super-tech man that could have proven to Philo he was definitely stuck in the future.

"Greetings, I am Ronald Swift, the Skyborne representative of the Atlantic Law and Technology Institute. Founded in 2410, ALTI is the

THE VALEDICTORIAN & THE FROZEN PRINCESS

newest major dioka university and we reside on the skisland over the Atlantic Ocean. We have the highest test scores, a state-of-the-art data storage wing, and are constantly inventing new technologies for the planet. Our institution has had a troubled past in accepting trioka students. However, over the recent centuries, trioka minds have enlightened and enriched our Skyborne classrooms. Students may enroll in classes of Data & Technology, Political Law, Global Government, and Electrical Coding. We welcome the logical minds of SIYT's 3451 graduating class to join us in building an efficient society. *Forward, Upward, Onward.* That is all."

As the bionic man stepped down, a stylish, youthful man in vibrant pastels took the podium. He had tall, gelled hair that seemed shaped underwater and a sing-song voice that made Philo smile.

"Hello to all you beautiful humans! My name is Fineus Tide, and I am the headmaster of PUAE, the Pacific University of Artistic Expression. Founded in 2395, our campus's underwater dome lives on the ocean floor outside Saltwater City, capital of the Pacific. Our graduate program is both secluded from the distractions of the surface, but at the center of Earth's creativity. If you are an artist, no matter if you are dioka or trioka, you belong with us!

"Painters, photographers, filmmakers, and illustrators will find their home in our Image Capture courses. Singers, actors, dancers, comics, poets, and any other entertainers will love to hone their craft in our Performance Program. Thirdly, our Production & Media courses are perfect for those artists who prefer to stay behind the scenes to construct the business of entertainment. This year we have exciting new courses from every program, including *Intricacies of Kelp Fashion, Historical Films of the 3000s,* and *Underwater Music and Vocals.* Thrilling! Until we meet again, *May Artistry Flow Within Us!* Thank you."

Headmaster Tide sidestepped from the podium, gave a dramatic flowing bow, and the entire Oceanite section jumped up to cheer.

Suddenly, the twenty warrior women from the Frozen section stood to make deep, grunting chants in unison. The noises were fearsome but still somehow melodic and pleasing. They were dressed in white leather battledress with sharp protruding spikes. Their thick, long braids reached the floor. The chant started to swell in pitch as one woman stood out from the rest to grace the stage. This woman's military uniform had an additional white fur coat that looked so dense it

CHAPTER 7

might deflect bullets.

"I am Grayda Michaelson. Co-General of The Winter Thorns Army and Commanding Officer of the Antarctic Martial Defense Academy. AMDA's educational base is situated around the South Pole Headquarters of Antarctica. We train Earth's elite fighters, athletes, explorers, security, and law enforcement. Our impenetrable compound is the perfect place to become one with your body and learn how to safeguard yourself, your loved ones, and our beloved planet we would die to protect. Both dioka and trioka students can enroll in our programs of Law Enforcement, Sports Training, and Global Defense. Our graduates are placed worldwide, protecting the well-being of Earth's citizens, preventing crime, and taking down any threats to peace. Join us to honor your duty of service. *We Do Not Melt.* Good day."

General Michaelson nodded as the warrior women restarted their chant. She rejoined her Winter Thorns as Superintendent Pearl returned to the podium.

"Thank you, General. And thank you to all of our esteemed Heads of Education. Our five universities have been in a proud partnership for centuries. However, as we all know, trioka students may also choose to continue their studies here at the Superior Institute of Young Trioka. SIYT is the first graduate program dedicated to trioka-specific studies. We were founded in 3100, only a decade after the government gave trioka equal protection under global law. Our Human History Program will allow students to focus on humankind's historical significance and ancient knowledge. We preserve ideas, stories, and customs of the humans who came before us and reiterate the life lessons that often become forgotten. There is not a more valiant pursuit than becoming a student of history, for what has taken place in our past foretells our future."

Philo's eyebrows raised as he hung on Superintendent Pearl's every elegant word.

"Our Human History students will forgo their formal allegiances to their birth origin to preserve and protect all origins equally. They will take a wide range of historical courses to widen their abilities in global cultures, artistic expression, survival skills, and kineoka training. Our graduates go on to discover solutions for the world's greatest problems, serve society within the global government, and defend history against those who dare to harm it. At SIYT, students will learn more about this vast world and more about themselves. To all those who seek truth, we welcome you."

Philo's ecstatic mind was bursting with so many questions. This time, he actually clapped as loud as Blinda did.

"Before we move on to each student's graduation walk and declaration of university, I must announce the Principal Scholar of the class of 3451." The superintendent opened up a personal holoscreen display of notes.

Binda grabbed Philo's hand, raising her voice over the cheering crowd. "Ever since he started his primary classes at three years old, Xendo has worked so hard to become Principal Scholar, he even has a speech ready. It *has* to be him."

Blinda squeezed Philo's hand tighter as Superintendent Pearl looked out to the crowd.

"The Principal Scholar of the 3451 class at the Superior Institute of Young Trioka is… Alani Adalaide!"

Xendo heard the words but couldn't believe them. *Alani Adalaide? Who's that? How could she have better grades than me?*

As Xendo tried to stay composed in his defeat, a slender, short girl with pastel glasses from the Oceanite section stood up, raised her fists and belted a cheer. The tips of her brown hair were dyed seafoam-blue to compliment her Oceanite jacket. As the exuberant girl skipped toward the stage, she high-fived everybody along her path. Jasper Finn, the Skyborne bully who had tormented Xendo for years, turned around from two rows ahead.

"See Xendo, you're not as smart as you think you are. Losing to an Oceanite girl? Pathetic!" snickered Jasper. Xendo sulked down into his seat and scowled at the girl with blue-green hair.

Alani Adalaide was handed her small graduation plaque as she arrived at the podium. She raised her arms like a victorious wrestling champion and twirled in a circle embracing the crowd's applause. She pointed to the Oceanite section like a rock star as her rabid fans jumped up to cheer even louder. Xendo rolled his eyes. When Alani tapped the microphone, a screeching noise rippled across the auditorium.

"Woah! A Skyborne didn't get top scores? I can't believe it!" Alani cheered. "Thanks, SIYT! I didn't really prepare a speech… but, why not? Let's wing it!"

CHAPTER 7

The Oceanite section roared with pride.

"I'm so proud to be your Principal Scholar this year. I can be silly sometimes, but there is nothing I love more than learning! I come from a big dioka family that has never left the ocean! I have eight siblings, but I was the only one to be born trioka. I guess I had to stand out somehow! I am forever grateful my parents believed in me enough to let me study here! And now I have an award! So, take that, Haru!" Alani belted, pointing to a large family of equally cheery people with glasses in the crowd.

"Haru is my snotty older brother, who didn't think this was possible! Anyhoo, thanks for this! Oh! And my little piece of advice for the graduates is... don't listen to me! Listen to yourself! I don't even know you! So, make your own choices!" Alani giggled as the Oceanite and even the Grounded sections laughed with her.

The girl backed away from the podium with delight. Superintendent Pearl was confused for just a millisecond, then stepped up to the microphone.

"Thank you, Miss Adalaide, and your choice of graduate program?"

"Oh right, gosh," Alani choked and made an awkward sound. She rushed back to the stand with a stumble. "I'll be choosing to study Human History here at SIYT! Gonna learn a bunch of top secret shizz!" She flipped her hair, posed, and then raised her hands up in celebration with the cheers of the Oceanites.

"How wonderful, Miss Adalaide, we're glad you'll be joining us. Please return to your seat now." Superintendent Pearl directed.

Alani headed back down the stairs and off the stage while pumping her graduation plaque in the air like a sports trophy. Superintendent Pearl took control of the room once again.

"Excellent, now let's move on to the rest of the students. We are excited to partake in your declarations! An exciting step for all young trioka." Superintendent Pearl looked down at her personal display.

"Let's start with the Skybornes: Scott Anders!"

Xendo sighed. It was over. How disappointing. Four rows ahead of him, Scott Anders stood up and went to the stage. He chose to attend the Skyborne University, ALTI. No shocker there. His emotionless Skyborne peers never let him join in their virtual reality gaming, robot building contests, or coding challenges. They shunned him because of his father's failed mission. Every day Xendo was reminded of how inescapable the Quaker name was.

Up in the balcony, Philo strained to see down below. The twentieth Skyborne to cross the stage was a blonde girl with a bare face who seemed pretty grumpy. She also chose ALTI.

"Why are they all choosing the same school?" Philo asked Blinda.

"Ehh, some people like to stay comfortable, trying something new scares them," she responded. "The best choice I ever made was choosing a different origin to study from. It allowed me to discover more versions of myself. To not fit the same old mold and actually grow. That's so valuable."

"Yeah, seems like it," Philo agreed.

Suddenly, Superintendent Pearl called out, "Xendo Quaker," and Philo had to dodge to the right as Blinda literally bounced to her feet to holler and cheer. Everyone around them glared at Blinda with shock and disgust. Philo smirked. He loved how Blinda was unabashed in her love for her son.

Philo smiled as he watched Xendo's tall and slender frame nervously saunter up the stage to shake hands with the superintendent. In a surprising display of emotion, Superintendent Pearl gave Xendo a pat on the shoulder. Xendo approached the podium.

"I choose Human History here at SIYT," his voice said, amplifying out from the microphone.

No one in the huge auditorium cheered but Blinda. However, she cheered so loud, Philo was sure Xendo heard her all the way from the rafters. The boy dashed off the stage staring at his feet, ignoring his mother's embarrassing hurrahs. Philo clapped along.

"Wow, following in Jerome's footsteps." Blinda sat back down and shrugged her shoulders happily. "I knew it! That boy has a couple of wild years ahead of him."

"If I were up there, that's probably what I would choose," Philo threw in.

"Really? Well, it does make sense," Blinda considered. "Your parents did. You also could learn about everything you've missed these past 1,400 years," she chuckled.

"Yeah, I might need to know some of that," Philo joked back.

Over the next hour, most of the graduating fourteen-year-olds just chose the universities from their own origins. Only a handful of students chose Human History, or swapped to a different graduate pro-

CHAPTER 7

gram across the world.

"Aren't they at least curious about something new?" Philo asked, trying not to yawn.

"Oh! I'm sure they are. But taking that leap is scary. They may feel bound by family norms or fearful of making the wrong choice on a whim. So they stay safe." Blinda shrugged as the last Frozen student finally received their plaque. "Even trioka have a fear of change."

Philo glanced over to look at all the Grounded teens smiling down below, perfectly happy. That security and acceptance would have tempted him to stay safe as well.

Superintendent Pearl returned to the dais to speak.

"To close our Primary Advancement ceremony, we have a rare delight. For the first time in our school's history, members of the Frozen Royal Family have joined us for today's festivities. His Majesty, Bernard Arctikon, the King of the Frozen, has asked to say a few words," Superintendent Pearl announced, beginning a round of applause.

The warrior women's thunderous chants rang again as the Frozen king and the young girl stood up. General Grayda and four female soldiers surrounded the royals as they walked to the center of the crimson stage. With a husky deep voice, the mountain of a man began to speak. He seemed frigid, but peaceful.

"Friends, thank you for this kind welcome. My daughter and I have traveled all the way from Rosennie, our royal Frozen capital we constructed surrounding the North Pole. Superintendent Pearl has made our first journey up above the clouds a memorable one. From afar, up at the Northern Palace, Princess Raelyn and I have greatly admired all that your institute offers and represents. It is a beacon of knowledge and kinship to both the dioka and trioka of all four origins."

The King paused to gesture toward his daughter.

"Princess Raelyn is the first trioka born to the Frozen royal family. The Arctikons have always been dioka. Unfortunately, our governing ancestors did not look favorably on your people. However, my parents were the first who strived to break that mold. Our past fears of trioka were fears that held us back. We Frozen can be solid and stubborn individuals, but even glaciers inch forward as the world turns."

The King paused with a hesitant inhale. The princess, who had been standing still and staring at the floor, lifted her chin toward her father.

THE VALEDICTORIAN & THE FROZEN PRINCESS

"My late wife, Semira, was the epitome of a powerhouse mother and an *almost*-unstoppable force for good. But illness can halt even the mightiest of us. If she was standing by my side today, she would be endlessly proud of our daughter," King Bernard stated firmly.

Superintendent Pearl could tell that the princess was struggling to hold a stern face and not show any emotion. King Bernard carried on.

"Were it not for her royal duties and our safety concerns, Princess Raelyn would have joined you students in your classes here at SIYT at age three. Previous Frozen monarchs may have ignored this new trioka heritage in our family, or even snuffed it out. However, Queen Semira would not allow such nonsense. Upon the first glimpses of Raelyn's glowing genetic mark and propensity to levitate as a newborn, my wife reached out directly to Superintendent Pearl to secure the best tutors to educate Raelyn with the same SIYT courses you all learned here. It was a tricky balance to strike, but my daughter, like her mother, can never back down from a challenge." King Bernard informed, proudly. Princess Raelyn remained rigid and closed her eyes.

"When Princess Raelyn first asked to journey to this ceremony all the way from the Northern Palace, I was hesitant. She had already passed all her courses and been given her advancement plaque. However, my Raelyn has always been graciously humble and a fighter for fairness. She desired to graduate amongst her would-be classmates and proudly declare AMDA her future university for all to see. My daughter spoke of showcasing a new era for the Arctikon Family that not just quietly tolerates the Frozen trioka among our ranks, but one that *celebrates* all our trioka brethren. It was this moment that confirmed to me that Raelyn will one day become a more virtuous monarch than myself, and possibly even more than her wonderful mother." He turned to share a glance with his daughter. She smiled back with a tear of gratitude streaming down her cheek. "Now, I grant the rest of my time back to the magnificent Superintendent Pearl."

As King Bernard stepped back from the spotlight, Superintendent Pearl bowed at the waist in his direction then went to read off the final name on her list of graduating students.

"Raelyn Arctikon, Princess of the Frozen," Superintendent Pearl announced. She then turned to join the line of professors in the back as the auditorium's applause commenced.

Princess Raelyn, who was tall, dark-skinned, and beautiful with

CHAPTER 7

elegant passion twists in her onyx hair, peered out at the expectant audience. Her opulent tiara was made of spectrolite gems and clear white crystals. Wrapped in a shawl of white arctic fox fur, she lifted her gown of snowy lace and stepped up to the microphone to clear her throat.

"I will be studying Human History here at SIYT and not returning back to the palace," Princess Raelyn uttered. The microphone projected her quiet voice and the entire room gasped.

"Oh my data!" Blinda muttered in surprise. Philo was confused.

Raelyn immediately retreated from the podium, dodging the rays of extra spotlights rushing toward her. An awkward, dead silence hit the auditorium. No one knew how to react. The king opened his mouth in shock, lifted an angry finger of objection, but then lowered it, noticing the crowd. Chattering swelled as Superintendent Pearl glanced at the other professors with a split-second of unease.

"Uh, thank you all for your time today," Superintendent Pearl declared with a voice she strained to keep normal. "We are so proud to witness the start of your next chapters. Farewell."

The king urgently gestured for Princess Raelyn to come toward him. She quietly obeyed. The Winter Thorns surrounded the royals and shuffled them out the back door in seconds. Philo realized they were stuck up in the balcony for quite a while as the crowds dispersed.

"I can't believe the nerve of that dear girl. The news will be all over this," Blinda spoke through her hands in a state of disbelief.

"What's the big deal?" Philo questioned. "I get she's royalty, but it's just school."

"No, it's not *just* school!" replied Blinda, eyes darting to Philo in surprise. "The Frozen Queen died from a rare disease only ten years ago. The princess is the last Arctikon heir. The Frozen people have split opinions of her upcoming leadership as the first trioka monarch. However, that's all out the window now; they're all going to despise her. If you join Human History at SIYT, you must revoke your formal origin allegiances. That girl just abdicated her throne!"

"*Damn*, no way!" Philo gasped. "Why would she do that?"

"She must have her reasons… or she *really* doesn't want to be Queen." Blinda shook her head and leaned back in her seat. Philo couldn't imagine the pressures that would have caused the princess to break such tradition.

"Hey, guys," Xendo interjected, approaching their seats.

THE VALEDICTORIAN & THE FROZEN PRINCESS

"Oh! Xendo!" Blinda yelped. "Come here, you!"

Blinda flew past Philo to give her son a gripping embrace so forceful his arms flailed about.

"Oh, honey, History?" Blinda laughed, "Your father would be so full himself right now if he'd been here!"

"Yeah," Xendo sighed. "I wish Jasper and his cronies didn't *also* pick History, but, at least, I'm no longer with just Skybornes. And I figured there's no sense in fighting it, I always craved to learn what Dad knew, and I need a fresh start."

"Congratulations, Xendo," Philo offered warmly, slinking in next to Blinda. "I'm sure your speech would have been nice."

"Well," Xendo shrugged with a scoff, "of course, when *I* want to be Principal Scholar, it's the year that a Skyborne gets passed over. Typical. That Oceanite girl is lucky."

"I loved her seafoam hair—you think she dyes her ends that blue-green color?" Blinda asked.

"I don't know," Xendo replied curtly, glaring at his mother.

"She seemed like lots of fun," Philo added.

"No! She did *not!*" Xendo huffed. "Whose side are you two on anyway?"

Blinda and Philo laughed. Blinda squeezed Xendo again.

"Don't worry sweetie, you can fight her to the nerd death very soon. Think of it as homework motivation," Blinda joked as Xendo's wrist started to buzz.

"Your bracelet thingy is doing something again," Philo interrupted, pointing to the boy's wrist. Xendo squirmed out of Blinda's tight grasp as she turned to Philo.

"Technoband, sweetie." Blinda patted Philo on the shoulder.

"Right." Philo nodded. "I need to remember that."

Xendo turned his hand over, tapped his technoband, and a small hologram screen shot from his wrist to his fingertips, covering his left hand like a smartphone.

"It's an EDM, from SIYT admissions," Xendo told his mother.

"A what?" Philo questioned.

"EDM, Earth Database Message," Xendo informed as he stretched the image slightly larger and scrolled down like he was reading a web page.

"Like your 'emails.' No, 'texts'!" Blinda smiled toward Philo. "Or

CHAPTER 7

maybe a 'booty call'?"

"Definitely not the last one," Philo smirked.

"Superintendent Pearl already sent our course list and our supplies will be provided in our dorms," Xendo exclaimed. "Philo, look! Pearl already got you enrolled!"

"Really?" Philo peered over Xendo's shoulder at the hologram message:

Human History Subjects and Materials, Year 1:

Kineoka Martial Arts 1
Kineoka Physical Training 1 by Arther Argent
Morphstaff Weaponry by Clara Dobbins

Kineoka Mental Arts 1
Elemental Cores by Vaughn Elliot
Trioka Meditation 1 by Tyler Roburn

Artistic Expression 1
Dioka Artistic History 1 by Claudette Turk
Musical Performance by Amir Robbins

Ancient Survival Skills 1
Dioka Survival History 1 by Ronald Mayj
Ancient Healing by Nanci Pikit

Global Government 1
Governments of Earth 1 by Rebecky Parsons
Origin Relations by Lyle Johson

Mechanics of Time Travel 1
Mechanics of Time Travel by Hardy Flep
Continuum Missions: Case by Case by Angelina Marcus

Human History 1
Human History, Unity Era: 2750-Present by Boris Cline
Human Evolution: Dioka to Trioka by Shelly Horknight

Wardrobe:
5 SIYT black student suits
2 crimson history jackets
2 pairs of combat boots

Recommended Education Tools:
1 technoband
1 libe
1 Earth Database tablet

Xendo Quaker will board with **Philo Jonathan** in dorm 13B. Thank you, **Xendo Quaker**, for your time as a primary student, we hope your next five years of study are just as rewarding!

Nova Oliviana Pearl
Nova Oliviana Pearl, Superintendent of the Superior Institute of Young Trioka

THE VALEDICTORIAN & THE FROZEN PRINCESS

"Mechanics of Time Travel? Elemental Cores? Kineoka? Origin Relations? Continuum Missions? This is so cool!" Philo exclaimed. "What's a libe?"

"Electronic libraries. Nobody these days lugs books around, so we have libes to read those school texts, take notes, write essays, and watch educational videos. Everything we need for school, really." Xendo beamed as he patted Philo on the back.

"What is your SIYT dorm number, boys?" Blinda asked.

"The acceptance letter says Room 13B," Philo pointed to Xendo's holoscreen.

"I think your fathers shared a room on the thirteenth floor!" Blinda perked up. "Ava was also somewhere on that level!"

As the boys buzzed about the possibility of their next five years living on the same dorm floor as their fathers, Blinda started heading down the stairs.

"Let's get some lunch at Superior Bazaar!" Blinda yelled back at the boys, already walking down the arena steps. "We have to have Philo try one of the classic burgers at Bazaar Bistro."

Xendo shut off his technoband, put his arm around Philo, and the boys followed Blinda out of the auditorium.

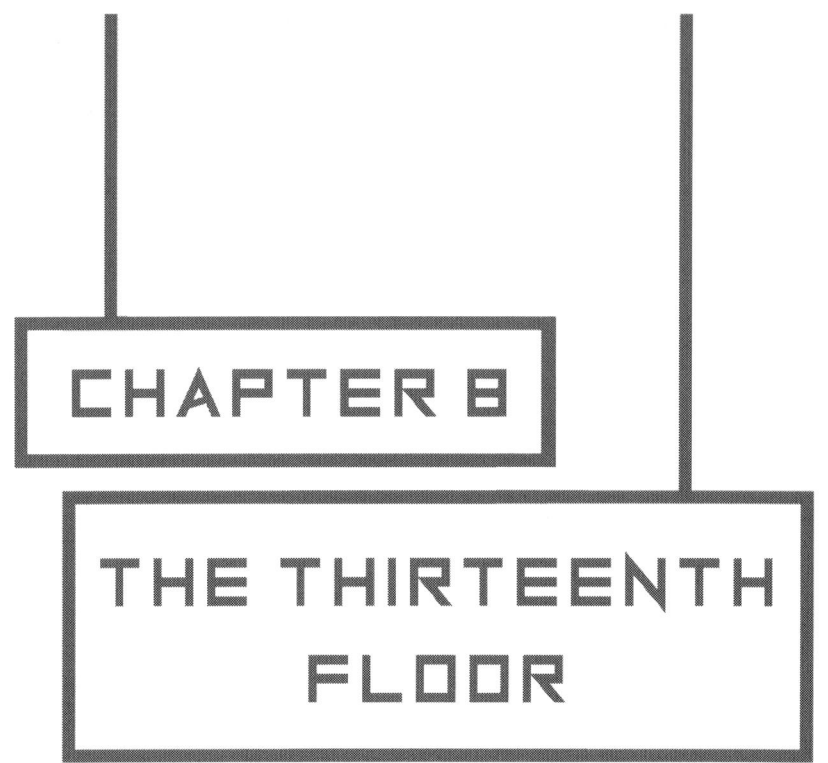

CHAPTER 8
THE THIRTEENTH FLOOR

Princess Raelyn Arctikon had been dreaming of this day for years. However, she never thought her plan would actually work or that it would be this painful. Her father, her personal guards, and the Frozen council had rushed her off the SIYT stage in a frenzy. They managed to sneak into a private room to discuss the damage of her Human History declaration. None of them foresaw her making such a disastrous blunder, but how could they? She had routinely lied for months and consistently misled everyone who had ever protected her. King Bernard could not bring himself to even look at his daughter. This choice could destroy him. But it was Raelyn's only option, her only way.

Her father and his royal inner circle had kept the assassination attempts of the Frozen monarchy secret from the other origins, and even their own subjects down in Antarctica. The world was blissfully unaware of the complications and confident in the king's leadership, but Raelyn knew it would soon come crashing down like an avalanche.

The crown's royal advisers would not stop pontificating around her. How could she betray her people? Had she lost her mind? How

THE THIRTEENTH FLOOR

can she be protected halfway around the planet? Raelyn was expected to answer them, but she kept her mouth shut. She knew she only needed to endure the anger and confusion. The declaration was final: it was too public to retract, and the entire world knew it.

She had studied the rules over and over. She's fourteen, so she now had authority over her own choices. She was no longer at the Northern Palace. They had no right to take her back if she refused to leave. They would never make a scene in such a public space, and now that she separated from her origin, she was under Global Government jurisdiction. If she wanted to train to be an agent, they could not stop her.

Raelyn still said nothing until everyone stopped trying to change her mind. The council members eventually allowed her to change out of her ornate gown, take off her makeup, and wear civilian clothes. The Winter Thorns would escort Raelyn to her new dwelling, Room 13C. Before she left, Raelyn put her hand on her father's shoulder.

"Stay strong," Raelyn whispered to him, trying to remain calm herself. "This is the only way to keep the peace and not get in your way. I love you."

The king did not speak. He was turned away from her. But after a few seconds, he lovingly placed his hand on hers for a heart-wrenching last moment together. She pulled her hand away, exhaled painfully, and joined her escorts.

Most students would take the main skytube up, so her guards chose the stairs to conceal the princess. The thirteen flights would have winded anyone else, but not Raelyn and the Winter Thorns. This many stairs was a breezy workout for the athletes.

As they entered the thirteenth floor's lounge, Raelyn peered around the room. A smile came to her face for the first time that day. The crimson lounge was warm and inviting. There was a big wooden dinner table and matching chairs with cushions. A cozy kitchen contained a double refrigerator, a stovetop, and wall ovens. The lounge was filled with comfy couches, small end tables, and an electric fireplace.

There were four dormitories on the thirteenth floor. Raelyn opened her room, 13C, and saw two sets of everything for her and the roommate she hadn't met yet. The Winter Thorns placed her belongings from the Northern Palace around the chambers. Raelyn tried to catch the gaze of the Winter Thorns to smile and thank them. However, they

CHAPTER 8

all avoided her attempts, finished the work, and left the room. Only one of the guards remained.

"Give them time. They will come to respect your decision. They're just upset at the moment."

This Winter Thorn was named Trayda Michaelson, Co-Commander of the Winter Thorns Army, Captain of the Royal Guards, and twin sister to General Grayda. She had a thick, long, brown braid tied into a bun for fighting. If there was someone who came close to a maternal figure for Raelyn, after her mother Semira passed away, Captain Trayda made a valiant effort. She had trained Raelyn to be a fighter ever since Raelyn could stand on two feet and throw a punch.

"If I stayed, the OMNI knights would have kept trying to attack the palace until the end of my days," Raelyn reasoned. "I need to know the truth. I can't stay hidden anymore. I must take control over what happens next."

"Every warrior must learn if they can handle the battle alone," Trayda agreed sorrowfully. "I have faith in your future, Little Snowflower. Even if others do not."

Trayda outstretched her arms for a rare hug. Raelyn entered her warm embrace. She looked up at her mentor.

"I will be safe here. The council may not be telling me the truth about my mother, but I will learn what really happened and bring a more stable peace to our people."

"Be careful who you trust," Trayda warned, "but I know your aim is noble. I will convince the others."

"I also...," Raelyn was almost embarrassed to admit it, "I also just want to be a normal teenager."

"Ah, yes," Trayda agreed. "A soul needs moments of freedom to breed clarity."

"I might even learn a few new battle tricks to best even you," Raelyn nudged. "I am trioka after all."

"Don't make me retract my well wishes, Princess." Trayda smirked as Raelyn laughed.

Trayda joined the other Winter Thorns as they left like a pack of wolves down the thirteen flights of stairs and out of Time Tower. Once they were gone, Raelyn checked the floor to see if any other students had arrived yet. No one. She went back to her empty room. There were no parents, no tutors, no guards, and no large crowds to judge her ev-

THE THIRTEENTH FLOOR

ery move. She didn't even know how a space like this would feel. Raelyn realized she was now finally alone for the first time in her entire life.

She gave a tiny yelp of joy and leaped onto her empty mattress bed, jumped up and down, and danced like an awkward flapping duck. She dismounted the bed and admired the view out her window and released a satisfied sigh of relief. This was the start of her new life! However, as quick as the blissful solace had come, it drifted away. Raelyn heard the doors of the skytube open. A pair of Oceanites entered the lounge to set up their own dorm on her floor. Raelyn tried to act normal, pretending to unpack her clothes and make her bed.

Raelyn heard the skytube open once more and a third student, a girl, immediately knocked something over and made a loud and boorish noise. *Did she just break something?* Raelyn was hoping this was not her new dorm mate, but, of course, it was.

"Well, bless my seawater!" the loud girl screamed, wide-eyed. "My roommate is the Frozen Princess?"

"Not anymore, I'm not," Raelyn muttered more to herself than this rambunctious stranger with seafoam hair.

"Oh right! Abdication and all that. The *draaaaaama* of it all!" the girl with glasses singsonged as she threw two duffel bags on the second bed with another loud thud.

"I'm Alani Adalaide," she beamed, stretching out her hand. "A^2, if you like math!"

"Hello, Alani," Raelyn replied kindly, shaking Alani's hand donned with agate rings.

"Just to get it out of the way, I'm trans. My parents are wonderful, but their boy name was far too boring for someone as fascinating as me," Alani confidently said with a flip of her blue-green hair. "Being male never felt like home, so I became Alani around age seven and never looked back!"

Raelyn nodded with a smirk, "Alani does seem to fit you well."

"You bet your sweet ass it does!"

Alani then twirled and swan-dived onto her new bed. Raelyn chuckled. She had never in her life been spoken to this way. This girl treated her like she was just a regular person. Raelyn couldn't quite tell if she disliked the crudeness or had been craving it for fourteen years.

However, she ended up hating it because Alani asked Raelyn too

CHAPTER 8

many personal questions. After the third one about Raelyn's skincare routine, Raelyn gave up answering. She just grunted in return. Alani didn't stop talking for the next hour while they decorated their dorm.

Annoying chattering aside, Alani was a master at making their room aesthetically beautiful. Raelyn was impressed. She hung tiny seashell lights around the room, watered aromatic kelp plants, and placed stunning hand-drawn artwork on their walls. As they continued to chat in the now-gorgeous room to Alani's calming oceanite music, Raelyn understood that Alani wasn't too bad. She may just need to procure some earplugs.

The girls heard some electronic beeping and turned around. Into their room rolled a mini humanoid robot. It was about two feet tall, constructed of white and gray metals, and had blue lights for eyes. Raelyn would venture to think it was actually... cute.

"I will dispose of this waste for you, students," the robot vocalized with mechanical beeps.

It trailed around the dorm picking up the girls' small pieces of trash. A compartment from the robot's stomach opened up and dropped the junk inside. The robot's middle section lit up, incinerating the unwanted materials.

"Oh! They have quality droids here," Raelyn noted.

"Perfect, I hate cleaning up!" Alani cheered as she walked over to the little robot and squatted down. It continued to clean as she spoke to it.

"Hey, buddy. What's your name?" Alani asked sweetly.

"I am called Quality Droid 313," it beeped and turned to scan her face. "May I ask your name and pronouns?"

"Of course," Alani chuckled. "Alani Adalaide. She/her."

"Hello, Alani Adalaide," Quality Droid 313 beeped in a mechanical voice. "Would you like to hear my list of functions?"

"No! Please, no," Raelyn called out hastily from her bed while putting clothes away.

"We're all right, but thank you," Alani smiled. "You are much more adorable than other quality droids I've seen. I'm going to call you QD. Like cutie, okay?"

The robot incinerated their last piece of trash in its stomach and replied, "I will log 'QD' down as a term I respond to."

"Perfect," Alani laughed and looked back at Raelyn. "These ones

THE THIRTEENTH FLOOR

are smart too!"

The skytube opened again. The girls looked out their door as an eager Skyborne boy and his shy Grounded roommate entered the common area. Quality Droid 313 beeped and exited their room.

The little robot rolled across the lounge to introduce itself to the two new male students on its floor.

"Hello. I am called Quality Droid 313," the robot beeped out. "May I ask your names and pronouns please?"

"Xendo Quaker. He/Him."

"Philo… Jonathan. He/Him."

"Welcome Xendo Quaker and Philo Jonathan. My records indicate you will be in room 13B. Follow me."

The boys followed the robot as it rolled ahead of them. Philo was in awe! He had never seen an actual working robot. Philo was shocked this was becoming his normal life! At their door, the robot stopped and beeped out, "Would you like to hear my list of functions?"

"No!" Xendo groaned.

"Yes!" Philo answered at the same time.

"Fine," Xendo looked at Philo. "Since it's your first quality droid."

The robot perked up. It rarely gets to share its spiel.

"My identification number is 313 and I am the droid that preserves the quality of the thirteenth floor of Time Tower at the Superior Institute of Young Trioka. I am responsible for dorm maintenance, package delivery, student protection, simple healthcare, and cleanliness. My 126 other specific functions include the followi—"

"Oh," Philo laughed. "Oh no…."

"Hey, 313," Xendo cut it off. "Actually, I think we're good, right, Philo?"

"Right," Philo agreed. That was far too many functions.

"But, 313," Xendo prepared to ask, "which room on this floor did a history student named Jerome Quaker stay in a few decades ago?"

Philo's eyes lit up, knowing what Xendo was hinting at. The quality droid cocked its head, computing an answer.

"Students Jerome Quaker and Daniel Nockby stayed in room 13A during the class years of 3425-3429. They often wou—"

"Shoot, it's 13A. Let's go," Xendo whispered to Philo.

The boys left the droid talking to itself at the doorstep of 13B to approach the adjacent room of 13A. The door was open and two stu-

CHAPTER 8

dents were unloading their own followpods. One was a plump brown girl with thick, straight, long black hair. The other was a androgynous person with a bright blue mini dress, a bowtie, a colorful vest, and pink stockings. The boys put their plan in action.

"Hello," Philo cheerfully greeted their new classmates. The roommates turned around in surprise, "I'm Philo and this is Xendo."

"I'm Skyborne and he's Grounded. Or I guess we were," Xendo reflected. "What are your names?"

"I'm Jade," the plump girl answered, "Oceanite."

"And I'm Naomii, also Oceanite," the quirky one responded.

"Oh! So you girls were in primary together?" Xendo asked.

"Yes, we've been friends for as long as I can remember," Jade answered.

"Most people think I'm odd," Naomii added. "Jade's the only one who doesn't ignore me."

They all laughed except Naomii. With a peaceful, dazed expression, Naomii just stared deeply at the boys with a peculiar smile. It was like Naomii knew they were already going to laugh and didn't need to exert the effort. It was a bit odd. Philo felt like Naomii stared into his eyes, down through his stomach, and found his soul. Naomii must do this to everyone.

"Also, my pronouns are they/them," Naomii corrected Xendo.

"Oh, cool. Thanks for telling us," Xendo nodded. Naomii smiled.

"Do you need something?" Jade asked.

"Yes." Philo didn't know how to start. "You see…um, Xendo?"

"My father actually stayed in your dorm, 13A, when he studied here," Xendo took over. "We don't know who the other roommate was…, but my dad for sure lived in this dorm. Would you mind if we switched? We're 13B."

The two friends looked at each other. Then back at the boys.

"We did hear this room was haunted and unlucky because it was Jerome Quaker's old room," Jade thought aloud. "Was he your father?"

"Haunted?" Philo responded, shocked. He felt Xendo sigh sadly on his right.

"Yeah, he was," Xendo lamented. Naomii was staring in a different direction.

"We're sorry for your loss," Jade offered kindly. "People must be cruel to you with the conspiracy theories and everything."

THE THIRTEENTH FLOOR

"All the time," Xendo chuckled.

"The haunting rumors don't bother me," Naomii responded suddenly, entering the chat again with a slow wave of their hand. "I also don't believe anything that angry people scream at me. If they were ever right, they wouldn't need anger."

"Very wise," Philo replied. Naomii nodded and turned to him, staring deeply without blinking.

"I guess the biggest issue is we're already unpacked," Jade mentioned, then gestured to all their belongings around their feet. "If you help us move our stuff to 13B, then 13A is yours."

"Deal!" Xendo exclaimed.

Naomii then stopped what they were doing and stared off distantly in thought again.

"I just realized. This is the beginning of it all," Naomii pondered.

Philo and Xendo were lost on what Naomii meant. They looked to Jade, who just shrugged and shook her head with a chuckle.

"I don't know either, I just let them say what they want." Jade smiled at her best friend. Naomii now seemed to be smiling and waving as if someone else was watching what they were doing. Jade handed her suitcase to Xendo. "We'll switch rooms with you two."

The boys carried all of Jade and Naomii's dormitory items from 13A to 13B. Jade helped transfer their provided school supplies to their new room and Naomii and just watched Philo and Xendo sweat. Eventually, the boys had 13A all to themselves. They looked through their libes at their electronic textbooks, tried on their SIYT crimson jackets with origin stitching, and Philo finally got his own technoband. As they finally unpacked everything and rested on their beds, a floating storage container appeared outside at their window. Xendo opened the glass panel and the self-piloting suitcase floated into the room.

"This is a followpod for carrying or sending luggage," Xendo explained to an awe-struck Philo. "Mom must have gotten back home and sent the rest of my stuff."

"Is it weird that I'll miss your mom even though I just met her?" Philo pondered aloud as Xendo pulled out his street clothes and old books.

"She works in the cafe downstairs every day," Xendo grunted. "That feeling will fade."

As daylight darkened into night, Philo and Xendo went over their

CHAPTER 8

SIYT course materials on their libes for their first day of classes tomorrow. Xendo was relieved he was the only Skyborne on their floor. He no longer had to endure Jasper and his cronies constantly tormenting him, or at least not after classes. They'd be in room 13A for five more years until they graduated. All Human History students went through this program and stayed in these dorms. His father did. Philo's parents did.

Eventually, the boys got comfortable in their own beds and turned the lights off. Philo heard Xendo's breathing become steady with quiet snores. However, Philo could not fall asleep. He was too anxious about his first day in the morning. *What if I can't keep up with the other kids? What if they discover I snuck into SIYT? Find out my real name?* His mind wouldn't calm down. *Is this how nervous mom and dad felt before their first day? Would they be happy I followed in their footsteps?*

Just twenty-four hours ago, Philo was alone, lost, and didn't have a clue what his future would be. 2019 was a nightmare, but at least he understood it. Philo hated leaving the comforts of a familiar foster home, even if it was terrible. He hated having to start over and over again. But this time was different.

Philo finally had a chance to make his life *mean* something. He had a chance to learn about his parents! Somehow he ended up in this future and he vowed not to squander this dream. Philo looked over to Xendo snoring. He still did not have a room to himself at night, but he finally had a space he didn't mind sharing. Philo was eager for the new futuristic adventures tomorrow would bring. However, he had to be careful he didn't make mistakes.

Philo promised himself his secrets wouldn't ruin this new life before it even started.

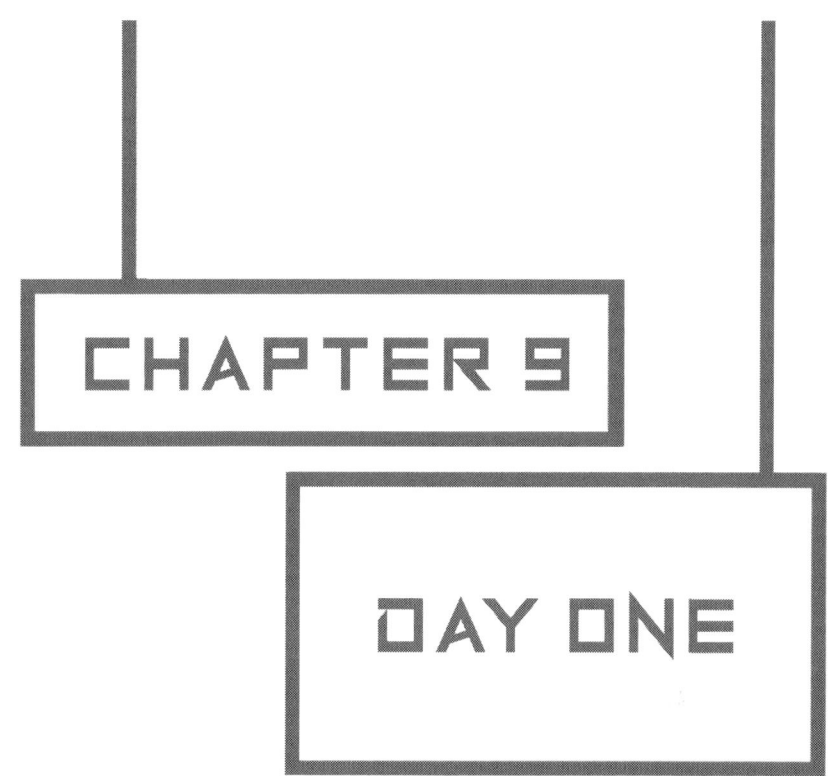

CHAPTER 9

DAY ONE

Philo was woken up on his first official day of SIYT trioka classes by a pillow being whipped at his head. Philo sat up in shock as Xendo chortled.

"Get dressed, grandpa," Xendo chuckled while rushing to put on his SIYT uniform. "We didn't set an alarm. The first orientation starts in ten minutes. We're late!"

Philo jumped to his feet wearing only his underpants. Xendo laughed and turned around as Philo put on his SIYT suit and crimson jacket with green stitching. They dashed out of their room. All their classmates had already left for their first class, Kineoka Martial Arts. Philo was furious he slept in. He didn't want to stand out on their first day.

As they sprinted through the hallways, Xendo shouted out important school landmarks.

"That's the cafe where Mom works. We can get food there each day," Xendo pointed to the large dining area, "but let's pretend we don't know her."

"Out that window is the massive vertical garden where fresh produce is grown year-round."

"That staffball hexagon is where the younger primary kids can

CHAPTER 9

practice our sport, but the actual SIYT staffball team is terrible."

"Okay, and now we're approaching the elemental sanctuary chamber and the kineoka sparring room."

The boys opened big black doors and entered a wide gymnasium with padded walls, floor mats, and huge windows. Ten slender humanoid robots stood solid in the far corner. They were menacing even when shut off. Philo's eyes also fell upon strangely twisted black poles leaning against one wall. Their fellow classmates were waiting on mats next to an elevated fighting stage in the center of the room. Philo and Xendo spotted Jade and Naomii and sat next to them.

"You both sure like to break the rules don't you?" Naomii joked while scooting closer to Jade to give the boys space.

"Did we miss anything?" Philo asked.

"Not really. Professor Bryne told us all to sit down here," Jade explained. "She said she'd be right back."

"I can't wait to meet *the* Uma Bryne. She's a *kineoka master*!" Xendo said to their group. "She's legendary."

"What for?" Philo wondered aloud.

"It's all rumors," Jade informed, "but apparently when she was an agent she went back in time to terminate assassins traveling to active battle zones during the Third World War."

A girl with seafoam hair sitting behind them leaned forward to join their conversation. "They call her the *Lethal Lady!*"

The boys turned around and realized it was the same girl that beat Xendo for top marks. Philo nodded in amazement at the nickname. Xendo grunted at her and turned back to face Philo.

"Her entire team of twenty agents were murdered in battle, but she was able to take down the final assassins by herself before they did too much damage," Xendo continued. "She was the only one who returned alive."

"Wow!" Philo marveled. "That's insane."

"She actually was able to *complete* a mission, unlike other failed agents," a familiar voice sneered.

The boys looked past Jade and Naomii to see a posh boy with sandy light-brown hair and a menacing smirk. Jasper Finn, the same angry teen from the bazaar. Behind him was a glamorous gothic girl with a purple streak in her silver Skyborne hair. There were two tall boys on either side of her: one boy had a thin mustache, and the other had too

DAY ONE

many muscles. All four had yellow stitching in their jackets like Xendo, and were glaring at him like he was garbage.

"Your father was an embarrassment to the Skyborne, this school, and all trioka," the posh boy insulted.

"I find *you* embarrassing, Jasper!" Xendo shot back.

Jasper laughed and his gang followed suit. The bully completely ignored Xendo and turned to Philo.

"Luther Wyatt tells me your name is Philo Jonathan. Meet Ivy, Damian, and Russell," Jasper gestured to his friends behind him. Ivy waved with a sly grin while the boys kept scowling at Xendo.

"You must have been a gifted fighter or wicked smart if they let you come here from a lowly Grounded primary program," Jasper snarled. Philo didn't know how to respond to any of that.

"Don't tell me you're rooming with Xendo on the thirteenth floor? With the rest of...," Jasper cringed, then tilted his head toward Naomii and Jade with disgust, "*them*."

Xendo tried to keep his cool. "None of your business. We—"

"I wasn't talking to you anymore," Jasper cut Xendo off forcefully. Xendo huffed but stayed quiet.

"Philo, you're Grounded, so you must not know Xendo's reputation. Switch with Luther and room with me on fifteen. You need stronger friends. After all, only *one* group of us can become active agents when we graduate. Join us, and no one else in our year will stand a chance."

"Only one group?" Philo asked, confused.

"You didn't know?" Jasper scoffed. "Figures. Quaker doesn't have my connections that know how this world works. Most SIYT students are only offered historical documentation jobs. The HTPA selects only one team each graduation to train for active duty. Competition is stiff to become an agent. There's no use keeping around dead weight. Xendo and Luther... they're more fit for desk work."

Philo looked around the floor mat.... *Where was Luther?* He stretched to look over Jasper's cronies and saw Luther Wyatt with his legs close to his chest, sitting in a little ball by himself. He must have been ridiculed right before Xendo was. Philo didn't understand why Jasper could be so cruel to someone so timid.

"I'm happy where I am," Philo answered back. "I'm sure Luther can't say the same."

CHAPTER 9

Jasper scoffed and crossed his arms. He wasn't used to people telling him no. The gymnasium door opened and all the students stopped whispering.

"Fine. Be that way," Jasper snarled at Philo, "but you just made your road to becoming an agent impossible. Stupid mistake, you can't trust a Quaker."

Philo ignored him and Xendo huffed as they faced forward. Professor Uma Bryne walked in front of the class followed by a man sitting in what looked like a floating wheelchair. Uma Bryne was a tall, muscular woman with subtle streaks of gray in her hair. She was stoic, firm, and carried her own black triple-helix-shaped staff.

"Hello, first-years, Professor William Ruiz will be joining us to share this hour of class, as our kineoka courses work in partnership," Bryne explained.

Professor William Ruiz was the peaceful older man in the hovering wheelchair. He wore pastel tunic robes wrapped around his body and held a sheathed staff base on his lap. Professor Ruiz must have been injured years ago, for his legs were frail and paralyzed.

"Good morning, students. Like Professor Bryne, I will be training you in the art of kineoka," Professor Ruiz glanced across the room at his new pupils. "However, while she focuses on the physical fighting side, in my class, you shall learn the mental and emotional sides."

Philo heard Jasper and his gang snicker a bit at the words "emotional side." He didn't understand why they thought that was funny. Philo was intrigued.

"Kineoka is the martial art of the trioka people. It is the powerful force combining the movements of mind and body with the world around you. The first trioka warriors morphed the best aspects of global fighting tactics and restorative yoga into an original combat style of our own. These movement disciplines, along with proper focused meditation, can absorb the power that even the Earth itself provides. This allows us trioka to harness all our enhanced abilities to defend ourselves from those who wish us, or our society, harm."

Uma Bryne cleared her throat. "For the next five years in Kineoka Martial Arts, you will learn the thirty stances of kineoka, how to bond them together into fluid fighting movements, and how to wield our sacred staffs."

Professor Bryne held her own staff horizontally in her arms for

DAY ONE

the students to see. The long spiraling bo-staff looked heavy and forceful. The middle handle contained red liquid and connected to triple twisting ends that were a black graphite color. It was a contraption of dominant beauty.

"This weapon is called a morphstaff. The knowledge of how to build it has been passed down by kineoka masters throughout the centuries. It is *not* the same as the flimsy toy sticks you will practice with; even dioka use those for silly sporting matches. The *real* morphstaffs are much more powerful. Observe."

She twisted the morphstaff in her hand and pushed it out vertically in front of her. It was as tall as she was. She closed her eyes and took a deep, meditative breath. The dark staff began to emit an aura of white energy. All twenty-four students gasped.

While doing a series of different stances, Professor Bryne's weapon somehow melted into the base and re-morphed into new shapes. She first molded the morphstaff into a long, flat sword. Then it separated into two fighting batons, which shortened to daggers, which linked as nunchucks, which she finally stretched to become a bow and arrow. Professor Bryne took her now-glowing archer's bow and torpedoed shining arrows to all corners of the gymnasium. *Thud, thud, thud, thud, thud,* the darts hit the walls.

Bryne inhaled deeply, closing her eyes. The multiple arrows around the room dissolved into tiny luminescent cubes that shot back to her like a homing beacon. The bright-white cubes reattached themselves to the bow as it shape-shifted back to the original triple-helix morphstaff. Finally, Professor Bryne exhaled and the staff shrunk back into its handle. She holstered it to her belt as she stepped back to line up with Professor William Ruiz. The students' mouths were agape, awestruck by her mastery.

"All trioka have the capacity to connect with their telekinetic abilities," Uma Bryne informed, still speaking between deep breaths, "but you must unlock a deeper connection between your mind and the earth around you."

Professor William Ruiz floated forward in his hoverchair.

"In my class, Kineoka Mental Arts, you will discover the earthly elements that energize your fighting, grow your emotional intelligence, and build your own version of this weapon piece by tiny piece. With the correct amount of time, meditation, and introspection you will un-

CHAPTER 9

derstand your individual morphstaffs as deeply as your own limbs."

Philo had no idea what any of this meant, but he was enthralled.

"Follow me," Professor Ruiz instructed.

The students rose up from the mats and trailed behind Professor Ruiz as he floated down the hallway. Philo saw Ruiz move his hand with a wiping motion and a door ahead swung open like magic. They entered a peaceful room filled with calming plants and daylight spilling through wide windows.

"This is the elemental sanctuary chamber," Professor Ruiz explained.

In the room, there were thirty pedestals in an irregular grid position, each about as high as Philo's chest. The pedestals contained either a small vial of gas, a colored rock, or piece of metal. Professor Ruiz turned his hoverchair around to address the class.

"Through practicing deep meditation and connecting with nature around the globe, the first kineoka masters learned that the emotional states of the human mind can tie directly with the chemical elements of the periodic table. Not only can earthly substances affect our bodies and inner mental health, but our own powerful emotions can change the nature we touch."

Philo was confused. *Is Ruiz saying that fluorine could make us sad, or phosphorus could make us happy?*

"Dioka cannot harness this power. It takes a trioka person years of kineoka training to be able to understand the depths of their own mind and body. But once we discover our true selves, the very atoms in each cell of our bodies *unlock*."

The crowd of trioka students were perplexed. Blinda and Xendo never told Philo about any of this. *Maybe the ways of kineoka were kept hidden from them too?* Philo wondered if his parents had learned all of this on their first day at SIYT.

"May I have a volunteer?" Professor Ruiz asked.

Every single student raised their hand except Philo. Some were eager, like Xendo and the valedictorian girl, Alani. Others were more sheepish like Jade, or Luther Wyatt in the back. Philo was shocked. He had never been in a class where his peers actually appreciated learning this much and stayed engaged. Philo would never *volunteer* to be the center of attention; that was his worst nightmare. Philo planned to lay low, since everything was so new to him.

DAY ONE

"You, the small Grounded boy!" Professor Ruiz gestured. He looked directly at Philo. All the color in Philo's face vanished. *Why did I get picked?* Philo lost all motor functions. Xendo gently pushed Philo ahead when he didn't move. Everyone was staring at him. This was the last thing Philo wanted.

"Come here," Professor Ruiz requested, Philo walked up to the Professor, separating himself from his classmates. "What's your name?"

Philo paused. He almost let his real last name slip. "Philo. Philo Jonathan," he replied.

The other students looked him up and down, making Philo avert his gaze. Professor Ruiz held up a small, black cube for everyone to see.

"Each morphstaff that a trained kineoka fighter wields is built from hundreds of these small cubes of fortified graphite, which are made of 100-percent pure carbon."

All the first-years leaned in to peer closer at the tiny object. It looked like a black dice cube with no dots on it.

"Carbon is the king of the elements and the most common in everyday life. It is nonmetallic and tetravalent. It's the sixth chemical element of the periodic table. It was first discovered in 2,500 BC, about six thousand years ago. Carbon cannot be created or destroyed. It just continually morphs into a new form as needed. The food we eat, the ground we walk on, and even the cells in our own bodies contain carbon. It can form a limitless amount of compounds and easily bonds with almost every other element of the periodic table. In my class this year, you will each attempt to bond *yourself* to your first carbon cube."

Professor Ruiz brought his arm back down and held the cube in his palm close to his face. Philo did not know what to expect. Ruiz inhaled slowly, and as he did, the carbon cube expanded with his breath. As he exhaled, the cube shrunk back again. Professor Ruiz closed his eyes to begin meditating and the cube began to glow a pale translucent blue. The entire class was mesmerized. In and out, it rose and fell in perfect sync with Ruiz's breathing. "Once we calm our minds, we are able to make brand new connections."

Professor Ruiz gestured for Philo to step closer and the boy nervously obliged. Ruiz, still breathing deeply, placed the glowing, pulsating cube into Philo's hand. The cube switched from emitting its baby-blue shine to an emerald-green color. The light from the cube matched the exact green from the Grounded stitching in Philo's uni-

CHAPTER 9

form. The class oohed and aahed.

"Now, move to the center of the elemental core pedestals," Professor Ruiz directed.

Philo drifted through the many pedestals that housed various periodic metals, stones, and gas vials. He recognized a few of the common elements like gold, lead, and copper and glowing gas tubes of neon and xenon. Philo approached the center of the pedestals and stood waiting for instructions.

"There are 118 elements in the periodic table. Ninety-four organic, twenty-four synthetic. However, for kineoka, we only focus on the thirty organic elements that are essential to human life. We call these the Sacred Thirty. The remaining elements do not suit our craft," Professor Ruiz informed and turned to Philo. "Being surrounded by the elemental cores and their charged energy, what sensations are you experiencing, Philo Jonathan?"

Philo was quick to assume that he wouldn't feel any sensations, but then, he actually did! The warm carbon cube radiated energy into his skin that seemed like it was pulsing through his veins and into his nervous system. He sensed new stimuli and vibrations flowing in the room around him. It was indescribably strong, pleasing, and confusing. Philo closed his eyes and tried to mimic the pulsating pattern of the glowing green cube with his own breathing like Professor Ruiz had done.

"I feel...," Philo tried to articulate what his body was sensing. "I feel like I'm being pulled, in many different directions, from every angle, so my body is... stuck. I can't move."

"Exactly," Professor Ruiz stated. "An unbalanced mind in a chaotic world tugs at *all* our emotions. We become paralyzed not knowing which step leads toward the next correct decision or the next wrong direction."

Ruiz stopped his meditative breathing and the carbon cube in Philo's hand stopped glowing and returned to its normal dull black. Philo no longer felt trapped on his feet. He had zero control over the cube; only Professor Ruiz was making it work. Philo returned to stand by Xendo, still holding the cube.

"Every human has *four* periodic elements that determine their position within the world," Professor Uma Bryne spoke up. "We call these our *cardinal elements*."

DAY ONE

Professor Ruiz gestured to a giant compass painted over a map of their future world on the sanctuary wall. The land masses of the seven major continents were familiar to Philo, but there were new labeled markings around the arctic poles and oceans. As Professor Ruiz indicated each cardinal direction, the corresponding wall section lit up.

"Our Northern Emotional Element draws us forward, or *motivates* us. The Southern Element holds us back, or *terrifies* us. The Western Element defines how we judge the world, and the Eastern Element is how the world views each of us."

The professor explained the first-years would study the chemistry of how atoms bond together to form each element and how their emotions were created by similar chemistry within our own brains and environments.

"In the corner, you will find a container of carbon cubes. Each of you may grab one cube to start. You must hold it close to you at all times and practice trying to activate it through meditation," finished Professor Ruiz.

Philo already had his own cube, but followed Xendo as he grabbed one with the rest of the class. Philo was shocked the other kids seemed just as perplexed by all this ninja voodoo as he did. *They're from this future! Shouldn't they know at least some of this stuff already?* Xendo noticed Philo's confused face.

"We all know vaguely about time travel, morphstaffs, and kineoka," Xendo whispered, "but it has always been so mysterious, like some secret, untouchable legend. My dad was an actual agent and I still didn't even know how all this worked. I guess people were satisfied with the flashy rumors and never needed to dig deeper."

Xendo grabbed a cube. And next to the pile of cubes were small necklaces that easily attached to the cubes so they wouldn't misplace the precious pieces of carbon.

"The world is amazed by the mystery of kineoka," Professor Uma Bryne grunted, "but you will soon learn the truth of how much struggle and inner growth is needed to reach that level of mastery, *if* you can even achieve it."

"If you seek to become a continuum agent and preserve the world's history, you must first understand your *own* history," Professor Ruiz explained, finishing up the class.

CHAPTER 9

The next subject Philo and Xendo attended was *Ancient Survival Skills*. This first year they had *Ancient Healing* with Professor Mortha Plimkit. Philo and Xendo sat down as all the other seats filled up. The classroom's double doors burst out as Alani Adalaide kicked them wide open. The confident valedictorian flipped her blue-green hair and fluttered from one group to the next, gathering laughter like currency. Alani approached Philo and Xendo's table because it had the only empty seat remaining. She flashed the boys a charming, cool smile. Philo felt like he *needed* Alani to like him. Xendo was annoyed that she was so popular on day one.

"What up nerds?" she joked with a cheeky grin. "Can I sit here? I was going to sit with Lina Castellano, but her table is full. I'm Alani."

"We know," Xendo grunted as the girl held out her hand.

"Okay...," Alani retorted, raising her eyebrows and turning to Philo. "What's stuck up his ass?"

"He just worked hard to be Principal Scholar," Philo replied, almost ignoring Xendo, "but you can still sit with us."

"Thanks! Philo and Xendo, right?" she asked and sat down as Philo nodded. Xendo shot Philo an upset look.

"Ooh, testy," Alani laughed, noticing the glare. "Don't worry, we're all bookish. No need to hate."

"Exactly," Philo nudged Xendo. "We're all lucky to be here."

"Yep, fine," Xendo nodded, reluctantly.

"I do love a good ol' rivalry to make homework a challenge! Try and keep up!" Alani taunted with some dancing eyebrows as Xendo rolled his eyes.

Professor Mortha Plimkit meekly stepped into the room. She was an old, frail Grounded woman whose big nostrils were perpetually runny. She had a tight bun of gray hair and a tacky necklace. Professor Plimkit started to read every boring line of a thirty-seven-page syllabus for the year. Philo prided himself on being a good listener, but even he found it hard to not yawn.

"Thank data we already skimmed this last night," Xendo mumbled to Philo while Professor Plimkit droned on in a monotone voice. "I think I may actually fall asleep."

Philo agreed. He already knew they would learn about ancient medicine, surgeries, and mental health practices from around his time and before. The professor called all the medical practices that Philo

DAY ONE

knew of as "archaic." Trioka and dioka rarely get sick in this time, heal quickly, and are covered under global healthcare. However, Human History students must study ancient survival skills at SIYT to understand what their ancestors suffered through before the modern advances of the thirty-fifth century.

As old Plimkit droned on, Philo observed Jasper and his cronies in the back, definitely not paying attention. They sat with the quiet Luther and Ivy's Grounded roommate, Lina Castellano. Lina was fair-skinned, had loose curly-brown hair, and didn't seem to like Ivy very much. At Philo's table, Jade was following along with the professor like a pious student, but Naomii was in their own little world, daydreaming. Occasionally, Philo caught Naomii staring at him like *he* was the syllabus to be studied, which weirded him out.

Alani pointed out her roommate, the Frozen Princess, to Philo and Xendo up in the front. Today her hair was styled as an artistic afro and she kept her attention on Plimkit. Philo thought Princess Raelyn was so beautiful that he was glad she was at a different table; he would never have the courage to speak to her.

"Raelyn's having a tough time acclimating to life with us normal peasants," Alani shrugged with a chuckle, "but she'll come around. I try to treat her like one of my sisters."

For the rest of Ancient Healing class, Philo and Xendo kept each other awake by scoping out the rest of their classmates.

Next was *Artistic Expression*. For the first-year class of *Musical Performance*, the whimsical Professor Ophelia Willow spoke passionately about how music was a global language that humans understood no matter the era of history. Alani sat next to Philo and Xendo another time, bouncing in her seat with her love of music. Even though Xendo wasn't enjoying her presence, Philo was warming up to Alani quite nicely. It was so easy for her to make him laugh.

In *Global Government and Cultures*, the intense Professor Bartholomew Franklin was an elderly, heavy-set Frozen man who lectured sitting down from his desk. From him, the students were going to learn how politics evolved from mere nation-wide governments to the current global origin system in place today. Franklin described how the government's Historical Time Preservation Agency employed historians, researchers, and documentarians, and only rare SIYT gradu-

CHAPTER 9

ates could become continuum agents like Philo's parents. These HTPA agents traveled back in time on dangerous missions gathering first-hand information from the past to fill Earth's Database. Zero communication with the future was possible unless the travelers returned safely. Franklin confessed sometimes even the best agents couldn't survive difficult missions and some had sacrificed their lives to protect history. Xendo looked at Philo. They knew this first hand. Their parents had been talented young agents, but their skills weren't enough to keep them alive.

In *Mechanics of Time Travel,* Professor Merlin Boyle was a short, nerdy, Skyborne man who disliked direct eye contact. His class taught how time travel functioned and discussed case studies of the most successful missions. Philo noticed that all the students around the room, even Jasper and his cranky friends, seemed dazzled by the idea of traveling through time. *This is why they all chose SIYT's History Program. They all want to be agents!* If the HTPA only chooses one new team of agents from their year, he and Xendo were in trouble. Philo could feel the mounting sense of competition in the room.

Professor Boyle described why successful missions were the best way to study history. When agents return from the past, they upload all their body cam footage, copies of lost documents, and photos of ancient artifacts to Earth's Database. They studied prehistoric animals, filmed world-changing events, and even recorded secret discussions with historical figures. All this first-hand intelligence preserved in the ED is then analyzed by HTPA's historians. However, all the knowledge from failed missions was lost in the past with the agents who never returned. Philo realized this is why there was so much mysterious shame tied to his parents' unsuccessful mission. No one knew what happened or what was lost.

The last orientation class for the day was *Human History* with Professor Edgar Blaise. He was middle-aged with brown hair, a neatly trimmed beard, and sharp spectacles. Philo was surprised by how attractive the teacher was. Professor Blaise asked everyone to share an unexpected fact to introduce themselves to their new classmates.

"My dad does interior design, my mother is a painter, and I have eight brothers and sisters," Alani offered. "So, growing up, our seadome was jam-packed."

"Preserving my family's Catholic traditions back in Spain is very

DAY ONE

important to me," Lina Castellano quietly shared.

"I like old martial art movies," Damian, Jasper's strong minion, called out on his turn.

"Man, I was going to say that!" Russell, his buddy, grunted after him.

"I love to sit in the grass and read romance novels from the ED," Jade revealed.

"My family is one of the richest trioka families on the planet," Jasper Finn bragged.

"I really want to travel more around the world. I haven't been able to do that in my life," Raelyn explained. The class seemed quite disappointed with her simple answer, given her royal status.

"I enjoy talking to myself. I'm great company," Naomii revealed on their turn. The class was not shocked by this statement.

"My father is the CEO of Nurture, Inc. and my mother is Ambassador Irwin's Secretary," Luther Wyatt nervously added. This shocked Philo. *Luther's family was important?*

"I collect a lot of old books," Xendo contributed to the list of personal facts when Professor Blaise pointed to him. "I love reading from the old paper pages!"

Shoot! Now it was Philo's turn. He knew nothing about his family and had only been in their future a few days. He had been told to lie about everything to protect his secrets. What could he possibly mention that wouldn't reveal he's a fraud who doesn't belong here?

"I had a difficult childhood," Philo ended up saying.

The Professor moved on to the next student. Philo looked to Xendo, who nodded in relief. Philo was going to have to be very careful with how he answered questions at this school.

"Thank you all for sharing a tiny sliver of your own history." Professor Blaise moved on. "You see, history teaches us the consequences of human nature, both at the height of its creativity and the depths of its cruelty. History helps us understand how we've progressed slowly over time and what will never change."

Professor Edgar Blaise locked eyes with Philo as he roamed near his desk.

"And unfortunately, no matter how hard you hope for the lessons to sink in, history always forgets its shortcomings and is doomed to feel pain again."

Alani raised her hand and was called on.

CHAPTER 9

"Then why do we bother trying to record everything?" she asked.

"Because if we don't preserve our past, our future is in danger. The pain of unending struggle throughout history reminds us there is always more to share and always more to learn," Professor Blaise responded.

Most of the students were completely transfixed by Professor Blaise's stories for the remainder of the orientation class. As they walked out of the room, Xendo whispered to Philo, "I'm sorry, but Professor Blaise was too hot. I couldn't focus!"

At the end of their school day, the first-years were next expected to go to the Continuum Café for the congratulatory banquet celebrating the new school year. Xendo mentioned how his mother prepared the food with her kitchen staff over the entire day in order to feed the students. Philo was ravenous; he couldn't wait to have more of Blinda's food.

As the boys found their own small square table, Alani entered the café to sit with them again. Philo was beginning to love having her around, and Xendo realized he had no choice. As Princess Raelyn Arctikon walked by, Alani waved her over to join them. Philo's brain froze in nervousness. Raelyn exchanged kind greetings to Xendo as she sat down on Philo's right side. He decided to do as Alani did and just forget her royalty. *Raelyn isn't a beautiful princess. She's just another classmate.*

The four strangers' nerves soon melted away as their conversations discussing their first day became surprisingly natural. Before Philo knew it, the clock struck six and small drones flew out from the kitchen to deliver platters of food to their table. Philo, Raelyn, Alani, and Xendo all gasped as succulent entrees and side dishes were revealed and pleasing aromas graced their nostrils.

Philo looked around the other tables and recognized a few authentic global meals from his favorite food books he never dreamed he could taste. The ancient dishes must still be favorites of the Grounded people. Jade and Naomii sat with shy Luther and the reserved Lina, and their table had Korean pork bossam with kimchi, Turkish kebabs, and Nigerian egusi soup with pounded yam. Jasper's gang seemed unimpressed with their English beef wellingtons, Kashmiri rogan josh curry, and Mexican red chicken tamales with melted cotija cheese.

DAY ONE

At Philo's table, he did recognize some Ethiopian injera and doro wot, Luxembourgish rieslingspaschteit, and Dominican mangú con los tres golpes, but there were also dishes Philo had never seen before.

"Oh, wow!" Raelyn gushed, unexpectedly. "Creamy winter parsnips! Cured salmon! They have all my favorites from back home!" Raelyn pointed out. "And oh! Spicy bear stew! Our cook used to make this when I was a kid! Us Frozen people like meat, starches, preserved foods, and lots of spice to keep us warm!"

"My mom likes to show off with food," Xendo shrugged, then nudged Philo. "This roasted quail and decorative vegetable platter is typical Skyborne. So is this spirulina honey lemonade. We're all about nutrition."

"You guys have to try these fresh oysters that come from the Pacific Coast!" Alani beamed excitedly showing some Oceanite favorites on the table. "I think this salad has hydroponic produce. And, oh my data! Fish cake skewers!"

Philo, Raelyn, Alani, and Xendo devoured all the food in front of them and laughed while sharing childhood memories. Philo couldn't even imagine how much global food he had happily wolfed down. All the students eventually cleared out of the Continuum Café and headed back to their dorms.

The boys turned off the lights, peeled off their clothes, and went to bed fully tuckered out. Philo was proud that he survived his first day with his new classmates. Since all the subjects were new to even students in this time, he seemed to fit right in. None of the first-years seemed suspicious of him, yet. They didn't somehow discover his secret, or act like he was out of place. Mission accomplished.

If Philo stayed focused, maybe he could make this school his first permanent one.

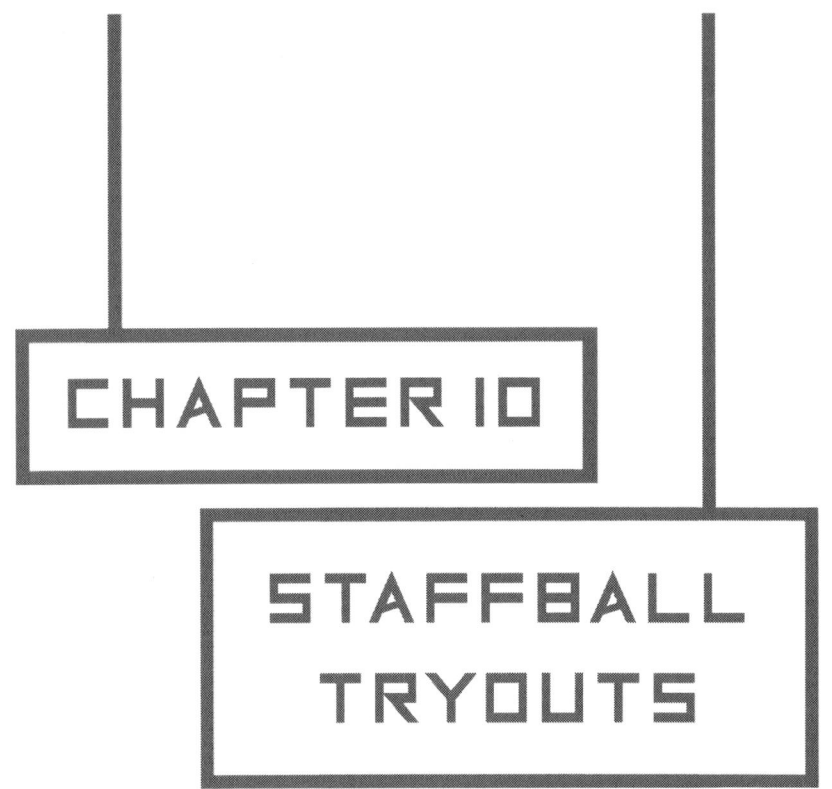

CHAPTER 10
STAFFBALL TRYOUTS

Philo's next few weeks of life ended up being some of the most exciting he'd ever experienced. Each weekday, their courses started with the boys joining their classmates in the sparring room for Kineoka Martial Arts with Professor Uma Bryne. Philo and the other first-years practiced the Sacred Thirty Stances, connecting each natural element of the periodic table to a matching fighting pose. Every stance of kineoka could flow into another to create a series of powerful movements to defend yourself and attack an opponent.

Like a drill sergeant, Professor Uma Bryne would stand at the head of the gymnasium, call out a periodic element, and demonstrate its corresponding kineoka pose. The students would replicate each stance, punching, kicking, or blocking for the full class hour. Philo couldn't help but compare himself to the other students in his class. Jasper Finn and his friends were annoyingly skilled at kineoka and would snicker each time Philo or Xendo made the slightest mistake. Raelyn Arctikon was a complete natural; she was born to become a kineoka master. Alani, however, often made embarrassing blunders. She'd lose her balance, fall down, and then crack a joke. Philo admired her ability to get

STAFFBALL TRYOUTS

right back up and keep fighting.

As time went on, the class grew more in sync with their combat poses. Professor Bryne would call out a string of random elements and all twenty-four first-years would powerfully strike in unison. They became a flowing force of attacks that moved as smooth as dancing. Philo felt himself getting stronger and developing muscles he didn't even know he had.

In Kineoka Mental Arts, it also took a few weeks for Philo and his peers to even begin to grasp the emotional and psychological side of their training. With Professor Ruiz, they studied the actual chemistry behind the periodic elements. Even if they'd only ever use the Sacred Thirty in kineoka, they still had to study the properties of all 118 elements. Understanding all the chemical compounds helped clarify why the Sacred Thirty were indeed essential for human life and kineoka.

Apparently, hydrogen sparked joy, zinc spawned grief, lead brought apathy, and oxygen fueled fear. It was fascinating! Philo and his classmates meditated daily with their carbon cubes to strengthen their mental connections in kineoka. Philo assumed they would be allowed to visit the sanctuary room to practice, but they were not. All students had to first activate their carbon cubes, getting them to glow and vibrate, before they were granted permission by a professor to attempt to connect with the elements in the sanctuary. Many of the elements were rare or dangerous, so they were kept safe in their guarded containers.

Professor Ruiz kept reiterating to his class that morphing their carbon cubes was one of the most challenging mental feats on earth, so they shouldn't fret. It would take time and patience. Naturally, the students didn't listen and placed bets on who could master their meditations first. Ruiz promised that if they bonded with the correct four elements, they would feel a beautiful sense of peace, and could move on to their next stage of training.

In their dorm late at night, Philo would meditate so hard his brain hurt. He tried not to laugh as Xendo would squint and scrunch up his face trying to remain pensive. Philo could never clear his mind. He couldn't feel any strong emotions. As soon as he'd start to focus successfully on his breathing, a question would pop in his head. He'd get distracted by a random sound, think about his parents, or start getting hungry. Philo never thought that embracing peace would be

CHAPTER 10

such a challenge.

As late autumn approached, a buzz started to circulate around school about the upcoming staffball season. Xendo eagerly introduced Philo to the futuristic sport by watching multiple historic matches in Earth's Database. Staffball was complex, intense, thrilling, and it dazzled Philo. Xendo needed to explain the rules a few times in order for Philo to understand.

"Here's a guide from the ED," Xendo began, tapping his technoband to bring up a visual. A giant holoscreen expanded in their dorm room:

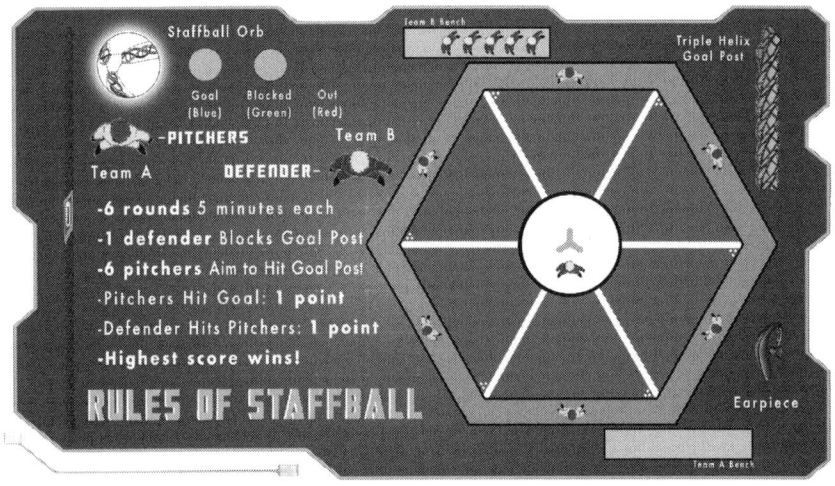

"Each round, Team A's six *pitchers* stand behind the hexagon's side walls and pelt white glowing orbs at the triple-helix post, earning one point per hit. Team B's single *defender* blocks the post from all angles using their sportstaff, hands, or feet. The orbs turn blue if the pitchers score a goal, green if swatted away, and red if they hit the defender, disqualifying the player for the round. If a defender can smack an orb back to hit one of the pitchers, then the defender gains an extra point for *their* team. Each team's turn lasts until the defender is knocked out, or after five minutes expire," Xendo explained. "The teams then switch, and Team B becomes the pitchers and a player from Team A becomes their team's first defender. After six rounds, the team with the highest point score at the end of the match wins the game."

"So it's like a mashup of dodgeball, racquetball, and a light-up video game?" Philo asked with a beaming face. "That's awesome!"

STAFFBALL TRYOUTS

"I don't know your old sports, but sure!" Xendo shrugged with a smile. "Everyone in our time loves staffball, even the dioka play."

Xendo decided to take his chance to join SIYT's staffball team, but Philo was too nervous of looking like a fool and chose just to watch in support. On tryout day, they walked out to the huge hexagon-shaped building behind Time Tower on campus. Philo saw the court had six zones and a giant triple-helix post in the center that stood six feet tall. A holographic netting encased the hexagon to prevent flying orbs from crashing into the audience.

Philo already saw some students practicing as Xendo led them to the SIYT staffball captain running the tryouts. The eighteen-year-old student in his fifth year was tall, burly, and had white stitching in his suit. He seemed grumpy and annoyed.

"Hello! Rodger Gorn, right?" Xendo greeted the captain. "We're here for tryouts!"

"Humpf," the young man grunted as he pointed to the stands. "Go sit with the rest of the newbies on the benches."

To their surprise, Philo and Xendo saw a few of their fellow first-years in the stands; some were clearly trying out, while some just came to watch like Philo. Jasper and his gang were lounging in the back with their arms crossed. Poor Luther sat behind them like he was put in a timeout. Lina Castellano, the Grounded girl who usually sat alone in their classes, observed everyone from her own bleacher far to the left. Alani Adalaide chirped eagerly with older students as Raelyn Arctikon sat next to her, focused in thought. Raelyn's usually voluptuous coiled black hair was cornrowed into a tight bun. Philo noticed that the princess enjoyed switching up her hair every few weeks and must have changed the style for today's tryouts.

Rodger and two other fifth-year boys addressed the chatting crowd.

"Okay, okay, quiet down!" Rodger called out. "I'm the captain of SIYT's graduate staffball team." He pointed to the boys on either side of him. "This is Juo Mikaski and Pauli Simons. The rest of our team all graduated last year. We are looking for three new players."

Philo looked over to Xendo, who nodded with ambition. Xendo really wanted to make the team.

"For tryouts today, you'll each be defending the helix post. Since there are only three of us as pitchers, it should be easy enough. Don't

CHAPTER 10

mess up," Rodger Gorn concluded. "Who's going first?"

While half of the crowd raised their hands to volunteer, the cunning Jasper Finn just strolled down the bleachers to seize control. Rodger liked Jasper's power move and nodded with approval. With a smug look on his face, Jasper brushed forcefully past Xendo's shoulder on his way down to the court. Xendo winced in pain.

Rodger handed Jasper a sportstaff and the bully sauntered out to the hexagon's center circle. Rodger, Juo, and Pauli took their positions behind three of the six short walls on the perimeter. Jasper struck a pose holding the staff, ready to play as the holoscreen scoreboard counted down.

The starting buzzer went off, and all three pitchers threw white orbs at the triple helix post as fast as bullets. Jasper sprang into action, masterfully deflecting the balls in every direction. The orbs turned green, fell to the ground, and rolled to the court's edge to switch back to white. It was annoying to admit, but Jasper Finn was brilliant at this. After five minutes, another bell sounded and all the orbs turned white and the pitchers stopped throwing. Not a single orb had hit the post. The bully's friends cheered in the crowd. Xendo rolled his eyes.

"Great job, Jasper Finn. Excellent start!" Rodger called out from the field. "Someone else come down!"

Damien, Ivy, and Russell all had their turns next, but the lackeys couldn't keep up with Jasper's stellar performance. Luther was too nervous to try out. Lina Castellano also just watched from a distance as some of the older students stumbled through the challenging sport.

"NEXT!" Rodger screamed from the hexagon.

"I'm going," Xendo muttered aloud, getting up from his feet. Philo watched as Xendo was handed a morphstaff and stepped into the hexagon.

The pitchers pummeled the orbs toward the center post and, with a determined look on his face, Xendo used the staff to swat them all away. He smiled, a first small success under his belt. Philo struck a fist in pride as his friend continued to narrowly hit, kick, and swat orbs away from the helix for the next two minutes. Philo snuck a glance behind him to watch the bullies' eyes angrily darting back and forth following the action. *BUZZ!* Philo turned back to see two red orbs at Xendo's feet. One had struck Xendo in the shoulder and the other smacked his leg. Xendo hung his head in disqualified defeat.

STAFFBALL TRYOUTS

"It was still really impressive, Xen," Philo comforted his friend as he sat back down in the bleachers. Xendo sighed.

"Maybe for a pathetic dioka!" Jasper coughed loudly behind them as his whole posse snickered. "All the Quakers are useless."

"Hey! Leave him alone!" Philo snapped before he could stop himself.

"Oh, I'm sorry. Did I hurt your boyfriend's feelings?" Jasper glared at Philo.

"He's not my boyfriend," Philo shot back. "Jealous, much?"

Xendo choked with glee at Philo's fiery retort.

"NEXT!" screamed Captain Rodger Gorn from the court.

"You know what, I *will* try out," Philo whispered to Xendo before standing. Xendo perked up and patted Philo on the back in encouragement.

"This oughta be rich," Jasper grunted to his friends. "Who wants to bet the Grounded boy gets hit in the first minute?"

Philo grabbed the morphstaff and stepped out to center court. He could still hear chuckles coming from the bullies in the stands. Philo realized—a few seconds too late— that this was his first time holding an actual morphstaff. He may have been too brash in wanting to spite Jasper; now he was worried he'd fumble and embarrass himself. Philo's hands were shaking as the starting bell chimed.

The pitchers chucked the glowing orbs and, a bit spooked, Philo contorted to dodge the balls. Another orb was pelted toward the helix post. Philo gasped and reached out to smack the orb, launching it far away. The next two orbs he blocked in simple succession. This gave him a bit more confidence. He started to flow smoothly between blocks and attacks. All sounds and visions outside of the hexagon faded away as Philo laser-focused on defending the triple helix. Philo soon forgot he was even holding the morphstaff it felt so natural. He cracked a sly smile. Philo's mind and body were in sync with his surroundings in a way he had never experienced before. In what felt like seconds, the round was over.

Xendo cheered while pumping his fist in the crowd.

"Fantastic job!" Rodger Gorn proclaimed, glancing down at his notes, "...Philo Jonathan, great work! NEXT!"

Raelyn Arctikon stepped down toward the court. Philo had felt pleased with himself and confident, but that pride soon vanished when Raelyn looked him directly in the eye. Philo melted. She was beautiful

CHAPTER 10

as ever, but also had a strangely serious look on her face. *Why is she walking toward me?* Raelyn outstretched her hand as she stood two feet in front of him. Philo felt his stomach jump and got nervous. *Oh no! Does she want to hold my hand?* His palms were sweating. He didn't know what to say, so Philo just stood still in confusion. Raelyn stared at him with a blank face.

"Hi, can I have the staff? It's my turn," Raelyn questioned.

"Oh!" Philo laughed nervously, "Here you go! Knock 'em dead!"

Wow. Philo hated himself. *Why did I say that? What an idiot!*

"Thanks," Raelyn chuckled. "Those orbs are going to be so... dead."

She reached to grab the sportstaff and her hand brushed his. She walked out toward the court, leaving him standing alone. Philo felt himself blush.

"Phi! Where did that come from?" Xendo exclaimed, fistbumping Philo as he sat down. "I think you might actually make the team!"

"Don't hold your breath," Jasper sassed behind them. "They're only choosing three people. And there's no way they're picking more than one first-year. I was miles better."

"Yeah, and then once these fifth-years graduate," Ivy Bates sneered to the bully's left, "Jasper will be captain and the rest of us will join next year!"

Damian and Russell backed the first two in scowling down at Xendo and Philo with haughty amusement. The boys glared back.

"You don't make the decisions," Philo argued weakly.

"Yeah, they'll want team members they can actually trust!" Xendo supported.

"No. You're both wrong," Jasper mocked with a confident scowl. "This team hasn't beat another school in years. They want to win. They'll choose me."

The alarm sounded again, signaling that Raelyn's turn was about to begin. Jasper and his cronies chuckled as Philo and Xendo couldn't say more. The boys turned around in a huff.

The pitchers hurled their orbs in Raelyn's direction. Without missing a beat, Raelyn created a whirling shield with the morphstaff, knocking multiple white orbs in various directions turning them all green. She easily moved from orb to orb pelting toward her, not just blocking them from the helix, but actually smacking them back toward the walls of the hexagon. Only skilled players aimed to hit pitchers from the very

STAFFBALL TRYOUTS

beginning. Rodger Gorn seemed surprised and upset by Raelyn's tactics. His eyebrows furrowed and he grunted as he whipped more orbs with increasing force. The other two pitchers followed his lead. Philo looked to Xendo with an apprehensive expression. They were *definitely* going harder on Raelyn than the other candidates.

Beads of sweat started trickling down Raelyn's brow. She contorted her body to smack orbs that kept inching closer to the helix. Even Jasper and his minions held their tongues to watch the heated round. Rodger seemed angry that Raelyn could keep up with him. Raelyn swung and missed an orb whipped at her from the right, but she turned around and banged the next orb straight back toward its thrower. Juo had to duck to prevent getting hit in the head. The orbs came so fast at Raelyn from all different directions she had to resort to hitting and kicking. Juo and Pauli started panting from exerting so much energy, but Rodger wasn't slowing down. Raelyn only had about thirty seconds left on her clock.

While Pauli hurled three orbs in a row at the post, Rodger found a window and whipped an orb at Raelyn's back, hoping to oust her. She ducked just in time and glared back in a huff. Rodger pelted another orb directly at her face. Raelyn whipped around with the staff like a baseball bat and cracked the orb right at him, catching Rodger by surprise. Raelyn's orb smacked Rodger squarely in the chest, making him fall backwards into the wall behind him, gaining a rare point of her own.

Alani Adalaide shot to her feet and roared with triumph. Philo and Xendo hollered in gleeful support as Jasper and company pretended they weren't impressed. Rodger stumbled back to his feet to bitterly throw some last orbs toward the helix in desperation. Raelyn smacked his downward, punched an incoming orb from her left, and twirled to roundhouse kick one to the right. *DING*! Her five minutes were up as she swatted a final orb down and away from the helix with the morphstaff.

The fact that Raelyn actually scored a point as a defender was so impressive. She was a shoo-in for the team!

"NEXT!" Rodger hollered, annoyed and trying to gather himself.

The crowd watched as the remaining students tried out. Some dodged too much or let the helix post turn blue multiple times. Most of the older students just performed sloppily and got knocked out with

CHAPTER 10

surprise orbs.

However, one girl named Jessica Boone was extremely talented with a morphstaff. Xendo whispered to Philo that since Jessica was in her fourth year, she probably had already built her own morphstaff and knew how to use one well. Jessica actually turned more orbs green than Philo, Jasper, or even Raelyn was able to. She wasn't as aggressive as Jasper, or as smoothly dynamic as Raelyn, but just calmly blocking orbs with the staff was still extremely effective. When her round concluded, Jessica Boone didn't let a single orb hit the post.

After a few final students failed miserably, Alani Adalaide was the last to anxiously stand up. She was hilariously horrible. In the beginning, she started off confident and danced around light on her feet. But as soon as one pelted orb almost hit her, Alani resorted to dodging, screaming, laughing, ducking, and hopping away from the rest of the balls.

"Ah! This is way scarier up close!" Alani screamed jokingly. This sport was not for her.

The crowd laughed as she ran around the center hexagon, hiding behind the helix post she was supposed to be defending. Philo couldn't help but chuckle and Xendo looked pleased that he was at least better than Alani at something. Only forty-nine seconds into her round, two orbs pelted her in the back. The buzzer rang and Alani was disqualified.

"Well, I've never really been one for boys and balls," Alani joked with a shrug.

Alani romped back to her seat with a spring in her step. She made a mock-cocky face and brushed off her shoulders as if she had done a spectacular job to make the crowd laugh even more. Jasper and his friends were disgusted that she made light of the tryouts. Every student hopeful had now been given a chance to join the staffball team. All that was left was to hear the results.

They waited for ten minutes as the three current players chatted amongst themselves in the court's corner. Philo wanted to ask Xendo if they could go sit with Alani and Raelyn to chat. However, Xendo seemed content with just staying a duo. *It's probably for the best*, Philo thought. They did have a really big secret to keep. Xendo often got annoyed with Alani, and Philo didn't want to look more foolish in front of Raelyn. He sulked a bit. *Why is making friends so hard!*

STAFFBALL TRYOUTS

"Okay, quiet down!" Rodger Gorn called out. "We've chosen our three new teammates."

Xendo placed his arm over Philo's shoulder in anticipation. "Remember, it's not just a point total they're looking for," Xendo comforted himself out loud. "It's how skilled we were overall. We both did good!"

Philo nodded, but secretly, he really didn't think they even had a chance.

"We choose Jasper Finn," Rodger declared, looking down at his technoband screen.

"Damn!" Xendo cursed as Jasper stood up with an arrogant scoff.

"Jessica Boone," Rodger continued. Jessica politely rose and followed Jasper to the front. As Jasper passed Xendo and Philo, he glared them down with a pompous sneer, relishing Xendo's contempt. Everyone watched Juo point to a name on the holoscreen in Rodger's hand urgently, but Rodger shook his head.

"And our last new team member is…," he double-checked how to read the name, "Philo Jonathan."

Xendo and Philo looked at each other in shock, then shot to their feet in victory. Xendo reached in for a hug and Philo laughed in surprise. As they embraced, Xendo twisted toward Jasper's cronies to make a vindicated face to gloat. Ivy twisted her silver hair and rolled her eyes in annoyance, and her sidekicks scowled at Xendo.

"Well, get your butt down there!" Xendo chortled. He gave Philo an encouraging push down the bleachers. Philo hated everyone staring at him and he couldn't help but turn red from nerves. He joined the other five members and shook Rodger's hand to thank him. As Philo turned around smiling, most of the crowd was gathering their belongings to leave. Raelyn and Alani, however, looked a little confused. Raelyn took a deep breath and sunk her head in disappointment. Alani shot up like an angry rocket.

"Are you *delusional*?" Alani spat out at Rodger, her eye twitching. "Did Raelyn's orb damage your head?"

"Excuse me?" Rodger scolded back, getting defensive. Raelyn tried to hush her roommate, but Alani ignored her.

"Raelyn is the only one to actually score a defending point. She did the best out of *everyone*! She was like an angelic badass ninja out there!" Alani argued while pointing to the hexagon court. "She deserves that spot more than any of them!"

CHAPTER 10

Philo gasped in shock. He looked to Xendo on what to do, but Xendo just rolled his eyes at Alani's outburst. Raelyn put her head in her hands out of embarrassment. Alani realized everyone was now watching her yell from the bleachers and saw Philo look disheartened.

"Oh…," Alani winced. She didn't mean to humiliate him. "Sorry, Philo."

"*You* can leave now!" Rodger stated firmly. "*You* did the worst out of everybody!"

"WOW!" Alani shouted back with raised eyebrows, insulted and riled up even more. The rest of the students rushed to the exit to avoid the kerfuffle. Alani angrily plodded down from the bleachers to Rodger Gorn. Raelyn and Xendo jumped to follow behind, trying to stop her. Alani passed by Philo in a huff. Rodger was almost twice her size, but that didn't stop Alani from standing at his feet and sticking an assertive finger in his face.

"Give me a good reason Raelyn didn't get in," Alani bellowed, first poking his chest, then crossing her arms in protest, "or we're not going anywhere!"

Rodger scoffed and looked at his teammates. Juo and Pauli were displeased that this blew up into an argument.

"You're embarrassing yourself," Jasper rebuked Alani in disgust. "Why don't you and your loser friends just go back to the thirteenth floor?"

Alani made a *close your mouth* gesture at Jasper without a word to waste on him. He swatted her duck hand away.

"It's not about Arctikon's performance," Rodger countered. "Of course, she'd be good. She lived in a castle her whole life being trained to fight by the Winter Thorns."

"Uhh…," Raelyn interjected finally, growing suspicious. "Why should that matter?"

Rodger didn't want to look at her, but he finally did.

"Betraying your entire kingdom in public wasn't good enough?" Rodger asked spitefully. "You need to make more of a scene? We can't have a traitor on our team."

Alani's mouth dropped. Raelyn's eyebrows raised as she nodded in comprehension. Now she understood what went wrong.

"You don't know the full story," Raelyn responded, "and that has nothing to do with staffball. I'm a student here just like everyone else."

STAFFBALL TRYOUTS

"You're supposed to renounce your origin when you join SIYT," Alani argued, getting more furious with the injustices by the second. "You're a fifth-year! You should know that!"

Philo didn't like seeing the girls getting so upset, but they were right; this *was* unfair.

"No one really gives allegiances up," Jasper griped, fully annoyed by all this. "Stop being sore losers. You b—"

"She didn't lose," Philo interrupted. "She *did* perform better than all three of us." He looked at Raelyn for a second, then sighed. "So, she can have my spot."

Raelyn raised her eyebrows, shocked by the gesture. Philo could hear Xendo facepalm himself, but he didn't care as he saw Raelyn smile. Raelyn earned this more than him, and it was worth it to make her look at him this way.

"She'll do better on the team than I will," Philo admitted to Rodger, Juo, and Pauli.

"Yeah!" Alani backed Philo up with a swing of her finger at Rodger again. "With Raelyn, maybe you'll actually *win* a game this year!"

The three senior team members argued in the corner amongst themselves until Rodger stormed off in a huff. Juo and Pauli returned to tell the first-years that Philo could indeed give up his spot to Raelyn. As everyone separated, Xendo congratulated Philo for his noble decision, but still joked that it was stupid. They laughed about remaining social outcasts and the downfall of their fantasy staffball careers. On their way out of the hexagon court, Alani pounced on Philo and Xendo with a giant bear hug. Raelyn followed behind.

"Philo, that was *so* amazing of you," Alani tousled his dark brown hair. "You have officially earned my friendship!"

"You didn't have to do that for me," Raelyn bowed her head, "but you did. Thank you, Philo Jonathan."

Philo smiled and hid a wince. They thought he was kind, but he was still lying to them about his real last name. He nodded in return, grateful to just speak more with the girls. Alani draped her arm around Raelyn's shoulders, pulling her closer into a big group hug with the boys.

"You know? I *like* us," Alani beamed, looking around the huddle. "The four of us, together. The SIYT Human History Program is hard enough. We can't also let people like Jasper Finn or Rodger Gorn

CHAPTER 10

get us down!"

"It is very stressful sometimes," agreed Philo, "stiff competition."

"What are you suggesting?" Xendo asked her suspiciously.

"Don't act like I'm an alien, Robot-hair," Alani joked back at Xendo, punching him in the arm just like his mother always did. "You'd be lucky to have Raelyn and me as friends."

"Philo and I are good on our own," Xendo responded reluctantly.

"Are you sure?" asked Raelyn. "Good allies are always needed."

"For our time here, we'll have your backs, if you boys have ours?" Alani offered.

"Deal!" Philo smiled. Xendo grunted on his left, annoyed that Philo agreed so easily.

"Fine," Xendo lamented. "I guess I'll survive."

"Perfect!" Alani concluded with a chuckle. "Now, you're stuck with us!"

They opened up the huddle and started walking back together toward Time Tower. They talked about how great Philo and Raelyn performed, and how Alani should never, ever, ever attempt the sport again. Before they separated in their dorm's lounge, Alani spoke up once more.

"Do you guys want to have some Oceanite snacks and watch a movie in our room?" Alani suggested. "I have nori crisps, ocean-salted popcorn, and I think some of my mom's shrimp shumai she teleported me in the freezer."

"That sounds fun!" responded Philo. He could never turn down food.

"Yeah, okay sure," Xendo squinted playfully. "What movie would we watch?"

"How about something we've never seen?" Alani thought aloud, "We have the whole ED gallery to choose from."

"I think Philo should choose," Raelyn offered with a grin. "He's earned it."

Alani and Xendo agreed and all four walked into the girl's room. They pulled the pillows and blankets from both beds onto the carpeted floor to make a cozy fort. Raelyn tapped on her technoband and projected the holoscreen onto the ceiling for them all to watch. There were literally millions of movie options that were made in the thousand years since Philo's digital era. Philo ended up picking a movie he

STAFFBALL TRYOUTS

recognized, but that meant it was from the 2010s.

"Ooh, vintage!" Alani cooed as she brought in their snacks.

"Yeah," Philo responded, hoping his choice didn't seem suspicious. "I love old films."

At first, Raelyn, Alani, and Xendo couldn't stop joking about the "archaic" way movies used to be made. But soon they all laughed at the funny moments, and handed each other tissues during the sad scenes. Philo's life had changed so much since he first watched the movie in secret as a foster kid. He exhaled peacefully as the movie ended on a bittersweet note. Alani openly wept next to him. She was a snotty crier. She blew her nose awkwardly loud and they all chuckled as the credits rolled. This was the best Saturday of Philo's life. He couldn't help himself from feeling giddy and grateful.

Philo Nockby finally had some friends to share his weekends with.

CHAPTER 11

THE AMBASSADOR'S ANNOUNCEMENT

As December began, Philo waited for snow to start falling down. But even on the most frigid of days, nothing fell from the sky. One particular evening, the boys were dictating essays into their libes for their musical performance class. Philo looked out their window and finally asked Xendo why the snow hadn't come down yet; winter was clearly here. Xendo glanced over from his essay entitled, "The Downfall of Boy Bands."

"Philo, we are *on top* of the clouds," Xendo chuckled. "Snow only falls down if more clouds form *above* us!"

"Oh, right!" Philo facepalmed. Four months in and this future still befuddled him.

Xendo was constantly assisting Philo in learning the customs and history tidbits he missed. So far, none of the SIYT teachers or students suspected that Philo was out of place in their future. Even Raelyn and Alani believed Philo was just an always-curious exchange student from the Grounded primary program.

Every weekend the four friends grew closer. Philo, Raelyn, Alani, and Xendo snuck around the buildings of SIYT decoding the centuries

THE AMBASSADOR'S ANNOUNCEMENT

of history in its walls and records. They perused Superior Bazaar, visiting artisan shops and tasting food from all around the world. Raelyn's staffball team transitioned from practices to actual matches against the major dioka universities. However, they had lost every single match so far, because the team was abysmal at working together. Raelyn told her friends she'd quit if it weren't for the kind Jessica Boone.

For their kineoka training, the students were now able to move on from practicing the Sacred Thirty Stances to start sparring with each other. Philo had never been in an actual fight before; he wasn't sure if he was ready. The morning of their first sparring session, Professor Uma Bryne sat the students down for a demonstration. She gestured to the tall humanoid robots in the corner of the kineoka gym.

"When you do not have a partner to spar with, our friends at AMDA and ALTI collaborated to create these combots," Bryne explained.

The robots were programmed with all thirty kineoka stances and were safely designed for students to train with. They had a sturdy metallic skeleton and silicone musculature, creating a genderless shape. The combots also had a thick outer padding that was soft, like skin.

"If you punch them, you won't break your fist," Professor Bryne summarized. "But they'll punch you right back."

Bryne stepped onto one of the wide mats on the sparring room floor. She tapped her technoband and one of the combots lit up from where its brain would sit. A kaleidoscope of lights streamed down the combot's extremities like veins to its robotic fingers and toes.

Philo squinted as Professor Bryne adjusted the combot's performance gauge on its touchscreen forehead all the way to level ten, the highest intensity. The professor explained that combots did not attack unless engaged, and, like real kineoka fighters, they focused on defense. Bryne inhaled deeply, placed her hands by her sides, exhaled, and bowed at the waist toward the combot. The machine gracefully mirrored her bowing gesture.

"All opponents deserve our respect," Professor Bryne stated, returning to her standing position, "or we have already lost the fight."

The combot relaxed into the hydrogen pose, the first sacred pose of kineoka: feet together, arms in praying position, and the head facing forward. Professor Bryne chose the potassium pose. Her legs were far apart, left foot forward, right foot back. The left hand pushed forward

CHAPTER II

with two fingers raised, and the right hand pushed backward. Combots never struck first, so Professor Bryne sprang into action.

The class stared in amazement as Professor Bryne and the combot flowed in a flurry of fighting poses. They swiped, kicked, and punched toward each other, attacking and blocking back and forth. Bryne expertly maneuvered around the vicious strikes the combot threw her way. The students roared every time Professor Bryne secured a strong blow and gasped every time she was swiped by mistake. Philo was mesmerized by the beautiful, dangerous dance.

For every smack the professor landed, a yellow progress bar on the combot's touchscreen face increased in damage percentage. After many violent minutes, Bryne was able to catch the combot's metallic kick mid-air, knock out it's opposing knee, and yanked the machine over her shoulder. The combot flew through the air, and landed on its back. Bryne jumped up and elbowed the combot in its chest, forcing it to reach its full damage amount. The lights flowed back to the combot's head and it turned off. Signaling it had been defeated. The class cheered.

The students were next split up into pairs to engage in their first sparring match. Jade Mahala was placed with Ivy Bates. Naomii Clover was with Russell York. Alani was matched with her friend Lina Castellano. Xendo was with Luther Wyatt, and Raelyn was paired with Damian Gomez.

"And Philo Jonathan," Bryne called out, "your sparring partner will be Jasper Finn."

Philo turned to find Jasper Finn, and the boy glared back with an evil smile. Philo didn't understand why Jasper hated him so much. But then again, the feeling was becoming mutual. The bully and his cronies never missed a chance to make fun of Philo and his friends.

The only direction that Professor Bryne gave the paired-off students was to get their opponent to leave the mat or give up by tapping out. They must focus on maintaining the good form of their thirty kineoka stances. Their goal was to subdue each other, not hurt their partner.

Philo stood across from Jasper. The bully struck the arsenic pose, the element of hatred. This stance placed his feet far apart and his fists were held below his glaring, angry eyes. It was one of the more forceful poses to intimidate others. Jasper couldn't stomach losing to someone

THE AMBASSADOR'S ANNOUNCEMENT

as lowly as Philo. However, Philo refused to let Jasper shake his focus. Philo decided on the common carbon pose, the stance of trust. His feet were spread comfortably, his forearms blocked his head with his hands flattened.

"Remember your stances!" Professor Bryne announced, lifting her hand up. "Keep your balance of flow, monitor the emotions you experience, and fight with honor!" She grunted a deep battle cry and brought her hand down signaling for them to begin.

Before Philo could even glance back from Professor Bryne, Jasper lunged at him with a kick. Philo grunted as Jasper's foot banged into his oblique. Jasper smiled devilishly and followed with an onslaught of quick punching motions. Stinging pains hit Philo all over his body as he recoiled. Philo held up his arms to block, purely on the defensive. He couldn't get in any counter attacks because Jasper was moving so fast.

After getting punched in his shoulder, Philo noticed the bully's back leg placed wrong in the arsenic pose. Philo kicked the side of Jasper's knee, making the bully wobble. Philo twisted and kicked Jasper's chest. Jasper fell to the floor. A bit shocked the move worked, Philo took a deep breath and steadied himself back to carbon pose.

"You're *hiding* something, Jonathan!" Jasper spat as he got off the ground. "I know it!"

"What?" Philo jabbed back, anger mounting. "No, I'm not!"

Jasper Finn lunged at Philo with a strong right hook. Philo ducked. Finn grunted and swung his other fist.

"We looked into it," Finn growled as he missed Philo again. "Ivy is a master of digging up dirt. We couldn't find any record of you from any Grounded schools!"

Jasper broke through Philo's blocks and landed a wicked sucker punch to his stomach. Philo hunched over, his abdomen throbbed in pain. He couldn't let Jasper get the better of him, especially about his past.

"It's not my fault you don't trust anyone!" Philo shot back. He sent an uppercut to Jasper's chin, but the boy caught his fist.

"It's pathetic how behind all of us you are," Jasper twisted Philo's arm behind his back. "You don't belong at SIYT. Is there even any proof you are trioka?"

Philo yelped in agony as Jasper twisted his arm even further.

CHAPTER 11

"You reek of weak dioka to me."

Jasper kicked the back of Philo's leg and pushed him to the ground. They were entangled on the mat. Jasper laughed as Philo began to lose energy, struggling in his grasp.

"How embarrassing," Jasper maniacally smirked. "Just quit and tap out. Go back home to your little village in the dirt."

"No!" Philo grunted. "I'm not letting you beat me!"

As Philo tried to squirm out of Jasper's grip on the mat, he glanced around the sparring room. Most of the other pairs had already finished fighting. Ivy Bates had easily beaten Jade Mahala. Luther Wyatt lost to Xendo. Raelyn was rubbing a hurt shoulder after defeating Damian. And even though Lina Castellano had flipped Alani to win their match, the two seemed to be laughing about it to themselves as friends. The only other pair still sparring was Naomii and Russell. Naomii peacefully weaved and dodged all of Russell's exasperated attacks like a feather in the wind. The entire class laughed as Russell kept losing energy and Naomii stayed breezy as ever. Professor Bryne, however, was not watching Naomii. She was honed in on the spar between Philo and Jasper, analyzing how Philo was struggling.

Philo was desperately trying to push Jasper off of his back, but Philo's limbs were locked in place by the bully's heavy weight. Jasper was bulkier and stronger than Philo could ever hope to be. He was stuck. Philo was beginning to think his only option was to tap out on Jasper's arm and admit defeat.

Uma Bryne called out to the boys, "When the end to your path is inevitable, your only hope is to accept a new direction."

What? Philo thought as his muscles strained and ached. The only other direction Philo could go was... *down?* That wouldn't help him escape the hold Jasper had on him. Then it dawned on Philo.

Philo relaxed all his muscles. He winced in pain as Jasper's strength overpowered his own, twisting his frame further. However, with Philo no longer struggling to hold them up, both boys dropped to the mat with a loud thud. Caught off guard, Jasper let go of Philo's left arm to catch himself. Philo elbowed back at Jasper, smacking his bully square in the eye. Jasper cursed foul words as he recoiled.

Philo rolled out of the way and tried to recover his breathing. The boys wobbled back to their feet.

"What a cheap trick!" Jasper shot at Philo, gripping his left eye that

THE AMBASSADOR'S ANNOUNCEMENT

was beginning to swell. "Pathetic."

Jasper leaped toward Philo again. Philo blocked his next three punches and kicks. Philo jabbed across Jasper's face and kneed his stomach. While exhausted, Philo tried his best to keep his stances strong, maintain his balance, and keep his form steady. Jasper didn't care about kineoka foundations anymore. He was switching tactics to an all-out brawl. Jasper swung over and over at Philo in desperation. Philo backtracked as he tried to dodge. Jasper's fist knocked him so hard across the jaw, Philo almost fell over again, teetering close to the mat's edge.

Philo heard gasps from his friends and classmates watching them spar. Instead of letting Philo reset and regain his balance for a fair fight, Jasper growled in anger and dived toward Philo. Jasper grabbed him by the shoulders and aggressively shoved him. Philo fell backwards onto the gymnasium floor outside the fighting pad. Jasper Finn won the sparring match.

Philo groaned as Xendo rushed over to help him up. Jasper clutched his hurt eye, but threw his other arm up in victory. The Skyborne bully walked away from the defeated Philo to join his cheering gang of cronies. Alani and Raelyn came over to console Philo and check his injuries. Philo didn't care about the pain; he was angrier at himself for losing.

For the rest of his classes that day, Philo couldn't even focus on lectures or his assignments. His sore jaw and aching stomach thankfully healed up sooner than he expected, but he felt embarrassed and didn't want to talk. Raelyn, Alani, and Xendo could tell he was downtrodden as they walked to the café for dinner.

"Don't worry, Philo, we can train with the combots, spar with each other, and we'll all do better next time," Xendo comforted his friend.

"Finn is such a slime ball!" Alani added. "I lost my match too, but Lina is honorable, she beat me fair and square. Jasper definitely did some shady, sneaky moves!"

"He was desperate to show his dominance," Raelyn commented with curiosity, "like he's trying to prove something. I wonder what he's on about."

Philo didn't want Alani or Raelyn to be suspicious of him, too. *Would they ditch me if they knew I was an imposter at their school?* Philo finally found some good friends; he couldn't stomach losing them. He

CHAPTER 11

was also running out of white lies to distract the girls.

"I'm tired of thinking about Jasper," Philo sighed. "Let's just focus on dinner."

Smells of delicious food hit their noses as they entered Continuum Café. Philo breathed it all in with relief. Food always helped him forget his problems.

"I'm so hungry," Philo said, "I think I could eat a whol—"

"Shhh," Xendo shushed him and the girls. "There's Mom. No! Don't look!"

But they did. Sure enough, across the dining room, Chef Blinda Quaker was standing in the doorway that connected the café's seating area to the kitchen in the back.

"Why is she out front? She never does that. Let's wait a bit to go in," Xendo directed.

"But we haven't met your mother yet," Raelyn reasoned politely. "We should introduce ourselves."

"No, no need for that!" Xendo flailed. "She's busy!"

"Xendo, she's not embarrassing at all," Philo laughed. "You're too hard on her."

After refilling the salad bar with more produce, Blinda turned around. Xendo tried to hide behind the tiny Alani, but it didn't work. Blinda's face brightened and she waved them over. Xendo groaned and rolled his eyes.

"See, she loves me," Philo said, leading the way to Blinda.

"I don't understand your fear of her," Raelyn expressed to Xendo. "Your mother seems more relaxed than most parents. Surely more than my own."

"Ugh, fine," Xendo groaned, "but no personal questions."

"Ummm…, request declined," Alani mocked. "I need to know if you were this much of a pain as a kid as you are now."

Xendo grumbled a quiet retort and stomped behind his friends as they hurried over to his beaming mother.

"Give me a hug, kiddo," Blinda cooed to Philo as she embraced him. "Xendo tells me your first months have been good! Well, that is when he actually responds to my ED messages!"

They all laughed, except Xendo.

"Yes, I'm learning *so* much." Philo gave Blinda a knowing look that signified he was learning much more than the normal SIYT

THE AMBASSADOR'S ANNOUNCEMENT

history major.

"I bet you are," Blinda chuckled. She turned to Alani and Raelyn. "And ladies, Philo has told me great things about you both. Thank data you two are around to keep the boys on their toes."

"Yes," Alani crossed her arms proudly, "I knock 'em down a peg every single day."

"Atta girl." Blinda held out her hand for a high five and Alani smacked it with glee.

"Mrs. Quaker, we joke around, but your son is a wonderful friend," Raelyn snuck in, noticing Xendo's unease.

"Oh, thank you, my dear," Blinda responded. "I'm glad he chose some good friends. Now, before you eat, I actually have a bit of time. Would you like a little tour of what I do?"

Blinda took her son's friends outside to her massive vertical garden towers that grew produce for the entire school. In Blinda's state-of-the-art kitchen, her staff was preparing food, plating dishes, and cleaning. Philo was glad that even though this future was so advanced, the SIYT students were still taught to appreciate homemade food and its history.

While waiting for their dinners, Alani coerced embarrassing stories about Xendo's childhood out of Blinda. Xendo covered his face in shame as his mother described how her son used to escape baths as a toddler to run naked in her backyard. Alani was having the time of her life soaking in every hilarious, mortifying detail. However, a cook soon came to pull Blinda back to the kitchen.

"Well, your mom is my new best friend," Alani joked as they sat down to eat.

"She truly just gets better and better," Philo confirmed. Raelyn nodded.

"Repeat any of those stories and you're all dead." Xendo glared at them with a smirk.

Like every other evening, the four friends shared their dinners so they could each taste different flavors from above, below, and around the globe. Philo loved the sweet and pungent flavor of Xendo's air-fried turkey wings, had his first-ever bite of walrus meat from Raelyn's spicy Antartican stew, and loved how fresh the eel maki roll tasted from Alani. By the time he finished his roasted buffalo with wild rice, Philo completely forgot about stupid Jasper Finn.

A notification alert rang from Raelyn's technoband.

CHAPTER II

"Ambassador Irwin is running for president?" Raelyn announced with shock.

"What?" Alani peered over while the boys chatted. "Really?"

"Yeah! Look!" Raelyn tapped her wrists together and spread the holoscreen out so they could all read.

Trioka Ambassador of the Global Government's Peace Department, Daryl Irwin, has announced his candidacy for President of Earth under the Freedom Party. Watch the first campaign speech <u>here</u>.

"Finally! A trioka for the top office! He'd be so great!" Xendo exclaimed.

"He's the last one to be nominated. So, if he's under the Freedom Party, that puts all five parties in play with candidates for the election," Alani mentioned.

"President Kanosha has been doing a splendid job," Raelyn noted with intrigue. "She's from the Restorative Party, but stated she just wants the best next leader for the role. Irwin could certainly be a great follow-up to her two terms."

"I definitely want Irwin," Xendo expressed, "but any of the nominees are better than that Duke Denholm guy from the Common Party. He wants to bring global capitalism back. That's insane."

"Yeah, that worries me. My father is sure that Denholm is hiding something behind all his family's construction company money. They aren't supposed to have that much," Raelyn sighed remembering her last conversations with her father before parting ways. "Should we watch the speech here or back in the lounge?"

"Let's watch now," Xendo urged. "Click it, Rae."

"It'll be fun to have an Oceanite president again," Alani shrugged, "but everything has been perfectly fine around the world for centuries. I'm not worried. We have those history papers for Professor Blaise to get done tonight. I don't want to hear a long speech."

"I do," Philo contributed to the conversation. "It could be important."

Raelyn pressed the link with her finger. "I may not hold my ruling title anymore, but I still need to ensure Irwin promises to uphold the treaties my father signed for the Frozen Kingdom," she reasoned.

"I don't think he would change any treaties," Alani assured. "Irwin is, like, all about peace."

THE AMBASSADOR'S ANNOUNCEMENT

"I'm less worried about how Irwin will perform, and more worried about how the dioka candidates will debate against him." Raelyn squinted at the screen. "Most dioka secretly don't want trioka people in positions of power. I'm fearful of how certain groups will try to take him down."

The video began with Ambassador Daryl Irwin's secretary organizing a podium in an Oceanite underwater dome. Behind the glass wall backdrop there were colorful fish, rock formations, and strands of swiveling kelp. Daryl Irwin walked out onto the stage and the small crowd of supporters began to cheer and whistle for him. Philo noticed how Ambassador Irwin was poised, confident, and genuinely pleased to be there.

"Hello, Croiley! It means so much to be here with all of you on this special day. Every time I return to my homedome in the Atlantic Ocean, I am reminded of my family and friends who shaped my childhood dreams. For the rest of you who have been supportive of my work, nothing has made me prouder to serve you in my years of fighting for peace and advocating for the trioka people of Earth.

"When I was young, I was as free and reckless as waves in the ocean. I dreamed of glorious adventures and making a big difference in the world. I soon found myself at the Superior Institute of Young Trioka studying to become a continuum agent. I worked for the Historical Timeline Preservation Agency. Imagine my delight when, a few years in, three talented peers and I were selected for a mission to try and protect our past from terrorists who sought to abuse it for their own advantage. I was prepared and excited to do my duty.

"But then, as you all know, the mission to 2005 became one of the deadliest missions the HTPA has ever known. To this day, we still have not discovered who was behind the attacks, and how they were able to kidnap and torture my brave team of fellow agents."

Irwin bowed his head and side-stepped from the podium so the crowd and cameras could see his full frame. He pulled back his Oceanite robes to reveal that both of his legs were robotic prosthetics from the thigh down.

"I lost my legs on that mission, but that was nothing compared to the pain of losing my friends in that final battle. When I woke up alone, screaming in anguish, all hope of succeeding our mission was lost. I was just lucky to still be breathing. My fellow agents Daniel Nockby,

CHAPTER 11

Ava Harlow, and Jerome Quaker were on the ground, slain in front of me."

Philo glanced away from the holoscreen to lock eyes with Xendo. Alani and Raelyn also turned his way, knowing this must be tragic for him to hear. Alani patted Xendo's hand on the table as Raelyn rubbed his shoulder in support.

Xendo felt embarrassed. He wished he could share the girls' condolences with Philo, but the girls could never know Philo's secret. All the boys were able to share was a silent, depressing nod. The girls turned back to look at the holoscreen as Irwin continued.

"I had to escape and return to our time as the only survivor. My childhood dreams of adventure had become so twisted, and it broke me. I learned that none of our days are ever guaranteed. I must make the most of each day I am lucky enough to have. I knew I must do something good. Something more.

"I transferred from the HTPA to the Peace Department of the Global Government. I spent a decade promoting peace discussions and resolving diplomatic conflicts in each of the four origins of our great planet. While being trioka is only a tiny part of who I am, it is something I declare proudly. So, when the position was offered to me three years ago, I took on the mantle of Trioka Ambassador of the President's Parliament. My mission was to educate the governing body on trioka interests and ensure that my people have a voice in global affairs.

"It has been an honor to serve under President Namid Kanosha. As her time in the role comes to a close, we need to stay the course and continue the strength in leadership she demonstrated. Which is why, today, I am announcing my candidacy for President of Earth!"

The room erupted with applause. Philo and his friends clapped along with the video.

"Join me in building a stronger world that protects us all."

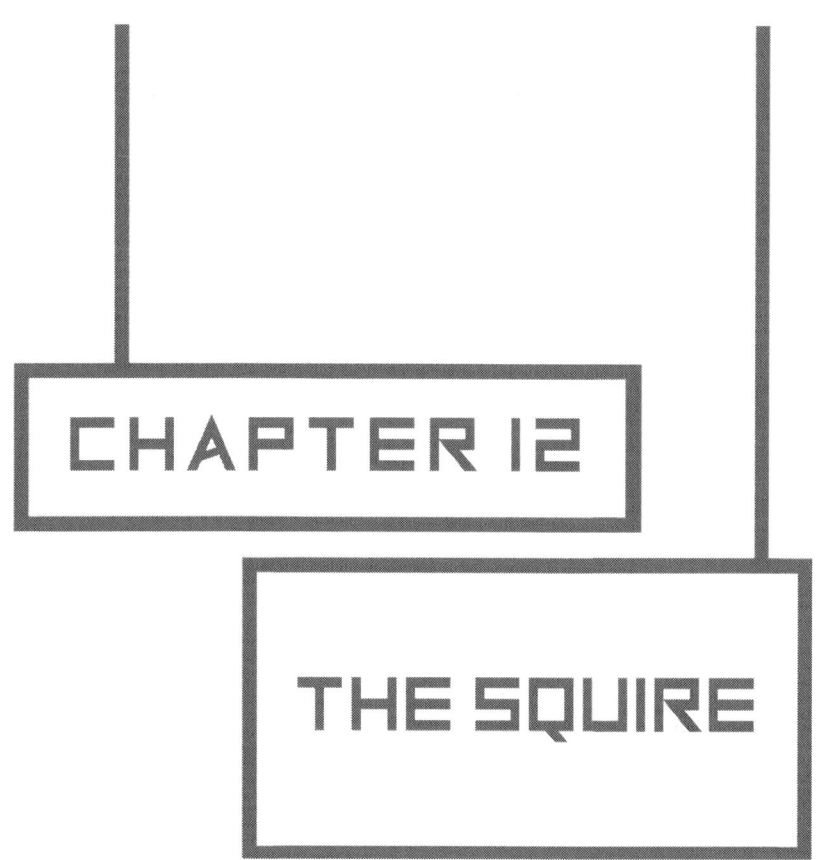

CHAPTER 12
THE SQUIRE

As dusk approached the Denholm Industry Headquarters in southern RAs dusk approached the Denholm Industry Headquarters in southern Russia in the Grounded region, a frustrated Viktor Dimo sprinted down the hallway toward Robin Alcroy's office. He was supposed to give his boss the classified files ten minutes ago, but hate-watching Ambassador Irwin's announcement speech made him lose track of time. Mr. Alcroy had just forced Viktor to drop everything for a sudden secret emergency meeting—luckily, Viktor knew *who* and *what* the meeting was for—and he had no choice but to agree.

Instead of attending a graduate program, Viktor worked for Denholm Industries as a construction laborer, building homes around the world. The Global Government promised every citizen on earth basic living quarters once they turned twenty-one as part of Earth's Universal Basic Income. Denholm Industries was the non-profit company that built all the government-subsidized apartment buildings for all four origins.

Duke Denholm, the CEO, was a god to Viktor. He inspired poor

CHAPTER 12

dioka like him around the planet, and he wasn't afraid to speak his mind when it came to trioka people. Duke Denholm also wore fancy suits, had a beautiful young wife, and owned multiple luxury hovercars, sailing yachts, and private jets. With his wealth, Denholm could actually enjoy traveling around the world, instead of just using public teleporting like everyone else.

Duke Denholm was one of the few billionaires left on Earth. This feat was next to impossible in the past few centuries due to high wealth taxation to help fund global infrastructure and education. Even though Denholm's family somehow held onto their wealth for generations, Denholm wanted every average dioka to have financial freedom and live as lavishly as they wanted. He was everything Viktor wanted to be one day! However, that freedom would take decades of hard work as a faithful Denholm employee. Viktor Dimo was so dedicated to his construction job, he would sacrifice everything for it.

Mr. Alcroy noticed Viktor's dedication and ambition right away, and started to give Viktor more responsibility. When Viktor had discussed their CEO's desire to bring capitalism back to Earth by removing wealth caps, and the possibility of a Denholm Presidency, Alcroy seemed impressed by Viktor's opinions. When Duke Denholm did announce his run for Earth's presidency a few months back, Alcroy invited Viktor to become a Common Party intern for Denholm's campaign. Viktor happily signed on for the extra work. Robin Alcroy also mentioned he had some *clandestine* opportunities available for him. Viktor agreed again, and soon joined a secret order within the Common Party doing private political research for Denholm. Viktor, like always, worked harder than every other intern, and he soon got a pay raise and a promotion over his old corporate coworkers.

If Viktor wanted to keep rising in the ranks of Denholm Industries and the Common Party to one day meet Duke Denholm, he had to keep Mr. Alcroy satisfied. So far, it was proving successful; Mr. Alcroy even recently started calling him his "squire." However, being late to this secret meeting would make his boss irate. Viktor narrowly dodged other campaign staff as he sprinted down the hall.

"Hey! Slow down!" one of the Common Party campaign managers yelled. Viktor reduced his speed to a power-walk and turned to apologize.

"Ow!" a woman cried out. Viktor had crashed into a person round-

THE SQUIRE

ing the corner. Her folders and tablet fell to the tiled floor.

"Urgh!" Viktor cursed, having dropped his campaign documents.

Viktor bent down to pick up his precious file before the woman could read any of the classified information. He helped to awkwardly scoop up the woman's strewn papers and handed them to her. They stood and collected themselves.

"Careful with going too fast, young man," the woman warned, patting him on the shoulder. "You never know what danger you'll bump into."

Viktor nodded without listening. He continued to power-walk down the hallway again until he arrived at his boss's office. He paused for a second to shake out his nerves. Viktor lifted his hand to knock.

"I can already hear you!" Mr. Alcroy bellowed from inside the metallic doors. "Get in here!"

Viktor winced and shuffled into the room. Robin Alcroy, a balding, scruffy man with dark ruby rings on his fingers, had his feet up on his desk watching Ambassador Irwin's speech. He was angrily chewing some gum with his mouth open, glaring at the screen with contempt.

"The infection never stops spreading. *Trioka Pride?* Ha!" Mr. Alcroy snorted. "When will people get it? These freaks are taking us all down the wrong direction."

"Yes, sir," Viktor whispered, checking back toward the hall to make sure no one could see or hear them. "They won't have much pride for long."

"Do you have the printed papers on the girl?" Alcroy grunted without tearing his eyes away from the screen. "The higher-ups will be here shortly."

Viktor showed off the tan folder in his hand and whispered, "Yes, the last digital copy is on your tablet. The full outline, map of the school, the kill strategy, everything."

"The rest is wiped?" Alcroy asked under hushed tones, picking up his tablet.

"Yes," Viktor confirmed, "I deleted all remaining files."

"Good. Now is our time," Alcroy stated. "After years of keeping her hidden and evading our combat team's attacks, he just let her *leave*? For trioka school? The Frozen King is an idiot."

Viktor nodded in agreement as Mr. Alcroy pointed to Trioka Ambassador Daryl Irwin speaking in the telecast.

CHAPTER 12

"I wonder who is in charge of handling this mess. It better not upstage my pitch," Alcroy bemused as he put his tablet in his satchel. "Let's be there before the Director arrives."

Viktor nervously trailed behind Mr. Alcroy as he barged down the corridors to the restricted wing of Denholm Industry headquarters. Viktor had never been in this part of the building; no lower employees were allowed to enter. However, Mr. Alcroy placed his technoband against the door's lock pad, and it lifted to grant them access. They approached the outside of a conference room Viktor didn't even know existed.

"This is the big leagues, boy. The Director hasn't called an in-person meeting in years." Robin Alcroy stopped and turned back to Viktor, whispering, "You've been a trustworthy page. Taking you on as my squire was a risk. Do not screw this up... or you're out."

Viktor nodded, staring sternly into his boss's dull green eyes. Alcroy turned around to open the conference doors as Viktor gulped down his nerves. It was dark inside the meeting room; only the pale blue light from the mounted holoscreen upfront illuminated the dim space. Just a few members of the order were present so far. Mr. Alcroy took a seat toward the head of the conference table. Viktor pulled out the chair next to his boss to sit on his right.

"No, go to the side!" Robin Alcroy scolded Viktor as if he were an annoying mosquito. "This table is for knights only."

Viktor bowed his head in embarrassment and backed to the wall to sit in an empty hard chair. Soon, a flurry of society members entered the chambers. Political squires rushed to sit along the walls and soldier squires wearing dark gray camouflage uniforms queued in rigid lines. The higher-ranking knights, of both the political and military wings of the order, filled the cushioned chairs at the wooden conference table.

A harsh whistle sounded and the room fell silent. The Director strode in to stand behind the final seat. Viktor had never seen the Director before—no one had. He wore a light-gray ski mask that covered his entire skull. His dark camouflage uniform, black boots, and gloves concealed his entire body, so not even an inch of skin was showing. For all Viktor could tell, the Director could be aged twenty-five or seventy-two. The only embellishment the terrifying leader wore was dark sunglasses engraved with a gold eagle. The Director slowly sat at the head of the table and scanned the room before he spoke.

THE SQUIRE

"Nothing you will witness in this room ever happened. If you are here, it is because you have been vetted extensively, even if you do not know it. We, the knights of *Omnipotence,* are constantly under attack. Our government may accept the disgusting changes to how the world has always worked, but we will not. *Omnipotence* was first to stomp out the rising trioxyribonucleic acid infections centuries ago, after the wars and pandemics of the digital era. However, our work was never fast enough. No one listened to our warnings. Our knights were forced into the shadows. The corrupt leaders, and the sheep who followed them, eventually succumbed to politics and labeled themselves *dioka*.

"Our enemies call themselves *trioka*. As if the spreading disease of mutating genomes across our planet is new and improved. This delusion will be our end. These trioka mutations want to *replace* us. Our kind has created human civilizations for thousands of years, and now they want to benefit from our hard work. But we will wipe them out. We are not *dioka*. We are *humans*. They are *abominations*."

Viktor nodded in agreement. He looked around the dim space to see the rest of his comrades staring intently at the Director with grins as he continued.

"When Omnipotence was first founded in the Roman Empire, our imperialist conquests shaped the world in our own glorious image. It was the only time this planet was truly powerful. Morally superior people controlled a public full of savages. Nothing tested our organization more than uprisings in the digital era. Our early efforts were successful in keeping the spreading trioka infections at bay; we secretly terminated any infants who were spreading the virus, but it soon grew beyond the control of just our covert organization.

"After our secret soldiers faced devastating defeats by the so-called 'kineoka masters,' savage vigilantes of the trioka elites, we had to hide and better strategize our return. Duke Denholm is an inspiration to many of our people across the globe. He is the perfect political figurehead for us to control and change public policy in the centuries ahead. After years of our knights rising through his company, we convinced him to run for president and further our ideologies. We dedicated our order to do whatever it takes to win him the global election, but with the disgusting Ambassador Irwin announcing his own candidacy, we may need to accelerate our campaign's strength. Mr. Duke Denholm has sent us a message to thank you all for your hard work thus far."

CHAPTER 12

Viktor's ears perked up. Duke Denholm not only knew of Omnipotence but was also asking for their support? *This is perfect!* The holoscreen behind the Director lit up. An image appeared of Duke Denholm at his giant rally in Canada in the Grounded origin last week. He's had many extravagant rallies touring all four origins to meet his supporters these past few months. He was a thick, heavy, aging man, but he had a smile that had gotten him far in life.

"Here is his recognition of our work." The Director zoomed in on the rally image on the holoscreen. Duke Denholm's left hand at his side was making an "O" shape with his five fingers and pointed the face of the O directly to the camera.

"Our men in his inner circle showed him our signal and, after our commitments to tearing down his competition, he accepted our proposal. Here, he proved it."

The room erupted into cheers, celebrating the secret hand symbol of OMNI members. Viktor clapped along as the photo zoomed back out to normal. The Director spoke again.

"Namid Kanosha and other global presidents have made our efforts almost impossible. However, the soon-to-be President Denholm shall turn our righteous goals into a reality. We must move on to the next stage of our operations. I need updates on the Frozen Kingdom missions, and we must now take down Ambassador Irwin. Let's hear your pitches."

Mr. Alcroy stood up and cleared his throat.

"Robin Alcroy, Third Degree Knight, Grounded, OMNI Political Unit. Our destabilization and public conditioning efforts increased this past decade, proving particularly effective within the Grounded and Frozen origins. A large number of the citizens at the South Pole continue to have purely pro-dioka interests and they resent the royal family and the Winter Thorns for living in the north. They have been losing faith in King Bernard's lazy leadership and are open to our influence. The OMNI military team's secret attacks on the Northern Palace to try and capture the trioka princess have not succeeded. However, Queen Semira's death by our soldiers has been successful in further disrupting the Frozen Kingdom. The foolish King blamed her death on the simple illness of frost decay. Many Frozen people fell for this declaration, but they question why the daughter has been kept hidden in the Northern Palace.

THE SQUIRE

"There is growing underground support for the end of the Arctikon Dynasty. The princess abandoning her people to study at the trioka academy was the final push in betrayal. If Denholm wins the election, one of our own Omnipotence knights of Frozen origin can challenge King Bernard's claim to the throne. All we would need is Denholm's endorsement and a successful attack. Soon all of the Frozen Kingdom will fall under our control!"

The room exploded with deep cheers and chants again. Mr. Alcroy cocked a smile as the ruckus died down as he continued.

"Our time to strike the trioka princess and officially terminate the Arctikon royal family line is *now!* The stupid princess is now on her own, in North America, on a small trioka skisland over Lake Superior. An easy target for a sneak attack by our military knights and squires. We are hoping to strike before the princess returns home when the school year ends. Some of our spies are gathering info as we speak."

"Excellent work from our political unit," the Director confirmed as Robin Alcroy sat down, pleased with himself. "Military unit?"

Viktor Dimo looked down the table as another man stood up. He was strong but slim, had pale skin, a stern face, and was half the age of the other knights. Viktor was jealous he was a knight so young. The fit man had zero nerves before speaking.

"Judd Stemson, second-degree knight, Frozen, OMNI Military Unit. Our findings indicate that in just the few short hours since the announcement, public excitement for our rival Ambassador Irwin is growing over the candidates from the other parties. Irwin appeals to the flimsier origins, to all trioka people, and even some progressive dioka. Instilling fear and uncertainty around his leadership may make his followers distrust him. In the past, the OMNI military has sent in secret agents to turn simple protests into riots, has co-opted rallies, and even assassinated rivals."

"Yes, Irwin must be stopped by any means necessary," responded the Director. "Where is he going for his next speaking engagements?"

"For now, he is touring more of the Oceanite Metropolis Domes," Judd Stemson explained. "However, he plans to also attend trioka-specific locations to appeal to his base."

"Will he visit the trioka school mentioned before?" asked the Director, clasping his gloved hands together.

Viktor darted his eyes toward Mr. Alcroy who seemed a bit taken aback.

CHAPTER 12

Judd Stemson answered, "Our information suggests his team is planning on an event there this spring."

The Director thought to himself for a moment. Weighing his thoughts, he turned back to Viktor's boss to ask, "Knight Alcroy, do you have your maps of the school and the girl's assassination plan with you?"

"I memorized as much as possible sir," Mr. Alcroy replied. "My squire has the last printed copy. I felt tha—"

"If we attend that event and cause a stir," Knight Stemson interrupted, "we could take down Denholm's lead competition and announce OMNI's return to stroke trioka fears."

Mr. Alcroy hated being interrupted. His fists balled up near his sides and he tapped his foot. The Director seemed intrigued with this new plan of action. Mr. Alcroy attempted to regain the floor.

"But, sir, that would expose us to the public too soon and risk our mission with the girl we've waited so long for," Mr. Alcroy argued. Judd Stemson interrupted again, trying to convince the Director to side with him.

"The dumb girl is stuck at the school with no deep security for months, if not years," Stemson doubled down, "and the school itself is a hotbed of trioka history. The perfect place to undermine Irwin's authority. We may only have one chance to strike them both in an impactful way."

"Do you suggest assassinating the ambassador at the school?" the Director looked at Knight Stemson, impressed. "How so?"

"We teleport into the school. We sneak in concealed sniper rifles. We take Irwin out," Judd Stemson granted himself a sly grin. "We've been training our men with the weapons."

"Guns?" Mr. Alcroy scoffed. "Isn't that a bit outdated and childish?"

"That's why it's perfect," Stemson shot back with a smirk. "No one expects them anymore. It'll be more of a show."

"I think it would risk our longer-term goals with the Frozen throne." Mr. Alcroy was growing a little too passionate.

"This is of more importance, old man," Stemson stated, raising his voice.

Mr. Alcroy slammed his fist down on the table. "Under whose authority?"

"Enough!" the Director condemned in a booming, deep, but mea-

THE SQUIRE

sured voice. Both men quieted.

"The world may have forgotten guns, but they are an ancient weapon that are tradition with the old OMNI," the Director continued. "It could be a clever way to announce our return."

"But Sir, I—"

"Knight Alcroy, we will kill the ambassador first. The girl can wait," the Director spoke over Alcroy, silencing him.

Robin Alcroy bowed his head in shame.

"Where is your squire?" the Director was growing impatient. "Have him hand over the files on the school."

Alcroy began to fidget. His face twitched and his eyes bulged. This was strange. Viktor could tell his boss was losing power.

"No, I refuse," Robin Alcroy stated in a strangely forced voice. "My squire is on *my* side. Besides, I am the only one that knows the true secrets of the Arctikons. We—"

Viktor Dimo stood up. This was his chance to seize an opportunity.

"Here, sir," Viktor called out, interrupting his own boss, his own senior Omnipotence knight. "Here in my hands are the files on the trioka school. Whatever is best for OMNI, I will abide by."

"No! I can fix this!" Mr. Alcroy complained again. "There must be something else I can do!"

The Director held out his hand. Viktor couldn't see any sort of smile or expression under the gray ski mask the Director was wearing, but he hoped the Director was pleased. Viktor approached the head of the table. A loud *thud* shook the chamber as Mr. Alcroy threw his chair across the room and fractured the huge mounted holoscreen. Robin Alcroy made strange growling and wailing noises as if in pain. The screen's blinking lights made Mr. Alcroy's deranged screeching sounds even more frightening.

Something was very wrong. Alcroy had drool foaming from his mouth and his eyes glowed red with rage. The Director hardly seemed phased. He tilted his covered head to the side, watching this mess unfold while the rest of the OMNI political members fled. The Mr. Alcroy beast leaped high into the air toward the Director to attack. Out of nowhere, five harsh gunshots fired. Viktor Dimo flinched in shock.

Blood spurted as Robin Alcroy crashed into the side wall and toppled to the floor. Judd Stemson had somehow brought a concealed rifle into the chamber and was the one who pulled the trigger. Viktor turned

CHAPTER 12

to Stemson, wide-eyed and slack-jawed. The young knight shot one last bullet into the corpse on the ground to make sure this mess was finished.

"See, we should have done things my way from the get-go." Jedd Stemson sat back down casually.

The Director sighed. He turned his head toward Viktor Dimo and took off his dark sunglasses with the golden eagle. Behind the pieces of tinted plastic was still nothing but the covered gray mask that hid the Director's face and secrets.

"Squire, what's your name?" the Director asked in Viktor's direction. Viktor gulped. He tried to stop his hands holding the files from shaking.

"Viktor Dimo, sir," Viktor replied, regaining his composure.

"Well, Viktor Dimo, welcome to Omnipotence." The Director held out his hand again for the papers. "You've just been promoted."

Viktor smiled and stepped forward to present the assassination files.

CHAPTER 13

THE FIRST ATTRACTION

"**W**ow! I never thought meditating would make my ass so sore," Alani Adalaide griped to her roommate with her eyes closed. She had tried to focus all her mind's energy, but had no spark of success. Alani opened one eyeball and peered over at Raelyn meditating on the other side of their dorm. The princess was silent and did not even chuckle at Alani's quip. Alani felt most embarrassed when people didn't laugh at her jokes. She hated the silence.

Alani glanced down at the little black trinket hanging from her neck. Her carbon cube didn't glow or pulsate to match her breathing. It was as dead as a rock. She groaned. Studying for classes, finishing assignments, and acing exams was a breeze for Alani, but *why* couldn't she morph her cube? Professor Ruiz said if they cleared their minds and connected with their honest emotions, it would unlock deeper memories of their true selves. But Alani was pretty damn sure her mind was clear about her feelings of boredom right now. Somehow that wasn't working.

Alani looked over to Raelyn, calmly breathing in and breathing out. Inhaling and exhaling. She at least *looked* the part. Maybe after

CHAPTER 13

three months of meditation practice, Raelyn would be the first classmate to make a breakthrough. Yet, Raelyn's carbon cube was still inactive.

Alani checked the time on her technoband and smirked. She tiptoed across her dorm to get closer to Raelyn. She was as royal, peaceful, and flawless as ever. Alani leaned in close to her face and took in a silent breath.

"Time to go to class!" Alani screamed in her ear.

Raelyn jumped in surprise, flailing in fear, and fell backward on her own bed.

Alani burst out laughing so hard she hunched at the waist, grabbing her stomach, and almost knocked over the paint brushes on her desk.

Raelyn clutched her heart in shock as she tried to catch her breath. She rolled her eyes and jokingly threw her shoe at Alani.

"I'm already prepared to go!" Raelyn shot back, starting to chuckle.

"Sorry! I had to," Alani giggled while swatting the shoe down. "Seeing your flabbergasted face was so worth it!"

Alani grabbed her tablet and put on her Oceanite blue-lined jacket over her black SIYT uniform.

"Did you almost get there?" Alani questioned, mimicking Professor Ruiz's elderly voice, *"Did you unlock your secret self?"*

"No, I did not," Raelyn sighed, shaking her head. "I've mastered other breathing methods for fighting in seconds, why is carbon cube morphing so hard?"

"I don't know. This trioka mental magic is new to all of us. Alani handed Raelyn her shoes with a smirk. "I just want to do it before Philo and Xendo!"

"Yeah!" Raelyn agreed with a chuckle, "We must win!"

"Do Philo and Xendo act weird around you sometimes?" Alani asked. "I feel like they're hiding something?"

"Everyone acts weird around me," Raelyn shrugged, "but, they do whisper a lot."

"Are they dating?" Alani guessed, "Do you think Philo is gay too?"

"I'm not sure," Raelyn tried to pinpoint what was most suspicious about the boys. "I really enjoy Philo, but I feel like I know nothing about him. He's definitely nervous about something."

"He is quiet… and Xendo talks too much," Alani laughed.

"Sounds like we have a mystery to solve." Raelyn raised her eyebrows.

THE FIRST ATTRACTION

"Indeed," Alani crossed her arms, "and a meditation race to win!"

The girls fist bumped and left their dorm to meet the boys in the thirteenth-floor lounge. Alani and Raelyn gave each other sly smiles as the boys also complained of their meditation struggles.

After a full morning of sparring and history lectures, the four friends' final class for the day was Kinoka Mental Arts. Yesterday, they took a surprise exam on all ninety-four organic periodic elements. The answers ranged from matching the elements with their assigned properties to complex chemical equations of theoretical isotopes bonding under certain organic conditions in nature. The exam also quizzed them on the essential functions the Sacred Thirty Elements performed in the human body, as well as the emotions they induce. Alani was positive she aced it.

"Do you think he'll give back our graded exams?" Alani whispered to Raelyn in class. Professor Ruiz was discussing how the electrons orbiting in the outer shells of atoms directly translate to our ever-changing feelings and mental health.

"He usually does the next day," Raelyn responded.

Her friend was right. After his lecture the students received their exam results on their libes.

"Booyah!" Alani cheered, seeing a perfect score on her test. She then scrunched her chin down to scream at her necklace. "Take that! You stupid little cube. I do understand the mental side of kineoka!"

"I also got one hundred," Xendo leaned forward to show off his tablet, "which means we're still even for marks in every class."

Alani cursed as Philo and Raelyn laughed. Xendo smirked with pride.

"This is one of our neutral classes," Alani reasoned to him. "If you think you'll beat my score for our ancient instrument recital next week your head is in the clouds, Robot Boy!"

"Then, I'll just get a higher grade on our next debate in Government," Xendo countered. The two bright students glared at each other with increasing tension.

"Gosh, the rivalry never ends," Raelyn sighed to Philo as they shared their grades with each other.

"I'm just glad we scored in the high 80s," Philo added.

Looking to her right, Alani saw Naomii drawing small doodles of weird animals on the margins of their tablet. The top corner of the exam page showed their score of 51, just enough to pass the exam in-

CHAPTER 13

stead of failing.

"Ooof, that's rough. Sorry, Naomii," Alani mentioned empathetically. "You and Jade can come study with us next time if you want."

"Oh, I don't waste time with studying," Naomii brushed off casually as they finished an intricate sketch mixing a cat and a horse. "I'd rather waste time thinking about life's mysteries I don't know… ya know?"

Naomii intently resumed doodling as Alani scoffed, "Don't you want to learn all this important information for class?"

"Naomii has a perfect memory," Jade chimed in from Naomii's right. "They have never needed to study; they know all the answers."

"I see, smell, hear, taste, or feel something once and I never forget it." Naomii shrugged as if it were the most normal thing in the world. "I just got bored halfway through the test and didn't want to finish it…. I don't need approval from teacher's grades like you and Xendo."

"Oh…," Alani responded, not sure if she was offended or not. She decided Naomii wouldn't realize their words were rude. "I wish I had a perfect memory."

"It is handy when trying to read something dense, because that can often be a chore," Naomii agreed as they finished their drawing. "The readers get it."

Alani squinted at Naomii completely befuddled. She opened her mouth to ask more questions but just shrugged and gave up.

Jade poked Naomii on the shoulder as Professor Ruiz floated by on his hoverchair.

"Are you going to tell Professor Ruiz?" Jade whispered to Naomii. "I think we have enough time during this class period."

"If we must," Naomii relented with a sigh. They both turned to Professor Ruiz who, shockingly, was already facing them.

"No need," Professor Ruiz spoke before the two friends even asked for his attention. "Naomii Clover is ready to activate their carbon cube. I can sense it."

"Yes! Last night in our dorm, Naomii's cube flickered and made a buzzing noise while they were meditating," Jade responded in nervous wonder. "How could you tell?"

"Ah, young one. After decades of teaching many students and morphing the mind myself, I am keenly aware when the energy needed is present." He lifted a slow finger to point to Naomii's carbon cube

THE FIRST ATTRACTION

dangling from their necklace. "That cube's first reaction with Naomii was strong. It is already attempting to attract your friend's cardinal elements to complete the bond."

"Woah," Philo responded without stopping himself. "Naomii's the first one?"

"Damn it!" Alani and Xendo both cursed in unison under their breaths. They glanced at each other in surprise then looked away to hide their jealous reactions. Raelyn and Philo laughed. Alani and Xendo finally weren't the best in class at something. Jade was ecstatic!

"Are we allowed to watch the attraction process take place?" Jade asked the professor.

"Certainly!" Professor Ruiz replied. "If Naomii doesn't mind an audience."

"We never *don't* have an audience for our story," Naomii replied while looking into the hallway, far from the conversation. She gave a knowing smirk and nodded to no one in particular. Philo and his friends followed Naomii's odd gaze to nowhere. They shrugged. Naomii's strange habits and imaginary friends were becoming their norm. Everyone looked to Jade.

"That means Naomii is fine with it," Jade translated.

"Excellent!" Professor Ruiz smiled. "Follow me, students!"

The entire class got up from their seats and followed Professor Ruiz out of their kineoka classroom to the elemental sanctuary. All of the students gathered near the edge of the chamber as Professor Ruiz guided Naomii into the center of the room to stand on a small, raised circle step among the pedestals. Alani saw Jasper and his gang walk to the back corner, grumbling to themselves, upset that their time was wasted on Naomii.

"Today is a special day, students," Professor Ruiz informed his class. "Young Naomii Clover is ready to activate their carbon cube. Today, you will witness how their four cardinal elements reveal for the first time. This is a somewhat private experience; some find it too revealing to share their most primal and emotional secrets with others. Naomii, for a final time, are you sure you don't mind us all discovering your cardinal emotions with you?"

"Everyone will discover them eventually," Naomii peacefully reasoned. "What's the point in me hiding them?"

"You see!" Professor Ruiz smiled toward Naomii then turned to

CHAPTER 13

the rest of the students. "This is why Naomii is first to connect with their cube, they are unashamed of their inner thoughts and open to all emotions. Naomii is completely honest with themself, fully free!"

The class clapped eagerly as Naomii blinked. Naomii seemed hardly bothered, as if they were still thinking about their cat-horse doodle.

"To fully master every step of kineoka, to unlock our mental powers, we must be completely *honest* with ourselves and with the world around us. Kineoka is impossible if one cannot accept the truth," Professor Ruiz explained.

Alani nodded while listening until she caught Philo and Xendo glance at each other with worried expressions. *That was weird.* She didn't like the thoughts that were coming into her head. *What are they hiding?*

"Every year you study here at SIYT you will discover deeper levels of connection and memories within your own mind," Professor Ruiz continued as Alani shook off her suspicions.

"Eventually, the simple power to activate your carbon cube will evolve into mastery of a full morphstaff of your own. Let us begin."

Professor Ruiz floated to the edge of the room with the rest of the students to leave Naomii alone in the center with the organic periodic elements. Naomii closed their eyes, took a deep breath in, and struck the carbon pose with their hands pressed together in front of their heart. Naomii breathed in through their nose, held the air in their lungs, and pushed a long exhale out their mouth.

"Who are you, Naomii?" Professor Ruiz called out as Naomii entered a meditative state. "What emotions are tugging you forward in this life? What holds you back? What has this world taught you and what have you embraced about yourself?"

The room was dead silent. Alani feared the process wasn't working. Naomii scrunched their brow briefly and a tear fell down their cheek. A small buzzing noise joined the room. Alani squinted to see Naomii's carbon cube vibrating. A soft blue light began to grow from the object. The class gasped. The glowing cube slowly rose up from Naomii's chest to float at eye level. Naomii kept steady with their breathing. Inhale and exhale. Inhale and exhale.

The shy Skyborne boy, Luther Wyatt, absent-mindedly whispered, "Look!"

Luther pointed toward the periodic pedestals. Four of the Sacred Thirty Elements also started to vibrate. Alani could recognize each of

THE FIRST ATTRACTION

them immediately. Lithium, iron, gold, and boron. Next, the elements levitated from their stands and hovered to Naomii meditating in the center. They were attracted to Naomii and the carbon cube like moths to a flame.

"Wow...," Alani uttered in quiet amazement.

Philo watched in astonishment as the four elements began to orbit in a circle around Naomii. They sped up faster and faster. The cube tugged upward at their necklace, expanding and shrinking to morph with Naomii's breathing chest.

With a surge of energy, the elements froze in mid-air. All four sat perfectly still to Naomii's north, south, east, and west. Lithium was in front, Iron on their left, boron on the right, and gold floated behind Naomii's head. Naomii opened their eyes and their carbon cube began to glow an even brighter bubble-blue.

The students' jaws fell open. Jade clasped her hands together and squealed in happiness for her friend. The glowing blue cube produced a melodic ringing sound. On Naomii's left thigh, under their SIYT leggings, a randomly shaped patch of light shone through. *Naomii's trioka genetic mark was also glowing!* Philo was in total awe.

"Congratulations!" Professor Ruiz spoke out, snapping all the students back from their wonder. "Naomii Clover, you are this year's first freshman SIYT student to have activated your carbon cube!"

Everybody in the room clapped. Philo was completely blown away, but Naomii's stunning mental powers also made him a little bit depressed. *I'll never be able to do that.* Philo thought as the class continued to applaud Naomii. *I still don't know who I am! I need to learn more about my parents. I hate keeping these secrets. I'm lying to everyone!*

Philo would never be as free as Naomii. He wasn't allowed to be honest, even with his closest friends. It could ruin everything. *If I told the truth, would SIYT kick me out? Would I get sent back to the past?* Philo had absolutely no idea. He just wanted to keep learning and become an agent like his parents. But *these secrets are making everything impossible. It's just all too much*! Philo thought.

"As you can see, Naomii's cardinal elements have aligned themselves," Professor Ruiz stated. "To their north hovers lithium, the element of passion. What drives Naomii forward in their life must be the pursuit of new discoveries, something fresh and fascinating other peo-

CHAPTER 13

ple overlook. To Naomii's east floats iron, which breeds the emotion of distraction, meaning Naomii is aware the world views them as if they are somehow not paying attention."

Jasper scoffed in the corner with his arms crossed, clearly agreeing that Naomii was a distracted weirdo. Philo looked over and saw Jasper whispering insulting jokes to Ivy, Damian, and Russell. Philo hated that Jasper could be so rude to someone so kind and free-spirited. Sure, it was a bit odd that Naomii liked to stare at people for extremely long periods without blinking. However, Philo knew Jasper was just jealous he wasn't first to activate his carbon cube.

"To Naomii's south is the precious metal gold," Professor Ruiz paused, intrigued and curious. "Meaning what holds Naomii back is love? Or possibly, their *fear* of love? Fascinating."

This caught Philo's attention and drew him back to share a glance with Xendo, who beamed eagerly at him, just as excited about the dazzling show as he was. Philo looked over to Raelyn, who was radiant and calm as the blue light graced her face. Philo blushed.

"And finally, to Naomii's west floats boron," Professor Ruiz continued, "meaning that Naomii finds much of the current world, and many people around them, insufferably boring and monotonous."

The room laughed. Even Naomii, who was still trying to focus on their meditation, was able to let out a smile.

"You should all be proud of Mx. Naomii Clover," Ruiz urged his class. "The most confusing journey in life is striving for our greatest purpose while accepting gratitude for our own imperfections. Most humans are unable to achieve both. Naomii took a great step forward in that journey today. Let their honesty of self be what you all strive for this year."

The four glass vials of pure elements floating above Naomii's head slowly descended into Naomii's open hands near their heart. Naomii exited their kineoka pose to stand normally again. They clasped their fingers around the vials. Their carbon cube stopped glowing blue and fell back to their chest, becoming a regular necklace again. Naomii looked at all the other students gawking back at them with wide eyes and open mouths.

"Well," Naomii shrugged nonchalantly, "that felt refreshing."

CHAPTER 14

UNDERWATER GRATITUDE

Philo, Raelyn, Alani, and Xendo congratulated Naomii one final time, waved goodbye to Jade, and headed off to have dinner in the Continuum Café. The four friends sat together at their favorite table near the large windows overlooking Lake Superior. As per usual, they each ordered something new off the menu from their home origins and shared their dinners. While discussing their Human History essays on the first Global Peace Summit after World War III, Alani got a buzz on her technoband. She tapped it to illuminate the incoming message on her palm.

"Is something wrong?" Raelyn asked as Alani read to herself.

"No, not at all!" Alani responded eagerly. "My mom just told me about some of our family's plans for Gratitude Week!"

"Gratitude Week? What's Gra—," Philo asked, confused. Xendo stepped on his foot under the table to silence him.

"THAT sounds great! Tell us more!" Xendo raised his voice over Philo's question. Philo grew quiet in realization of his stupid mistake. Raelyn didn't seem too bothered, but Alani squinted deeply at them.

"Why are you two being weird?" Alani interrogated the boys.

CHAPTER 14

"We are perfectly *not* weird," Xendo replied. "Right, Philo?"

"Oh yes, so normal," Philo agreed awkwardly, hoping Alani wouldn't ask more. She glared at them with suspicious eyes for a while longer, making the boys nervous. However, soon she shrugged her shoulders and slurped more of her Oceanite fish head soup.

"My mom wanted to know what you three are planning for Gratitude Week?" Alani asked the table. "We have extra space if you three wanted to come celebrate with us!"

Raelyn, Philo, and Xendo all perked up.

"Every year my mother and I just spend the holiday in our little cottage. She has always wanted to cook for a huge family to celebrate, but we're always alone. It's kinda depressing," Xendo explained with a sigh. "Could I bring my mom along?"

"Duh! My family can't cook at all. My parents would be thrilled to have her make the food!" Alani laughed with growing excitement. "Raelyn?"

"Things are still tense with my father and the Frozen Royal Council. I'm afraid if I go back now, they won't let me leave again," Raelyn lamented. "I was just going to spend the holiday here in our dorm," Raelyn admitted.

"What? You psycho!" Alani spurted in shock with a fish's eyeball jiggling on her dinner spoon. "You can't be alone on New Year's! You are coming for sure!"

"Okay, thanks, Alani," Raelyn blushed with a smile. "I'd be honored."

"And Philo?" Alani looked over to him hopefully. "Can you come? What does your family usually do to celebrate?"

"Oh…, y-you know…," Philo stuttered nervously, trying not to glance over to Xendo to help him lie. That would be too odd again. "We just do normal Grounded stuff… boring really. I could use a new adventure!"

"They wouldn't mind if you came with us?" Alani questioned.

"No…, I think my parents would just be happy to see me spending time with new friends," Philo worded cleverly. He then had a moment of sadness as the girls brightened with excitement. Xendo secretly patted Philo on the back to comfort him.

"This is going to be incredible!" Alani resounded.

UNDERWATER GRATITUDE

Later that night, Xendo shared the basics of Gratitude Week to Philo to arm him with specifics in case he got caught in conversation again. The holiday was a seven-day celebration in the final week of December that all four origins took part in. The holiday developed because, as dioka continued to settle upon more uncharted locations of the planet, people of varying ethnic backgrounds argued how to blend their family traditions. However, back in 2340, the first President of Earth, Alondrima Consuelo, created a perfect solution by accident. The President came from a mixed family of different origin heritages herself and casually shared with the public how her family celebrated each year's end; the holiday, which her family lovingly called their "Week of Gratitude," took off globally.

Each day of Gratitude Week honored a specific aspect of humanity. The first day started with reflecting on the personal *history* that allowed each family to evolve over the millennia; it was a perfect time to engage in any ancient customs or religious practices the family's ancestors held dear. The next five days were filled with activities that honored *family*, *body*, *mind*, *nature*, and *community*. Finally, on New Year's Eve, people honored the *future* with a huge feast where everyone expressed what they were most grateful for in the previous twelve months and what they hoped to accomplish in the upcoming year. Xendo mentioned that they'd probably follow the Adalaides' usual family traditions.

Philo had never celebrated a regular holiday in his life, and soon he was about to celebrate a *week's* worth? Philo was excited but apprehensive. He was scared of letting anything slip about his past and didn't know how to act at a normal family function. Waiting for the end of December was all Philo could think about.

"Oh, dang!" Xendo exclaimed, as he packed the last of their items the morning of their trip. "You've never traveled by teleportal before!"

"No, I haven't," Philo winced in apprehension. "Is that what we're using?"

"Yes, I swear it's just like your...," Xendo paused, tilting his head in thought. "How did you guys travel in your time again? The digital era went by so quick. The locomotive? Helicopter?"

"Oh, no. Ummm," Philo never had to answer a question like this before, "I guess the most common was just various cars and airplanes."

"Right. Right," Xendo nodded and opened their door to leave. "Teleportals are just like those, but they transport you instantly and are

CHAPTER 14

less stupid."

Philo shook his head in amused annoyance and Xendo chuckled as they left their dorm to exit the building.

Alani, Raelyn, and Blinda were waiting near the outgoing teleportal station just beyond the entrance to the SIYT compound. Behind the girls were wide steps leading to a raised area with five teleportal platforms. Philo saw some older SIYT students stepping onto the small round platforms, and within a few seconds, they completely vaporized into thin air. Philo tried to hide any shock his face might exhibit.

"Okay, team! My parents are waiting for us at the teleportal station of Saltwater City where we'll take our seashuttle to my homedome of Lisoo!" Alani told them.

"Where is Lisoo again?" Raelyn asked as they all moved as a group toward the platforms.

"It's a domed metropolis on the floor of the South China Sea. It's between a bunch of Grounded nations: Vietnam, China, Taiwan, and the Philippines." Alani mapped out with her hands in the air.

"I've never been to any of the Oceanite Domes!" Blinda chirped. "I can't wait to meet your family!"

"Can we take the group portal?" Xendo suggested to Alani and Raelyn. "Mom sometimes gets nauseous and vomits if she does it alone."

Both girls made faces in slight disgust. Blinda's beaming face turned sour as she sadly nodded in agreement.

"All right," Alani called out as she led them up the platform steps. "The group portals will take longer than us each going solo, but I'd say that's a win if we avoid puking!"

Xendo leaned over to Philo's ear, trailing behind the group.

"Just let Alani do everything with the controls," Xendo whispered to Philo. "If you get confused, just nudge me and I'll cover for you."

Philo nodded with realization. He was so lucky he had Xendo. That was such quick-thinking to use his mother's portal sickness so they could all travel together. Philo certainly didn't want Alani or Raelyn to see him fumbling with the solo portal and get more suspicious.

Everyone squeezed into the group portal platform. A pale teal holoscreen wall surrounded them and a digital menu appeared. Philo watched as Alani selected *Oceanite Origin > Pacific Ocean > Saltwater City*. The teal wall buzzed with the submissions and turned a brighter vibrant green.

UNDERWATER GRATITUDE

"Here we go!" Alani beamed excitedly. "Let's keep all the puke inside our bodies, people!"

Their view of SIYT's Skisland Station immediately disappeared. They shot across the world's skies as if flying through endless amounts of nature paintings at lightspeed. The images of sky, mountains, forests, and rolling hills transitioned to sandy beaches as they approached wide, open waters. Binda and Philo winced as they plunged into the Pacific Ocean. Philo's jaw dropped at what he saw.

Along the sandy ocean floor ran a vast network of giant domes and glass-tube pathways spanning hundreds of miles. As they barreled toward the largest of the glass domes, Philo, again, braced for impact, but they passed right through the thick, clear barrier like ghosts. When they came to a halt, the holographic wall dematerialized around them.

"Whoa!" Philo marveled as his eyes soaked in their new view.

They were now in a busy travel station under the sea. Philo inhaled sweet smells of sea salt caramel, coconut, and tropical fruit. Oceanite kids were frolicking about with shaved ice desserts and fish-shaped pancakes on sticks. There was a huge, gorgeous kinetic art sculpture in the center of the chamber made of colorful clay fish swimming in a mesmerizing pattern. All the travelers were fashionably dressed in long-flowing vibrant robes or asymmetrical swimwear. To Philo's right was a dark blue stage with a full orchestra playing majestic music on whimsical instruments to entertain the tourists.

Philo tilted his head back. The outside of their glass dome was the dark navy blue of the ocean they sat beneath. Philo couldn't see any sunlight peeking through from above; it didn't exist down here. However, what replaced the sun was even more breathtaking! Different forms of billowing jellyfish, neon eels, and glowing coral were so bright, they resembled shooting stars within the dark waters. The bioluminescent aquatic creatures gave off just enough light to make this Oceanite habitat a magical home that astounded Philo.

Blinda immediately stepped out from the teleportal and vomited loads of spew into one of the platform's nearby disposable puke bags. She had gotten portal-sick after all.

"I'm sorry," Blinda sighed as she wiped off her mouth and threw the spew bag in the nearby incinerator. "I have mints in my bag."

Down below the steps of the teleportal station was a couple holding up a kelp-paper sign that read *Welcome Home, Alani!* decorated with

CHAPTER 14

colored agates and tiny seashells. Alani squealed at full volume and dashed into her parents' embrace. Alani's gleeful father had brown-gray hair, thick glasses, and a radiant smile as charming as Alani's. His attire was a blend of orange and purple robes folded in clever designs to wrap tightly around his torso and legs. Alani's mother was quieter and more reserved. She had a long braid studded with seashells draped over her shoulder. Her colored robes embraced a flowing freedom that reminded Philo of a dress. She looked so elegant and serene.

"This is my father, Junsu, and my mother, Manoba," Alani introduced as her parents smiled warmly.

"We hear this is your first time visiting Oceanite life underwater. If you like fish and art, you should survive," Junsu commented with a boisterous laugh just like Alani's.

"Our family is so pleased to share Gratitude Week with the people who have brought so much joy to Alani's time at school," Manoba added.

"Thank you for sharing your home with us," Blinda responded cheerfully as Philo, Xendo, and Raelyn all grinned.

"All right, people, let's go to Lisoo!" Alani clapped her hands together.

They walked through vibrant mural-lined halls until they came to a garage of submarine ships that were wide and flat like stingrays. The entire group filed into the Adalaide's seashuttle. It began to auto-pilot itself to Alani's podhome.

The seashuttle picked up insane speed as they shot like a harpoon through the ocean. Philo saw rainbows of fish whizzing by so fast it looked like they were falling sideways. On either side of the ship, Philo saw other glass-domed cities scattered about the ocean floor.

"Now we're in Lisoo!" Alani nudged Philo from the side while pointing. "There's our pod! Next to Apo Reef!"

Up ahead was a collection of glass pods and some tubular aquatic buildings nestled in between curves of a dazzling, coral reef network. Their seashuttle pulled into the back of a vibrantly painted pod with wide aquarium windows that stood out from its neighbors. A door sealed behind them and their surrounding water drained out. Alani led her friends out of the seashuttle to open her family's water-sealed door.

Immediately, Philo, Raelyn, and Xendo's faces lit up as they stepped in. Alani's childhood home was an artist's paradise. Upbeat, jazzy music was playing that made Alani start snapping her fingers

UNDERWATER GRATITUDE

and shaking her booty. The cozy space was a stunning mix of blues and purples with subtle accents of white, gold, and sea-tinted greens. Gorgeous paintings of aquatic animals hung on the walls and abstract sea sculptures were placed on side tables. Every piece of marine furniture looked as if the family designed it themselves. No wonder Philo's friend had such an eye for beauty.

"Alani!" a bunch of kids screamed as they ran over and hugged her. Alani lined up all her siblings from youngest to oldest, nine in total. Alani stood eighth in the line.

"Here we have Tori, Shanzo, Kagami, Tamo, Piao, Morika, Yasuko," Alani named her siblings one after the other, then gestured to herself, "then me and Haru."

The younger siblings scurried off to continue playing and Alani's parents guided Blinda to their spare bedroom. Blinda couldn't help herself from commenting on every piece of beautiful artwork as they passed by it. Haru, Alani's oldest brother, helped Philo, Xendo, and Raelyn transport their belongings to Alani's childhood bedroom. He set up the same gray rollout pads Philo had slept on in Xendo's room in the Quaker's cottage.

Haru told them that he just turned eighteen, was in his final year at Pacific University of Artistic Expression, and was majoring in Post-Modern Art and Virtual Reality Filmmaking. Philo noticed Xendo was staring a lot at Haru, and Philo couldn't blame him. Haru was physically attractive, had a strong swimmer's build, and an endearing smile. He had tousled hair that draped to the left and short sides buzzed with designs.

"Alani, Haru is kinda hot," Xendo whispered after Haru left the room, raising his eyebrows to her.

"No, no, don't get your hopes up," Alani sighed with an eye roll. "He's straight and boring. You can do better."

"Holy frostbite! Was this you?" Raelyn cut off the jabbering to point to a painting of Alani's first day at SIYT, pre-transition, done by her parents. "So cute, Alani!"

"Yeah, what happened?" Xendo joked, looking at the sweet painting. Alani punched him in the arm.

"You wish you were as cute as me," Alani casually clapped back to Xendo with a flip of her hair. They all laughed.

The Adalaide family and their guests spent the rest of the evening

CHAPTER 14

getting to know each other better. Junsu and Manoba discussed their work creating art pieces for the metropolises in all five ocean basins and Alani's siblings shared their little adventures as young Oceanites in Lisoo. However, since Alani was the first trioka born to their family, the Adalaides were dying to hear more about kineoka, staffball, and their trioka classes.

Raelyn discussed how her team struggled to win even just one game so far this year, Xendo shared his love of studying old continuum missions, and Alani made her family laugh with silly ways dioka made mistakes in distant history. Philo even mustered up the courage to show how he practiced his stances for kineoka each morning.

"Have your classmates been keeping up with the presidential campaigns?" Junsu asked his daughter.

"We discuss it here and there," Alani responded, "but everyone at SIYT is trioka, so we're all for a President Irwin."

"Denholm is super popular at other universities, though," Xendo commented.

"As dioka, do you think Duke Denholm would be a good successor to Kanosha?" Blinda asked the older Adalaides.

"Some Oceanite dioka think so, but most of us would rather vote for a fellow Oceanite like Irwin. It doesn't matter if he's trioka."

"In Antarctica, it is a factor," Raelyn tacked on. "Many of the dioka there don't want a trioka president. Even with me, they were upset I was born trioka."

"It's similar with some of my neighbors in my Grounded village near Superior Skisland," Blinda added with a sigh. "The idea of a trioka at the top is so new to them, they fear it. They say they have nothing against Irwin, they just feel more comfortable with one of the other dioka candidates, like Denholm. Irwin is definitely behind."

"Isn't Ambassador Irwin coming to speak at SIYT?" Haru asked Alani. "He came to PUAE just a few days ago before winter break started for Gratitude Week."

"Yeah, he's coming in the spring," Alani answered while trying to confirm with her friends. "March, I think. Right?"

Xendo and Raelyn nodded. Philo then nodded after them quickly as if he had actually known that information. Honestly, Philo had been focusing so much on trying to keep up with all his SIYT coursework, he didn't have time for politics.

UNDERWATER GRATITUDE

As Philo tried to fall asleep that night, he wondered what his life would be like back at Mr. Kelly's foster home right now. Tonight was technically Christmas Eve. Philo remembered hearing stories from childhood classmates of holiday meals, gingerbread houses, and cookies for Santa. They all had bright green Christmas trees, stuffed stockings, and tons of Christmas gifts. However, for Philo, Christmas always had bad memories. Several of Philo's foster homes had kicked him out at the end of the year. The orphanages he was sent to during transfers could only afford to give Philo a pair of socks, trinkets from the dollar store, or nothing at all. Mr. Kelly's foster kids told Philo that since Mr. Kelly's wife passed away, they didn't even bother celebrating Christmas.

Philo never realized just how tragic his holiday memories really were until he had escaped them all. *Raelyn, Xendo, and Alani all have it so easy.* Philo thought. *They're so lucky.* As he lay on the ground of Alani's bedroom, he couldn't stop his eyes from shrinking closed to let tears leak down his cheeks. He tried not to make any noise, crying silently to avoid waking his sleeping friends.

The next morning, Philo sat up in shock from a bad childhood dream, waking all his friends with gasps. Philo was damp with sweat and had puffy cheeks from crying as he realized where and *when* he was. However, as he took in the worried faces of his new friends, Philo felt a wave of comfort wash over him and his fright dissolved away.

"I'm sorry," Philo offered up. "Crazy weird nightmare."

"You scared us, Philo," Raelyn breathed as she relaxed.

"Do you wanna talk about it?" Xendo comforted while giving Philo a knowing look.

"No, no," Philo sighed, returning back to normal. "I'm fine, really."

"Well, good! We can't have you feeling down!" Alani cooed as she patted him jovially on the cheek. "Gratitude Week starts today!"

Philo had barely enough time to get dressed before being swept up in all the busy holiday excitement in the Adalaide home. Day one was dedicated to honoring *history*. Junsu and Manoba pulled out their ancient heirlooms and art pieces that had been passed down for generations to show their guests. The entire creative family put on a silly performance to demonstrate the migration of their ancestral history. They

CHAPTER 14

dressed up in traditional East Asian attire from the various mainland countries surrounding Lisoo that they originated from.

Junsu's family had roots mostly in Korea and China before the migration, while Manoba's side of the family stemmed from Japan, Vietnam, and the Philippines. Centuries ago, in the 2280s, their ancestors joined the expansion of artists to build the new underwater civilization that eventually became the Oceanite origin. The family's play shared how Junsu and Manoba fell in love, how each of their grandparents met, and all the exciting cultural traditions their family had passed down over the millennia. Philo, Raelyn, Xendo, and Blinda all loved watching Alani's adorable siblings perform the stories. Alani's parents had taught their children all these important Oceanite traditions so they would never forget the sacrifices their artistic forebears made to safeguard the family's future. To understand where you come from is such a gift. Philo felt a little bit left out, but he had to keep that secret; he'd give anything to know his ancestral history.

The rest of the Gratitude Week brought fun new adventures each day. Day two of Gratitude Week was for honoring *family*. They spent the day together telling funny childhood memories, making snacks, crafting each other thoughtful presents, and playing games.

Day three was dedicated to honoring *the body*. Philo and his friends taught Alani's family basic fighting stances for kineoka, they swam in races in the ocean surrounding Alani's home, and got full-body massages to relax their tired muscles.

Day four was all about the *mind*. They played Oceanite puzzle games, competed in math tournaments, did kineoka meditation, and made homemade art in Manoba's painting studio.

Day five was dedicated to honoring *nature*. The Adalaides helped clean Lisoo's huge water filters with a crew of friendly neighbors. These massive steel filters were secured around the five oceans and collected any possible contaminants from humans or wildlife and burned them as fuel to keep itself consistently powered. Before the waters got too dark at night, Philo and his friends swam around the glowing Apo Coral Reef to revel in its natural beauty.

Day six was devoted to cherishing *community*. They made some Oceanite dried spiced fish to give to Alani's neighbors. In return, they received saltwater taffies and candied kelp. Everyone joined Blinda at Lisoo's hydroponic farm to purchase all the ingredients they would

UNDERWATER GRATITUDE

need for the final big feast tomorrow. At night, the entire town threw a huge talent show with singers, poets, dance groups, comedians, and all different forms of rare talents Philo had never seen. His favorite acts, by far, were when Oceanite drag artists performed on the enormous seashell stage. The drag queens and kings were dressed in over-the-top, glorious costumes. In a single performance, they would lip-sync, do crazy dancing stunts, and make Philo cry with laughter!

Finally, day seven of Gratitude Week, New Year's Eve, was for honoring *the future*. Families traditionally dressed up, made celebratory feasts, and partied until the dawn of New Year's Day. Philo and Xendo put on formal Grounded and Skyborne attire they hadn't worn for school yet. Philo was wearing a green button-up shirt with a slim brown tie and dark emerald blazer. Xendo wore a sunrise yellow dress shirt with a super fashionable patterned gray suit. Philo was sent to get the girls from Alani's bedroom; he knocked on her door.

"Come in!" Alani called out and Philo entered the room. Alani was wearing a festive Oceanite gown that wrapped around her whole body in an ombre of blue and teal shades. She had shiny pearl earrings, a purple agate necklace, and long, winding rings embedded with aquamarine gems on her fingers. Alani was standing behind Raelyn, helping to style her friend's hair in front of the bedroom mirror. Raelyn was wearing an onyx cape with geometric patterns and a white fur collar draped over high-waist slacks, and an aurora-colored blouse. Her Frozen jewelry was made of arctic rainbow spectrolite gems. Raelyn's black hair was in thick, long twists styled artfully to the side. Philo had never seen anyone so beautiful.

"I've been teaching Alani how to do my hair and we wanted something special for the New Year's Eve feast," Raelyn explained to Philo as Alani gently tugged and folded her stunning coiled hair into thick, styled plaits.

"The possibilities are endless," Alani shared eagerly while finishing up a twist that tapered into a thin end, "but we settled on doing asymmetrical goddess braids."

"Growing up, the Winter Thorns taught me how to shape my hair for combat. The council maidens did traditional Frozen updos for events," Raelyn reminisced while supervising Alani's progress in the mirror, "but my favorite designs are the more traditional African hairstyles that my mother taught me, and her mother taught her."

CHAPTER 14

"Queen Semira Arctikon always wore goddess braids like these," Alani mentioned warmly without taking her eyes off of the three strands of hair moving in her hands. "In almost all the Frozen Royal telecasts, she styled them in a new glorious way."

"Yeah, they were her favorite," Raelyn breathed poignantly, remembering her mother. "But it's very hard to do alone. I thought I'd have to do them all by myself at school."

"Nope! Not while I'm here!" Alani interrupted with a braid tug. "Great, I think we're done! Philo, doesn't Raelyn look gorgeous?"

Raelyn swiveled around to show Philo the final design of the goddess braids as Alani put her arm over Raelyn's shoulder. They both giggled when Philo looked nervous and caught off-guard by the question. He would never have the courage to even look at a girl like her in his old time period. She was beyond beautiful, but that was actually the most lackluster part of her shine. What really made Raelyn so extraordinary was that, even though she was a literal princess, she somehow was still proud to be his friend.

"Yeah, she does," Philo responded. That's all he really could put into words. The girls took one last check in the mirror and then followed Philo back out to the dining room.

"Blinda, you have really outdone yourself!" Manoba mused happily as everyone pulled out their cushioned glass chairs to sit down for the gratitude feast.

"I haven't had homemade galbijjim, bulgogi, banchan, and daikon kimchi since my own mother used to make it!" Junsu commented on the Korean food with elation.

"Wow! Osechi Ryori! Blinda, you were able to fit so many colorful little dishes in here!" Alani chirped excitedly, then turned to her friends. "We all share the cute little snacks from this one layered jūbako box! Ancient Japanese New Year's tradition!"

"These gyoza are folded so perfectly and the Rellenong Manok is stuffed beautifully!" Manoba marveled at the Japanese pork dumplings and Filipino meat-stuffed chicken.

"Well, food is my love language," Blinda told the hungry people, all praising her beautiful creations. "We don't always get to choose the family we're given. So, when I have the chance to grow my circle of loved ones, I spoil them with love and happy stomachs. I hope we can all share more dinners as the years go on!"

UNDERWATER GRATITUDE

The adults and teens raised their Oceanite sparkling wines and clinked their glasses together in celebration. The Adalaide family and the four SIYT kids all agreed they should spend their future Gratitude Weeks together, sharing their four families' traditions and customs. Philo nodded along with everyone else to agree, even though he had no idea how he'd even contribute down the line. Each of the well-dressed people at the table stood up to declare what they were most grateful for during 3451 and shared their future goals for 3452.

After dinner, the party guests talked, played games, and danced all night long. When the clock struck midnight, they popped some Champagne and cheered! Blinda poured them each a glass. Philo had never drunk Champagne before, much less underwater! It was so sweet and bubbly. He felt like an adult! Then, much to Philo's surprise, Blinda put the empty Champagne bottle in a cloth bag and smacked it against the table. Everyone cheered again. The bottle shattered into tiny pieces in the bag of fabric. Blinda then reached in, took a piece of the broken bottle, and put it into her mouth! Philo was horrified, but she chewed it as if it were completely normal. When Philo looked at her like she had lost her mind, she leaned in close to him.

"We make the bottles out of sugar now, dear," Blinda whispered to him secretly. She then called out to the room, "Who wants some Champagne candy?"

She passed the bag around and everyone grabbed a piece to taste. It looked like a combination of rock candy and fizzy pop rocks. Philo was nervous it would cut him like glass, but when he put the shard in his mouth, it started to fizzle on his tongue. Philo couldn't believe how good it tasted! It was super sweet, carbonated, and tangy, just like Champagne. Philo eagerly grabbed a few more pieces of the candy as he watched Junsu and Manoba walk around the room to give their kids adorable little smooches on their cheeks. Then the couple came together for a sweet romantic kiss with each other. Just like holiday movies, this festive night felt like a beautiful fantasy.

"It's tradition to give kisses to the people you love and care about most at midnight on New Years' Eve during Gratitude Week," Xendo shared with Philo, turning and staring at him unflinchingly in the eye. Philo caught himself blushing out of nervousness. Xendo didn't seem anxious at all as he slyly smirked. "It's good luck!"

Before Philo could think of something to say, a dancing Alani and

CHAPTER 14

awkwardly swaying Raelyn bumped into them. Philo smelled Raelyn's perfume and was instantly transfixed. Even though she couldn't really dance and seemed to be nervous, she was trying her best to fit in with the party-loving Oceanites. Philo tried to think of something clever to say to impress Raelyn, but Alani reached past him to put her hands on Raelyn's shoulders.

"Raelyn, can I kiss you?" Alani asked. "You're my best friend, I love you, and I couldn't have survived these past few months of school without you!"

"I knew you'd ask me, you dork!" Raelyn chuckled in return, and then she shrugged. "Sure, I'd be honored."

Alani leaned forward and gave Raelyn a small, cute peck on the lips, then they touched their foreheads together. The girls smiled and gave each other a tight hug. Alani exhaled a victorious sigh and turned to Philo and Xendo to give a snarky look.

"I just got to kiss the prettiest girl at SIYT!" she gloated to the boys while Raelyn rolled her eyes. "What can I say, the ladies love me!"

They all laughed. Philo wished he was as carefree as Alani to randomly ask somebody for a kiss. It was so bold and brave! He had never kissed anyone before. Philo was much too shy for anything like that. Soon, Alani's youngest siblings ran up to the girls, who picked them up, and they continued dancing toward the rest of the Adalaides.

Philo looked over to Xendo. They were alone again as a new, peppier song came on. Xendo bobbed his neck back and forth to the music and dashed a big, charming smile toward Philo. His silver, coiffed hair bounced up and down with his dancing shoulders. Xendo breezily lifted his arms up into the air as he grooved. Philo watched a bead of sweat slowly fall down to the jaw of his friend's handsome face. Xendo tilted his head down and his cheeks dimpled into a smile when his sparkling blue eyes connected with Philo's hazel ones. Xendo's gaze momentarily dazzled Philo, making him lose his train of thought again.

Maybe the Champagne candy was beginning to affect him. Philo returned the smile back to the boy as he swayed awkwardly to the music. Xendo nudged Philo as they danced to encourage him, which made Philo laugh. Xendo was always fun, adventurous, and seemed so sure of himself. Philo loved that about him. He was everything Philo wished he could be.

It was shocking just how close they had become in just a couple

UNDERWATER GRATITUDE

of months. Xendo always had Philo's back, even when Philo didn't realize he needed it. Philo never had anyone care about him this much before. It was... hard to get used to. Philo realized in any other period of his life, it would be insanely awkward to be standing with another boy with everyone else kissing all around them. But Xendo never made things feel awkward for Philo. Xendo always made him feel safe. *I'm so lucky he found me,* Philo thought. *He basically rescued me! Gave me a whole new life! Should I thank him for how much he's helped me? Show him how much he means to me?* Philo felt lost on what to say or do as Xendo continued to look endearingly at him.

Blinda came out of nowhere and grabbed Xendo by the face and gave him a huge smooch on his forehead.

"I love you, my son," Blinda cooed to Xendo, clearly enjoying the Champagne.

"Ewww, Mom," Xendo cried out, ending his moment with Philo to wipe his forehead and shudder. "You gotta warn a guy if you're gonna pounce on me like that."

"Better than no kisses at all, mister." Blinda laughed as she leaned in to give Philo a peck on the forehead as well. "Happy New Year, boys. I can't tell you how thankful I am to be sharing Gratitude Week with each of you."

Blinda gave them both a hug with a hiccup. She then pulled Xendo away with her to open another sugar bottle of Champagne.

Every holiday of Philo's childhood was either nonexistent or painful to remember. So, as Philo looked around, it was hard for him to not cry. Blinda popped open the next bottle of Champagne as everyone cheered again. Philo watched as Alani, Raelyn, and Xendo clinked their flutes together and raised them up in the air. They glanced around the room until they found Philo. They beamed with huge smiles and waved him over to come join them.

These wonderful friends will never understand how much they changed Philo's life for the better.

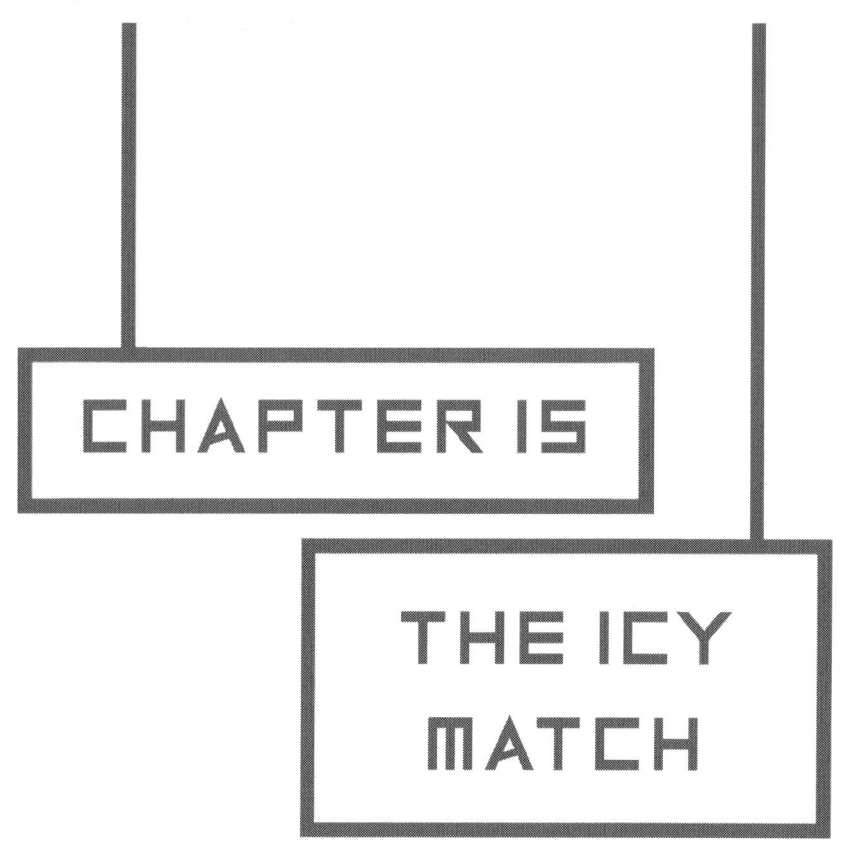

CHAPTER 15
THE ICY MATCH

The magic of the holidays soon transitioned back to Kineoka sparring and challenging SIYT coursework for Philo, Raelyn, Alani, and Xendo. Before they knew it, it was March.

One morning in their Human History course, Professor Edgar Blaise described how Earth's Database came to be. Philo had no idea just how damaging the faulty internet was in his past. Xendo and Blinda had rescued him merely months before his old world descended into chaos.

"What humans always fail to understand about history, is how easily we can be deluded into despising our own people, performing superiority to hide our insecurities," Professor Blaise lectured while coasting around the classroom, "but, when we put ourselves in a superficial hierarchy, the tower inevitably comes crashing down, damaging us all."

Xendo was almost drooling listening to Professor Blaise's rusty, deep voice. Alani noticed Xendo's doe-eyed crush and poked him with her electric pencil.

THE ICY MATCH

"Pull it together, Quaker!" Alani hissed at Xendo.

Xendo sat up, not realizing his dazed affection was so obvious, and then covered his eyes with a little embarrassment as Professor Blaise glanced their way. Philo tried really hard not to laugh.

"The invention of Earth's Database helped the world heal and rebuild after the collapse of The Digital Era. The ED was completed in 2029 by Recollection Computers, Inc. after forty years of trying to perfect its fact-checking algorithm. The new program was backed by the United Nations in order to prevent the spreading of falsehoods and corruption with a more trusted global information resource."

The biggest shock Philo found with Earth's Database was that it could not be abused. Which, in turn, prevented the damages of social comparison, financial swindling, and misinformation from affecting humans for over 1,200 years! Professor Blaise emphasized to their class that *this* was the ED's greatest achievement: that its sanctity was protected.

"Are there any questions the ED can't answer?" Lina Castellano asked, "or a result we can't find?"

"Oh, of course!" Professor Blaise jovially mused. "They are rare because the ED is filled with eons of accurate knowledge. However, nothing in this world is permanent. Answers must be updated once we learn more. There are endless moments in history still yet to explore, and each passing day, humans learn new lessons and create new art! We haven't even come close to solving all the secrets of life's many mysteries. Which is good. Why would we want our quest to end?"

Half an hour later, Philo, Raelyn, Alani, and Xendo left the lecture room and Raelyn pulled up her technoband to read off some messages she missed during class.

"I can't believe him!" Raelyn griped while looking ahead at the fifteenth-floor Skybornes strolling around the corner. "Jasper is driving me insane!"

"His face makes me feel the same way," Alani added casually.

"Jasper told our team he's bringing his rowdy friends to our next match. Ivy and the hench-boys encourage Jasper to show off, which always makes our team mess up and lose."

"Rodger Gorn isn't on your side?" Philo questioned, being supportive. "You'd think he'd want the team to play better."

CHAPTER 15

"No, he just messaged our group giving Jasper permission. Rodger has basically given up as captain since we aren't winning. He doesn't care."

"Jasper is used to doing whatever he wants; his parents spoil him. He's always been this way." Xendo shook his head in annoyance.

"I'm nervous about playing at AMDA this weekend," Raelyn admitted, anxiously. "The team is Frozen, but almost the whole school hates me for deserting them. I think the game might get intense."

"They *are* the best dioka university team," Xendo said under his breath. Raelyn nodded in sad agreement.

"Maybe I should just quit," Raelyn sulked, dropping her head as they walked. "No one even wants me to play."

"Hey!" Alani Adalaide called out, stopping dead in her tracks to turn toward a surprised Raelyn. "Who is this sad sack in front of my face right now? This isn't you, Raelyn. Show those numbskulls who the real leader on your team is!"

"Alani," Raelyn scoffed with a smile, "I am not the staffball captain."

"Not with that attitude you won't be!" Alani shot back, placing her hands on her hips to glare at her friend.

"Yeah!" Philo and Xendo agreed in unison. Raelyn crossed her arms with a chuckle and smirked back.

"What do you suppose I do?" Raelyn asked.

"Stomp into that icy hexagon, wave that toy stick around like only you can do, and show those chumps how a warrior princess kicks major ass!" Alani sassed with so much enthusiasm that Philo's and Xendo's eyebrows raised in giddy surprise.

"Fine…," Raelyn rolled her eyes adorably. "May as well go out with a bang."

"Maybe we can come and cheer you on!" Philo suggested to the group.

"YES!" Alani pointed toward him with big, excited eyes. "Stellar idea, Philo!"

"You guys have time to come all the way to Antarctica with me?" Raelyn perked up, looking around at her friends.

"I will *make* time if you promise to play better than Jasper," Xendo challenged with a raised eyebrow. Raelyn laughed.

"We've only seen your home games so far. We can definitely cheer better than Jasper's sidekicks can," Philo added with growing excite-

THE ICY MATCH

ment.

"I smell a plan formulating," Alani continued. "Should I invite Lina? No, she doesn't like group activities." She then saw Jade and Naomii in the hallway and shouted toward them humorously. "Fellow Oceanites, I require your assistance!"

Jade and Naomii walked over.

"Clear your schedules this weekend! Can you come cheer for Raelyn at her final staffball match at AMDA on Saturday?"

"Oh! That could be educational! I haven't been to Antarctica yet!" Jade reasoned while holding her libe close to her chest.

"Sounds like a YES to me!" Alani cheered and twirled around to point at their other Oceanite classmate. "Naomii?"

"I guess I can't say no, can I?" Naomii replied in her usual odd, distracted tone. "I can't be the downer that stops this journey."

Saturday morning, the students each chose their own solo portal to teleport to Antarctica. The destination menu materialized on the digital wall in front of Philo and he selected *Frozen Origin > West Antarctica > Antarctic Military Defense Academy*. He pressed the submit button and, to his surprise, the ring holding up the holoscreen surrounding him lowered with a snap. As soon as it re-entered the base, Philo was in a brand-new location. He traveled over 20,000 miles to Antarctica in milliseconds.

"Wow!" Philo remarked as his teleportal subsided.

Rhythmic drum music played in the chilly AMDA station that was filled with museum displays of Antarctic rock and taxidermy animals. Smoky dried meats, pungent cheeses, fresh yeasty breads, and savory streaming stews were being eaten around the station. The Frozen locals wore thermal suits with geometric patterns, warm furs, or thick leather coats as they walked outside to the freezing Antarctic landscape.

"Welcome to my Southern home!" Raelyn cooed to her friends with awe-struck faces.

The students bundled up in rented winter wear and stepped to the frigid outside to find what Raelyn called an ice buggy. The winter-white public transport vehicles could hold up to twenty travelers and had wide rounded windows for soaking in the snowy scenery. To Philo's amazement, the ice buggy completely drove itself! No driver was needed.

CHAPTER 15

As they sped across the open Antarctic land toward the AMDA campus, Philo watched endless amounts of snow constantly being swept up by gorgeous gusts of blizzard winds. However, this Antarctica wasn't the same empty wasteland Philo remembered in his early geography textbooks. There were now dark steel buildings and white concrete igloos scattered around the icy hills. Every edifice had thermal solar panels and thick tinted windows to soak in as much sunlight as possible. Philo saw everything from small residential homes for Frozen families, to large community centers, science labs, and office buildings.

"Aren't they damaging all this untouched land?" Philo whispered to Xendo as the girls were chatting on the other side of the transport buggy. Naomii was drawing doodles on the frosted windows.

"Well, I mean, it hasn't been 'untouched' for over 1,500 years now," Xendo quietly responded and then shrugged. "People lived on Antarctica back in your time too, Philo."

"Oh, right," Philo pretended he was aware of that fact.

"They train the world's best athletes and soldiers here," Xendo continued, "but Antarctica is also where some of the most cutting-edge science comes from."

"But… how do they get electricity, gas, and clean water out here?" Philo wondered next, "And what about getting rid of garbage or… waste?"

"Naturally, duh," Xendo said as if it were obvious. "Power is generated from the sun, wind, and flowing ocean water. And they burn waste safely for heat and energy, or use it as fertilizer for sheltered crop gardens like Mom has."

"What? Gross! Why?" Philo responded a bit too loudly. The girls didn't hear them, but Naomii glanced their way in suspicion.

"Open your ED," Xendo whispered out of the corner of his mouth. "Read it all in there."

Philo tapped his technoband to read more about Antarctica's modern advancements as their ice buggy sped to AMDA. He was completely engrossed with what he had missed. Even in his time, scientists adored Antarctica because it was home to rare microscopic organisms that could thrive in frigid temperatures. The scientists on the Antarctic research base built their own ecosystem to live and study on the continent full-time.

After hitting a snow bump, Philo looked up to see a huge, dark

THE ICY MATCH

steel compound surrounded by thick, icy walls four times the height of their buggy. This Frozen fortress was the Antarctic Martial Defense Academy.

As they drove past the various science labs, weapons storage buildings, athletic obstacle courses, and battle arenas of the AMDA campus, Philo was reminded of why the Frozen people were hard as nails. Xendo pointed out a firm line of students jogging in the freezing winds wearing heavy weighted backpacks to build stamina. Philo thought Professor Uma Bryne was tough on them in Kineoka Martial Arts back at SIYT, but now he was grateful they had it so easy.

Raelyn told them she visited all the Antarctic cities near the South Pole as a child on royal diplomatic trips with her parents. However, she hasn't been able to leave the Northern Palace since her mother passed away a few years ago. Philo smiled watching Raelyn beam with pride while sharing old stories of their surroundings.

"That, over there, is the main school building with most of the academic classrooms," Raelyn described to her friends while pointing, "but the AMDA staffball hexagon is over this way."

AMDA's stadium was draped in stark-white banners picturing a black frostbitten fist dripping with icicles. When the ice buggy dropped them off at the front doors, the six friends rushed inside the arena before they could get too cold again. When they entered, a friendly face awaited them.

"Jessica!" Raelyn chirped as she reached to give her teammate a hug. "Sorry we're a little bit late."

"I had to travel here with the boys all by myself." Jessica Boone shook her head, smirking to Raelyn. "You owe me, Princess!"

"I know, I know," Raelyn mused as her guests happily waved hello to Jessica. Naomii did an odd half-bow, half-curtsy. "But if Jasper can bring his rowdy gang, I can bring mine too."

"I'd like to see them try and cheer louder than me!" Alani challenged while crossing her arms confidently.

"Perfect! Our team could use that energy," Jessica Boone approved with a smile as she gestured for the group to follow her.

Jessica was already wearing her bright crimson SIYT staffball uniform, extra padding, and carrying her morphstaff. She led them down the busy stadium hallways toward the main hexagon court. The open arena was huge! Philo craned his neck upward to see giant float-

CHAPTER 15

ing screens showing the six-sided court from all angles. Twinkly holographic lights fell from the ceiling like magic sparkling snow. The crowds were dancing to Frozen music and drinking spiced hot chocolate with flavored marshmallows.

Jessica and Raelyn said goodbye as they headed to their locker room to prepare for the match. Philo and his remaining friends looked for their own bleacher seats in the packed visitors' section of the arena. It was far from the hexagon court down below, but all the hovering holoscreens around the stadium would still show close-up views of the action.

"Oh! For data's sake!" a female voice snarled near them as they walked by. "It's Princess Icicle's motley crew of servants."

Philo and his friends turned to their left to see Ivy Bates, Damian Gomez, and Russell York sitting behind them in the visitor's section as well. Luther sat quietly on their left. As Alani and Xendo sighed in annoyance, Philo watched Ivy roll her eyes and cross her arms. Ivy Bates had a purple stud in her nose, dark red lips, and had the same Skyborne silver-gray hair as Xendo. Philo realized, just now, that barely any people wore makeup in this future, but Ivy's gothic glamour did grant her a powerful dominating presence.

"Why are you nerds here?" Ivy confronted with a raised eyebrow as the taller Skyborne boys backed her up with scowls.

"We're here to watch Raelyn make Jasper's performance look like a six-year-old still doing algebra," Alani retorted with a smile.

"As if!" Ivy scoffed. "The SIYT team doesn't even like Little Miss Icy."

"Jessica does!" Alani shot back defensively. "And, so do we!"

"I meant people that matter…," Ivy trailed off with an evil grin as she looked away from them and back toward the field. Alani breathed in, wanting to hurl one more comeback, but Philo and Xendo just dragged her down the stairs to find seats. Philo locked eyes with Luther. The quiet boy seemed to be apologizing to Philo for Ivy's behavior with his glance. Philo knew Luther was kinder than the rest of Jasper's gang, but he still never stopped them from being cruel.

"Yeah! 'Cause you losers don't matter!" Damian tacked on stupidly as Philo and his friends walked away.

"Dude!" Russel sighed, let down. "I was gonna say that."

Philo's group finally found five empty seats together in one row. Gratefully, they were now out of earshot of the Skyborne bullies. As

THE ICY MATCH

they relaxed in their cushioned seats, Philo noticed that the AMDA helix post in the center of the staffball hexagon was only a double helix, not a triple helix like the one they had at SIYT. Philo's brow scrunched up in confusion as he leaned over to Xendo.

"Why do they only have a double helix, I thought you said staffball was invented by trioka warriors training in kineoka?" Philo asked his friend.

"Ah, that's what we call revisionist history, Philo," Xendo sighed. "The masses appropriate traditional customs, but they always ruin it a bit."

"Just because they're dioka they erased the triple helix?" Philo confirmed, slightly annoyed.

"How can you blame them?" Xendo shrugged while shaking his head. "First they pretended we didn't exist, then they thought we were freaks. They used us as science experiments, and then when trioka got a tiny sliver of equality, they take what we create and make it palatable for their own people."

"That's so unfair," Philo murmured.

"Yeah, most dioka keep forgetting that we contribute so much to the world," Xendo mentioned casually, "but I've given up fighting it."

Philo sighed and then turned his head to notice Naomii staring at a group of Frozen students sitting in the row in front of them. The three friends all had puffy coats, rosy cheeks, and were gawking around the arena like they had never been to their own sports stadium before.

Naomii was analyzing the students with a tilted head and wide eyes and Philo had an uneasy feeling that Naomii was going to bother them somehow. Seconds later, he cringed as Naomii tapped the closest Frozen kid on his shoulder.

"Ummmm, hello?" a pale, chubby boy with freckles turned around. His two female friends also faced Naomii.

"I couldn't help but notice you three seem as out of place as I feel," Naomii postulated airily. "Aren't you AMDA students? Don't you watch sweaty people throwing balls around *all* the time?"

"Oh, they do sweat a lot at AMDA," one of the girls with curly blonde hair and a gem necklace answered, "but we actually go to Antarctic Science University. It's on the eastern side of the continent."

"Yeah, AMDA does most of the athletic and military training," the third slender girl with a half-shaved head added, "and ASU is for the

CHAPTER 15

few of us Frozen who prefer scientific pursuits."

"Oh, wow! How interesting!" Jade joined in. "I'm Jade, and your poker was Naomii. What are you each studying?"

"I'm Charlie. I'm majoring in cultured meat production," the chubby boy answered.

"Danika here. I'm studying to be a solar engineer," the slender girl followed next.

"And I'm Grace. My passion is waste efficiency," the curly-haired girl finished.

"Thank you for all that your school does for helping the planet," Jade offered, as Naomii seemed to lose interest and looked away at something else.

"You're welcome!" Danika responded kindly. "You and your friends must be visitors too; most AMDA students would think it's embarrassing that we enjoy Environmental Science."

"Oh? Then why did you come to the match today?" Philo asked. "Especially if you don't like sports."

"We heard Princess Raelyn Arctikon was coming today!" Charlie replied, beaming. "The South hasn't seen her in ages!"

"We love her!" Grace added on. "We were hoping to even just get a glimpse of her. She's *beyond* mesmerizing!"

Philo and his friends all whipped their heads to look at each other. They all shared huge smiles, except for Naomii, who did not notice or care. If they told these royal superfans that they were Raelyn's actual friends and they all came from SIYT together… how would they react?

"That's funny! We actually know R—," Xendo began before Alani suddenly kicked him in the leg to shut him up.

"We all love her too!" Alani interrupted while putting her arms behind her friends and squeezing their shoulders to secretly quiet them as well. "Do some people *not* support their own princess in the south?"

Grace, Charlie, and Danika all slouched a bit and glanced toward each other.

"Well, some do and some don't," Danika replied.

"*Our* families are loyal to the Arctikons," Grace contributed. "They've done so much for Antarctica over the centuries and helped save the planet from destroying itself."

"But many people felt slighted when the monarchy moved to the North," Danika added. "Some Frozen subjects now refuse to be ruled

THE ICY MATCH

by any trioka. They think Raelyn betrayed her origin by going to that mysterious trioka institute in North America."

"But we don't feel that way!" Charlie urged. "We think Princess Raelyn could help bring us all back together and help the Frozen people be more accepting of trioka."

Alani didn't need to silence her friends now. They knew to keep their mouths shut. They were in a huge crowd of strangers who might hate their trioka guts.

"We're all Oceanite," Alani lied carefully, making sure Xendo's winter hat was covering his silver hair. "I thought the world was beyond all that discrimination?"

"Most of us are," Grace sighed. "We haven't meant any trioka in person before, but we're okay with them; we think they're so unique!"

Alani nodded. The rest of the SIYT students remained silent.

"Yeah! And if Princess Raelyn is trioka, they can't be too bad!" Danika replied.

"Which is why we're here to cheer on her team today," Charlie finished.

Philo had no idea what to say. Luckily, Naomii hadn't blown their cover. He was so glad Alani was quick enough to catch on.

"Well, cool! We support trioka, too," Alani replied carefully. Down below, the Frozen staffball team jogged out from their dugout as the arena full of dioka students leaped to cheer for their team. Alani smiled at the three ASU friends. "It's gonna be an exciting match, that's for sure!"

The Frozen scientist students smiled in reply and turned back around in their seats as the match was about to begin. All the SIYT friends shared glances of concern, wondering if they had missed a chance to defend their identity or dodged a dangerous bullet.

For round one, the AMDA home players would defend first and the SIYT guests would pitch. Rodger, Juo, Pauli, Jessica, Jasper, and Raelyn all took their positions on the hexagon's perimeter in their bright crimson uniforms. They wore small earpieces to communicate with each other across the court while pitching. Philo watched the SIYT players bounce in place, amping themselves up to pitch the white staffball orbs at the goal post.

The AMDA player defending the center helix was a huge, muscular Frozen student named Jeremiah Frost. He wore a stark white

CHAPTER 15

staffball suit with black padding and black combat boots. He held the morphstaff like it was a twig and glared daggers at his opponents. If the entire Frozen team was this intimidating, SIYT was in trouble. Alani stood up to wave toward Raelyn, but the three ASU students in front of them beat her to it.

"Go, Princess Raelyn!" all three shouted in unison with their fists up in the air.

Alani looked back at her friends and gave a surprised expression. She then continued with her own cheer.

"WE LOVE YOU, RAELYN!" Alani shouted with glee at the top of her lungs, then started chanting Raelyn's name over and over again. Philo and Xendo laughed. The boys, Jade, and Naomii got out of their seats to join Alani in waving wildly and shouting support for their friend. They were cheering so loud that the Frozen dioka nearby thought they were all lunatics, but the five friends didn't care. Floating cameras flying around the stadium zoomed in on Raelyn and her image popped up on the largest holoscreen. Philo and the SIYT kids shrieked even more obnoxiously seeing their friend's face amplified. Raelyn didn't wave back at them because she was trying to stay focused on the match; however, Philo noticed Raelyn blush from the adorable support and cracked a grateful smile.

"You've got this, Rae!" Alani squealed to the screen. "Give 'em hell!"

As the match's starting bell rang, all six SIYT team members sprang into action and whipped their white orbs toward the helix. Jeremiah Frost effortlessly batted the six orbs away like he was swatting flies. The SIYT team continued to chuck more and more orbs at super speed to hit the post, but they failed with every throw. It was almost a joke how masterful Jeremiah was at defending.

Raelyn, growing annoyed, stopped throwing orbs for a moment and watched how Jeremiah Frost was using his body. The machine of a man seemed to flow so quickly because he never stopped his momentum of kicking, punching, and blocking the orbs. Raelyn couldn't see any possible openings, but then she slowly turned to glance at Jessica Boone.

Philo watched Raelyn put her hand to her temple to intently whisper into her earpiece while looking across the field. A second later, Jessica Boone also stood completely still. The two were locked in secret

THE ICY MATCH

conversation, communicating from opposite sides of the hexagon. Philo saw Jasper scream into his own earpiece at the girls while continuing his assault of throwing orbs. Juo and Pauli seemed very confused, and now Rodger was shouting at Raelyn as well. The girls were downright ignoring the commands of Jasper and Rodger as the boys continued to pitch. Philo sighed. It was only the first half of round one and SIYT was already arguing!

While Jeremiah kept smacking down all incoming orbs, Raelyn and Jessica nodded toward each other. Raelyn reached down, grabbed a new white staffball orb, wound up, and viscously pelted the glowing orb harder than Philo thought possible. The ball catapulted toward the ground then bounced high up in the air above the helix post. Raelyn completely missed! Most people in the crowd booed and Philo even heard Ivy laugh out loud behind them at the terrible throw.

However, the lobbed orb fell at increasing speed toward the helix post. Jeremiah looked up, unsure of where it would land, while still batting away other oncoming orbs. Jeremiah needed to look up, down, up, down, up, down, as Raelyn's orb barreled toward him from above. Philo got excited; it might work! But the crowd laughed again as the orb landed a few yards away from the goal post.

BUZZZ! The helix post glowed blue! SIYT's first point appeared on the scoreboard! Alani, Xendo, Jade, Naomi, and the Frozen ASU students leaped to their feet and cheered. Jeremiah looked shocked and confused. So did Philo.

"Where did that point come from?" Philo poked Xendo hurriedly. "Raelyn was way off...."

"No! Raelyn's brilliant!" Xendo screamed back over the Frozen crowd's shrieks of disappointment. "Jessica snuck in an orb while the defender was distracted by Raelyn!"

Philo's eyes and mouth widened in glorious realization. He shook his head in beaming disbelief as the stadium holoscreens shared an instant replay of the moment he missed. While Jeremiah watched Raelyn's orb bounce high in the air, Jessica whipped a swift underhanded pitch that smacked the double helix near Jeremiah's feet without him even noticing. Raelyn really *was* a genius! She knew, as the Frozen Princess, the crowd's attention would be on her. Deciding to be the distraction to give her teammate Jessica an opening to score was a sublime strategy.

CHAPTER 15

"WOOHOO!" Philo jumped up to scream at the top of his lungs, "Go SIYT!"

Soon, the first round ended, and SIYT had only gotten the one point. However, their team almost never scored pitching points at their matches so this was a small victory!

"I hope Raelyn defends that well in her round," Xendo leaned over to Philo. "We need her to prove she's better than Jasper and win the match. That's the whole reason why we came!"

"No, we came to support Raelyn, no matter what," Philo chuckled.

"Yeah." Alani poked Xendo. "Deflate your ego, please."

"Right, that's what I meant…," Xendo backtracked with an awkward grin.

"Do you think they still have a shot at winning?" Philo asked their group over the noise of the crowd.

"Not a single chance," Naomii answered flatly, stunning the four others that they were even listening to the conversation.

"Naomii!" Jade playfully nudged her friend as the other three laughed.

"What?" Naomii shrugged. "You may all live in a fantasy world, but I only speak the truth."

Alani was barely paying attention as the intense match progressed. Instead, she started to peer around the stadium. Many of the dioka were visibly outraged at the trioka team as Jasper performed well defending the helix in his round. She noticed some obscene gestures and heard AMDA students start to scream trioka insults like "Triple Freak!" or "Germ!" as Jasper smacked the AMDA team's orbs away. Alani had only ever heard those harsh virus-related terms used in her history books. Alani was getting worried. Since Philo and Xendo were fully engrossed in the match and Naomii was busy ogling the floating action cameras whizzing by, she leaned over to Jade to share her concern.

"The diokas here are much angrier than they are on the skislands or back in the oceans," Alani whispered to her fellow Oceanite.

"I've noticed that, too," Jade muttered back. "Where did they even hear those curse words? Do they not know how disrespectful they are?"

"We can't be the only other trioka in this entire stadium, can we?" Alani fretted as she and Jade inspected the arena again.

Half of the cantankerous crowd was shouting in anger not only at Jasper, but the entire SIYT team. This was getting a little bit out of

THE ICY MATCH

control.

"Gross! Who even let these infectious Germs in our stadium in the first place?" Alani heard a gruff dioka boy complain to his jock friend.

"No more Germs!" the athletic friend screamed, trying to start a chant. "No more Germs! No more Germs! No more Germs!"

As other crowd members joined in the chanting. Jade and Alani wondered if they should grab the rest of their friends and escape the stands. Then, a familiar angry voice started yelling behind them.

"You idiots! Trioka are more evolved than you in every conceivable way!" Ivy Bates screamed at the chanting dioka in the visitor's section.

Alani's face went white with fear as she turned to watch Ivy, Russell, and Damian converge on the chanters in the stands. Luther trailed behind them fretting. Before Alani even grasped what was happening, it already went too far.

"You pathetic dioka should be extinct!" Russell threatened as Damian sucker-punched one of the AMDA students right in the face, knocking him over. The strong dioka athletes yelled at the Skybornes and some tried to punch Damian and Russell back.

Alani looked at Philo and Xendo. They were so engrossed in Jasper's defensive round that they had no clue what was happening around them.

"We have a situation." Alani tapped the boys. "The Skybornes are arguing with the dioka."

"What's new about that? Ivy's always picking fights," Xendo squashed her comment without looking away from the game. "Raelyn's up next, she has to try and hit a pitcher to do better than Jasper!"

"Xendo! Don't ignore me," Alani demanded as Philo turned to see the brawl. "We can't have SIYT students acting like *that* at other schools."

"Let's go help," Philo agreed, standing up and dragging Xendo from his staffball trance.

"This is why you're my favorite," Alani thanked Philo as they moved up the stadium steps. Jade and Naomii followed behind. They winced as an AMDA student punched Russell square in the jaw, but it didn't seem to affect Russell's thick skull.

"Don't even waste your time," Ivy pulled her burly boys back from the fray. She turned to ridicule the dioka students, "Trioka are

CHAPTER 15

smarter, stronger, and better than any of you!"

Philo and his friends passed Luther to step behind Ivy, Damian, and Russell.

"If you're so perfect, why do you freaks still have the virus in your blood, huh?" an AMDA boy that Damian had elbowed yelled at Ivy, clutching his bloody nose.

"Haven't you Neanderthals ever read the ED?" Ivy laughed with maniacal pity, "Our ancestors evolved *from* fighting the virus, your kind couldn't handle it. We're twice as strong now!"

"Stop trying to spread your sickness to the rest of us!" a Frozen girl in the AMDA crowd screamed at them. Philo and his friends knew this needed to end.

"Hey! Hey! Everyone, quiet down!" Alani screeched. "Stop fighting!"

"Get lost, losers!" Ivy cut Alani off, waving her away.

"Ivy, you're just proving them right," Xendo intervened. "We can't stoop to a lower level."

"Oh! So, we're beneath you?" The angry AMDA dioka turned to Xendo. "Are you all Germs too?"

"That's not what he meant," Philo tried to back his friend up.

"You all should just leave!" the Frozen girl pushed. "Go back to your school in the sky and leave u—"

DING! The alarm bell rang, interrupting the argument and signifying the end of the SIYT's final defensive round. Everyone in the crowd turned to witness the final score. SIYT still only had one point while AMDA scored three. SIYT had lost the match.

"Damn it!" Ivy cursed as the AMDA section cheered.

As the AMDA students jumped up and down, Philo, Alani, and Xendo looked at Ivy, who just rolled her eyes. She grabbed Damian and Russel and stomped off to find Jasper and head back to SIYT.

"Sorry, I wish they didn't do things like that," Luther quietly admitted to Philo and his friends as he turned to leave too.

"Why do you hang out with them?" Xendo asked, annoyed.

"They're awful," Alani cautioned, "even to you."

"Stay with us," Philo offered to Luther. "You're not like them."

"I can't be with you all," Luther sighed and dropped his head. "Jasper is my oldest friend, I don't want him to be upset with me."

Luther left to follow Ivy and the henchboys. Philo sighed and shared a sad look with his friends, grateful they were nothing like

THE ICY MATCH

the Skybornes. As the group walked back down to their seats, they bumped into the nerdy ASU students.

"Oh! We were just coming up to defend you guys against those AMDA kids," Charlie told the group of SIYT students.

"You were?" Alani asked, surprised.

"We're sorry the Frozen students acted deranged like that," Grace mentioned. "We don't all think like them."

"We didn't realize you five were trioka earlier on," Danika stated sheepishly. "We probably should've guessed."

"That's all right," Alani offered, finally relaxing. "We didn't tell you, either."

"Our whole mission in life is to make the planet a better place," Grace added.

"And that means for *everyone*," Danika finished. Alani and Xendo grinned.

"Well, now you three can say you actually *do* have some trioka friends," Philo responded with a smile.

"Oh, Yeah? Wonderful!" Charlie beamed as the ASU girls nodded.

"Since you actually go to SIYT…," Danika pondered, "do you know if Princess Raelyn is locked away in a special part of the school to be tutored alone, or does she actually mingle with regular people?"

"Oh my! I haven't even thought of that!" Grace's eyes widened in wonder. "Have any of you ever actually gotten to talk with her?"

Philo, Alani, Xendo, Jade, and Naomii all looked at each other with sneaky smiles. They weren't exactly sure how to break the news to the royal loyalists.

"Do they actually get to talk to *who* now?" someone replied behind the Frozen students.

Raelyn Arctikon, who was still dressed in her badass SIYT staffball uniform, walked into their group conversation. She put her arms around Alani and Xendo and smiled at the new strangers gawking at her. The ASU students were starstruck.

"Well, we lost again!" Raelyn took a deep sigh and looked back and forth to each of her friends. "The staffball season is over, but I did play the best I have ever played because I could hear you maniacs screaming all the way from up here. So, thanks for that."

Raelyn's friends laughed. The three ASU kids stood like dumbfounded penguins, watching the Frozen princess in front of them. Al-

CHAPTER 15

ani laid her head lovingly against Raelyn's cheek as Xendo patted her arm around his shoulder. Philo gave Raelyn a fist bump.

"Look! We made some new dioka friends." Alani gestured to the flabbergasted Frozen teenagers, pointing them out to her roommate. The ASU students gasped.

"Um, hi. Nice to meet you three," the princess stretched her hand to her awkward fans. "I'm Raelyn."

Danika and Grace squealed with joy. Charlie fainted and fell to the floor.

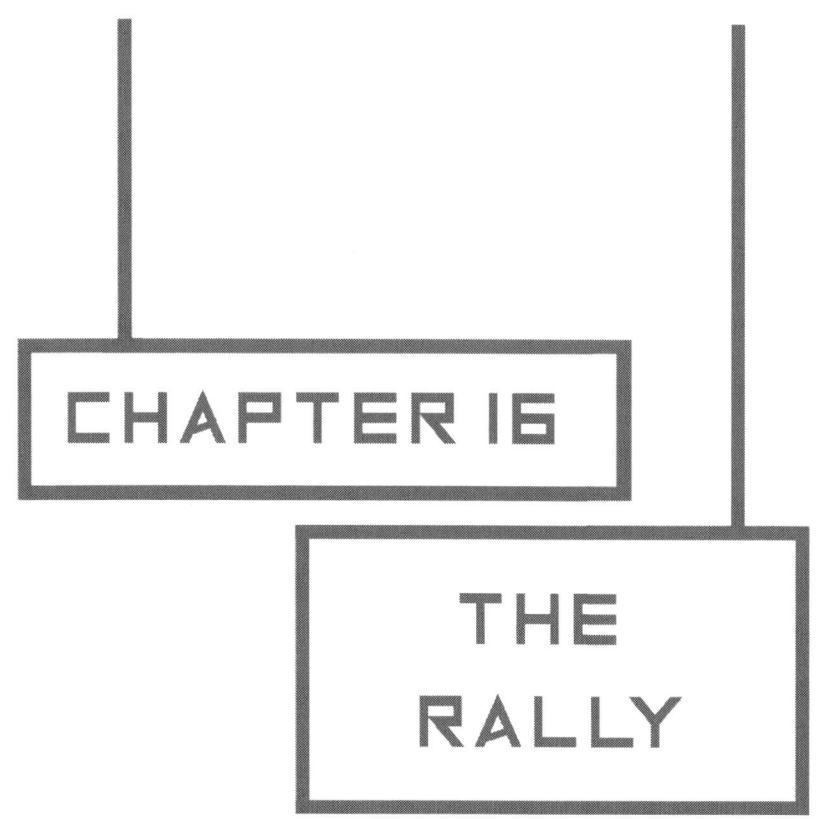

CHAPTER 16
THE RALLY

As April approached, the excitement around the upcoming global election was growing to full force. The morning of Ambassador Irwin's special rally at SIYT, Philo woke up early, made his bed, and picked up some food before Xendo even woke up for the day.

"I brought you some breakfast." Philo entered their dorm room as Xendo changed into his SIYT uniform.

"Oh, perfect. I slept in!" Xendo thanked, rushing to put on his pants. "We gotta find seats before all the good spots are taken!"

"The girls saved us some, let's go!" Philo handed Xendo his breakfast in SIYT's reusable containers.

"Oh! You got my favorite!" Xendo beamed as they jogged out the door.

"You order this almost every day!" Philo laughed.

Indeed, Xendo loved having toasted bread with various spreads and veggie toppings with one of Blinda's probiotic fruity yogurt drinks. Every day in the Continuum Café, there was a huge salad bar full of fresh veggies grown from Blinda's garden as well as homemade condiments to personalize their meals. Today, Philo added sliced avocado, pickled jardinière vegetables, sprouts, and red chili flakes to his

CHAPTER 16

friend's two pieces of breakfast toast.

Philo laughed as Xendo moaned in pleasure taking bites of his food while they hustled down the school hallways. He also got his friend one of his favorite yogurt drink flavors: strawberry. Xendo realized Philo was quickly growing to know him surprisingly well. He never had anyone like that besides his mother.

As the boys entered the auditorium, they noticed there were more SIYT security guards around the auditorium than Philo had ever seen on campus. The ambassador's staff must have requested more support during the busy event. Raelyn and Alani waved over to them.

"Awesome! They got us great seats!" Xendo chirped as he downed the last of his drink and followed Philo to meet their friends.

Philo was pleased to see Jade and Naomii in their row, and strangely, Lina Castellano and Luther Wyatt also sat chatting with Raelyn and Alani. Lina usually kept to herself and didn't hang out with anyone, even her roommate Ivy. Philo did know Lina enjoyed talking with Alani and was a great kineoka fighter, but she didn't speak much in their classes. If she did, it was always a blunt addition to the conversation. She seemed content strutting her own path in training to become a historical agent.

Luther Wyatt, on the other hand, was always trailing behind Jasper and his gang. He seemed desperate to be their friend, but also terrified of them. Xendo told Philo that Luther and Jasper had been stuck near each other since birth because their fathers worked together. Philo thought Luther was kind and had wanted to coax him into their friend group, but it was almost like Jasper wouldn't allow Luther to make other friends. Philo and Luther would often nod at each other as a quiet hello, but they barely said any words to each other.

"Hey, everyone!" Philo greeted the group. "Big crowd for Irwin, right?"

"Yeah, people are really excited." Alani smiled back.

"Some more than others," Lina replied curtly. "Ivy thinks Irwin has it in the bag and it's *tacky* that we're out here with his dioka fans."

"Same with Jasper," Luther nodded nervously, looking around as if Jasper would somehow spot him. "He says his dad already has assurances that Irwin will win, so there isn't any point mingling with all the visitors coming to SIYT for his rally."

"Is that why you left him to come here?" Philo asked Luther.

THE RALLY

"Yeah," Luther Wyatt replied softly. "I just needed a break from him."

"Well, you are always welcome to hang out with all of us," Philo offered. "We wouldn't make fun of you like Jasper always does."

"Yeah, we'd just make fun of Jasper to you," Xendo laughed from the side.

"That might be good for me," Luther smiled sheepishly, "and I really want Irwin to win. The world needs him."

"We also have some other guests here," Raelyn mentioned with a poke to Xendo and Philo.

"Oh? Who would that be?" Xendo looked around, puzzled.

Alani leaned back to reveal the group of strangers in their row.

"Oh wow! Hi, guys!" Philo vocalized, fully shocked. "You came all this way?"

Danika, Charlie, and Grace nodded eagerly on the other side of Alani. Philo hadn't recognized the dioka Antarctic Science University students without their Frozen snow pants, puffy bright jackets, and rosy cheeks. They all wore slim, geometric, temperature-regulating body suits like Raelyn sometimes wore.

"We teleported here last night, stayed at the Superior Inn, and were first in line to get in the auditorium four hours ago," Charlie beamed, eyes bright with glee.

"They screamed when they saw Raelyn and asked to sit with us," Alani mentioned, raising eyebrows at the boys. Philo chuckled while Xendo nodded in comprehension.

"We wanted to support Ambassador Irwin's campaign," Grace added cheerfully, "but who knew we'd actually get to sit with *the* Princess Raelyn!"

"You did climb over some seats to hunt us down," Alani replied with a feigned smile.

"Fair point," Danika admitted. "We are trying to keep calm. All this trioka history around us is so amazing!"

"Well, I'm glad you three came all this way," Raelyn gracefully thanked them. "It means a lot to me to have more Frozen friends supporting Ambassador Irwin's presidential bid. We need all the help we can get."

The three ASU students inhaled sharply and looked at each other with a giddy rush of pleasure, mouthing to each other silently, "She just called us *friends!*"

CHAPTER 16

Cheers erupted from the crowd. Philo and his row of friends looked forward as Daryl Irwin strode onto the scarlet stage. His staff and security stood behind him in the wings. Daryl Irwin's secretary, a svelte middle-aged woman with long, black hair was passing out pamphlets to the SIYT professors behind the podium. Superintendent Pearl whispered a couple last words that made Daryl Irwin laugh before he stepped to the microphone.

"Students of SIYT, I am so pleased to meet you all today!" Ambassador Irwin proclaimed as the audience bellowed with applause. "I never tire from returning to this incredible institution. So much potential in this room!"

Philo caught himself smiling at the ambassador's charm without even realizing it.

"I am here, today, to talk about our *future*, the future of our planet. But to truly strategize for what we have next to build, we must honor what we have left behind. Earth has taken too many centuries to finally unite together in our shared humanity. The world was not always as peaceful as we maintain it now. Eons ago, petty squabbles held us back from realizing we all desire the same freedoms in life. Some of our very ancestors believed that you can only obtain liberty if you steal it from those around you, that you won't be abused if you abuse others first. However, these were all lies told to them by a fearful world that stamped out their individual gifts that could inspire evolution. If only we knew then that expanding the dinner table doesn't mean you will go hungry. Planting diverse seeds provides a shared harvest for us all."

Philo looked around the huge auditorium. All the trioka students were nodding in agreement.

"No origin, no country, and no person can ever live peacefully if they pull others down to climb higher themselves. Taking advantage of others inevitably leads to your victims praying for your downfall. However, if we build a just society that protects the entire community, we all float with the rising tide to higher ground. Today, we take our Global Government, technology, and factual information for granted. I have traveled to a time where truth was manipulated. The people felt lost and confused. One of the other candidates in this election, Duke Denholm, wants to bring back these loose structures to our world. We cannot let that happen. As your next president, I promise to—"

A booming gunshot made Philo jump in his seat. Ambassador Ir-

THE RALLY

win winced in pain and clutched his right shoulder as blood oozed between his fingers. Dead silence hit the room as the shocked crowd watched Ambassador Irwin crumble to the stage floor. Superintendent Pearl shot to her feet, deployed her morphstaff, and scanned the auditorium. Philo had no idea what was happening.

A second gunshot exploded as a bullet hit the stage floor inches away from Ambassador Irwin's head. Irwin reflexively covered his skull with his bloody arms in fear. The entire auditorium erupted with thousands of screams. Philo peered over to meet eyes with Xendo; his friend had pure fright and confusion on his face. *Someone's trying to shoot the ambassador.*

Another gunshot was fired. Superintendent Pearl lunged forward with her staff to swat away the lightning-fast bullet from hitting Irwin. It fell to the ground, smoking.

"WILLIAM!" Superintendent Pearl bellowed with a grunt.

Professor Ruiz scrunched his brow to focus, raised his hands, and the morphstaff in his lap suddenly de-morphed from its long triple helix shape into glowing blue dust. It expanded around the entire crimson stage to create a growing psychic barrier. Three booming bullets hit the expanding force field and bounced off. Pearl tracked where the shooter was hiding.

"UMA!" Pearl yelled, pointing up high to the very back of the auditorium. "The Skyborne rafters. Go!"

Without a second thought, Professor Uma Bryne leaped off the stage with her morphstaff like a hound on a hunt and barreled toward the stairs. Philo looked back to where he once sat during Primary Advancement. There was a masked man dressed in dark gray military camouflage holding a sniper rifle. Philo's eyes widened. The nervous, elderly Professor Plimkit performed some emergency first aid on Ambassador's Irwin's bloody shoulder with a medical kit attached to the stage. Superintendent Pearl scurried to the microphone.

"Everyone remain calm, and get on the ground!" Superintendent Pearl commanded the audience. Philo's group immediately tucked in front of their auditorium seats and got as low to the ground as possible. In the rafters, Philo saw Professor Uma Bryne throwing morphed daggers at the intruder as he turned to shoot toward her.

"How'd she already get up there?" Alani whispered in shock. Philo watched Professor Bryne masterfully deflect all the attacker's bullets

CHAPTER 16

as she narrowed in on him on the balcony.

More gunshots fired from new locations in the gigantic chamber, causing more terrified screams from the crowds. Everyone looked in different directions as they realized there wasn't just one shooter. Philo noticed at least four masked men standing in dark gray camo gear in all different parts of the auditorium.

Wailing SIYT students and dioka visitors pushed each other out of the way to escape their seats. Superintendent Pearl huffed on stage as the crowd ignored her safety orders. Pearl morphed her staff into an archer's bow and fired glowing green arrows toward each shooter.

"We've gotta get out of here!" Alani screamed to her friends over the pandemonium. Behind her, Lina, Naomii, Jade, and Luther were crouched and frightened. The ASU girls, Danika and Grace, were fretting, and Charlie was frozen in shock. The noise of gunshots and screaming people was deafening.

"But Pearl said to stay down!" Philo dissented to Alani, Raelyn, and Xendo. Another thunderous round of bullets fired off. All four friends huddled closer together, covering their heads.

"That was before all hell broke loose!" Xendo yelled back to Philo. Jade screamed as a bullet hit the balcony over her head, making debris fall down near her and Luther. She grabbed onto Naomii for support.

"We need better cover! Now!" Raelyn decided, taking charge. She glanced back at Jade, Naomii, Lina, and Luther behind her. The three ASU students looked at Raelyn as their last hope. Philo felt Raelyn slip her hand into his. He felt shivers travel up his spine. She placed Philo's hand into Xendo's.

"Everyone link up!" Raelyn called out to the rest of their group. "On the count of three, we *all* dash to the exit. Stay low. Stay together. Meet back at floor thirteen!"

Philo, Alani, Xendo, and the others nodded in unison. Shot after shot from the gunmen continued at a deafening volume as Pearl's green arrows whizzed after the attackers. Xendo squeezed Philo's hand tight as they looked at each other. Somehow that tiny gesture made Philo's stomach flip. He had never been in so much danger. Since he was closest to the aisle's exit, Philo realized he'd have to lead his friends out of the auditorium.

"ONE!" their row chanted together. "TWO." They all braced for the leap. "THREE!"

THE RALLY

The SIYT and ASU students crouched low on their feet and trailed behind Philo as he led them out of their row. The attackers weren't shooting into the actual crowds; the scary men in dark camouflage only assaulted the stage. *Why would they want to kill Ambassador Irwin?*

As Philo pulled his friends out of their row, frantically escaping guests swarmed the main aisle. Philo stayed low and held tight onto Xendo's hand. Another bullet fired. This one was so ear-splitting, Philo couldn't stop his head from looking toward the noise. When he turned to his left, Philo locked eyes with one of the shooters not far from them. He was just a boy, barely older than they were! Philo was terrified. The attacker seemed surprised for a second before a menacing scowl returned to his freckled face. He pointed the gun toward Philo. Philo felt his muscles go limp as the shooter stared him down.

"The princess is down here!" the young shooter yelled up to his fellow attackers. Philo whipped his head around to see Raelyn crouched directly beside him. The shooter didn't want to suddenly kill Philo. *He had his eyes on Raelyn.*

"Nooo!" Philo bellowed.

The shooter started running toward them, assault rifle in tow.

"Go! Go! Go!" Raelyn screamed in desperation to her friends. "Go now! He's getting closer!"

Raelyn had tears welling on her cheeks as if she knew this was coming. Philo, Alani, and Xendo were petrified with panic, but Raelyn pushed them to keep moving. All four of them tripped, dropping each other's hands. The stampede of escaping Irwin supporters banged into Philo and knocked him down to the dirty floor. The mob of screaming people blocked the light from above and all Philo could sense were dark legs about to step on him. As he stumbled to his feet, Philo was carried away like a fish failing to swim upstream. Yet another bullet was fired and a student wailed in pain nearby. *Was Raelyn shot?* Philo wriggled within the pandemonium and craned his neck to find his friends, but Philo couldn't spot them anywhere. No Xendo, no Raelyn, no Alani. He couldn't even find the Frozen ASU students. Philo felt completely alone in the sea of strangers.

The swarm shoved Philo through the tight doorway of the auditorium exit. Without the walls holding them in anymore, the screaming crowd dispersed into the wider SIYT hallways. The trioka students ran back to their dorms and the dioka visitors bolted to the teleportals to

CHAPTER 16

escape campus. Philo backed up against the corridor wall outside and heaved in shock. Suddenly, Lina Castellano popped out from the same doorway. The drove of escapees knocked her onto her back near Philo. Lina was shaking with fright as Philo helped her up.

"Did you see anything?" Philo questioned her right away. "Where are the others?"

"They're still stuck back there!" Lina wailed. "It's a madhouse! I got pushed out!"

"We have to go back in!" Philo fretted. "We have to make sure everyone else is safe!"

"Screw everyone else!" Lina cried, pushing Philo off of her. "I'm not going back in there!"

"What?" Philo was stunned. "They're our friends!"

"No, they're *your* friends!" Lina pointed at him as she turned to hide in her dorm. "Not mine!"

"How can you say that?" Philo hollered as she ran away. Lina stopped for a split-second, and looked back at him.

"Sometimes you can only protect yourself, Philo," Lina fretted, completely drained. She took off out of sight.

Philo kicked the wall behind him. *How could Lina just leave? It was so selfish!* But maybe she was right. Could he actually do anything to help? Philo had no idea what was going on. *Should I leave too?* Just when he finally was happy with his miserable life, *of course* something had to mess it up! Death, tragedy, and mayhem followed him wherever he went! It was *his fault* the shooter saw his friends in the first place. It was *his fault* they could be hurt back there! If he went back now, would he just make things worse? Maybe Philo was better off alone. At least then, he couldn't screw his friends' lives up even more.

"Philo!" a voice called out. As more of the crowd passed by him, Philo saw Xendo! Next to him on the ground was Alani, they were the only two to find each other in the stampede. Philo ran to his friends and gave them a huge hug on the ground. Xendo squeezed him back. Philo was grateful he hadn't run away.

"Raelyn!" Alani screamed as their royal friend trailed out of the doorway, separating from the mass of escapees. Raelyn was frantically looking around for them.

"Oh, good. You're safe!" she panted, swiftly approaching them as the crowds continued to leak out of the auditorium.

THE RALLY

"Are you okay?" Alani reached out to her. "I was worried he shot you!"

"Damn it. *I'm* fine!" Raelyn lamented, "Why is everyone always worried about how I am? Charlie jumped in front of me and got shot in the leg! We're trying to carry him out now. Come help!"

"We can't go back in there!" Xendo replied in horror. "The teachers should handle it!"

"We have to," Alani reacted, getting up on her feet. "Our friends need help."

"Are you sure? Can we really do anything?" Xendo questioned as Raelyn stepped closer to him.

"If they die, and we do nothing, we're going to regret it for the rest of our lives." Raelyn pressed her finger on Xendo's chest sternly. "*Trust me*, I've made this mistake before."

"I'm coming," Alani agreed, moving next to Raelyn, who nodded.

"C'mon!" Raelyn urged the boys, "We need your help to get them out!"

Xendo looked to Philo for guidance. Philo felt every cell in his body tell him to run away to safety, but the last thing Philo wanted was more regrets.

"Let's go!" Philo decided.

The four friends pushed through the screaming stragglers leaving the assembly hall. They crouched behind the first seated section to gauge what was still going on in the chaotic chamber. Everything was happening so fast. Professor Ruiz's force field was still holding strong on the stage. Irwin was hurt and had Plimkit fussing over him. Two of the shooters were laying on the ground in pain with glowing green arrows in their chests, having been immobilized by Superintendent Pearl. Much of the ambassador's security team were racing around looking for shooters that were trying to escape.

Alani gasped and pointed. The young shooter who ambushed them was now fist fighting with Luther, Jade, and Naomii. His rifle had been flung a few yards away. Behind them, Danika and Grace struggled to carry a bleeding Charlie toward the exit. As the young shooter brawled with their friends, he still searched for Raelyn, annoyed he had lost sight of her.

Suddenly, a white rope-like projectile flew from above them and wrapped around the shooter. The young man grunted as he tumbled to the ground, unable to move in the restraints. Philo and his friends looked behind them in the rafters. Standing there with her morphstaff

CHAPTER 16

blazing a blinding white was Professor Uma Bryne. In her arms, she was lugging the first shooter who she had knocked out.

The room finally fell silent. Philo and his friends kept nervously peering around the room for more secret shooters. They cautiously stood up, wanting to help their friends carry Charlie to the medical wing. However, before they even took two steps, Philo put his arms out to stop Raelyn, Alani, and Xendo. The disabled shooter on the ground was laughing, of all things. A small metallic canister fell out of the shooter's pocket as he wriggled around in his restraints. It bounced out a few paces and exploded.

A thick, orange-colored gas discharged from the object and surged to fill the air near their friends. Luther, Jade, and Naomii started coughing within a second. Danika, Grace, and Charlie violently wheezed and clutched their throats.

Philo watched in horror as they all collapsed to the ground, unconscious.

CHAPTER 17

A HAZARDOUS THREAT RETURNS

A complete blur of depressing chaos ensued as the cloud of orange gas dispersed into the air around the shooter. Stray guests close enough to the poisoned friends also wheezed and passed out onto the floor. Raelyn wanted to barge over to the scene to help, but Alani pulled her back. They had no idea if being even this distance could poison them as well.

Philo glanced over to Raelyn and noticed she wasn't really looking at their friends, she was studying the shooter on the ground. He lay just as motionless as his group of twenty victims. Raelyn scanned the chamber searching for any remaining gray soldiers. She had both a confused fear in her eyes and a fire of contempt. The stage's force field faded away, as the SIYT professors realized the gunshots had stopped. Philo, Raelyn, Alani, and Xendo, unsure of what to do, called the adults for help.

"Stay there! Don't move!" Superintendent Pearl commanded, hearing Philo and his friends from the stage. "Cover your mouths and nose! Mortha, go test the air."

Philo and his friends lifted their SIYT suits over the bottom half of their faces. Now that Professor Plimkit had bandaged up Ambassador Irwin, she unfolded a techy, sealed gas mask from the med kit and

CHAPTER 17

put it over her face. She grabbed some testing gadgets and slowly approached the area of the auditorium where the toxin was released. Philo was surprised the elderly trioka professor was this agile. She wasn't as frail as he had assumed.

Plimkit, now standing over the depleted gas canister on the ground, pulled out a small tube-like gadget that sucked in air where the gas once billowed. The tiny vacuum beeped, and she read its message. Plimkit gestured to the room that the nearby air molecules had returned to safe levels, but the students were still poisoned. Superintendent Pearl rushed to whisper with Ambassador Irwin and issued assignments to her staff. The surrounding professors and campaign officials nodded, taking their orders.

Superintendent Pearl sent over SIYT's security team to carry the wounded students—and even the young shooter—to the medical wing at the school. The remaining security members rounded up the intruders that Pearl had shot with arrows to send to law enforcement. Before leaving with Daryl Irwin to the medical wing, Superintendent Pearl whispered to a burly security guard and gestured to Raelyn. The guard hurriedly walked over to Philo and his friends.

"Are they alive?" Alani pleaded. "Let us know what happened!"

"The superintendent has requested I escort you back to your dorms," the beefy security guard responded stoically. "This predicament is no longer of your concern."

"It's not *our* concern?" Raelyn questioned firmly. "They attacked us, too."

"Your Highness, you will be safest back in your dorm. A larger team will come to guard you, but for now, I will protec—"

"I do *not* need protection," Raelyn stopped him, surprised with her own volume. "We need answers. How did OMNI get into SIYT?"

Philo looked at Raelyn with a confused face. *What is OMNI? What does she mean?*

"OMNI?" Xendo gasped in shock. "It can't! How did—"

"No more talking," the guard interrupted. He peered around as if more attackers were hidden. "Please. It is for your own safety."

Philo and his friends reluctantly agreed to stay silent as they were ushered back to the thirteenth floor. While passing through the emptied hallways, Philo saw Alani, Xendo, and Raelyn exchanging worried glances, as if they knew something he didn't. When they entered their

A HAZARDOUS THREAT RETURNS

lounge, the guard turned to speak to Philo and Xendo.

"Gentleman, please return to your room and stay there. Superintendent Pearl will soon be giving a school-wide announcement and you must remain in your dorms."

"No, we're staying with our friends," Philo responded before he could stop himself.

"Yeah!" Xendo agreed. "We're not splitting up again!"

"That goes against my direct instructions from the superintendent," the guard stated, a bit less assured this time.

"No one knows what's going on!" Alani pushed, while Raelyn seemed deep in concentration. "We need support from each other, our friends were just poisoned!"

"The boys are coming with us," Raelyn anxiously spoke up.

"I cannot sanction that." The guard shook his head. Raelyn lifted up her chin.

"You are Frozen, correct? Trained at AMDA?" Raelyn quietly questioned the guard, breathing in, raising her chest.

"Yes, Your Highness. Born Frozen in Atwell, Antarctica. Elite Forces at AMDA," the guard replied, squaring his shoulders. "Loyal to the crown. *We do not melt*."

"Then you *will* let the boys sequester with us in my room," Raelyn asserted. She had a slight quiver in her raising voice. "That's an order!"

The guard paused, unsure of what to do. He seemed like he wanted to reject their complaints once more, but then sighed and bowed at the waist.

"As you wish, Your Highness," he replied, looking down at the floor while bowing, then returning Raelyn's gaze. She nodded solemnly.

Alani opened their dorm and the four friends hastily packed into the girls' room before the guard could change his mind. Raelyn locked the door behind her. Alani immediately tapped her technoband on her wrist to start playing some current Oceanite pop music so the guard couldn't hear them talking. Raelyn leaned back against their wall and released a deep sigh of relief.

"I've never done that before," Raelyn admitted, growing embarrassed, "using the whole 'royal order' move."

"Yeah, it shocked us, too," Alani replied as the boys nodded.

"Something's up if OMNI's here," Raelyn whispered to them. She seemed to be tossing a thousand thoughts around her brain. "I knew if

CHAPTER 17

we were all separated, the guards would take me away."

"It can't be OMNI, they've been gone for centuries," Xendo replied worriedly.

"What aren't you telling us, Raelyn?" Alani asked with concern. "We're here to support you, but the whole world will freak out if it was them."

"It's OMNI, I know it," Raelyn whispered through gritted teeth. "That's all I can say."

"What the hell is OMNI?" Philo finally questioned, utterly perplexed.

Raelyn and Alani looked at Philo, wide-eyed and open-mouthed, as if he had just fallen to Earth from Mars and slapped them. Xendo sighed and glared at Philo with eyebrows raised.

"Oh, should I have known that?" Philo let out by mistake, then covered his mouth in surprise. He looked to his roommate. Xendo smacked his forehead and groaned.

"What is up with you two?" Alani proclaimed, fully irked, putting her hands on her hips. "Are all three of you hiding secrets from me?"

"No!" the boys both shouted too quickly.

"It is weird. You guys do whisper all the time...," Raelyn stated, taking an uneasy step backward. All four friends squared off and looked back and forth at each other cautiously.

"Why can't we trust you? What are you hiding?" Alani asked Philo directly. He turned away. Philo was so angry at himself. Lying to the girls was spiraling out of control. Hiding his true self was destroying the only life he ever wanted.

"ATTENTION STUDENTS OF SIYT!" Superintendent Pearl's loud voice was suddenly broadcast from the speakers of the thirteenth-floor lounge. Philo, Raelyn, Alani, and Xendo all stopped squinting at each other with distrust to listen to the blaring announcement, "At this time, we must request that you all stay in your dorms. The school is going on lockdown. As you are all aware, SIYT has been infiltrated by radicals seeking to harm the Global Presidential Candidate, Daryl Irwin. We do not yet know the identity of the violent intruders, but somehow they were able to illegally bypass SIYT's physical and technological securities with unregulated personal teleportal rings.

"All known intruders have been apprehended and sent to Antarctica's prison facilities, but we believe more individuals of the radical

A HAZARDOUS THREAT RETURNS

group might still be hidden within the buildings on campus. These individuals are violent, dangerous, and equipped with crude firearms. To prevent further harm, this lockdown is mandatory and all platinum doors to each floor have been locked. Only your professors and SIYT's security will be able to unlock them. While these measures may worry you, they are for your protection. SIYT staff will stop at nothing to defend you all. Please remain calm."

"Damn it!" Raelyn cursed as she started pacing back and forth, upset to be locked in their dorm. She put her head in her hands. Her mind was reeling with a million different things at once. Philo was confused. *Why wouldn't Raelyn want to have more protection?*

"I also regret to inform you that a second, biohazard attack by the intruders has been released in the auditorium. The hazardous gas travels through the air, so all ventilation at SIYT has been turned off as a precaution. Professor Plimkit is speedily working on an antidote, but the toxin does appear to be deadly. The infected individuals are being cared for now but are in critical condition and unresponsive. Again, we ask you to remain in the dorms to prevent further incidents while the threats are neutralized. All the SIYT staff and security will protect you. Updates will come in due time. Be safe."

"The patients are unresponsive?" Alani worried. "That's a really bad sign."

"We better hope that Plimkit can make an antidote, fast!" Xendo responded.

"So much is going on all at once," Philo fretted.

Raelyn, no longer pacing, sat on her bed in stoic silence. She stared at the dorm door with the SIYT security guard on the other side. Suddenly, all four of their technobands beeped. Raelyn snapped out of her daze and the four friends looked at each other. Without tapping them to activate, their technobands all released a small holoscreen with an image on it. Technobands didn't do this by themselves! On the image was a statement written with white letters on a dark gray camouflage-patterned background

CHAPTER 17

> **WE ARE OMNIPOTENCE**
>
> WE HAVE LIVED IN THE SHADOWS SINCE THE BEGINNING OF CIVILIZATION, MAINTAINING ORDER AND SUPPRESSING UNDESIRABLES. WITHOUT US, MODERN LIFE COULD NOT HAVE EXISTED. TODAY'S ATTACK WAS JUST A WARNING. IF THE TREACHEROUS DARYL IRWIN IS ELECTED, MORE ATTACKS SHALL OCCUR UNTIL ALL "TRIOKA" ABOMINATIONS ARE WIPED OUT. WE WILL NOT BE REPLACED!
>
> **JOIN US IN PREVENTING THE ENEMY'S TAKEOVER!**

Philo, Raelyn, Alani, and Xendo all read the words and glanced at each other with terrified looks.

"I need to go to the medical wing and talk to that OMNI shooter," Raelyn whispered out of the blue.

Her three friends' mouths fell agape, shocked to hear her insane utterance.

"Are you out of your mind?" Xendo let out. "You're their second target!"

"I think someone needs a nap," Alani joked, a bit concerned about her friend.

"Raelyn, we're stuck in here," Philo reasoned. "There's a guard outside."

Raelyn looked over to the door. She seemed determined.

"I don't know how much time we have," she whispered distantly. "The other attackers are already gone. What if they take the sick one away, too?"

"Good!" Alani yelped. "Get that skinny little villain out of here!"

"No, he might have some info I need!" Raelyn confessed.

"Raelyn? You can tell us what's going on," Philo tried comforting her. Raelyn turned to her distressed classmates.

"I need you three to help me break out of here first," Raelyn challenged. "Help me get down to the medical wing, and I'll tell you everything."

A HAZARDOUS THREAT RETURNS

"But why?" Xendo argued. "Everyone is already being treated by medical professionals. We can't do anything useful."

"I can't stay locked in here and do nothing," Raelyn assured. "I'm going whether you all come or not."

Philo, Alani, and Xendo shared apprehensive expressions. Raelyn was beyond serious. If they didn't help her, she'd try to barrel through the locked platinum doors herself. Philo decided if he wanted Raelyn and Alani to really trust him again, secrets aside, he was going to have to prove he was their real friend first.

"I'll help you," Philo assured her. "Whatever you need."

"Fine," Xendo agreed. "We may as well put all this kineoka training into action."

"And if we're already down there, maybe we can help Plimkit save our poisoned friends, too," Alani chimed in.

Raelyn exhaled with a slight smile, returning a bit back to normal. She held out her fist in the center of their standing square, "In this together?"

Philo, Alani, and Xendo bumped their fists in the center against Raelyn's.

"Together!" The three responded with nods and building energy.

"Let's be like actual continuum agents," Xendo breathed in. "What's our plan?"

"To go down to the medical wing, so I can talk to that shooter before he dies," Raelyn started off.

"Right. I mean *how* do we actually do that?" Xendo reiterated.

"First, we have to get past that huge security guard," Philo reminded them. Raelyn nodded in agreement.

"By doing what?" Alani whispered, leaning in. "Like... *killing* him?"

"No!" Raelyn groaned, throwing up her arms. "Let's figure something else out."

The SIYT security guard had now waited outside the princess's dorm door for over an hour. The broadcast and OMNI alert unnerved him as well. He expected more guards to come help defend the thirteenth floor, but so far no support had arrived. The massive man suddenly heard the ongoing girlish pop music turn off behind him in the princess's room. A knocking noise sounded from the opposite side of the door. He guessed that meant the princess and her precocious

CHAPTER 17

friends wanted to speak with him.

"Princess?" the guard beckoned through the wooden material. He heard footsteps moving around the room inside.

"Hello, sir." Philo smiled as he opened the door, greeting the watchman.

"Is something wrong?" the guard asked. "You knocked for me?"

"Yes, we were wondering if you could guard us from inside the room? The princess would feel more comfortable that way," Xendo graciously mused.

"Oh?" the guard naively beamed, "but I thought she—"

"We were rude to you earlier because we were so stressed with everything going on," Raelyn played along. "We wanted to apologize and thank you for your service."

"Your Highness, I'm truly honored," the guard stepped into the room.

"You must be really overwhelmed; this is a tough job for you," Philo tacked on as he gestured to Alani's stool for the burly guard to sit down.

Alani, who now had a little bit of paint on her fingers, came over to the security guard holding a canvas.

"Also, this week I've been working on a painting of Antarctica for our wall and figured you may have some advice, since you've lived at the South Pole longer than Raelyn has," Alani kindly explained as she showed him an unfinished acrylic canvas.

"Alani is such a talented artist," Philo explained to the guard.

The painting showed a dark night sky filled with shining stars and a stunning array of Aurora Australis lights reflecting down onto the snowy flatlands of Antarctica. In the center was a small silhouette of a man next to a campfire looking up at the shooting stars above him. The layers of folding rainbow lights were famous down at the south pole.

"I'm trying to add details to the village below," Alani explained. "What would you add?"

"Well, it's already beautiful!" the guard breathed. "But that man wouldn't be alone, he'd be with some family and friends roasting food over the fire. And the Festival lights should be brighter."

Philo, Raelyn, Alani, and Xendo all looked toward each other. He was taking the bait like a fish to hook.

"Thanks! Raelyn has told us so many stories about her Aurora Festivals," Alani breezily mentioned as she turned to grab some tubes of

A HAZARDOUS THREAT RETURNS

acrylic paint from her side of the room. "To make the lights sparkle brighter, I'll add some more glitter."

The guard looked up with a big grin as Alani walked back toward him holding paints and her canister of glitter. Without warning, Alani yelped as she tripped on her wrinkled rug. The guard gasped and Philo, Raelyn, and Xendo all acted surprised. As Alani dramatically tumbled to the ground, she squeezed her paint tubes and let the container of glitter fly out of her grasp. The colorful art materials doused the beefy guard's face and torso, getting into his open eyes and mouth. The guard grunted in shock as the pain of stinging blindness hit him and he tasted the bitter acrylics on his tongue. As Alani hit the floor, the guard's big hands instinctively rubbed his eyes, making the mess even worse.

"Ptui! It's in my eyes!" the guard screamed and spat in disgust with his glittery, sticky tongue flopping about.

While the guard was distracted, the boys leaped into action. Philo jumped up to grab the earpiece out of the tall guard's ear, and Xendo used Alani's crafting scissors to cut off the SIYT encrypted access key from the guard's belt. Raelyn immediately played into the chaos.

"Oh no! Alani!" Raelyn gushed loudly, feigning embarrassment. "Look what you did! It's such a mess!"

"URGH! I am so, so, so sorry, Mr. Giant Guard Man, sir," Alani apologized profusely as she and her friends gave each other quick, hidden, fist bumps. "I am complete trash and so clumsy!"

The guard continued to grunt, spit out paint, and rub the mess all over his face. He couldn't help but stumble about the room in disorder as the four friends dodged around him, avoiding his path.

"Philo! Go get the nice guard some water to wash out his eyes!" Raelyn called out, "Xendo, go get him a towel!"

However, the boys didn't have to go anywhere. They were both already holding a bucket of water and towel from the girl's shared bathroom. They placed both near the stool for the guard to use after they were already long gone. Alani got up to her feet, not at all hurt or messy from her stumble. Philo snuck over to open the dorm door, silently. Raelyn waved for Alani and Xendo to come follow them.

"Don't worry, sir, the boys will be back with a towel in just a second!" Alani fibbed as she placed an apology note she had written on her end table.

CHAPTER 17

Hi!
Sorry for throwing glitter in your face!
...Princesses are so wild these days, huh?

Anyhoo! I hope you still liked the painting!
...please don't beat me up, BYE!

- Alani Adalaide <3

The four friends exited the dormitory and locked the guard inside.

"I hate us for doing that," Raelyn groaned as they scurried through the empty thirteenth floor lounge.

"I don't!" Xendo admitted. "I've never felt more *alive!*"

The guard's earpiece was buzzing in Philo's pocket so he put it in his own ear to listen. The four students dashed to the skytube to take them down to the SIYT medical wing, but a platinum wall blocked the exit. This was the first time the massive metal door was fully down and locked. Xendo pulled out the guard's encrypted access key to place near the door's magnetic sensor to read.

"If this doesn't work, we're *so* expelled," Alani mumbled. However, a small clicking noise went off and the magnetic sensor beeped a green color. The platinum door shot into the ceiling, granting them passage through.

"Yes!" Raelyn pumped her fist in victory as they walked over to the skytube.

Philo stepped with his friends into the white skytube but was quiet as he listened to the conversations happening in the earpiece. Xendo

A HAZARDOUS THREAT RETURNS

kept blabbing about how exhilarating this all was.

"Shhh!" Philo put a hand on his shoulder.

"What are you hearing?" Raelyn asked him, still in mission mode.

"The patients are still unresponsive," Philo informed them. "They're in a coma and need breathing tubes."

"Oh! How terrible!" Alani fussed. "Plimkit hasn't made an antidote yet?"

"What about the shooter?" Raelyn pushed. "Is he still alive?"

Philo paused as he listened a bit more. His eyes widened in worry.

"Plimkit keeps reaching dead ends, the guards are saying." Philo passed along. "The dioka are all worse off than the trioka students. They haven't mentioned the shooter."

"He's dioka, so my guess is not good," Xendo breathed.

"We have got to go now, before it's too late!" Raelyn pushed the button on the skytube to take them down to the first floor.

"It's Superintendent Pearl! On the coms!" Philo gasped, listening harder. Raelyn, Alani, and Xendo all turned to each other nervously.

"She's telling the guards that if Professor Plimkit can't get an antidote in time to counteract the toxin, all the patients will die," Philo relayed to them. "She's telling staff to call the patients' families to come in case the worst happens."

"Oh my data," Alani gulped in a sorrowful panic. "How much time do they have?"

"Pearl estimates they only have six hours...," Philo finished and looked at his friends with distress. Alani, Raelyn, and Xendo all breathed somberly in the skytube's chamber. If Raelyn was going to break the rules and interrogate the shooter, she needed her friends to back her up now more than ever. The mounting pressure of this hazardous countdown meant they couldn't afford any mistakes. The four friends turned forward as the doors closed and the skytube descended.

They only had six hours to rescue their friends and the boy who tried to kill them.

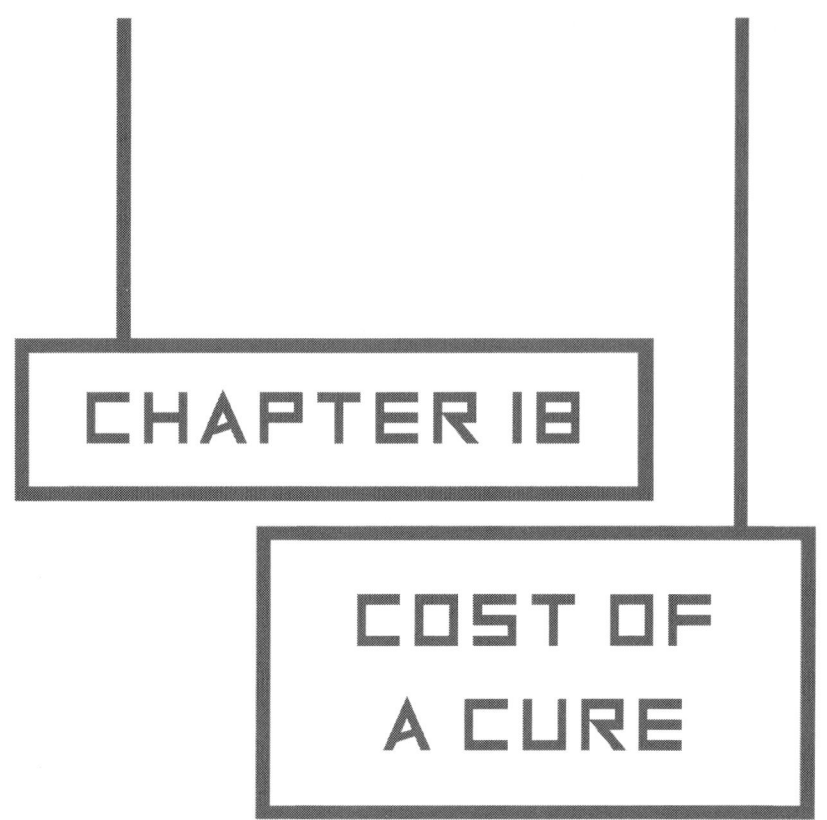

CHAPTER 18

COST OF A CURE

Philo, Raelyn, Alani, and Xendo raced down the first-floor corridors toward the hospital wing. They peered around each corner to ensure they were not ambushed by Omnipotence radicals or SIYT security. Philo tried to stay brave like Raelyn, but he did *not* want to be shot at ever again. They were still just first-years; their kineoka wasn't strong enough to stop a bullet.

They approached the medical bay, which had its platinum door shut, locking them out. Xendo pulled out the stolen access key to use again.

"Get ready to get yelled at," Alani sighed with a chuckle.

The platinum door retracted itself, and the first-years stepped inside the hospital room. The chambers reminded Philo of a hectic scene from a medical drama. Machines were blinking and the wounded rally attendees were sick on cushioned beds. Nurses in crimson-colored scrubs frantically buzzed around bandaging up the shooting survivors or typing information into floating holoscreens.

In the furthest back corner lay Ambassador Daryl Irwin and the poisoned patients, with some of SIYT's teaching staff standing around

COST OF A CURE

them. Philo saw Jade, Naomii, Luther, the ASU dioka students, and even the red-haired shooter lying motionless in their beds. Daryl Irwin, whose whole right shoulder was wrapped in thick bandages, was the only patient who was awake. He seemed to be focusing more on conversing with Superintendent Pearl and his aides than actually worrying about his own health. He was speaking firmly with Pearl about how they should best protect the school and alert the public. He wanted to get up and be proactive, but his staff kept urging him to rest.

The poisoned teens were so still Philo wasn't sure if they were even breathing anymore. Between Jade and Naomii's hospital beds stood Professor Plimkit. She hastily mixed vials of chemical powders and colored liquids together over a futuristic burner while speaking with other nurses. The professor was in her late seventies and walked around like a nervous snail; however, Philo was impressed at how Professor Plimkit pushed forward to brew the antidote. Plimkit went back and forth drawing blood from the poisoned patients as well as getting DNA and TNA samples. So much was going on in the small medical chamber that Philo hadn't seen Superintendent Pearl turn around to look at him and his intruding friends.

"Princess Arctikon? Miss Adalaide? Boys?" Superintendent Pearl questioned them, "How did you four get down here? You are supposed to be staying safe in your dorms!"

"Oh, long story…," Xendo began as the four friends stumbled to explain themselves.

"It's all my fault, Superintendent, you see—," Raelyn added.

"We just wanted to help—," Philo offered.

"The guard really was easy to take down—," Alani got in, before the superintendent raised her voice.

"You four cannot be in here," she interrupted firmly, turning to two of the SIYT security guards. "Please escort the children back to—"

"Wait!" Raelyn pushed forward. Everyone in the room turned to her. She sighed. "I just need to talk to him!"

Raelyn pointed to the young shooter in the corner of the room. He was not only passed out, but surrounded by SIYT guards carrying morphstaffs in case the attacker got violent again.

"Nobody can speak to any of the patients because they are in an unconscious state," Professor Plimkit warned, looking up from her antidote creation with her lab goggles askew. "Their bodies are struggling

CHAPTER 18

to survive. We only have a few hours to save them."

"Then let us help you!" Alani pleaded.

"We can be an extra pair of hands," Philo offered.

"No, we cannot risk more students getting injured," Superintendent Pearl replied without an ounce of indication she'd change her mind. "We have armed intruders still at large on campus. Back to your dorms, now."

Just as the four friends were about to object again, the huge platinum door of the medical wing opened up behind them. The SIYT guards immediately deployed their morphstaffs and pointed them toward the door. The superintendent jumped in front of Philo, Raelyn, Alani, and Xendo, blocking them from view of the doorway.

However, instead of more masked mercenaries, in walked Professor Uma Bryne, Professor Ruiz, and more SIYT security. The superintendent relaxed her stance and the guards blocking the patients lowered their weapons.

"Uma, what's the update?" Superintendent Pearl asked the kineoka master.

"We've searched the entire grounds of SIYT," Professor Bryne began with a displeased grunt . "Any remaining Omnipotence loyalists have escaped."

"They only had a quick window to attack the ambassador," Professor Ruiz continued from his floating hoverchair. "Without their cover of surprise, they realized they were outmatched."

"I don't trust a premature retreat," Superintendent Pearl responded, furrowing her brow in thought. "Are we certain Omnipotence won't return with larger numbers to withdraw their fallen enforcer here?"

Everyone looked to the red-headed shooter, poisoned and deathly motionless on the hospital bed. Philo breathed through his nose in worry. He didn't even consider the violent terrorist group would actually come into the medical wing itself.

"Possibly, if they think he has sensitive information. However, they have abandoned their other wounded minions," Bryne spat in disgust, "knowing they'd either die in action or be taken to prison."

"Let's leave nothing to chance," Superintendent Pearl decided. "Let's defend for the worst."

"General Grayda has requested you teleport to the South Antarctic Prison to help her interrogate the two shooters we were able to appre-

| COST OF A CURE |

hend," Professor Ruiz passed on. "They may have more details about the assassination plot."

"Yes. I must go," she agreed, checking her technoband. "William, you remain here to guard the medical wing. Uma, take your security team and guard all the entrances."

Professors Bryne and Ruiz nodded. Uma Bryne waved at the team of SIYT security she had been leading and they followed her back out the platinum door exit. Professor Ruiz floated his chair around as the superintendent turned to address the room.

"Mortha, how much longer do you estimate before the toxin's effects are irreversible?" Pearl asked Professor Plimkit, who was still mixing a possible antidote.

"Five hours...," Plimkit replied with a strained sigh. "Possibly four for the dioka."

"Affirmative." Superintendent Pearl nodded quickly like a commanding officer. "Keep working. Ambassador, are you able to travel with me to the AMDA prison?"

"I am," confirmed the ambassador. "We must assure the public that a terrorist attack like this will not go without rebuke."

"Take it easy," one of the nurses gently warned as the ambassador removed the blankets covering his robotic legs and slowly moved to stand up on his metallic feet. If Daryl Irwin had been a normal dioka man, his shoulder wound would have taken up to a month to heal. However, Irwin's bandage over his shoulder was no longer bleeding, even if he still winced. His small team of campaign staff fluttered nervously around him as he took a step away from the bed.

"A simple graze wound from a bullet is like a kitten's scratch after you've had your legs blown off," the ambassador grunted as he faced the superintendent. "Let's decipher what OMNI is planning. After the interrogation, we must update President Kanosha."

"General Grayda informed us that the President has already arrived by teleport to the prison," Professor Ruiz mentioned. "She is waiting for you both to provide your accounts of the attack."

"Thank you, William," Superintendent Pearl responded. She turned to face Daryl Irwin. "Let's go to my office; we can use SIYT's internal teleporter to head to Antarctica."

The superintendent turned on the thick gold heels of her dark maroon suit and led the way toward the exit of the medical wing. Irwin

CHAPTER 18

trailed behind, followed by his fretting campaign staff.

"Children, you come as well," Superintendent Pearl mentioned to Philo and his friends leading the way out the door. "The guards will drop you off at your rooms."

"I cannot go yet," Raelyn urged adamantly.

"Let us help out!" Alani pushed next. "We can't rest until we know they're safe!"

"Professor Ruiz is here; he's a kineoka master!" Xendo added.

"We're probably safer here than with that one guard upstairs!" Philo reasoned.

Superintendent Pearl shook her head in response. She was about to put her foot down again, when Daryl Irwin chuckled and placed his free hand on Pearl's shoulder.

"Let them stay, Nova," supported Daryl Irwin, shocking Philo and his friends. "After all, this is how great continuum agents are made, by being tested."

"They're first-years, Daryl, they wou—," Pearl turned to him in surprise.

"So were Daniel and Jerome when they broke into your office as a prank," Daryl quipped back with a cheeky grin. "You never punished them for being clever enough to get through your passcodes."

Xendo and Philo gasped silently and snuck a look at each other. *Their dads broke rules too?*

"Fine," Pearl ended the conversation. "Any misbehaving and you four will be banned from becoming agents—"

"I will watch over the students, Nova," Professor Ruiz promised from down below the steps. Superintendent Pearl grunted in acquiescence.

"Call me immediately if any danger arises," she ordered him. Professor Ruiz nodded solemnly.

The superintendent turned back toward the door and led her guards, Ambassador Irwin, and his campaign team out the platinum door of the medical wing. As Philo and his friends followed Professor Ruiz back to the patients, Philo looked over to their fellow sick SIYT friends. Sitting near their beds was a woman with sleek dark hair in a professional blouse and skirt. It was Irwin's dutiful secretary. She was almost always at her boss's side. Philo tilted his head in confusion.

"Why is she still here?" Philo whispered to Xendo, "Why didn't

COST OF A CURE

she go with Ambassador Irwin?"

"That's Bianca Wyatt, Luther's mom," Xendo responded as if it were obvious.

"What?" Philo questioned, shocked he never noticed.

"Yeah, she can be a parent and have a job, Philo," Xendo shrugged as they got to work in the stressful hospital.

For the next hour, Philo, Raelyn, Alani, and Xendo helped the SIYT nursing staff take care of the injured shooting survivors and their poisoned friends. Plimkit mixed blood samples from the patients to test with strains of the antidote.

Raelyn spent an odd amount of time around the OMNI shooter. Philo wondered what she was so desperate to discover from this young man who tried to kill her. Raelyn anxiously monitored his levels and studied his freckled face with disgust. Philo was unsure if Raelyn was longing for the shooter to recover or if she planned to finish him off herself.

They now had only three hours left and the poisoned patients just looked worse and worse. Philo was getting nervous. Jade and Naomii's breathing was so sparse he couldn't see their chests move. They were melting with sweat and all the color was draining from their faces. They looked like zombie versions of their normal lively selves.

Philo looked over to Luther, who was in the same perilous state. His mother held his hand and periodically peered around the room with her tear-soaked eyes, praying that someone would have an ounce of good news, to no avail. She'd whisper sweet things in Luther's ear to remind him that she loved him, no matter what happened.

The triokas' afflictions were nothing compared to how sickly the diokas were becoming. When Philo would dry the faces of Charlie, Danika, and Grace, he couldn't help but feel hopeless. Their skin was turning a mucus-green color and seemed to be breaking out in allergic rashes. It all looked so painful.

Suddenly, Philo heard a gasp from Professor Plimkit at her lab station. Professor Ruiz, Philo, and his friends went over to her straight away.

"I think I have found a possible formula for the toxin's cure," Professor Plimkit informed with hesitation.

"Yes! That's great!" Alani yipped, shaking Xendo next to her.

CHAPTER 18

"Who should we prepare first?" Raelyn asked. Professor Plimkit looked at the five of them with a worried expression.

"Why do you say *possible* formula, Mortha?" Professor William Ruiz questioned.

"The toxin released a very complex and volatile combination of chemicals into the patients' bloodstreams," Professor Plimkit explained while removing her lab goggles. "Deciphering each of them was almost impossible. The antidote could neutralize all the foreign irritants and counterbalance their blood's pH to return to normal levels," Professor Plimkit informed. "Or, if just one isotope bonds incorrectly, it could make their toxin spread at triple speed, most likely killing them."

"Oh dear," Professor Ruiz sighed and rubbed his forehead.

"Are there any other formulas that might be safer?" Xendo asked.

"I'm out of supplies in this lab and this antidote alone took hours to perfect," Professor Plimkit reasoned, looking up at the clock. "We may not have time for other options."

"Test it!" a woman's voice called behind them. It was Luther's mother. "We can't just sit here and do nothing."

"Mrs. Wyatt…, do we have your permission to test the antidote on your son?" Plimkit asked cautiously. "I have no guarantee of the outcome."

Mrs. Wyatt's face flooded with anxious dread. She took a deep breath and dropped her chin in worry. She looked to her son lying motionless in the bed next to her. She squeezed Luther's hand and got no response back.

"Yes, I need to know we did all we possibly could before time runs out," Mrs. Wyatt responded solemnly.

Professor Plimkit nodded and prepared their antidote. The potion was made of a purple liquid, thick as heavy cream. She walked back over to Luther and his mother with the filled syringe.

"Wait!" Raelyn called out in desperation. Everyone side-stepped and turned to look her way, surprised. "Can we test it on the OMNI shooter instead?"

Everyone's mouths fell open, shocked with her cruel and perilous suggestion.

"I can't ask his permission to do so," Plimkit reasoned with the syringe in her hand.

"He tried to kill us," Xendo yelled out. "He's lucky we're even

COST OF A CURE

trying to save him!"

"Why should Luther risk getting sicker?" Philo added. "Luther is innocent in all of this!"

"Do the intruder first, Mortha," Professor Ruiz stated, taking the burden of the final decision onto himself.

Plimkit nodded with a deep sigh and moved to the motionless OMNI shooter tied down in his hospital bed. Everyone watched as Professor Plimkit gently inserted the syringe's needle into the shooter's blood vessel and administered the antidote into his system. They all held their breath. Nothing seemed to change, not for better, not for worse.

Soon, the boy's heart rate began to rise. His rosy inflamed rashes started to fade, and his greenish skin returned to its normal pale color. Alani nudged Philo and Xendo and gave them a hopeful expression. Philo looked over to Raelyn who, again, looked conflicted. She seemed pleased that he wasn't gone just yet, but angry that he was no longer suffering. Plimkit was dabbing more perspiration off of the OMNI shooter's chest and face when his eyes suddenly shot open with shock. Plimkit gasped as everyone else took a step back. The shooter winced in pain as he looked with worry around the strange room. His confusion then switched to anger. The young man struggled with the metallic restraints pinning down his limbs and thrashed about when he couldn't escape.

"Who the hell are you people?" the boy bellowed at them. "Where am I?"

"You are at the Superior Institute of Young Trioka," Plimkit calmly responded.

"Where is my team?" the boy complained. "Get me outta here!"

"We're just trying to heal you." Plimkit urged him to relax as she studied which symptoms faded and which remained.

"Don't touch me, Germ! I don't want to catch whatever you have!" the deranged boy spat at Plimkit's feet as if he was the victim here.

"Hey! You already poisoned yourself!" Alani interjected.

Raelyn's fists clenched in frustration as the shooter ignored Alani to scowl at the princess.

"I wish I had shot you instead of that fat kid!" the boy barked at Raelyn from his restraints. "I'd be a *hero* if you were dead."

"Well, you missed!" Raelyn scolded back. "Who else was here

CHAPTER 18

from Omnipotence?"

"I'm not telling you anything," the shooter snarled. "They'll be back for me soon. You'll all die for this!"

Raelyn broke from the crowd to approach the crazed OMNI boy.

"What's your name?" Raelyn demanded. "Tell us now!"

"It doesn't matter," the boy cursed. "I'll be gone soon."

Raelyn was upset he wasn't answering her questions. She pointed a furious finger toward the shooter's freckled face.

"Who killed my mother?" Raelyn screamed at him. "Which OMNI knight murdered Queen Semira Arctikon? I know OMNI did it!"

The boy stayed silent and glared back at her. The air was filled with chilling tension as thick as frost. Raelyn huffed in anger.

"Tell me. Now," Raelyn forcibly urged. "I need a name!"

"Your family will be *replaced* soon," the boy muttered with gritted teeth.

Raelyn lunged toward him. Philo and Xendo grabbed her shoulders to hold her back. She struggled in their grasp, reaching to kick or scratch the shooter. Professor Ruiz threw his hands in the air.

"SILENCE!" Professor Ruiz demanded from his floating chair nearby. He moved closer to the shooter and closed his eyes to focus. The kineoka master began to meditate.

"I don't have to listen to any of you," the shooter spat.

Professor Ruiz's carbon cube and morphstaff started to glow bright blue. The square-shaped genetic mark on Ruiz's arm illuminated as he reached out a hand toward the boy's forehead.

"Don't touch me, you decrepit old Germ!" the shooter screamed, terrified and disgusted. He leaned away to escape the touch of Professor Ruiz as a mystical blue aura grew around them.

"What freak magic is this?" the boy shrieked.

As soon as Professor Ruiz calmly touched the angry boy's forehead, the yelling stopped. The room was silent again. The shooter's tightened, scared posture relaxed back into its neutral position and his eyes became a cloudy white. Professor Ruiz had put the shooter in some sort of trance. Philo's eyes widened as he marveled at Ruiz's kineoka powers. While straining to hold his mental focus, Professor Ruiz took a long, deep breath.

"Now ask your questions, young Princess," Professor Ruiz voiced to Raelyn. "May his truth offer you peace."

COST OF A CURE

Philo, Alani, and Xendo let go of Raelyn as she stepped forward. Raelyn cleared her throat, looking at the boy who wanted her dead.

"What is your name?" Raelyn asked slowly with a sturdy face. The boy seemed to be resisting whatever words wanted to escape his lips, fighting his own brain.

"V… V… Vik…." The boy was strong. Professor Ruiz pressed harder on the shooter's forehead.

"Viktor Dimo," the shooter finally confessed. The entire room glanced around at each other to see if that unknown name would somehow hold meaning to the Frozen Princess.

"Viktor Dimo," Raelyn began, "who murdered Semira Arctikon?"

The boy resisted Professor Ruiz's powers again. The shooter seemed to be both peaceful and in excruciating pain.

"Viktor Dimo," Raelyn repeated, raising her voice slightly, "which Omnipotence knight murdered the Queen of the Frozen?"

"I… I… I do not know," the shooter released in a huge exhale of energy.

If it was impossible for the boy to lie, the young shooter was useless in finding the answer Raelyn craved. The princess now felt uncertain and disorganized.

"Why don't you know?" Raelyn demanded, "You are one of them!"

"The palace attacks were before my time…," the boy revealed like a broken robot. "Omnipotence knights always use code names…. I am only a squire."

"Who would know? Is there someone who was there?" Raelyn stepped closer to the shooter, crouching down, looking into his dead eyes. "Do you know anything that's useful?"

"I know *one* person," the boy let go with a small wince. "I only know *one* name."

"Tell me," Raelyn coaxed him again. The boy was still trying to repel the kineoka magic and keep his mouth shut, but he was losing his resistance.

"Omnipotence hates traitors. They'll kill me…," revealed the young shooter as tears fell down his cheek. "I'm scared."

Even though this damaged person in front of them was hell-bent on killing them only a few hours ago, Philo now just saw a weeping child. He felt sorry for him. Raelyn sighed with heartache, but remained persistent.

"I need a name," she urged, "any name."

CHAPTER 18

"Judd... Stemson," the boy exhaled faintly. "That's all I know."

"Judd Stemson?" Raelyn repeated to herself, hundreds more questions arose on her face.

The shooter was losing all his energy. He couldn't keep himself from losing focus, but none of this was from the kineoka trance. The boy's head was drooping. Alani started to fret.

"Professor, something is happening to him!" Alani interrupted, tapping Plimkit on the shoulder as the medical historian took notes on her floating holoscreen.

"He's slipping out of consciousness again," Professor Plimkit informed as she raced back to her lab station. "I may need to give him a second dose."

Philo and his friends backed away to give her more space. Raelyn was still locked in thought. Professor Ruiz opened his eyes and all the blue light faded away. Professor Plimkit inserted the syringe's needle into the shooters left arm again.

"The antidote seems to either be fading too quickly or the virus is mutating within the patient's bloodstream," Plimkit observed as she pushed a second round of the purple cure into his system.

Immediately, the shooter's face returned to a sickly green and he convulsed on the table. Plimkit cursed as the shooter foamed at the mouth. Philo and his friends looked away from the disturbing sight. Professor Plimkit dashed to get IV fluid to try and replace all the moisture he was losing. However, by the time she got back, the shooter had a blank look on his face, vomit all over his chest, and had stopped moving. The heart rate monitor rang a dull chime as his heart rate flatlined.

"Damn it. As I feared," Plimkit lamented with a defeated exhale. "We can't even use their own blood to bloom the antidote. Their blood is too contaminated. It just pushes the toxin to eat at the brain quicker. Poor boy, even he didn't deserve this."

Philo had never seen someone die in front of him before. It was horrifying. What shocked Philo the most was how quick it happened. The shooter went from yelling at the Frozen Princess one minute, to being completely gone from this world the next. Philo didn't want to accept that life was so disposable.

"What do we do now?" Alani asked, turning away from the shooter in sadness. "What about the others?"

"I only have enough supplies down here to make one more round.

COST OF A CURE

We'll need non-contaminated blood that matches their own," Professor Plimkit sighed.

"That sounds impossible," Xendo remarked.

"Close relatives may work if they are the same blood type," Plimkit noted, turning to her staff. "Holocall the families that are on their way here and double-check if their blood matches with their children."

"Luther and I are both B negative!" Mrs. Wyatt called out anxiously to Professor Plimkit behind them. Everyone turned to the mother sitting next to Luther's hospital bed. Professor Plimkit's eyebrows raised as she walked toward the ambassador's secretary.

"Mrs. Wyatt, do I have your permission to draw some blood from you?" Plimkit asked the woman.

"Yes! Do it!" Luther's mother responded immediately. "Whatever you need!"

Professor Plimkit drew some blood from Mrs. Wyatt and prepared an antidote with the last of the formula. Philo and his friends stood behind Luther's mother, who was still holding onto her son's hand in fear. Luther's skin looked pale green and had spreading rash marks, but he still didn't look as damaged as Viktor Dimo had. Plimkit injected the antidote into the inside of Luther's wrapped elbow. Nothing happened immediately.

"Don't worry, Mrs. Wyatt," Alani kindly assured. "It has to work this time."

"We just want Luther to be okay," Philo added.

"Thank you, children," Mrs. Wyatt nodded nervously, "and you can call me Bianca."

After several painstaking moments of the group studying every pore on Luther's face, they started to see his rash blemishes fade and his face flush with rosy colors again. His mother had desperate tears of anguish streaming down her cheeks. Luther took in a sharp breath and opened both eyes. The onlookers gasped and glanced at each other.

"Mom?" Luther whispered, tearing up. "I thought I would never see you again."

Bianca Wyatt rushed in to embrace her son, grateful she didn't lose him too soon.

CHAPTER 19

COUNTDOWN TO MADNESS

The antidote had worked! Professor Plimkit rolled back in her office chair and exhaled all her stress.

"Professor, may I take my son home to rest?" Bianca Wyatt asked.

"Yes, of course, Mrs. Wyatt. Whatever you wish." Professor Plimkit bowed her head kindly to the pair.

As Bianca and Luther Wyatt gathered the rest of their belongings to teleport to their home on Atlantic Skisland, Philo looked to their SIYT friends and the ASU dioka. They were still sweating through their clothes, sickly green, and in so much quiet pain. Philo glanced up at the clock. They now only had two hours left to save the remaining poisoned students.

"How can we help you cure the rest of them?" Alani asked Professor Plimkit.

"I'm all out of supplies down here. I need to brew another batch of the final antidote recipe," Professor Plimkit responded in an exasperated daze as one of the SIYT nurses walked near her.

"Professor, we have just confirmed that all the families should arrive any minute," the nurse relayed to Plimkit while holding his technoband to his ear, "and each patient does have a parent or sibling that matches their blood type."

"Excellent," Plimkit replied back. "As soon as each blood-matching relative arrives, draw five ounces of their blood and have it prepared for me when I return."

"Where are you going?" Philo asked worriedly. She was the only person here who knew how to cure the students.

"Back to my larger lab upstairs," Plimkit answered, standing up from her chair and grabbing a small lab kit from her desk. "I'll create a new batch of the formula."

"Can we help you with that at all?" Raelyn inquired of the professor. "We can help carry all the supplies back down."

"Fine," Plimkit acknowledged without stopping her hurried pace. "Having some extra hands would be useful."

"Professor Ruiz, can we help Professor Plimkit?" Philo asked their chaperone.

"Yes, go," Professor Ruiz approved, "but first…."

The elderly kineoka master rotated his hoverchair around, closed his eyes, and raised his hands in the air. The carbon cube around his neck glowed blue again. The four friends waited for something mystical to happen to their own bodies when, suddenly, four black morph-staffs flew into the room. He caught two staffs in each hand while his eyes remained closed. Philo couldn't even begin to guess how much brain power that must have taken. Ruiz opened his eyes and the blue energy faded.

"Bring these with you for protection," Professor Ruiz directed, offering the four students the defensive rods, "just in case."

"Are these staffs that can actually morph?" Xendo asked, squeezing the weapon forcefully and making a scrunched face.

"No, they're from the sparring room," Raelyn remembered.

"Correct, Miss Arctikon," Professor Ruiz concurred, quickly handing the last staff to Philo.

"Are we even allowed to use these training staffs as first-years?" Philo asked their teacher nervously. The beautiful, daunting weapon still felt alien in his grip. He had no idea how they were ever going to build something this intricate.

"You four have earned the opportunity," Professor Ruiz encouraged. "Protect Mortha and get that antidote as fast as you can!"

CHAPTER 19

Professor Plimkit waved a hurried goodbye to Luther Wyatt and his mother exiting the medical wing as Philo, Raelyn, Alani, and Xendo jogged up the steps to join her. Professor Bryne confirmed there were no more Omnipotence intruders on campus, but something still felt... strange.

Plimkit's chemistry lab was on the tenth floor so Philo and his friends stood guard around Professor Plimkit as they dashed through the dark corridors to the floor's skytube. Xendo looked up and down the hallways with paranoid dread and Raelyn passed Alani a stretchy hair tie. Alani knotted her hair up into a quick tight bun, now more ready to fight for survival if need be. His friends must have sensed danger looming as well. Philo gripped his training morphstaff tight, hoping he wouldn't need it.

When they arrived at the Ancient Healing classroom, Xendo used the stolen access key to let them in. Plimiket rushed to place all her supplies at her trioka chemistry table.

"Okay, kids, in the pantry are all the various substances we need to add to this beaker," Plimkit explained as she placed a small glass stein over an electric burner with a holographic flame. "Here, take this list."

Philo took hold of the sheet of paper she passed him. It contained hastily scribbled ingredients of the original formula that had cured Luther. Philo didn't recognize even half of these rare items. As Professor Plimkit continued to set up her lab station, Philo and his friends rushed to the panty. Inside, the shelves of ingredients traced fifteen feet up the wall. Some items were labeled, but most were not.

"Oh. My. Data," Alani muttered under her breath, annoyed with all the clutter around them. "I should have known. Plimkit does project messy old witch vibes."

"Let's get to work." Raelyn charged forward, starting to sift through the label names on containers.

Xendo grabbed a wide bin to place all their ingredients into "Come on, Philo. Read them off."

Philo, Raelyn, Alani, and Xendo quickly got into the groove of finding the simple items like dried berries, activated charcoal, herbs, and water. These added plenty of vitamins and antioxidants, as well as important structural isotopes for creating larger chemical bonds. However, there were also various powders, serums, and pill capsules that sounded like complex pharmacy drugs. Philo had a difficult time

COUNTDOWN TO MADNESS

pronouncing names like glyceryl trinitrate.

"Glyceryl... tri... what?" Raelyn called down from a top shelf, fifteen feet above them, hurriedly trying to make sure she didn't grab the wrong container.

"Trinitrate," Philo repeated up to her, craning his neck. "That's the last one."

"Plimkit mentioned some of these medications in Ancient Healing lectures, but no one has actually used them in centuries," Xendo breathed aloud while taking the jar of white pills from Raelyn and placing it in the large open tub he was carrying. "Man, she's making a very precarious potion mixing all of these together."

"Why do you say that?" Philo asked, worried.

"Almost all these drugs themselves are insanely strong antidotes for other deadly poisons used throughout history," Alani explained. "They may keep you from dying when used correctly, but their hazardous side effects alone are unpredictable."

"And she's combining them *together*?" Raelyn replied anxiously, jumping down from the highest shelf with ease. "No wonder that OMNI shooter couldn't survive a second dose..., but he chose his fate."

"I mean, one incorrect measurement and she could poison the students even worse," Alani whispered to her friends.

"Well, she's the only expert here," Raelyn surmised. "We just have to trust she can do it."

The friends brought the antidote ingredients back to the lab.

"Here you go, professor," Philo told Plimkit as Xendo placed their bin on the chemistry station. The Ancient Healing professor had thick glasses propped in her gray hair. Her wrinkled face was staring down at her libe full of chemistry formulas in deep thought. Plimkit gave no response to Philo. *That's weird. Is she getting tired?* The other kids waved to her and called her name. Still no response.

Philo looked to his friends. They awkwardly gestured for him to poke their teacher to get her attention.

"Professor?" Philo inquired again, carefully prodding her. Plimkit slowly turned his way.

"Oh yes!" The old woman snapped back to life. "You're back! Let's start."

Professor Mortha Plimkit began working and the friends shrugged, looking at each other with unease. Plimkit measured out the ingredi-

CHAPTER 19

ents and added them to the boiling beaker. The master chemists would call out for the students to hand her a new tool or clean up after her as she worked. In no time, the bubbling elixir turned the same deep purple color they had seen down in the medical wing.

"There. The pH balance is now perfect and the ratios are consistent," Professor Plimkit uttered, taking the elixir off the heat. "Help me fill these syringes."

The students gathered closer to Plimkit, grabbed empty syringes from a bowl, and quickly sucked the elixir into the twenty empty canisters. Philo, Raelyn, Alani, and Xendo then placed their finished antidotes on a transport tray. With only a few syringes left to fill, Philo noticed that Plimkit suddenly stopped her work and stared blankly forward.

"Professor? Guys, look!" Philo nudged his friends. Plimkit looked rigid and lost in thought again, as if a new idea derailed her from the vital task at hand. This was becoming… odd. The elderly professor was a ghostly statue holding a leaking syringe like she was brain dead.

"I swear, if I'm like this as a grandma, just drown me in the sea," Alani sighed with frustration.

Then, hearing a whooshing noise, Philo had to duck as Plimkit suddenly whipped the syringe filled with their precious antidote over his head and across the lab. It smashed into the mounted holoscreen in the front of the room, splattering small glass shards and purple goo all around them. Alani screamed in surprise.

"What are you doing?" Xendo cried out, looking in horror at their teacher. Like a zombie, Plimkit grabbed another perfectly filled syringe and crushed it in her hand with a popping noise. Philo and his friends all gasped and covered their heads to block getting hit with glass shards or purple muck. Plimkit's hand was now all scratched and bloody. They looked at Plimkit in terrified bewilderment.

"What the hell is going on?" Alani questioned in confusion. Plimkit reached for another antidote to destroy.

"Oh no you don't!" Raelyn objected and deftly grabbed the tray of syringes and held it out of Plimkit's reach. The professor then growled at Raelyn like an animal. This made all four students jump. They were completely lost on what to do.

"Professor Plimkit…, are you okay?" Philo asked.

Instead of answering Philo in her normal slow and quiet voice,

COUNTDOWN TO MADNESS

Plimkit turned and slapped Philo so hard across his face it knocked him off his feet and he fell to the floor.

"Oh, damn!" Xendo shrieked in shock as they all backed away in fear. Alani clutched her head in stress, messing up the blue hair bun on her head.

"Xendo, grab the staffs!" Raelyn called out, taking charge, immediately retreating into defensive mode. Xendo ran to the classroom door to gather their training staffs that they had stupidly placed down. Alani hurried over to Philo to check if he was hurt. He grunted in pain as she helped him up. Philo clutched the swollen side of his face and looked around. Plimkit started to slowly step toward Raelyn, who held the unbroken antidotes. The princess backed further away unsure of her next move.

"We can't let her ruin the antidotes, Raelyn!" Philo called out. "There's no way we can make any more in time!"

"I do realize this!" Raelyn called back, tensing up, as she continued to watch Plimkit carefully. Raelyn kept her distance as the old woman stalked closer like a carnivore on the hunt. Xendo returned to hand Philo and Alani their training staffs.

"Did we somehow poison her?" Philo asked his friends, growing stressed.

"I told you to double-check those drugs, instead of just rushing us!" Alani yelled at Xendo.

"I *did* double-check!" Xendo screamed back. "It's not my fault you can't read fast enough. You wer—"

"Don't argue now!" Philo hissed at them.

"Get it together, you two!" Raelyn demanded from the other side of the room, still maneuvering around a sloth-like Plimkit. She gestured forcibly to Xendo. "Throw me that staff!"

Xendo grunted and tossed a staff over to Raelyn. She caught the weapon with her spare hand and pointed it at their delirious teacher.

"Professor Plimkit, something is very wrong. Come back with us to medical and we can get you some help," Raelyn offered, "but we can't let you near these antidotes. We need them, remember?"

Instead of agreeing, Professor Plimkit reached out to grab the antidotes again. Raelyn's eyes widened and she swerved out of the way. Plimkit slashed her hand at Raelyn's face, but Raelyn crouched to dodge under her flailing arm.

CHAPTER 19

"Catch!" Raelyn called to Philo, as she gently tossed the tray of antidotes to him. Alani gasped as the tray flew in the air, but Philo somehow caught it softly.

Plimkit growled in anger and lunged toward Raelyn. The princess backed further away in shock and bumped into the wall behind her. As Plimkit wound up to attack again, Raelyn thwacked Professor Plimkit in the abdomen in self-defense. Plimkit groaned in pain and hobbled to the side.

"Raelyn!" Alani called out in surprise. Raelyn escaped her cornered position to turn around and block Plimkit from her friends, defending them and the antidotes.

Without moving, Plimkit turned her head like a demented owl, twisting almost 180 degrees to look back at the SIYT students. Plimkit's eyes had changed to a dark, blood-red color. The jaws of all four kids dropped in terror.

"Oh, frostbite!" Raelyn let out in fear and confusion.

Plimkit jumped toward them and suddenly started fighting with amazing mobility for an old woman. With every furious punch, slash, kick, and elbow thrown at Raelyn, all she could do was dodge and block the attacks with her staff. The onslaught was so shockingly strong that the combat-trained princess soon found herself outmatched. Alani let out a shriek each time Plimkit landed a dangerous blow to her best friend. Philo and Xendo didn't quite know how to break into the fray; the fighting duo were moving at lighting speed.

As Raelyn dodged a swinging left hook from the rampaging professor, Xendo found his opening. He charged forward and clumsily shoved Plimkit away from Raelyn as hard as he could. Plimkit lost her footing and crashed into tall chemistry cabinets nearby. Shelves of test tubes and beakers collapsed to the ground and shattered. There was broken glass everywhere, but Plimkit still rose in a bloody, disjointed daze.

Alani, seemingly shaken by all this madness, split away from their group and ran toward the exit. Philo turned to watch her leave, shocked and heartbroken; he never expected Alani to abandon them in their time of need! Philo called out to beg her to stay and help, but soon realized she was actually grabbing something. On a table near the door was a cloth bag filled with clean dish rags the students used to clean their stations after chemistry experiments. Philo had no idea what Alani was planning as she dashed back toward him.

"Let's put them in here!" Alani fretted, opening up the cloth bag.

Philo's eyes lit up as Alani took a dish rag, tied it around one of the antidote syringes and placed it into the bag on her hip. Alani was a genius! Philo quickly helped her hide and protect more syringes as he heard grunt after grunt coming from Xendo and Raelyn fighting off the vicious professor. Philo glanced behind him—Plimkit was possessed! She was in a ferocious daze, like she had no control over her own limbs. Plimkit wasn't speaking, just attacking. Her red eyes were emotionless and terrifying!

Raelyn and Xendo's impressively clean kineoka forms were a huge contrast to whatever perverse, brutish kineoka Professor Plimkit was attempting. While Philo was distracted watching the fight, one of the antidotes slipped out of his hand and hit the ground with a loud clinking noise. Philo gasped as the Plimkit monster turned his way. She snarled like a bull and charged toward him.

Before Philo could catch his bearings, Alani stepped in front of him to guard him from the stampeding Plimkit. Alani braced for impact, holding her staff up for defense. The supercharged professor bulldozed into Alani and swatted her away like a rag doll. Horrified, Philo watched as his friend flew through the air over Plimkit's lab station, knocking all the equipment off the table, and crashed to the floor in a heap of pills, powders, and glass shards.

"ALANI!" her three friends yelped in desperation, but there was no response.

Professor Plimkit stomped on the antidote Philo just dropped, crushing it under her foot. She dashed to attack Philo. He lifted his fists up to fight. However, Xendo swiftly threw his staff like a javelin to hit Plimkit in the back before she reached Philo. Plimkit fell to the ground. Philo breathed a short sigh of relief as Raelyn and Xendo approached closer to help keep Plimkit at bay. Philo subtly pushed the cloth bag of antidotes toward the door with his foot so it would be out of sight. As Plimkit got back up, hardly phased by the blow to the back, Philo, Raelyn, and Xendo stood around the monster in a triangle formation and gripped their morphstaffs tighter. The beast growled at them.

All three first-years charged inward at Plimkit with their morphstaffs at the same time. Philo, Raelyn, and Xendo desperately punched and kicked with all their might to try and knock Plimkit out for their

CHAPTER 19

own survival. Philo heard rustling by Plimkit's lab station over the loud panting of his own strained breath.

"We... we have to...," Alani's voice simpered out from the left. Her friends gasped and looked her way as they continued to fight Plimkit. Alani struggled to stand up. She clutched her head, "We have to subdue her, or we're not going to get out of here alive!"

"At least we're trying to fight her off!" Xendo asserted.

"You rest, we'll handle this!" Raelyn called out.

Alani shook her head. For some reason, these comments seemed to bother her. She ignored her friends and started limping around the laboratory, opening up drawers and cabinets, looking for anything they could possibly use.

"Alani! Stay put!" Xendo yelled over to her, still fighting. "What could you possibly fight with? Everything is broken!"

"Not helping, Xendo!" Philo scolded him as he and Raelyn both kicked Plimkit in her side, knocking her a bit away from the group. Philo could tell Plimkit's mind was no longer her own. Her body looked exhausted beyond measure, but she wasn't slowing down in the slightest. Nothing they were doing was working. Plimkit's dark red eyes and vicious attacks were growing wilder and more erratic. The beast wanted to *kill* them.

A loud clanking sound forced Philo to turn and look behind him. Alani had lifted her morphstaff over her head and smashed it down onto a locked first aid kit perched on the wall. The white, metallic box fell open and all of its contents spewed out. Alani grabbed all the gauze rolls housed in the kit.

"I got something!" Alani called out to them. "Get her ready!"

"For what?" Xendo replied after kicking Plimkit back.

"We have to disable her somehow," Philo reasoned, agreeing with Alani.

"Let's squeeze her in," Raelyn suggested. "One, two, three, now!"

Philo, Raelyn, and Xendo put their morphstaffs at chest level and pushed their triangle formation around Plimkit at the same time, trapping her body between their staffs. Plimkit wriggled and thrashed violently like a hooked fish. The three students struggled to keep the mad professor contained as Alani hobbled their way as fast as she could.

Raelyn grabbed Plimkit's left fist and twisted it behind her back. Xendo followed suit, grabbing her right fist. The Plimkit monster hissed at them and tried to headbutt Philo in front of her. Philo dodged her incoming skull and sucker-punched his teacher in the stomach.

"Ope! Sorry, Professor!" Philo instantly apologized.

"Philo, don't be nice!" Xendo yelled at him. "She's trying to kill us!"

Plimkit hunched over at the waist from Philo's punch. Raelyn then kicked the back of her leg and pushed the rabid professor to her knees. Alani stumbled behind Raelyn and Xendo. She took the roll of gauze material and started wrapping it extremely tight around Plimkit's hands, making them impossible to separate. Alani continued to wrap the gauze around Plimkit's waist, securing her hands so they couldn't budge her arms. Plimkit tried to hit them with her head again so Xendo moved to put his arm around her neck, holding her in place.

"Get her legs, Philo!" Raelyn demanded, still holding Plimkit's arms as Alani tied a double knot in the gauze and ripped off the excess with her teeth.

Unsure of how to best hold the squirming legs trying to kick them all, Philo ended up just plopping his rear end to sit on her legs, squishing them into submission. He moved to just hold Plimkit's ankles and got out of the way as Alani came down to wrap the gauze extremely taught around her ankles. Alani tied the final knot and blew her fallen hair out of the way. Finding herself stuck, Professor Plimkit's red eyes seemed to grow even darker as she bent her chin down and sank her teeth into Xendo's forearm holding her in place.

"OW!" Xendo shrieked. "The crazy old grandma bit me!"

"This is never gonna end!" Philo huffed in frustration, running out of energy.

"I got this!" Raelyn called out. "Everyone duck!"

The princess grabbed the end of her morphstaff, got up on her feet, and took a step to twirl in front of the Plimkit beast. In one fluid movement, Raelyn turned back holding her morphstaff like a golf club and slugged Plimkit across the face, hard. Philo, Alani, and Xendo's jaws all dropped as the hogtied Plimkit hit the ground with a deep thud. Raelyn knocked her out. The room was quiet again. The madness was over.

Philo, Raelyn, Alani, and Xendo slowly looked away from Professor Plimkit on the ground to instead look at each other. For a moment, it felt like time stood still. Their synergy and cooperation during that fight was a rush of adrenaline that astounded Philo. He smiled toward his friends and they all smiled back. *They didn't die!* At the exact same

CHAPTER 19

time, all four dashed together for a group hug. They squeezed each other so tight the wounded Alani winced in pain and started to tear up.

"Oh! Sorry, Alani," Raelyn commented. "Did we hurt you more?"

"My leg and my head do hurt, but no, that's not it," Alani smirked, wiping a tear off her cheek, then chuckled. "I just love you idiots."

The students all laughed as they backed away, smiling at each other. They did another four-way fist bump. Philo took a few steps to his left and picked up the cloth bag full of antidotes.

"What do you think happened?" Raelyn posed to the group. "I've never seen any medical condition so demented like that!"

"Did you see her eyes? Red as blood!" Alani added fearfully.

"We have to tell Pearl," Xendo offered. "She'll know what to do."

"Yeah," Philo agreed, walking back to them holding the bag up. "But first, let's get these down to our friends."

Alani tapped her technoband and then looked stark white, "We have less than fifty minutes left!"

"Then let's get a move on!" Raelyn urged, gesturing for them all to head toward the door.

"Wait!" Philo yelped out. "Look!"

Raelyn, Alani, and Xendo turned around to glance where Philo was pointing. In the back corner, they saw the rabid Professor Plimkit was awake again. She had managed to cut the bandages off her hands with the glass shards on the floor and had begun to take the wrappings off her feet!

"Go!" Raelyn screamed as they all ran out the door, hoping to beat the monster back to the medical wing.

As they were running down the tenth floor hallway to the skytube, Alani was limping and fell behind.

"Sorry, my ankle!" Alani shared with them as Raelyn and Philo stopped, looking worried. With a loud bang, Plimkit burst into the hallway. She was crudely hopping out of her bandages like an angry, flopping bear. To everyone's surprise, Xendo ran back toward Alani.

"Oy! What are you doing?" Alani berated him as he bent down and scooped her up in his arms.

"Carrying you so we can get out of here, dumbass!" Xendo responded as he started running to the skytube. Philo and Raelyn looked stressed, but raced on either side of the Skyborne boy carrying Alani.

"Gosh, my hero!" Alani teased. Even in deathly peril she thought a chivalrous Xendo was worth a joke.

"Shut up!" Xendo snorted as they finally got into the skytube.

"Close the door!" Raelyn told Philo as Plimkit continued to barrel toward them, growling and thrashing about.

Philo pressed the metallic button on the skytube and the doors shut just in time before Plimkit could barge in. She pounded on the closed doors as they descended to the first floor.

In the silence of the skytube, Philo and his friends tried to catch their breath. Alani looked at the rest of them and put her head in her hands.

"I'm so pathetic! Having to be carried like this," Alani whispered. "I was too scared to fight her."

"Are you making another joke right now?" Raelyn asked her friend.

"No, I'm not always performing, okay?" Alani responded. "That was scary. I freaked out."

Xendo gently set Alani down on her good leg. Philo and Raelyn gave Alani concerned glances.

"It's thanks to your quick thinking we even got out of there!" Xendo admitted. "I was wrong to yell at you. I didn't mean it was because you're bad at combat."

"But I am. I'm not strong like you three," Alani simpered, feeling ashamed.

"Alani, you jumped in front to save me from Plimkit!" Philo reminded her, shocked she was feeling insecure. He never saw her like this. "That was so brave."

"I got thrown across the room," Alani countered. "Real agent material right there."

"Look at me," Raelyn urged Alani, pulling her friend's gaze toward her. "Stop this. You are the strongest person I know. Not everyone needs to be punching through walls to be effective. You are a *defender*. You defend people who need protecting. And that's the strongest trait of all. Never forget that."

Alani looked at her friend for a moment, then sighed and reached in for a hug. "Thanks, Raelyn."

Raelyn nodded and gave her friend a kiss on the forehead. The doors of the skytube then opened up on the first floor. Xendo grunted and picked up Alani again.

CHAPTER 19

"I hate to admit this," started Xendo, while following Philo and Raelyn out of the tube with Alani in his arms, "but, the only reason I'm doing so well in our classes is because you are there to challenge me. Our team only works because we have you, Alani. We need you just as much as you need us."

Alani seemed surprised for a half-second. Then she smirked at Xendo and poked him on the nose. "See, I knew you liked me, Skyboy."

Xendo rolled his eyes as they followed their other two friends down the first-floor hallways, but Alani knew he was trying to hide a grin. When they arrived at the hospital chamber entrance, Xendo placed Alani back down on her feet and opened the door. The four students walked inside.

Superintendent Pearl had returned and was now speaking with Professor Ruiz. Families of their poisoned friends were having their blood drawn into little tubes by the SIYT nursing staff. As Philo and his friends jumped down the steps, everyone turned to look at them and were startled by their roughed-up appearance.

"Do you have the antidotes?" Superintendent Pearl asked hastily.

"Here they are," Philo held the sack of cleaning cloths.

The superintendent was confused until she looked into the bag. She passed the wrapped antidotes to the nurses who immediately went to combine each with clean blood from the patient's relatives.

"And where is Professor Plimkit?" The superintendent's eyes narrowed in suspicion.

As Philo and his friends tripped over each other trying to explain the chaotic mess that happened upstairs, they realized just how insane it all sounded. However, to Philo's surprise, Superintendent Pearl didn't seem shocked or upset. She remained calm as the friends were gesturing wildly explaining Plimkit's rabid rage in the laboratory.

"I think you children need a good night's rest," Superintendent Pearl extended calmly. "You've had a stressful day."

"Wait, you don't believe us?" Xendo asked incredulously.

"I'm thankful for what you all have contributed tonight by lending some extra hands," Superintendent Pearl encouraged, "but I've known Mortha Plimkit for over fifty years. She could never act like that."

"Superintendent, it's true!" Raelyn urged. "She wasn't herself!"

"All right, children, I'll send the SIYT security to go check on her," Pearl comforted. "Now that we have the antidotes, it is time for you

COUNTDOWN TO MADNESS

four to rest for the night."

"But there's more!" Philo insisted. "She—"

Suddenly, they were interrupted by a medical cart being loudly kicked across the room. In the doorway stood a heaving Professor Plimkit. Her body had developed bruises, her right hand was bloody, she had blue veins popping from her skin, and her eyes were still dark red with rage. The entire room looked in fright as the Plimkit monster ferociously growled at them. The SIYT security guards deployed their staffs and stepped forward to protect the innocent patients.

"STAY BACK," Superintendent Pearl commanded her security, holding up her hands.

Plimkit's red eyes stopped darting rabidly around the room and instead focused squarely on Superintendent Pearl. The frail and damaged old woman watched the superintendent for a brief moment. Superintendent Pearl showed zero fear as she studied Plimkit. The strange beast hissed at her, briefly unsure of itself. Slowly, a look of knowing dread creeped upon the superintendent's face. Then, as if hit with a painful jolt of electricity, Plimkit's dark red eyes opened wider. The beast lunged off the steps of the doorway and catapulted toward Superintendent Pearl to attack. Alani shrieked in terror as Raelyn and Xendo took defensive stances with their staffs. Philo's nerves failed him; he was immobilized with fear.

Superintendent Pearl took a deep breath, swiftly stepped forward with one foot, and threw forth a rigid hand with a stupendous amount of force. The monster stopped in her tracks, as if frozen in time and space. Philo's mouth dropped open. Superintendent Pearl, a kineoka master herself, was using telekinesis to hold Plimkit in midair.

Plimkit's red eyes were bouncing around as she was trying to make moves that her body was incapable of completing. Superintendent Pearl then took another deep inhale and forcefully pushed her left hand up and forward to join her right. As if repelled by invisible magnetic energy, Plimkit was hurled several yards across the expansive room, hitting the wall above the door frame. With a loud thud, Plimkit then fell to the ground, collapsing upon the entrance steps. Superintendent Pearl brought her back leg forward while shifting both hands facing outwards into a wrapping circle motion. She pushed her arms down with an exhale and Plimkit was plastered to the stairs on the floor and couldn't move. Superintendent Pearl's eyebrows were fur-

CHAPTER 19

rowed in concentration and her forehead leaked a few drops of sweat. Exerting this much energy was extremely draining and could not be held for long.

"William!" Superintendent Pearl called out to her colleague as she tried to hold the telekinetic trap. "Calm her."

Professor Ruiz hastily floated over to Plimkit in his hoverchair. The elderly kineoka sage put his right hand over Plimkit's cranium and placed his left index finger over Plimkit's damp swollen forehead. Even from afar, Philo was disturbed watching the old woman's engorged red eyes bulging in furious contempt, trying to escape the mental prison . Professor Ruiz closed his eyes and took a deep inhaling breath that raised his torso. On his exhale, blue kineoka energy and light shone from his cube and genetic mark again. Plimkit's head started to be coated in an aura of bright blue Oceanite energy.

"Be at peace, my old friend," Professor Ruiz whispered quietly as he continued to focus intently on the mental energy he was extracting from Plimkit.

The dark red color slowly drained from Plimkit's eyes. Her normal green irises returned, and the elderly Ancient Healing professor blinked in confusion. She then looked over to Professor Ruiz and started crying.

"She's back, Nova," Professor Ruiz stated as he let go of Professor Plimkit's forehead and sat back in his hoverchair.

Superintendent Pearl released her meditative hold, returning to her normal standing position. Professor Plimkit immediately regained control over her body, but just continued to lie on the steps and weep silently. Superintendent Pearl, now out of breath having exerted so much mental energy, turned to Philo, Raelyn, Alani, and Xendo.

"I owe you four an apology. I should have trusted your judgment," Superintendent Pearl stated solemnly, looking at them with new respect. "Even a master can make mistakes."

Philo and his four friends were so floored they didn't know how to respond. Raelyn took the lead by just politely bowing her head to their Superintendent, and Philo, Alani, and Xendo followed suit. As soon as the superintendent turned away, the four friends sneakily took a sigh of relief.

The SIYT security guards carried the sore and depleted Professor Plimkit to a fresh bed. Philo looked up toward the holographic clock on

COUNTDOWN TO MADNESS

the hospital's crimson walls. They now only had twenty-eight minutes before they passed the point of no return in healing the dioka visitors, and their trioka friends would fall soon after. Philo, Raelyn, Alani, and Xendo spread about the room to visit the patients.

The SIYT nurses wrapped the unconscious ASU students' upper arms in the compression bands, ready to administer the prepared antidotes. The dioka students would be treated first. Superintendent Pearl had just finished comforting Grace and Danika's stressed families and walked over to Charlie's two mothers. Charlie Randolph was the worst of all the poisoned students, because he also had a bullet wound in his leg. His swollen throat was gasping for oxygen. His skin had a greenish tint and was sweating profusely. Superintendent Pearl addressed one of Charlie's moms who had donated her blood for her son.

"Mrs. Randolph, just like the other parents' blood match samples, yours has successfully stabilized with the antidote, so we are now ready to administer the formula to Charlie," Superintendent Pearl explained.

Charlie's parents nodded worriedly as a nurse came over with the syringe filled with the purple serum to counteract the toxin. She slowly injected the needle into the inside of Charlie's elbow.

Philo, Raelyn, Alani, and Xendo held their breath in anticipation, waiting to see how the injections performed on all the other students. Then, just like with Luther and the Omnipotence shooter, the greenish color drained from the patients' skin, the puffy redness faded, and their heart rates gradually returned to normal. Charlie's parents squeezed his hand tighter in hopes he could feel their touch.

"Moms?" Charlie muttered softly, blinking his eyes. He then turned to look to his right. "Princess Raelyn?"

Raelyn, who was standing nearby, blushed and turned away as Charlie's parents rushed in to hug him. She didn't want this moment to be made about her. Charlie took some deep inhales through his nose as his face returned to its rosy plush fullness.

"Her Royal Highness helped create the antidote that saved you, Danika, and Grace!" Charlie's mother cooed in grateful admiration. Raelyn hurriedly shook her head to deflect the praise.

"Thank you for saving me," Charlie lauded toward Raelyn. "I am the luckiest guy in the world."

"Oh, goodness no." Raelyn couldn't help but step forward. "Charlie, you are the one who saved me from being shot! Professor Plimkit

CHAPTER 19

and my friends also helped make the antidote. I could never do it by myself, but it's thanks to you and only you that I'm standing here still alive."

Charlie's eyes widened, almost in shock. Raelyn, for a second, thought the antidote was reversing again, about to hurt the boy.

"....Hearing you say that just made it all worth it," Charlie responded to her compliment with a beaming face. "I'd get shot again!"

Charlie's parents chuckled at his charming admiration. Raelyn tilted her head with a smile and patted him on the shoulder.

"But jokes aside," Charlie then turned more serious, "thank you, Princess."

"Oh, I'm not technically a princess anymore. I abdicated," Raelyn sighed, "and now OMNI's back.... The world is becoming a mess and I—"

"What?!" Charlie interrupted, a bit shocked. "That's who the shooters were?"

"Yes," Raelyn answered, "they came to assassinate Ambassador Irwin."

"Well, then, screw OMNI!" Charlie declared, shocking Raelyn. "And... your actual title doesn't matter when you are a *true leader*. *You* are exactly who the Frozen people need, now more than ever! If anyone can take Omnipotence down, I have every faith it will be you."

Raelyn blinked. She didn't know how to respond. She didn't realize how much words like that could affect her. She thanked Charlie and his parents as the nurses swooped in to continue with fully recuperating the boy. Raelyn looked around the room and saw the rest of the poisoned patients all sitting up in their beds, awake, and returning to normal. Raelyn smiled. They did it. She glanced over to Philo, Alani, and Xendo. They walked toward each other to meet in the center of the room.

"Charlie's all healed up!" Raelyn told her friends.

"So are Danika and Grace," Alani added. "They can't wait to return to Antarctica."

"Jade took a while, but she's cured too," Xendo reported. "She was worried about Luther, before I let her know he's already back home resting."

"Thank goodness," Alani responded. "And Philo, how about Naomii?"

"Interesting as always," Philo laughed. "Naomii said it was obvious we four would be down here in the middle of all this," Philo

COUNTDOWN TO MADNESS

recounted.

"How would Naomii know that?" Raelyn wondered aloud.

"They said," Philo then mimicked Naomii's monotone voice and pensive demeanor, "'All four of you have insistent hero syndrome and an acute craving for drama. You rush into conflict despite normal social boundaries desperately hoping you stop.'"

The four of them laughed. Naomii always said the silliest things.

Philo heard someone clearing their throat. He saw his three friends' eyes widen and stand up straighter. Philo turned around to see Professor Ruiz floating behind him.

"Excellent work, students," Professor Ruiz offered. "You demonstrated incredible kineoka skills and critical thinking under pressure. You should be very proud."

Philo and his friends nodded to their professor in gratitude. The four friends took their strapped training staffs off their backs and held them out to the professor.

"I wish we didn't have to part with these so soon," Xendo said in a melancholy voice. "Why do we have to wait so long to build ours?"

Professor Ruiz smiled warmly. His carbon cube around his neck gave off a gentle blue light as he made a sweeping gesture to telekinetically pluck the four training staffs from the friends' grasps. He held the staffs in midair above them all. He then cheerfully looked to his own morphstaff and made it sparkle with blue energy. He smirked as the four students marveled at his little light show. Professor Ruiz was showing off.

"You'll each have your own morphstaffs soon enough," the professor chuckled. "Superintendent Pearl has tasked me with notifying you four that she requests to see you all in her office bright and early in the morning,"

"Oh?" Raelyn asked, looking around the room. "Did she already leave?"

"Are we in trouble?" Xendo sighed, rolling his eyes.

"The superintendent did not say. Once the poisoned students were confirmed to be healthy, she immediately teleported to the Croiley Dome on the Pacific floor to meet with Ambassador Irwin regarding today's attacks and how to address the public."

"She's so fast...," Alani breathed in admiration.

"The superintendent did stress that it was an urgent matter, and it is vital you all be there by nine o'clock sharp tomorrow morning,"

CHAPTER 19

Professor Ruiz reiterated as he floated through their huddle on his way toward the exit. "So, don't be late."

"Where are you headed, Professor?" Philo asked.

"Child, it is one in the morning," Professor Ruiz called back to them with the staffs trailing behind him in the air. "Kineoka masters need sleep, too."

Philo, Raelyn, Alani, and Xendo didn't realize just how tired and sore they were until they arrived at their dormitories on the thirteenth floor. As they exited the skytube, they noticed the platinum doors were now unlocked and there was a trail of glitter leading from the skytube toward the girl's dorm. Their little QD313 droid was buzzing around the floor vacuuming up the colorful sparkles with his tiny extendable arms.

"I guess the guard got out of our room eventually," Raelyn sighed.

"Today has been so crazy; I completely forgot we glitter-bombed him," Alani chuckled quietly as the four friends walked through their lounge.

"Do you think that's what Superintendent Pearl wants to talk about?" Philo asked.

"Probably…. We're dead meat. Pearl is notorious for her strict punishments," Xendo lamented as QD313 scurried around their feet vacuuming more glitter.

Alani crouched down to gently poke the pint-size white droid on its bulbous head.

"Good evening, QD, we're so sorry for the mess in our room. How long have you been cleaning?" Alani asked.

"Hello! - Alani Adalaide - the process of cleaning the mess in room 13C has lasted for precisely five hours, eighteen minutes, and thirty-one seconds so far," QD313 beeped. "Thirty-two, thirty-three, thirty—"

Raelyn's technoband made a dinging noise and blinked white. Raelyn brought her wrist up to check the incoming alert.

"Oh! Ambassador Irwin just made a statement on today's attack," Raelyn informed the others. "Should we watch?"

"Fine," Xendo groaned. "Then bed. I could sleep for a century."

Raelyn tapped her technoband, spreading the holoscreen wide to float in front of the warm electric fireplace of their dormitory lounge. Philo, Raelyn, Alani, and Xendo plopped down on the couch to watch the short address together. On the screen stood Ambassador Irwin in

COUNTDOWN TO MADNESS

front of an underwater building inside the Croiley Dome of the Pacific Ocean. He still had his shoulder bandaged in a sling under his deep navy Oceanite business robes. To his right stood Superintendent Pearl, in a fresh and crisp emerald blazer and slacks, representing SIYT in this address.

"No matter if it is in a school, in our workplaces, or even in our own neighborhoods, terrorism and hatred has no place in the year 3452. This attack on me and the trioka students of SIYT is an act of discrimination and fear mongering. Omnipotence is a threat the world all thought was vanquished. They are an ancient supremacy group that aims to divide us. The future we all want for Earth is a happier, safer, and more prosperous home to call our own. Omnipotence cannot silence our mission, and they have no place in our modern world."

As Ambassador Irwin continued, the news section of Earth's Database cut in clips from SIYT security cameras of the attack. Raelyn leaned forward in her seat as they showed closeup shots of some of the masked gunmen. Only two of the OMNI terrorists had been apprehended—most had escaped. Philo looked over at Raelyn's face as she intently dissected the images in front of her. She gasped as one one of the fleeing shooters took off his white ski mask. The leader of the crew was a young, handsome man with blonde hair and a strong wide jaw. He was belting orders at the rest of the escaping Omnipotence knights carrying ancient shooting rifles. Raelyn stood up, not taking her eyes off the angry mystery man on the screen.

"Do you guys think that's Judd Stemson?" Raelyn asked them, almost out of desperation. "The name that the poisoned shooter gave us?"

However, before any of her friends could respond, Raelyn immediately shushed them as the same OMNI intruders stepped into illegal solo teleportal rings to escape. Raelyn cursed under her breath. They could have teleported anywhere on the face of the planet. There was no way to track where they may have landed. The footage cut back to Irwin's address.

"These Omnipotence villains had apparently been planning this stunt for months, to make us question this upcoming election. However, we must not give into fear. Whether you are trioka or dioka, whether you support my candidacy for global president or not, we are all humans of this great planet. We must protect each other. The influence of these extremists will be snuffed out. Be safe and tell your loved ones

CHAPTER 19

you cherish them. Good night."

Ambassador Irwin and Superintendent Pearl walked away from the microphone and back into the underwater building behind them. The ED footage faded away.

"Just when you think the night can't get any more complicated," Xendo complained with worry. "This is just the beginning."

"I didn't even know some dioka hated us *this* much," Alani breathed, sadly.

"I knew," Raelyn responded with a depressing shake of her head. "Most people hide their hatred until it explodes and hurts us all."

"At least we have Superintendent Pearl and the ambassador on the trioka side," Philo added, gratefully.

"You're right, Philo." Raelyn lifted her head and turned to her friends. "As long as we have each other, we stand a fighting chance."

"We do make a fabulous team," Alani smirked.

"Let's remember that when we're defending ourselves tomorrow to Pearl," Xendo scoffed as the others chuckled. "I'm going to sleep now."

The other three nodded. They got up from the couch, waved goodnight, and parted ways to the doors of 13A and 13C. As Philo's head hit his pillow, he exhaled all the stress of the exhausting day. Xendo was snoring within seconds.

Philo dreaded tomorrow morning. He had no idea how they were going to explain the glitter bomb.

CHAPTER 20

MORPHING MEMORIES

After a café breakfast of spicy chilaquiles with queso fresco, Philo and Xendo met up with Raelyn and Alani on their walk toward Superintendent Pearl's office. The girls had not yet had time to have breakfast, shower, or properly do their hair. Philo knew that Xendo wanted to make a joke at their expense to lighten the mood, but as soon as he opened his mouth, both Raelyn and Alani stared daggers at him. It shut Xendo up before he even said a word. After entering the skytube, they stood in silence for a moment as they ascended, nervous of getting in trouble.

"I can't believe we're going into Superintendent Pearl's private office," Alani marveled, breaking the awkward silence. "No students ever go in there."

"Well, no one has broken as many rules as we have," Raelyn responded with a tilt of her head.

"I actually *have* been in there before," Xendo gloated gleefully. Philo shot him an angry look. Xendo was the one who messed up on revealing their secrets this time.

"Really?" Raelyn responded to him with suspicion. "Why?"

CHAPTER 20

"Yeah, what did you do wrong to actually go in there?" Alani asked with her eyebrows furrowed.

Xendo struggled to find an answer. Philo looked away to not be part of the lie.

"Birthday gift… for Mom," Xendo finally settled on. "My mom and the superintendent go way back."

The girls looked at Xendo, then at each other. They shrugged. That excuse seemed to work. Philo wished that he and Xendo could just tell the girls the truth! But it still felt too risky.

The skytube door opened to a crimson chamber with plaque portraits of previous SIYT superintendents on its walls. Xendo reached out to an intercom buzzer on the left of a platinum door to announce that they had arrived. Before he touched it, however, a voice came out from the speaker.

"You are two minutes late," Superintendent Pearl told them quickly. "Come in."

The four friends gave each other nervous looks as the platinum doors shot into the side walls, revealing the open office. Xendo and Philo walked to the superintendent's desk as the girls followed, glancing about the glorious room for the first time.

"Mom?" Xendo was shocked to see his mother sitting in one of the five chairs in front of Superintendent Pearl's grand oak desk. "What are you doing here?"

Blinda Quaker turned around to look up at her son with confusion, she had no idea either.

"Chef Quaker and I have a meeting after my discussion with you four," Superintendent Pearl informed. "However, since she is Xendo's mother, I figured it might be wise for her to join this conversation as well."

"Oh, wonderful," Xendo remarked through a strained smile, hoping his mother wasn't about to be fired.

Philo, Raelyn, Alani, and Xendo took seats facing the superintendent. After a few uncomfortable moments of silence, Philo wondered if they should say something first.

"Are we in trouble?" Philo asked finally, wanting to break the awkward tension. The other four guests in the room breathed out anxiously.

"Why would you ask that?" Superintendent Pearl replied, sur-

MORPHING MEMORIES

prised.

"Because you can be scary," Alani let out by accident, "that's why."

"Well, that sounds like your problem, not mine," Superintendent Pearl stated simply. Alani gulped down a startled chuckle as Superintendent Pearl continued. "Let's not waste time. There is too much to discuss."

Superintendent Pearl tapped her technoband and opened security videos from the day before. She took each holoscreen file and tossed them out into the air around the room.

"You four are here so that I may thank you for your work last night and ask for your discretion in what you experienced," the superintendent stated.

Philo, Raelyn, Alani, and Xendo all looked at each other with raised eyebrows and surprised smiles. Anything was better than getting scolded. Superintendent Pearl pulled over the security files showing closeup SIYT footage of the masked Omnipotence fighters, Viktor Dimo dying, and Professor Plimkit in her red-eyed zombie-like state. Xendo glanced over to his mother; she looked a bit alarmed by all the frightful images.

"Firstly, you should all be proud of the initiative you showed in not only your willingness to lend a supportive hand to those in need, but also your use of smart judgment in times of peril," Superintendent Pearl stated, as close to praise as Philo had ever heard from her. "The ambassador was correct. Sometimes you just have to break the rules to solve an impossible conundrum. You four are on track to be stellar kineoka fighters and, quite possibly, successful continuum agents one day."

Philo and his friends' small smiles now grew into wider grins as they realized all the drama wasn't going to get them expelled. Blinda rubbed Xendo's shoulder lovingly in support.

"However, you must keep secret anything sensitive you witnessed yesterday," the superintendent stated. "Professor Plimkit's strange affliction, your private conversation with the Omnipotence squire, any interactions with the ambassador, and how close the poisoned students were to death. All of it."

Philo sighed. More secrets. It was almost too much for him to handle. It was becoming hard to remember what Philo was allowed to even think about anymore without exposing all the clandestine truths

CHAPTER 20

locked in his mind.

"Why can't we tell people? Or tell our other friends?" Alani quietly questioned. "They saw this all on the news. They know what's going on."

"No, they only understand a fraction. The people of Earth only know what we've released publicly. They only saw that there was a small attack on SIYT, and that Omnipotence has unfortunately come out of hiding to execute a one-time terrorist stunt," Superintendent Pearl explained, gesturing to all the video clips around them on holoscreens. "None of *this* footage will *ever* be seen by the public. It will be locked away for the greater good. If the larger collective knew of all this, there would be pandemonium."

"Why all this secrecy?" Xendo asked, perplexed. "Isn't honesty better?"

"Yes, eventually. However, for the time being, the investigations into the motives behind these attacks are still ongoing. Professor Plimkit is still recovering, Omnipotence knights are still being interrogated. Everything must be handled delicately. More chaos is what this terror organization is trying to spread. We must remain steady in our pursuit of justice."

The four students nodded. Raelyn made a small murmuring noise, seemingly hesitant to say something. They all turned to her as she leaned back. She huffed and decided to go for it.

"Did you get any information from the captured Omnipotence knights about anything beyond the attack just yesterday?" Raelyn asked the superintendent.

"No, unfortunately, we did not," Superintendent Pearl conceded. "They barely gave us the small amount of intel we coaxed out of them. Extremely tight-lipped."

"Ah… okay," Raelyn sighed.

"I watched security tapes of what I missed in the medical wing," Superintendent Pearl told Raelyn, narrowing her eyes in thought. "You wanted *your own* information out of that young Omnipotence squire. May I ask…, what about the night of Queen Semira's death were you trying to discover?"

Raelyn took a breath. She looked between her three other friends. She hadn't told them the whole truth yet.

"My mother didn't die from sickness. She was murdered by a se-

MORPHING MEMORIES

cret OMNI ambush a few years back," Raelyn admitted to her friends, Pearl, and Blinda.

"That I gathered," Superintendent Pearl responded stoically. "What new information were you hoping to ascertain? What answer were you searching for that motivated you to lead your friends into such danger?"

"I... I didn't want anyone to get hurt," Raelyn struggled to speak. "I just needed to know...."

"Know what?" Pearl encouraged gently. "You can share within this group."

"Was it OMNI's *only* aim to attack the Northern Palace years ago? Were they trying to send a warning to my father or the Frozen council?" Raelyn uttered, starting to get emotional. "Had my mother just gotten in their way by mistake? Or, was it actually their true mission to kill *me*?"

Alani gasped and reached out to her friend. Blinda sighed in support. Philo and Xendo could plainly see how hard that was for Raelyn to actually ask. Superintendent Pearl breathed in slowly and leaned forward to look closer at the young princess. She dropped her steel demeanor for a gentle pout, showing the warmth she saves for the rarest of moments.

"My dear," Superintendent Pearl stated, dolefully, "I think you already know the answer to that final question."

Raelyn dropped her head, holding back tears. If Omnipotence's goal was to wipe out trioka influence, taking out the first trioka-born royal of the massive Frozen Kingdom was the only logical conclusion.

"I came to this school to learn how to be an agent and how to stop evil people like those that killed my mother," Raelyn explained through strained words. "I had no idea that after just a few months, the actual perpetrators would follow me to attack here, too."

"Was all this what you were keeping from us last night?" Alani said gently. "We still would have helped you."

"I couldn't trust anybody. My father and the Frozen council never wanted me to know the truth . Years of silence. As a kid, I had no idea who the masked killers were in the palace. Then, all of a sudden, the same men in sooty camo appeared here," Raelyn whispered. "I couldn't let them just attack the school and escape again. I had to do something before they got away. They were so close!"

CHAPTER 20

Pearl nodded. She understood Raelyn's urge to discover even a sliver of some real answers. *Not understanding our pain is what hurts the most.*

"The council told the world my mother died from heart failure, but I remembered so much fighting on that day. It all wasn't adding up. I need to find out for myself."

"You were so young," Blinda told her gently. "They probably just wanted to spare you any more heartache."

"But, she died protecting *me*," Raelyn whispered, ashamed. "It's all my fault."

"No, you were only a child," Superintendent Pearl assured her. "Omnipotence is to blame. Hidden in the shadows, Omnipotence has been suppressing progress that doesn't suit their own interests since the first empires in human history. And what they can't suppress, they destroy."

"Omnipotence was behind Xendo's father's death as well," Blinda added as a tear rolled down her cheek.

"They stole countless lives throughout time, which has crippled the freedoms of our ancestors. Even the mightiest of our agents can become victims of Omnipotence's violence," Superintendent Pearl uttered slowly, looking at both Philo and Xendo. The boy's eyes widened. They then looked at each other. *Was the superintendent about to share Philo's secrets?*

"You four have more in common than you even realize," Superintendent Pearl confided to the first-years. "Often, the world sends us friends to make sense of the journey we've been forced to travel alone."

Raelyn breathed in deeply and then exhaled slowly. She glanced over to the boys who gave her warm smiles. Alani rubbed her back.

"Tell me, children," Superintendent Pearl leaned back in her office chair and lifted her chin. "In your classes, have you learned the kineoka philosophy of *Odeterro* yet?"

Philo, Raelyn, Alani, and Xendo all took a moment to think, then all four shook their heads. They had never heard that word.

"The term essentially describes a trioka person's 'destiny for Earth.' We each have our own Odeterro in this life. Kineoka focuses on the peaceful movement of energy between the mind, the body, and the world around us. *Odeterro is that energy.* A trioka's mission in life is to fulfill their Odeterro, to find what energy they, alone, can contribute on

| MORPHING MEMORIES |

Earth to make it a better home for us all. Every tiny detail of this world, down to the tiniest atom, is forever connected. So, our Odeterro as humans is linked with the people who bond naturally to us within our lives. It is truly a beautiful thing. I sense a strong Odeterro connection blossoming within you four."

Philo, Raelyn, Alani, and Xendo all smirked and looked warmly toward each other. Their friendship did almost feel like destiny. If Odeterro was real, their horrible pasts had led them to this moment, despite their struggles and heartbreaks. They were stronger together than they were alone.

"Now that we've handled that, it's time for your punishments," Superintendent Pearl moved on casually. The four SIYT kids all jumped in surprise. Pearl glanced down at a small list she had prepared on her libe.

"Wait, I thought we weren't in trouble?" Alani spluttered, thoroughly shocked.

"You are nothing of the sort," Superintendent Pearl replied robotically. "However, breaking rules and getting in trouble are two very different things."

"Uhhhhh," Xendo vocalized in confusion as the other three were speechless.

"All choices have consequences, even correct choices," Superintendent Pearl explained. She gestured to the images around her. "According to all this, you four physically combated with a SIYT professor, broke the mandatory school-wide lockdown, and attacked a SIYT guard with colored paint and… glitter."

Philo, Raelyn, Alani, and Xendo all sat with their mouths fully open, feeling completely duped.

"All of that?" Blinda laughed with a facepalm and a smirk. "Kids!"

"For all of these infractions," Superintendent Pearl read off, "you four will not be allowed to leave campus. You will need to maintain the strict cleanliness of your entire dormitory floor yourselves for the remainder of the school yea—"

"What? No help from the quality droid?" Xendo interrupted with a groan, thoroughly annoyed he'd actually have to clean up after himself.

"Actually, we renamed it QD," Alani corrected him as he rolled his eyes. Philo, Blinda, and Raelyn laughed. Superintendent Pearl cleared her throat, not too happy with the interruption.

CHAPTER 20

"—*And* you four will be tasked with helping the professors with the voting ballots during global election week before your final exams in June next month," Pearl finished.

The superintendent put down her libe. Even though Xendo didn't seem pleased with these developments, Philo wasn't too shaken. Compared to how he used to be punished, these penalties were nothing.

"All right, that business has been sorted. Ladies, you may go," Superintendent Pearl gestured for Alani and Raelyn to exit as the metallic door at the end of the room opened on it's own. "I need to speak with Philo, Xendo, and Blinda in private for a moment."

"Why?" Alani asked, ever curious, eyeing her two friends suspiciously.

"Even though we cannot tell the world all our secrets just yet, I have some confessions of my own to share with these three," Superintendent Pearl tilted her head to Philo, Xendo, and Blinda.

"Oh? Is there more that we should know?" Raelyn asked the superintendent politely. Pearl paused to think and didn't make a sound for a few moments.

"I'll leave the decision of honesty up to the boys," Superintendent Pearl stated solemnly. "But out of respect, they may need some time to process before sharing."

"We… can tell them something?" Philo asked slowly, his eyes widening.

"No way!" Xendo looked at the girls with a growing grin.

"I do think they have earned our trust," Superintendent Pearl nodded. "A team can always use more allies."

The boys perked up, and Blinda laughed. Alani and Raelyn were smiling but had no idea what any of the other people in the room were talking about.

"Tell us what?" Alani eagerly pushed, fully lost. "Are you both princesses too?"

"The boys can speak with you after our own meeting," Superintendent Pearl suggested. "I can grant you four access to the soundproofed elemental sanctuary chamber to discuss what you wish privately. But for now, I only have half an hour before I must teleport to my next appointment."

"Thank you, Superintendent," Raelyn replied while bowing her head, respectively. She then grabbed Alani's hand to pull her to the

MORPHING MEMORIES

exit as she waved goodbye to the boys. "We'll meet you both near the sanctuary entrance."

"I *KNEW* there was something more mysterious going on between you two," Alani smirked in jest, pumping her fist victoriously toward her chest. "A² is never wrong!"

The platinum doors shut behind the girls, leaving Philo and Xendo alone with Blinda and Superintendent Pearl.

"Now, for my news," the superintendent began, immediately returning to her somber tone. "It has to do with Professor Plimkit's… outburst."

"It was so odd. It was like she was normal one moment, and a rabid dog the next," Xendo shuddered, remembering being hissed at and bitten by the old woman.

"The dead red eyes were what really frightened me," Philo added anxiously, "like a bloody robot, furious with rage."

Blinda, who had not witnessed the Plimkit monster in real life, was staring at the paused image of the gruesome red-eyed professor growling at her prey.

"I've never heard of OMNI doing anything like this," Blinda fretted. "Do you think she somehow poisoned herself?"

"No…," Superintendent Pearl stated slowly. She seemed reluctant to share her thoughts. "I have reason to believe Professor Plimkit was under some form of influence."

"What? Like mind control?" Xendo asked with horror and awe. "Some sort of zombie?"

"Negatory, that sounds cartoonish," Superintendent Pearl cut the boy off. "However, it reminded me of a strange phenomenon I heard being described long ago."

"How would Omnipotence be able to control someone?" Blinda asked, perplexed. "Is there technology for that?"

"I'm not certain just yet," Superintendent Pearl responded, lost in thought. "For eons, Omnipotence has executed messy massacres like yesterday's before the Third World War. However, they've done nothing this public for the last few centuries. They normally carry out their crimes covertly. An assassination attempt of a candidate for the highest office on Earth can not be discounted. President Namid Kanosha has given the HTPA her full support to investigate this matter. My next meeting is with continuum agents of their department to discuss how

CHAPTER 20

we should proceed."

"Woah! Real agents!" Xendo declared. "How cool!"

"Do you need our help with something?" Philo asked, worried for her answer.

"No, not at this moment." Superintendent Pearl shook her head. "You both should remain focused on your next few years of history education and kineoka training."

"Then, what does Professor Plimkit's rampage have to do with us?" Blinda wondered, innocently puzzled. "Particularly me! I can't do any sort of fighting or agent tactics."

Superintendent Pearl breathed deeply and then gave her longtime friend a sorrowful look. She tapped her technoband and a new holo-screen appeared in the air just in front of Pearl. She shuffled through a list of electronic files until she came to a section marked "CLASSIFIED." She dragged a video file into the air to float on her right. Philo saw a wooden table and chairs sitting in a nondescript room with bland white walls.

"This video contains a troubling, unofficial debrief of the HTPA time travel mission back to 2005 from a young Daryl Irwin, then just a junior agent," Superintendent Pearl explained cautiously, looking to Philo and Xendo with a slow sigh. "It mentions Jerome Quaker, Daniel Nockby, and Ava Harlow, your parents."

The boys gasped quietly in anticipation. Blinda's mouth fell open, expecting anything but that. Philo had never seen any sort of actual information about the 2005 mission. He had only heard rumors around school or the small snippets from Blinda and Xendo. No one seemed to know any real answers. Philo spent a portion of every day wondering about his parents and craved more pieces of this impossible puzzle.

"Why didn't you show this to us before, Nova?" Blinda asked the superintendent, almost in a demanding manner.

"I should not even be showing it to you *now*," the superintendent replied, very seriously. "These files are classified information of the HTPA, the only reason I have this shortened copy is because they filmed it here as soon as Irwin arrived back from 2005. At the time, it just seemed like a bewildered rant from a trauma victim. It made no sense. However, after seeing Professor Plimkit yesterday, I believe something sinister is afoot. I am making the decision that you three have the right to know at least this small amount."

MORPHING MEMORIES

"Nova, you are making me nervous," Blinda whimpered. Philo's stomach was boiling with anxiety.

"Well, press play already!" Xendo pleaded.

Superintendent Pearl touched the holoscreen allowing the floating clip to play. Immediately, a man and woman in matching dark suits burst into the bland room. Behind them, a nurse pushed in a levitating hospital bed with a person propped up, wincing in pain. The sweating and grunting patient had bloody bandaged legs and a bludgeoned, wrapped skull with black hair. Philo realized this must have been the young Daryl Irwin. The nurse left the chamber, leaving Irwin with the documentarians.

"Agent Irwin, we know your injuries are still fresh," the woman hurried, "but we must do your HTPA debrief before you go to the Grounded hospital in Mumbai for a droid limb surgery. If they put you under anesthesia we may lose information and vital details regardin—"

"Yes, yes, just get on with it." The young Irwin winced, trying to hoist himself up on the propped mattress. The woman nodded and pulled out a recording device and her own tablet to take notes. The man on her left looked directly into the lens of the camera of the video clip they were watching, to make sure it was filming. The female documentarian cleared her throat.

"This recording is the property of the Historical Timeline Preservation Agency. Everything you say will be documented and logged into the HTPA's classified time-travel mission debriefs of history. It will be analyzed by our division privately before possibly being approved for public release to Earth's Database. Our records indicate...."

Daryl Irwin's bloody head dropped back on his pillow for a moment and he seemed to lose focus.

"Let's skip ahead," the HTPA documentarian in the dark suit interrupted his partner. "He's going to pass out any minute."

"Right, yes. Agent Irwin, you just returned back to August of 3438 in SIYT's portal observatory. You came alone and severely distressed, please recount your statements on the record."

"After years... searching separately... we finally came back together," Daryl faltered, shaking his head aimlessly.

"Who? You and your teammates?" the male documentarian tried to clarify. "Where are they now?"

CHAPTER 20

"Dead!" Daryl yelled out loud, which seemed to make him woozy. "We... ambushed by time jumpers... they had guns... poisons... and red eyes."

"Did you get any ID of these jumpers you were tracking?" the woman pushed, seeing Daryl slipping in and out of consciousness. "What were they trying to find?"

"Never could outsmart them...," Daryl whimpered. "They got to Quaker."

"Agent Jerome Quaker?" the suited woman asked. "How did they get to him?"

"Red eyes!" Daryl raised his voice again, panting. He was barely able to look straight. "Quaker tried... kill us all. He slashed my legs off... grabbed the jumper's gun. Then... Nockby, dead! Harlow, dead!"

"How and why would Agent Quaker turn on his own team?" the HTPA man asked forcefully, leaning forward. Trying to pull all the necessary words out of the delirious agent.

"Quaker turned... ran away," Irwin struggled to say. "...Gone."

"Come on! Stay awake, now!" the suited woman urged, realizing Irwin was going to be knocked out any second, "Anything else you can tell us?"

"We failed... we never," Daryl Irwin muttered, "...knew the truth. Who was—"

Irwin's head fell back on his pillow. He was now fully unconscious.

"Agent Irwin?" the suited man asked again, as his partner walked closer to check on him. "Agent Irwin?"

The man shook Daryl Irwin's shoulder as the female documentarian called out for the nurse. She then told her partner, "That's all we can get, he needs medical treatment, now."

The SIYT nurse came in to pull the comatose Irwin out of the room on his stretcher. In all the shuffling and hurried movements, the camera was knocked over and it crashed to the ground, fracturing the lens. The recorded video ended.

"That's all I have," Superintendent Pearl stated, as Philo, Xendo, and Blinda tried to process that scattered information. "Daryl Irwin didn't wake up again until after his droid leg replacement surgeries and recovery from the head wounds. It took three months. When he finally was himself again, he barely remembered anything from the mission."

MORPHING MEMORIES

Philo was gutted. He refused to look at anyone else in the superintendent's office. He stared down at his lap in angry silence. *Jerome Quaker killed my parents? Then ran away?* Philo wanted to dash out of the room, escape out of the school, and never come back. *Xendo's father did all this? How could Blinda and Xendo not tell me? How could they have lied to me? They made me trust them, but it was all a lie.* Philo didn't know what was real anymore.

Blinda had tears in her eyes. She turned to Philo and extended a hand out to him. He pulled away from her touch, refusing to even look back in her direction. Philo was shutting down.

"Philo, I swear, we had no idea about any of this!" Blinda pleaded as the boy continued to sit in dejected misery. She turned to Xendo, who also sat in shock, learning his absent father was even worse than the world had been mocking him for. Blinda turned to the superintendent, "Nova, this can't be true! Jerome would never!"

"It didn't make sense to me either when I first saw this thirteen years ago," Superintendent Pearl told them all with a melancholy voice. "I didn't want to believe any agent could turn against their own team, let alone someone as carefree and valiant as young Jerome. So, I said nothing. I never pushed when the HTPA hid the mission details from the public. I made sure you and your baby son were taken care of. Then I let the story die, thinking it was all over, nothing to be salvaged."

Xendo sighed. No wonder the world mocks the Quakers. The shameful conspiracies the public believed were only a fraction of what happened. The truth was so much worse.

"However, then came Philo," Superintendent Pearl inhaled, turning to the young, Grounded boy. Philo didn't want to react, but he instinctively lifted his chin to look up to Superintendent Pearl. When his glance met hers, though, Philo pointed his head right back down to the floor.

"You changed everything, added more to the mystery," the superintendent continued. "Obviously, we missed something. This failed mission and its gruesome ending wasn't as simple as this old video made it seem."

"And now with the red eyes?" Xendo interjected. "How does it all connect?"

"Professor Plimkit told me she felt like she was being used like a puppet. She had no control over her own body. I think Jerome may

CHAPTER 20

have been manipulated in the same chaotic fashion," Superintendent Pearl concluded.

"So, Jerome didn't hurt anyone?" Blinda hoped, still teary-eyed.

"I cannot make that call," Superintendent Pearl clarified, "but there is now much more to investigate."

"Like what? Who could do something this maniacal?" Blinda asked, distraught.

"All of that is now *my* job to discover. We must uncover the truth behind the 2005 mission in secret. If the red-eyed mind controller is somehow working with Omnipotence, then their actions do not just affect SIYT, but all of Earth. We need to put an end to it all."

"What could it possibly be?" Blinda racked her brain. "I don't understand!"

"Something deeper and more mysterious is at play here," Superintendent Pearl theorized. "I am reluctant to even be pondering this, but… there is an evil side to kineoka, a toxic, inorganic side. It is called *syncontra*. This dark sect of our martial art is supposed to be long dead. No one even knows how to practice it anymore. However, mind control *would* fit into the perverted mental powers of a syncontra master. If yesterday's attack was a stunt to announce their return, then Omnipotence has only just begun."

A silence fell about the room. Philo could tell that the other three were waiting for him to share his state of mind. However, Philo didn't know how to vocalize his emotions. He just wanted to run away and escape back to 2019. His old life was excruciatingly miserable, yet, at the very least, Philo did have the tiniest bit of control over his own life.

Back in the past, he didn't feel overwhelmed all the time. His homework was easy, he wasn't getting bruises from fighting classes, or trying to make tiny cubes of carbon float and glow with his mind. He wasn't blindsided by people he thought he could trust. In the past, he wasn't afraid to be alone. He was *comfortable* being alone. Here, in this future, nothing terrified him more than being left to fend for himself with so much uncertainty.

Still stuck in his own mind, Philo remained shut down in his chair while everyone stared at him. Xendo decided to get out of his seat and crouched down in front of his friend.

"Philo, I want you to know that everything that we've experienced together this year was real and true," Xendo gently placed his hands on

MORPHING MEMORIES

Philo's knees. "Whatever happened between our parents, whether it be good or bad, will never change that you are my best friend, and I will always want you in my life. I am not my father and you are not your parents. We are Philo and Xendo. We make our own decisions, and I *choose* to always be here for you, now and always."

Philo lifted his head to look into the bright blue eyes of the silver-haired boy below him. Philo was confused and felt lost. He was still hurt. However, it wasn't actually Xendo who was hurting him. It wasn't Blinda, nor Superintendent Pearl. It wasn't even Jerome Quaker who may have killed his parents. What truly hurt Philo right now was that, yet again, he was on the cusp of being abandoned. He had felt this painful feeling so many times before, being discarded by caregivers for his entire childhood.

Philo could shut out Blinda and Xendo forever, refuse to talk to the superintendent, and disregard all the good memories he *did* create this year. He could push everything and everyone away again. That's what Philo should do, as retaliation for all this pain..., *but where would that actually get me? No.* This time, Philo realized no one was actually abandoning him. This familiar pain he was feeling, he was now preemptively doing to himself. If he gave everything up now, past or future, it didn't matter. He would still have even less to call his own.

There was also something different about this moment. This time, people were waiting on *his* input. He actually had the power to make his next move. Philo realized he didn't want to give up the future he was creating here. He cared about his friends. He loved kineoka. Philo finally felt like he belonged somewhere. Looking down to Xendo at his feet, Philo saw that his friend was showing him honest support. Philo concluded that no one here in this room desired to *hurt* him, they were trying to *help* him. Something in the boy switched. This recurring situation in his life finally made sense to him for the first time. So, Philo made his choice.

"What *I* want... is to find out what really happened to my parents. I want to become a kineoka master. I want to become a continuum agent one day," Philo declared softly, looking at Xendo in front of him, raising his voice with each statement.

"I want my life to be special. I want to do good to make up for all the terrible things in this world!" Philo kept going, finally feeling proud of himself as he looked at Xendo. "And I want to do all of that...

CHAPTER 20

with you."

Philo heard Blinda gasp with surprise on his right. The superintendent sighed with relief. However, all Philo was focused on was Xendo, his best friend. Xendo smiled, which made Philo smile.

"I want that for you, too, Philo," Xendo expressed, "and I want to be there, right by your side, to witness you doing it all."

Philo nodded. Xendo slowly got up and leaned in to give Philo a deep hug over his chair. This time, the hug felt more like home than ever before. Philo lifted his arms to put around Xendo to soak in the embrace. Blinda had her hands clasped together near her heart, and then couldn't stop herself from lunging in for a hug of her own. Philo chuckled. He took a deep inhale, feeling the warmth of security returning to him. All would be okay.

"What I don't understand is… why?" Philo pondered aloud, loosening the hug. "Why were *my* parents killed? What could be so important in the past?"

"The specifics, I do not yet know," Superintendent Pearl sighed. "However, there is something that humans are always after, something people are always trying to seize control of. Something that we never stop trying to change."

"And… what is that?" Philo asked.

"Time," she responded.

"What?" Philo replied, flabbergasted. "Time isn't even real. How can you steal it?"

"You are right. Time is not an object you can own. But it is a scarce commodity humans created to define our own existence," Superintendent Pearl stated, leaning forward in her chair, as serious as Philo had ever seen a person. "Time is a fickle and dangerous thing, especially in our line of work. Everyone is desperate to control it, to steal more of it, or to pretend they mastered each passing second. Yet, a person can never truly know if they spent their time correctly. When our days finally reach their end, some may even realize they wasted it all."

"Regretting our own decisions in life can lead people down a terrible road," Blinda added as she rubbed Philo's shoulder.

"Some time jumpers are desperate to change what cannot be altered," the superintendent explained. "Your parents fought people selfish enough to ruin reality for their own gain. The obsession of outsmarting time always fails. It isn't until we release the fears of our own

MORPHING MEMORIES

time ending that we can be grateful for the best moments this world gives us freely. And usually, those moments are all the time we need."

Philo glanced at Xendo and Blinda to his left and right. They squeezed him tighter. The superintendent checked the time on her technoband.

"Ah, I now must go to meet with the HTPA," she reminded them. Superintendent Pearl gave the young, Grounded boy a warm look of reassurance.

"Go find the rest of your team, Philo. Open up to Alani and Raelyn," the superintendent recommended. "I sense their support will assure you even further."

Philo and Xendo walked down to the Elemental Sanctuary Chamber next to the kineoka sparring rooms on the first floor. Raelyn and Alani were sitting on a small cushioned crimson couch near the chamber's locked platinum doors. As the boys came into their sights, Alani immediately pounced on them.

"Tell me everything," the girl pestered eagerly. "I am actually surprised you both could keep juicy secrets from me this long! I knew tha—"

"Calm down," Raelyn chuckled, placing a hand on Alani's shoulder. "Let's go into the chamber first, the superintendent wanted us to keep it all private."

"Pearl gave us the code: 54 - 15 - 21 - 3 - 42," Philo dictated from memory.

"Sweet, we can get in whenever we want to chat?" Alani asked.

"No, she says they change it daily," Xendo explained, typing in the password.

"Boo, boring," Alani scoffed.

The door to the chamber opened and the eerie lights of varying colors from the elemental sanctuary turned on. Xendo shut the door behind them and Philo and his friends walked further into the room.

"Okay, spill." Alani crossed her arms with one eyebrow raised. "Why do you two dumb-dumbs always give each other secret looks and whisper all the time?"

"Yes, I revealed my secrets like I promised, now it is your turn," Raelyn concurred to the boys.

"Well, how the hell do you even start, Philo?" Xendo laughed.

CHAPTER 20

Philo paused for a moment, unsure of how to actually say the words. He never even imagined he'd actually get to share his secrets in this new life at SIYT, much less how to boil it all down.

"Well, I guess we should start from the very beginning: my name," Philo mentioned slowly.

"Philo Jonathan isn't your real name?" Raelyn asked. Alani contorted her face in confusion.

Philo took a short breath and just went for it, "My real name is Philo Nockby."

Both Alani and Raelyn tilted their heads in thought. They looked at Xendo. Then back to Philo. They were unsure of why that was so important.

"Why does that sound familiar?" Raelyn wondered aloud.

"Like one of the other agents from the 2005 team?" Alani calculated with her forehead furrowed.

"Yes, Daniel Nockby and Ava Harlow were my parents, I was born in 2005, over 1400 years ago," Philo finally confessed. Xendo stretched his mouth wide with a knowing, cocky smile. Alani and Raelyn's faces slowly morphed from subtle confusion to complete amazement and curious wonder.

"Shut up!" Alani stamped her foot with nerdy excitement.

"I mean, what?" Raelyn coughed, racking her brain for a complete thought. "How is that even possible?"

"Tell us everything!" Alani demanded.

Philo then spilled all the information that he had been trapping inside his mind like a dam that finally gave way. The girls were beside themselves with disbelief. Philo and Xendo explained that any time the girls thought they were being suspicious was probably because one of the boys slipped up and almost revealed it all.

"Wow! That's… pure insanity!" Alani marveled, shaking her head with awe.

"I'm grateful you told us," Raelyn added kindly. "It does explain a great deal."

"Uh, yeah, no wonder you're always gawking at ordinary tech and common knowledge that everybody knows," Alani laughed, mimicking Philo's overly-curious, wide-eyed expressions he always made. "Because it's all new to you!"

"I should probably work on that," Philo chuckled as the other

MORPHING MEMORIES

three laughed with him.

"So, is there more?" Raelyn continued. "Anything else you want to tell us?"

"No, for the first time, I think I've told you everything!" Philo happily revealed. "It's such a relief!"

"Then let's make a pact," Alani suggested, placing her hand in the center of their square huddle. "That we'll be more honest with each other going forward. No more lies or secrets."

"Deal," Philo agreed, putting his hand on Alani's. Raelyn and Xendo followed suit.

"We only have five years at SIYT, we have to make them count," Raelyn surmised, as the rest nodded. "Let's set our goals right now, so we can work together to achieve them as a team."

Philo thought for a moment, then cleared his throat. "My goal is to make my parents proud by graduating from SIYT and becoming a continuum agent just like them... and I want us to find out who really killed my parents."

"I want to prove that my father didn't murder anyone or betray his friends," Xendo went next. "I want to discover the truth of how that mission went so wrong!"

"Omnipotence took my mother away from me, damaged my kingdom, and now is threatening the entire planet. My goal is to bring the entire disgusting organization to its knees and eradicate them for good," Raelyn stated firmly.

"Wow, um... I may not fight exactly like you three, but I am a strong protector," Alani began, looking at Raelyn. "I want to protect innocent people regardless of their DNA or TNA. I want to help convince the world that dioka are not obsolete and that trioka are not monsters. We can all live together in harmony."

The four friends nodded in unison.

"That's a lot of goals," Xendo sighed. "How the hell are we going to do it all?

"Trust me," Philo shrugged. "If this year has taught me anything, it's that literally anything is possible."

"No kidding!" Alani jested. "You're 1,450 years old!"

They all laughed. Philo felt so free and full of satisfaction that he was almost light-headed. He didn't realize just how much the burden of holding on to his secrets was weighing him down. Suddenly, Raelyn

CHAPTER 20

pointed to Philo's chest and gasped.

"Oh! Philo! Your cube just flickered!" Raelyn announced, "Look!"

Philo glanced down at his chest in surprise. His carbon cube dangling around his neck was vibrating and blinking green sporadically, like a small light bulb trying to turn itself on.

"Oh data! It's not just him," Alani called out. "They're all activating!"

Philo, Raelyn, Alani, and Xendo all looked down to see their four carbon cubes bouncing around glowing bright green, white, blue, and yellow. They all beamed at each other.

"Why weren't we honest sooner?" Xendo marveled with a laugh. "It's finally working!"

"Should we go tell Professor Ruiz?" Raelyn asked excitedly.

"What for?" Alani cheered. "We're already near the Sacred Thirty!"

"Okay, so let's focus. Try to attract your cardinal elements," Philo suggested to the group. "Let's grab hands!"

The young kineoka trainees clasped their hands and hustled to the center of the Sacred Thirty display of elements. Amongst the many metals, liquids, and noble gases on podiums, the kids stood in a square formation. They closed their eyes and focused intently, trying to clear their minds and stay peaceful. At first, Philo felt it was impossible, because really he was so excited he couldn't stop extra ideas from popping into his head. Then Philo remembered Professor Ruiz told them to follow their energies wherever they led. So, he embraced his curiosity and excitement!

Philo felt an immense sense of gratitude for even standing where he was. It took a lot of courage and grit to do all he had done this year, and no matter how many hurdles were thrown at him, he and his friends survived them all. Philo felt a wave of serenity pass over him.

Suddenly, a whooshing sound awoke Philo from his meditation. He opened his eyes at the same time as his three friends. Above their heads, sixteen elements flew from their podiums to start orbiting around them in the air. The four colorful carbon cubes were glowing bright and tugged on their necklaces wanting to float toward the elements. Philo felt a burning sensation on his chest under his left clavicle. He looked down and saw that his twisted heart shaped mole was glowing green so bright it shone through his black SIYT suit.

"Our genetic marks are glowing too!" Xendo pointed out as the

MORPHING MEMORIES

other three looked at their marks.

Alani looked down to her tear-drop shaped genetic mark on her wrist glowing a stunning blue. Xendo had two off-kilter dots shining like a yellow sunrise in the crook of his left elbow. Raelyn's squished snowflake on the back of her neck was brighter than white snow.

The cloud of sixteen swirling elements in the air separated, drifting to the particular student of their choosing. Philo, Raelyn, Alani, and Xendo each had four elements swirling around their heads.

"We did it!" Alani yipped in elation. "We attracted our cardinal elements!"

The dancing rainbow kaleidoscope of colored lights around them was mesmerizing to witness. Philo and his friends paced their deep abdominal breathing slowly and let go of each other's hands. The elements stopped orbiting and held still in the air. Each student had one chemical element to their north, south, east, and west.

"To my North is hydrogen for joy. South, sodium for sadness. East, magnesium for apprehension, and West, cobalt for courage," Alani called off, twisting her neck around to identify each periodic element and their corresponding emotion she had attracted. "I did *not* expect some of these!"

"Huh, if we're all going North, South, East, West, I attracted oxygen, iron, fluorine, and potassium," Xendo marveled with perplexity. "Those match with fear, distraction, desperation, and anticipation. Why are mine all negative?"

"It seems mine are phosphorus, zinc, calcium, and copper," Raelyn went next, seeming a bit confused, "which connect with anger, grief, serenity, and empathy. I'm not sure how I feel about anger in my North."

"I attracted gallium, carbon, iodine, and nitrogen," Philo informed them, double-checking his four elements. "Those should connect with curiosity, trust, insecurity, and surprise. Interesting...."

As their carbon cubes started to dim their shine and their glowing genetic marks faded, the four students reached out to gather their cardinal element vials one by one.

"Wow, that was intense," Alani uttered peacefully. "My whole body feels different."

"Yes, I can feel my blood pumping through every vessel from my toes to my fingertips," Raelyn described.

CHAPTER 20

"If this is how connecting with just our elements and tiny cubes feel, bonding with our full morphstaffs one day might knock me out!" Xendo burst with elation.

The four students returned the elements back to their rightful places on the Sacred Thirty podiums. The first-years then looked at each other with confident smiles. They were proud to have experienced this pivotal moment together.

"So, wait, you've already time-traveled before, Philo?" Raelyn wondered casually while they walked toward the exit. "You're probably the youngest trioka to ever do it, right?"

Philo blushed, "I guess, I don't really kno—."

"Uhhh! Not just him, remember? I also went! And Mom!" Xendo argued ahead of them as he opened the door. "We each technically time-traveled twice!"

"Wait, wait, now hold on…, I still have literally a zillion more questions to ask you both." Alani chuckled a bit behind them, still limping from her hurt leg the day before. "First off… did Blinda get time-sick and puke?"

The four friends left the chamber together, eager to tackle their shared destinies.

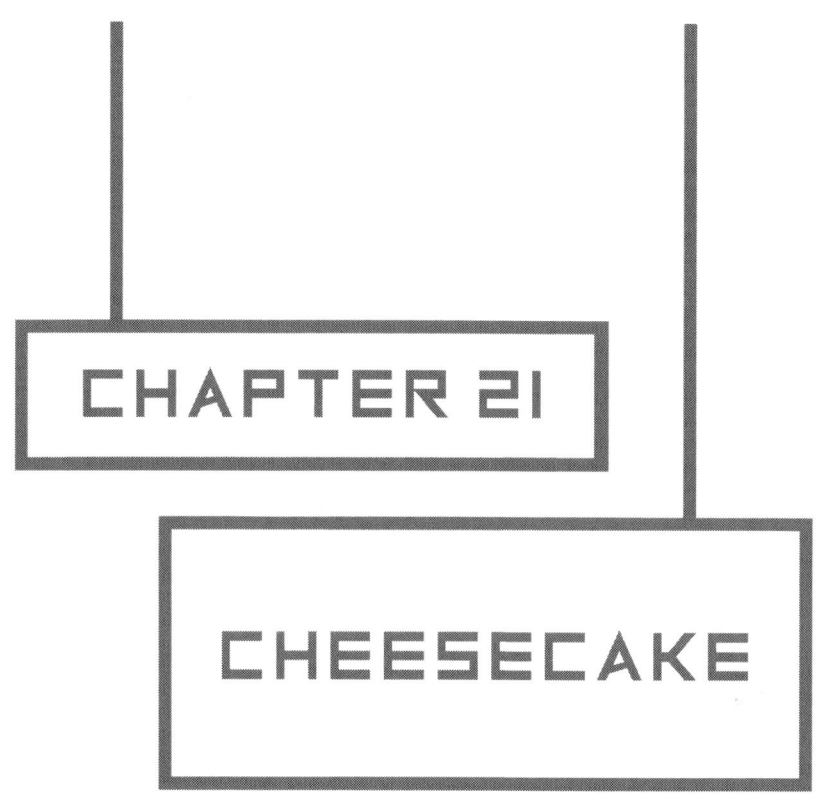

CHAPTER 21

CHEESECAKE

The last month of SIYT classes for Philo and his friends were wrapped up in studying for final exams and ensuring that floor thirteen—every single nook and cranny of it—was neat, organized, and polished clean. The group thought they'd be able to get away with skipping a few chores; however, QD313 pestered them to drop everything anytime the droid spotted a teensy smudge on the windows or a dust bunny under the furniture.

The four friends could barely keep their eyes from drooping during their late nights of studying until they retired to their dorms to fall asleep. Philo had learned so much in only his first nine months at SIYT, he was shocked he could still absorb more.

With all the anxious expectations from upcoming exams, the four friends completely forgot about the global election and their additional punishment of being student helpers. Early Saturday morning in the first week of June, Philo and his friends arrived in the Continuum Café to help the SIYT staff hand out supplies. As the SIYT students arrived to vote, they picked up a paper ballot, grabbed special voting markers, and sat down at one of the voting cubicles placed on the dining tables.

CHAPTER 21

Philo assumed future voting would be completely automatic, but saving physical copies of voting records is one of the few important traditions that remained from his old time period. Philo and Alani were tasked with refilling the stacks of ballots at the front table, and Xendo and Raelyn were the ones passing out the markers.

"We heard you losers got punished for breaking out on the day of the attack," Jasper's snooty voice insulted as he approached their table midday. "Being forced to drudge about as dim voting poll workers, that's a new low, even for you four."

Philo and his friends took a deep sigh of annoyance.

"Just take your ballot, your marker, and go vote, Jasper," Alani grumbled. "I don't have the energy to waste a clever insult on you right now."

"The insult is your wrinkled uniform," Ivy snarked at Alani. Before Alani could quip a comeback, Jasper interrupted by grabbing his papers.

"This whole charade is a waste of time anyway," Jasper complained.

"Yeah, we all know Irwin is going to win," Ivy agreed while handing a ballot to Russel, and Damian behind her.

"Gross, I can't believe we're voting for the same candidate," Alani shuddered with disgust.

"What was that, seaslug?" Jasper slighted.

"Do not call me that," Alani defended herself firmly as she squared her shoulders looking up at him. "I said I figured a capitalist fanboy like yourself would vote for Duke Denholm."

"A dioka?" Jasper scoffed as his friends laughed behind him. "Never."

"That's your *only* problem with Denholm?" Xendo leaned in from the side. "That he's dioka, not the terrible policy changes he wants to implement?"

"That sounds pretty prejudiced," Raelyn critiqued from Xendo's left.

"You think I care?" Jasper gloated. "Diokas have been running Earth for too long. Before this year, my father always just paid the fine to get out of the ridiculous international voting mandate. Paying only a few thousand elars is better than voting for another small-brained Neanderthal. Irwin is still too soft, but he will do."

CHEESECAKE

"Irwin *is* the better candidate, and not all dioka are as bad as Denholm," Alani argued to the bully. "You're speaking just like the bigoted dioka talk about us!"

"Just because your family are all under-evolved, doesn't mean you need to whimper about dioka equality here," Jasper shot at Alani. "We're at a *trioka* school, nitwit. Trioka are better than dioka in every single way. Or at least, *we* are. Not sure about you lot. Grow up, Adalaide, or get out."

Jasper then glared at Philo with the same suspicion and anger he always sent Philo's way.

"And who are *your* parents, Philo?" Jasper sniveled at the Grounded boy. "They're probably useless Neanderthals, too."

Xendo stood up in front of his friend as Jasper laughed at Philo's sullen reaction. Before Alani had the chance to throw an angry middle finger in Jasper's face, Raelyn caught her hand.

"Go vote, Jasper," Raelyn insisted, trying to be the adult in the conversation.

"Oh, touchy subject?" Jasper taunted as he refused to move an inch, standing his ground with an evil smile. "So many mommy and daddy issues with you all. Irwin is—"

"Hey! No talking about candidates," Professor Franklin called from a few yards away, realizing their conversation was holding up the queue. "Move along, students."

Jasper and his minions walked past them with audible scoffs and nasty glares. Philo caught his breath when he noticed a sheepish Luther Wyatt had been standing behind the gang of Skybornes the entire time. The small boy, who they had just risked their own lives trying to save from a poisonous death, had said nothing to defend them. Luther quietly picked up a ballot in shame without looking at Philo and his friends and followed Jasper like a lap dog.

Philo pitied Luther. He thought he and his friends had gotten through to him, but not everyone can break free from the bonds they've chosen.

After a full day of work, Superintendent Pearl told the kids they had officially finished their punishments and were free to leave after they voted themselves.

Philo sat down in an election cubicle for the first time in his life. He selected the candidates he and his friends had researched at the local,

CHAPTER 21

national, and Grounded origin levels. When he got to the global president section he saw Ambassador Daryl Irwin's name. Philo smiled. Irwin was always going to be his first choice. The ambassador had been through many complex hurdles, just like Philo, and was making the most of those hard lessons. Philo stamped his marker next to Irwin's name, proud of his parents' old friend for making it this far as a trioka.

The last week of classes for the SIYT school year purely consisted of the final exams for each course. Alani and Xendo were competing for top marks, where Philo and Raelyn just aimed for above average. Monday morning, in the hallway before they walked into their first final, Philo was surprised when Lina Castellano poked his shoulder. Lina was always such a lone wolf; he often didn't even notice her during lectures. Lina hadn't spoken to Philo at all since she ran away during the Omnipotence attack. He let his friends walk ahead to their Human History class while he waited back with Lina.

"Philo..., I've been avoiding you, and after meditating long enough to get my carbon cube to finally glow last week, I saw that my southern element is zirconium for greed," Lina explained with a sigh. "I guess that's proof of how selfish I can be."

"Ah. I see," Philo responded, unsure where this explanation was going.

"The day of the shooting, I freaked out and went into survival mode, but yet again, I was only thinking of myself," Lina confessed. "As soon as I left you there, I regretted it. I always push people away. Alani was trying to introduce me to you all, because, honestly, I need more friends," Lina shrugged nervously. "I really screwed that up."

Philo could tell Lina had never apologized before. He also was new to people even caring enough about him to make amends.

"I appreciate you telling me, Lina." Philo breathed in and offered her a smile. "We actually are a lot alike. I almost fled the auditorium myself. It was terrifying."

"Really? I admired that you stayed! That took bravery," Lina responded slowly, seeming to warm up a bit. "Almost the entire school ran away, and you actually were courageous enough to go back in there."

"Oh, well," Philo blushed. "Honestly, I only decided to return because my friends found me. We did it as a team."

CHEESECAKE

"You're lucky, then," Lina shared a small grin. "Not everyone can find their team in life."

After a moment of awkward silence, Philo then tilted his head in thought. "Would you like to sit next to me in Human History next period? Raelyn and I could use an extra friend to stop Alani and Xendo from bickering about whose exam answers are more accurate."

"Oh! Really?" Lina's eyes lit up. "Yeah! I, um, I would really like that."

Together they turned to walk down the hallway to catch up to their classmates.

"I'll keep Xendo from bringing up his higher History midterm grade," Philo prepared her. "You stop Alani from countering with her Artistic Expression midterm and shouting 'Robot boy' jokes at him."

"Deal!" Lina laughed with a surprising snort, eager to be included, even if it was in de-escalation strategies.

When the SIYT final grade point averages for the full academic year were released, the students were quick to discuss their results. Some got higher marks like Xendo, Alani, Jade, and, oddly, Ivy Bates, while other students just barely passed to move onto their second year like Damian, Russel, and Naomii. Jade told Philo that Naomii only answered the exact amount of questions they needed to pass each exam and left the remaining problems blank out of boredom. Naomii felt no need to prove their grasp of the material, not even to the SIYT professors.

The end of year feast at the Superior Institute of Young Trioka in the Continuum Café was beyond extravagant. Blinda and her staff went full-out with delicious foods from all four global origins. Superintendent Pearl gave a touching speech to the students from all five levels, wishing them a summer full of adventure.

On Saturday morning, all the SIYT students packed up their belongings as they had to teleport back home to their families before the weekend was over. Privately, Superintendent Pearl informed Philo he could stay in his dorm over the summer since he had no family to return to. Blinda sent a holomessage to Xendo inviting Philo, Raelyn, and Alani to come have one final dinner with her at Quaker cottage before they all separated. It would also be the perfect way to celebrate their accomplishments that year and watch the election results as a group.

CHAPTER 21

Blinda even teased a special sweet surprise she had baked for them all.

The four friends traveled down Superior Skisland's skytube, and peacefully walked down the lakeside shore of Duluth. When they arrived at Quaker cottage, Blinda already had some lively music playing and the whole house smelled of delicious roasted meats, caramelized vegetables, and sweet desserts. The four kids walked into Blinda's happy arms for warm hugs and kisses on their foreheads.

Soon, Xendo and Philo were munching on gravlax canapes and stuffed pasta chips on the couch, while Alani and Raelyn were swaying to the music and chatting with Blinda. Xendo tapped his technoband to turn on the election coverage and stretched the holoscreen wide for them all to view. The separate origins had just teleported their final counted ballots to the international capital in Luxembourg. The election results would soon be finalized. No false projections were ever promised before one authenticated verdict was reached.

As the music changed, Philo turned to notice Alani twirling around the living room. She held out her hand to Raelyn to join her. To his surprise, the princess dropped her proper etiquette to play in the frivolity. Philo smiled, Raelyn seemed so carefree.

The wafting aromas of smoky roasting beef, salty soy, and sweet vinegar pulled Philo to check on Blinda cooking in the kitchen.

"Hey, you," Blinda greeted Philo with a warm smile as he approached her at the stove. "Xendo and I were chatting, and instead of sheltering at SIYT over the summer with Nova as your guardian, would you like to stay with us here at our cottage?"

Philo's face brightened. He had never thought of that option.

"Really? I'd love that!" Philo beamed, but then he bowed his head in doubt. "I... don't want to be a burden. Are you sure?"

"Oh, Philo," Blinda tilted her head and rubbed his shoulder. "You are never a burden to those who love you. To us, you're family now. Which means you will always belong in our home."

Philo had never heard words that gave him this much comfort. To avoid tears from welling up, Philo reached in to hug Blinda. She squeezed him tight and patted his back. Blinda then chuckled as she witnessed her son get up to dance with the girls.

"Seeing you four together like this fills me with so much joy," Blinda cooed to Philo as they turned to the living room. "Life is nothing without friends you can be silly with."

CHEESECAKE

"If you had told me this is how my life would end up when you first rescued me from the past, I never would have believed you," Philo told her, shaking his head in amazement.

"Yeah, the best adventures usually are unbelievable, aren't they?" Blinda smiled. As he watched his three jubilant friends laughing, Philo felt a small ounce of insecurity drop into his mind.

"I don't know why, but this still doesn't feel real," Philo told Blinda quietly. "Everything moves so fast, I get worried things will all just slip away. I feel like I never have enough time to enjoy the memories we're making. I don't want to forget any of these small special moments. I don't want it to end."

"Oh, honey, I wouldn't really worry about it too much," Blinda comforted, looking at the boy with a sweet smile. "If you dread your time, it will last longer. If you enjoy your time, it speeds away. We can't control it. So, you just have to let go and enjoy what we're lucky enough to experience. That's the secret everyone forgets. Time just measures how much of life is worth remembering."

Blinda placed all the mouthwatering food out on her wide wooden dinner table. She had made a special global dish to honor each one of her son's friends. Philo's dish was cedar smoked bison with agave roasted turnips. Alani was delighted with her Hitsumabushi platter of grilled eel, rice, and garnishes. Xendo's Skyborne marinated chicken kale salad with cashew dressing was deliciously healthy. Finally, for Raelyn, Blinda made some traditional Buffalo Pemmican and sledging biscuits. Raelyn described how the meat paste should be spread onto the accompanying biscuits just like the first Antarctic scientists did centuries ago to keep satiated in the freezing weather.

While eating the tantalizing food, the four friends discussed their plans for the summer. Alani was excited to have a calm and peaceful summer in Lisoo, down under the Pacific Ocean with her family. Raelyn admitted she was dreading to return to life at the Northern Palace, but she hoped to finally have the time to explain her abdication decision to her father, King Bernard. Alani wished Philo luck in surviving a summer in such close proximity to Xendo with zero breaks. They all laughed, especially Blinda.

The mother then brought out the special dessert she had created for them.

CHAPTER 21

"Here you go, darlings," Blinda chirped. "It's a PRAX cheesecake."

On the table, she placed a beautifully decorated cheesecake separated into four colorful quadrants. Each section had its own alphabet letter placed above its flavored toppings; the P, R, A, and X-shaped decorations in each corner were made out of white chocolate.

"PRAX? What does that mean?" Philo asked, looking at the subdivided cheesecake.

"On the top left we have dulce de leche cheesecake with rosemary thyme caramel, candied herbs, and chopped nuts for garnish. The P is for Philo. Those are all his favorite sweet flavors," Blinda explained while showing off each special addition.

"Then for R, Raelyn, we have chocolate hazelnut cheesecake, with chocolate ganache and rainbow spectrolite sugar shards. Alani's section is blueberry and blackberry swirled cheesecake covered with blueberry syrup and fresh berries on top. Finally, for Xendo, I made lemon curd cheesecake with candied lemon slices, and whipped cream dollops. P-R-A-X! A section for each of you!"

"Wow! This is amazing!" Alani called out.

"How do you come up with an idea so brilliant, Mrs. Quaker?" Raelyn marveled.

"I am a sucker for lemon!" Xendo nodded as he shot a smile at his mother.

"I still want to try all four flavors!" beamed Philo, holding his fork at the ready.

The four friends bounced in their seats as Blinda sliced them each a chunk of their section of the cheesecake. The kids sampled their own corner and eagerly tasted the other three. Philo was floored by the sweet creaminess of the cheesecake and the salty, crunchy graham cracker crust.

"Oh! The voting counts are done!" Xendo declared, forcefully tapping Philo's shoulder. "Here we go!"

Everyone else's gaze followed Xendo as he sped toward the holoscreen and pulled it over through the air to their kitchen table. Philo was excited to finally know who their next global president would be, but that didn't stop him from continuing to chow down on his dulce de leche dessert. The news announcer from Earth's Database on the holoscreen announced that a winner has been decided and ratified. The election results then popped up for them all to see in big flashy letters. As

CHEESECAKE

the winning presidential candidate's face came on the screen, everyone in the room gasped and Philo choked on his bite of PRAX cheesecake.

This summer wasn't going to be calm or peaceful at all. The harmonious world of their future was about to change… *drastically*.

ABOUT THE AUTHOR

MATTHEW FRANCIS (1995-) was born in the lakeside town of Duluth, Minnesota. He grew up consuming all the fantasy stories he possibly could read and watched way too much food television to be healthy. He earned his bachelor's degree in Culinary Arts Management and Entrepreneurship from the Culinary Institute of America in Hyde Park, NY, in 2016.

Now, Matthew has his own production company, FrancisFilm, LLC, making recipe videos for multiple food media companies and building his own creative projects. He is the creator, host, and Director of a food interview show, DinnerViews. This novel, *PRAX and the Hazardous Countdown*, aims to be the first book in a six-part YA action fantasy series taking place in the fictional PRAX future. Later in life, Matthew plans on buying farmland in Minnesota to focus on creating a sustainable homestead, community kitchen, food studio, and building a family of his own.

Made in United States
Orlando, FL
02 January 2023